BLACKOUT AFTER DARK

GANSETT ISLAND SERIES, BOOK 23

MARIE FORCE

Blackout After Dark
Gansett Island Series, Book 23

By: Marie Force
Published by HTJB, Inc.

Cover Design: Diane Luger
Print Layout by E-book Formatting Fairies
ISBN: 978-1950654994

View the McCarthy Family Tree *marieforce.com/gansett/familytree/*

View the list of Who's Who on Gansett Island here *marieforce.com/whoswhogansett/*

View a map of Gansett Island *marieforce.com/mapofgansett/*

The Gansett Island Series

Book 1: Maid for Love *(Mac & Maddie)*
Book 2: Fool for Love *(Joe & Janey)*
Book 3: Ready for Love *(Luke & Sydney)*
Book 4: Falling for Love *(Grant & Stephanie)*
Book 5: Hoping for Love *(Evan & Grace)*
Book 6: Season for Love *(Owen & Laura)*
Book 7: Longing for Love *(Blaine & Tiffany)*
Book 8: Waiting for Love *(Adam & Abby)*
Book 9: Time for Love *(David & Daisy)*
Book 10: Meant for Love *(Jenny & Alex)*
Book 10.5: Chance for Love, *A Gansett Island Novella (Jared & Lizzie)*
Book 11: Gansett After Dark *(Owen & Laura)*
Book 12: Kisses After Dark *(Shane & Katie)*
Book 13: Love After Dark *(Paul & Hope)*
Book 14: Celebration After Dark *(Big Mac & Linda)*
Book 15: Desire After Dark *(Slim & Erin)*
Book 16: Light After Dark *(Mallory & Quinn)*
Book 17: Victoria & Shannon (Episode 1)
Book 18: Kevin & Chelsea (Episode 2)
A Gansett Island Christmas Novella
Book 19: Mine After Dark *(Riley & Nikki)*
Book 20: Yours After Dark *(Finn McCarthy)*
Book 21: Trouble After Dark *(Deacon & Julia)*
Book 22: Rescue After Dark *(Mason & Jordan)*
Book 23: Blackout After Dark *(Full Cast)*
Book 24: Temptation After Dark *(Gigi & Cooper)*

More new books are always in the works. For the most up-to-date list of what's available from the Gansett Island Series as well as series extras, go to *marieforce.com/gansett*

CHAPTER 1

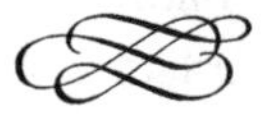

The invitation had arrived in that day's mail—a casual housewarming at the new seaside home of Charlie and Sarah Grandchamp. "The gift of your friendship is the only one we need," the invitation read. Linda McCarthy handed it to her husband, "Big Mac," over dinner.

"I can't wait to see the inside of that house," Big Mac said. "It's one of my favorites."

The huge contemporary had one of the best views of the Atlantic on the island. Its six bedrooms and seven bathrooms would allow Sarah and Charlie to have their whole family in residence for a visit, should the opportunity arise. Sarah had told Linda that'd been one of their primary goals in looking for a home of their own—somewhere the entire family could be together.

"I'm looking forward to it as well." Linda took a sip of the robust red wine her friend Carolina O'Grady had turned her on to during a recent get-together. "And may I add, no one in the entire world deserves happily ever after more than those two do."

"I agree. Rumor has it he told her to pick any house on the island she wanted, and he'd find a way to get it for her."

Linda fanned her face. "That's so romantic. He wants her to have it all."

"After the nightmare of her marriage to Mark Lawry, she deserves to have it all."

"Indeed, as does he. And I love that the state is footing the bill for their dream house."

Charlie had been granted a seven-million-dollar settlement from the state, half a million for each of the fourteen years he'd spent unjustly incarcerated. Their daughter-in-law Stephanie had worked tirelessly for all that time to try to free the stepfather who'd come to her aid and then been charged with the beating her late mother had actually inflicted.

Stephanie's husband, their son Grant, had written a screenplay based on Charlie and Stephanie's years' long odyssey. The movie, called *Indefatigable,* had been shot in Los Angeles over the winter and would soon be screened for the Gansett Island community. "I can't wait to see the film. Grant said it came together better than he could've dreamed."

"Has Steph seen it yet?" Big Mac asked.

Linda shook her head. "Apparently, she's trying to work up the courage to watch it. She says she lived it, and once was more than enough. But she wants to watch the film he worked so hard on, even if he's told her he'd understand if she never does."

"That's a tough one," Big Mac said. "I wouldn't want anything to set her back to where she was when we first met her. She had the weight of the world on her shoulders."

"I don't think that would happen, but she definitely needs to prepare herself emotionally to watch her story unfold on the screen."

"That'd be surreal—to see something you lived portrayed on film."

"I can only imagine."

"When is the Charlie and Sarah's party?"

"Saturday night. They waited until Grant and Steph would be back from LA."

"That's the day the new lighthouse keepers arrive, a married couple this time."

"You haven't said much about them."

Big Mac was president of the Gansett Island Town Council and had the inside scoop on everything that went on in their tiny corner of the world. He shrugged, fiddled with the stem on his wineglass and seemed sad for some reason.

"Did they send the usual letter to apply for the position?"

"They did."

"God, I'll never forget Jenny's letter."

Jenny Wilks had applied for the position nearly ten years after losing her fiancé in the 9/11 attacks in New York City. Her letter had been one of the most gut-wrenching things Linda had ever read. Since coming to Gansett, Jenny had become a close friend to the McCarthys and many others on the island. She'd also met and married Alex Martinez, and had a baby they'd named George, after Alex's late father.

"The new people have an equally gut-wrenching story," Big Mac said. "Like Jenny's, almost too much to bear."

"Do you want to tell me about it?"

"I do, but I haven't wanted to upset you."

"That bad, huh?"

Grimacing, he nodded, got up from his seat, went into his office and returned with two pieces of paper he handed to her. And then he refilled both their glasses.

"I'm almost afraid to look."

"It's pretty rough. I'm not going to lie."

Linda took another drink of wine to fortify herself before she began to read.

To the Gansett Island Town Council,

My name is Oliver Watkins. My wife, Dara, and I would like to apply for the lighthouse keeper position on your island, even though we have no experience with lighthouses. Do people with *experience actually apply? The opportunity for a change of scenery would be extremely welcome to both of us. Just over a year ago, we lost our three-year-old son, Lewis, in an accident that has haunted us every day since as we both blame ourselves for a tragedy that no one could have prevented. But when these things happen, you find yourself reliving every minute, trying to find the moment when you could've changed the outcome.*

We named Lewis for my hero, the late Rep. John Lewis, the Georgia congressman and Civil Rights leader. I worked as an intern in his office after college and met Dara at a party, when she was a law student at Howard.

Saddened by what she'd read so far, Linda took another sip of wine before diving back into the letter.

We were home on a regular Sunday. Lewis was napping in his room, and so was I, on the sofa while pretending to watch the Ravens game. Dara was on a conference call with work. She'd been crazy busy getting ready for a trial that was due to start in a few weeks. I woke out of a sound sleep when I heard our dog, Maisy, screaming. There's no other word for the sound she made, and when I realized it was coming from outside, I was up and off the sofa before I was even fully awake. I couldn't believe that the front door was standing open, but when I realized Lewis had let himself out of the house... My heart stopped. And then I saw why Maisy was screaming. Our baby had been hit by a car, and the driver was hysterical. The neighbors had come out, someone called EMS, but it was too late. We believe Lewis was killed on impact.

"Oh." Linda dabbed at her eyes with a napkin. "Those poor, poor people."

"I know. It's so awful."

Having to tell Dara what'd happened was the worst moment of my life. I'll never forget the way she screamed and tried to get to him, but I wouldn't let her. I didn't want her to see what I had, things I'll carry with me forever. The days and weeks that followed that awful day were simply horrible. In the year since we lost Lewis, our entire world has come unraveled. We've been unable to work, so we were forced to sell the home we'd once thought we'd own for the rest of our lives. Our marriage has suffered from an inability to share our mutual grief. She doesn't want to talk about it, and I do. We both blame ourselves. Me for falling asleep and her for working on a day that she feels should've been devoted to family. Our guilt and grief have caused a rift between us that we aren't sure we can overcome.

In short, everything is a mess, and we need a change badly, but we can't afford the cost of an expensive move. When I saw your lighthouse keeper ad online, I told Dara about it, and we agreed it certainly couldn't hurt to apply. That's the first time we've agreed on anything in a long time.

I'm not sure if our marriage is going to survive the devastating loss of our son. But I am sure that we can't go on the way we are. We appreciate your consideration of our application and look forward to hearing from you.

Sincerely,
Oliver and Dara Watkins

"I'm so glad you hired them," Linda said.

"We didn't hesitate to offer it to them after we read their letter."

"Gansett will be good for them. We'll surround them with friends and love and a whole new life. It worked for Jenny and Erin, and even Sydney when she came to the island after her terrible loss."

"I hope you're right. It sounds like they desperately need a fresh start. And thank you for rolling out the welcome mat for them."

"I honestly can't begin to know what they've been through. It was horrible enough losing a baby we never got to meet, but losing a three-year-old..." She shook her head. "Unbearable."

He scooted his chair closer to hers and held out his arms to her. "Completely."

Linda leaned into his embrace, appreciating the comfort after reading Oliver and Dara's devastating letter. "Why do bad things happen to good people?"

"I don't know, love. It seems so unfair."

"Sure does." After a long moment of contemplative silence, she looked up at him. "Did you see Mac today?"

"He was at the marina all morning but went home after lunch."

"That poor guy is still so wound up." They wouldn't soon forget the fright their oldest son had given them when he collapsed in the spring. Thankfully, he'd been at the clinic when it happened, and it had been determined he'd had an anxiety attack. "I can't wait to get those twin babies here safely so he can finally relax."

"I worry he's going to give himself a heart attack before they arrive," Big Mac said with a sigh.

"It's not as if he doesn't have good reason to be concerned after what happened when Hailey was born, as well as Janey nearly dying having PJ and Vivienne being born on the ferry." Linda let out a huff of nervous laughter. "Our grandbabies tend to arrive with a bit of drama. You can't blame Mac for being worried about what the twins have in store for them."

"At least they're leaving soon to move to the mainland for the last few weeks. Did you hear if they decided whether Thomas is going with them or staying here?"

"He's staying with Tiffany so he can start school on time," Linda said of their six-year-old grandson.

"That's probably what's best for him."

"But it'll add to his parents' stress, being separated from him for up to a month, potentially."

"Tiffany and Blaine and the rest of us will take very good care of him."

"Of course we will, but his parents will still fret. I hope the babies come early so they can get home and get settled in sooner rather than later."

"I hope so, too. If there's one downside to life on an island, access to hospitals and advanced medical care is it."

"For sure." Linda's cell phone rang, and she got up to retrieve it from the counter where she'd left it to charge. "Hi, honey," she said to her daughter, Janey. "What's up?"

"Joe and I were wondering if we could stop by for a minute."

"Of course you can. You know you don't have to ask first."

"We're all a little terrified of the second honeymoon you two have got going on over there at the White House."

"Oh hush. Are you bringing my grandchildren?"

"Yep. We'll see you in a few."

"I'll put the light on for you." Linda ended the call and turned to Big Mac. "They're coming by."

"So I heard."

They were always happy to see the kids, especially when they brought their grandchildren. Having all five of their children and Big Mac's daughter Mallory living on the island was a dream come true for them after their four sons had scattered as soon as they'd been old enough to leave home. One by one, they'd all come home, met the loves of their lives and settled into island life.

Janey was the only one who'd come home after college at UConn. A self-described homebody, she'd left the island to attend two years of veterinary school at Ohio State. She'd decided not to go back to school after her son PJ arrived in extra dramatic fashion with a placental abruption that had nearly killed them both. As Linda flipped on the front light for Janey, she shuddered as she relived the sheer terror of that day.

Big Mac came up behind her, placing his hands on her shoulders. "I hope she's not coming here to tell us they're expecting again."

His statement told her he, too, thought it was odd that the Cantrells were coming over so close to the kids' bedtime, which meant something was up.

"I hope not either. Joe was planning to get a vasectomy, but that hasn't happened yet." Their son-in-law, who co-owned the Gansett Island Ferry Company with his mother, Carolina, worked a lot during the summer when the ferries ran almost constantly.

"I vote to get a two-for-one deal for him and Mac after the season," Big Mac said.

"All in favor, say aye."

"Aye," they said together, laughing at their own foolishness.

"Who knew that having them all home would mean lots of worries about babies being born on a remote island?" he asked. They'd managed to have all of theirs in a hospital on the mainland, but that hadn't happened for their children.

"I have to confess I didn't really think too much about that until Hailey was born during a tropical storm with the only doctor off-island."

"That was a wakeup call for sure." He massaged shoulders that went tight with tension whenever she thought about the many things that could go wrong on an island with limited medical facilities. "We thought it was worrisome when they were teenagers, but it's even more so now."

"Definitely." She sighed with pleasure at the way he kneaded the kinks from her muscles. "It's the only downside to island life that I've ever found."

"Here they come." He kissed the top of her head. "Whatever it is, try not to worry. We'll figure it out. We always do."

Since that was the truth, she tried to take comfort in his assurances. But she wouldn't breathe easy until she knew what her daughter was coming to tell them.

CHAPTER 2

Janey's belly fluttered with nerves as they pulled into the driveway of her childhood home, and she saw her parents standing in the doorway waiting for them.

Joe put his warm hand on top of her cold one. "It's going to be fine. You know they want this for you as much as I do."

"It's true. They do, but they'll be sad, too."

"It'll be okay, Janey. I promise. Let's go get it over with so we can move forward with our plans."

She nodded and released her seat belt to get out of the car to fetch Vivienne from her seat while Joe got PJ. Both their kids had light blond hair, like their parents had as children, as well as their father's hazel eyes.

"Let's go see Grandma and Papa," Janey said to her daughter.

Viv let out a squeal at the words *Grandma* and *Papa*. Her parents gave all their grandchildren their undivided attention when they were with them, and the kids adored them.

At the front door, Linda took Vivienne from Janey while Big Mac relieved Joe of PJ. Seeing her parents as grandparents to her children was one of the most joyful things in Janey's life. The thought of what she'd come to tell them threatened to break her heart. But she and Joe had made their decision and were ready to implement it.

They just had to tell everyone, and that was the hard part.

"What's going on?" Linda asked, laser-focused on Janey.

They didn't call her Voodoo Mama for nothing. She always knew when something was up.

"We were hoping we could talk to you for a minute," Janey said, glancing at Joe.

He put his arm around her, reminding her they were a team and were in this together.

Thank God for him. She had that thought many times every day. When she recalled how close she'd come to marrying the wrong man…

"You're not pregnant, are you, Princess?" Big Mac asked.

"No, Dad!" Janey laughed. "I told you we're done with babies." Her daughter being born on the ferry after PJ's calamitous birth had cured her and Joe of any desire for more kids. They'd tempted fate twice. That was more than enough.

"Oh, thank you, Jesus," Big Mac said. "You two have already used up your share of my blood pressure medicine."

"Hush, Daddy. Your blood pressure is fine."

"Not when my baby girl is in danger, it isn't."

"I'm not in any danger." Janey followed them to the family room, where they put the kids down to play with the toys Big Mac and Linda had gotten for their grandchildren to have at their house.

"How about an ice cream sandwich?" Linda asked PJ, who got excited at the words *ice cream* no matter how they were presented.

He went with his grandmother to get treats for himself and his sister while Big Mac sat on the floor with Vivienne, the way he had when Janey and her brothers were little. "Just tell us what's going on so we can stop worrying about it."

"It's nothing bad," Janey said, glancing at Joe.

He sent her a warm, loving smile. His support had made so many things possible for her, and his sacrifices had gotten her halfway through vet school. "So Joe and I have been talking, and it looks like we'll be going back to Ohio this fall so I can get back to school."

"That's great news, honey." A big smile stretched across her father's handsome face. "You know we've wanted that for you since you were a little girl bringing home injured birds and squirrels to nurse them back to health."

"It's just…" She looked down at her hands as she tried not to give in to the tears that'd been plentiful since they made their decision a week ago. In the back of her mind, she'd hoped that OSU would tell her it was too late for the fall, but they'd welcomed her back with open arms. "It's harder to go this time around."

"Because you have two little ones," Linda said, tending to both kids as they made a disastrous mess with the half-size ice cream sandwiches.

"Who are deeply bonded to you, Carolina, Seamus, their aunts, uncles, cousins, friends. Not to mention how bonded *we* are to everyone." Despite her great desire to have this conversation without them, tears slid down her cheeks anyway. "It's going to be really hard to leave."

"It'll be hard for us to see you go," Linda said, "but don't worry about the kids. They'll be fine as long as they have you and Joe. Years from now, they won't remember being away from here. They'll only remember the love they always had from everyone around them."

"I know, and we've talked about that. They're too little to realize they won't see you guys or the others for a while, and that's a blessing."

"That's why I encouraged Janey to do this now," Joe said. "They're still young enough to roll with it. When PJ starts school, that'll complicate things even more."

"That's very true," Big Mac said. "I remember making vacation plans after Mac started school without giving a thought to the fact that he couldn't go then. It was a huge shock to our system that we couldn't do whatever we wanted anymore. You're wise to get this done before that's a factor. And if I could just add… I can't wait to call you Dr. Cantrell. I've been waiting a long time for that."

"I know you have." Her dad had been furious with her ex-fiancé, David Lawrence, when he'd talked her out of going to vet school after college. David had made the argument that paying off loans for med school and vet school would kill them financially. "And Doc Potter is getting closer to retiring whether I'm ready to take over the practice or not. He sort of gave me a bit of an ultimatum this summer. He said, 'If it can't be you, Janey, it's gonna have to be someone before too much longer.'"

"After he said that," Joe added, "I asked Janey how she'd feel about someone else taking over Doc's practice. That sort of got her seriously thinking about finishing school."

"I keep telling myself it's only two more years, but that seems like a lifetime right now. I'm homesick, and we haven't even left yet."

"You've always been such a homebody," Big Mac said. "Remember how you wanted to come home every weekend when you were at UConn?"

"I do, and I remember how mean you were, because you wouldn't let me."

"For two reasons. One, I had to go get you, which meant leaving my precious island to drive two hours each way, and two, I wanted you to make friends there and enjoy the college experience."

"I did make friends there, and I did enjoy the college experience, but this is the first I'm hearing that your precious island was more important than your precious daughter."

"She got you there, hon," Linda said, laughing.

"Now you know very well that nothing was or is more precious to me than my precious daughter, but I wasn't going to Connecticut to get you every weekend—and then taking you back two days later."

"Instead, you made me suffer away from my beloved island."

"I saw the pictures you sent your mother. You were *not* suffering. It's a wonder any schooling got done."

Janey could've play-bickered with her father all night, but Vivienne had a meltdown that led to Joe scooping her up to get her out of there before PJ could start up, too.

Linda produced a wipe from somewhere and had the kids cleaned up in no time.

That was just one of many reasons she'd miss her mother. Both her parents had a way of pitching in right where they were needed before Janey even knew she needed them. And then she was sobbing all over her mother.

"I'm such a big baby," she said, sniffling.

Linda patted her back and held her the way she had since Janey was a little girl with a skinned knee. "You're doing the right thing, sweetheart. Even though it's hard right now, you'll be so glad you did it." She pulled back and pushed the hair from Janey's face. "Think about what an amazing example you'll be setting for your own daughter by showing her there's no limit to what she can do if she dreams big and works hard."

"Your mom is right, Princess," Big Mac said. "It broke our hearts when David talked you out of vet school the first time around, and we understood why you took a break after you had the babies, but now it's time to go back and finish what you started. You'll always regret it if you don't."

Janey wiped her face and held her arms out to her son, who was studying her with his little brows knitted with dismay. "You guys will come visit, right?"

"Try to stop us," Big Mac said.

"Telling you our plan makes me feel better. It's been so stressful trying to imagine doing this with *two* kids and the menagerie." They had a squad of special-needs pets who would travel with them to Ohio.

"Joe will be right there with you to help with everything, and it'll go by so fast," Linda said. "You'll be back for next summer before you know it."

"I want to blink and be back." She kissed PJ on the top of his head. "Let's go rescue Daddy from your sister, buddy."

"Daddy!"

"He loves his daddy. Thanks, guys, for, you know, every single thing you've ever done and continue to do. I don't know what I'd ever do without you."

"No need to worry about that, sweetheart," Big Mac said. "We're not going anywhere."

They walked her out and stood in the doorway to wave them off as Joe backed their SUV out of the driveway.

Janey waved until they were out of sight and then broke down into tears again.

"I was hoping you'd feel better after you shared the news with them," Joe said.

"I do feel better. It's just hard to know I won't see them for months. That the kids won't see them."

"We'll see them. We'll FaceTime every week, and they'll come visit."

"I know. It just won't be the same as having everyone right here."

When they got home, Joe took Viv from her. "Go take a bath. I've got this."

"You don't have to do that."

"I know I don't. Go take some time for you." He kissed her cheek. "And then we'll have some time for us."

"Thank you." Janey kissed her babies good night and waited until Joe had taken the kids upstairs for baths before she went into the kitchen to pour a glass of wine and let out the dogs. She felt like a fool for being so emotional about something she'd wanted her whole life. Dreams had a funny way of changing to fit the circumstances.

Her dream come true was the man upstairs and the children they shared, their pets, their home, their extended family and friends nearby. She wanted for nothing, except for the unfinished business in Ohio that continued to rub at her like a wound with a scab that refused to heal properly. As the summer had progressed, the voice inside her that wanted her to finish what she'd started had grown harder to ignore, until she'd finally told Joe what had been weighing on her.

He'd responded with encouragement and support, even if her desire to go back to Ohio would turn both their lives upside down for the next two years. "As long as we're together, we'll figure it out," he'd said.

From the beginning, he'd been supportive of her desire to attend vet school, even going so far as to hire Seamus O'Grady to run the ferry company for him while he was with her in Ohio. That'd led to Seamus falling for Joe's mom, Carolina, which never would've happened if they hadn't gone to Ohio in the first place.

After she let in the dogs, Janey scratched Riley between the ears to console him. He always knew when something was bothering her.

Joe came into the kitchen. "There you are. I was looking for you in the tub."

She turned to face him. "I haven't made it there yet."

"So I see. You okay?"

"I'm better now that my parents know and that they're happy I'm going to finish."

"You know they've wanted it for you as long as you have."

"I do know that. They were so mad when I told them I wasn't going after college."

He put his hands on her hips and leaned his forehead against hers. "We all were."

"My babies went down fast."

"Faster than usual. Running them on the beach was a good idea."

She flattened her hands on his chest and slid them up to wrap around his neck. "I thought it might be. They were wound up today."

"Have you heard anything from Abby or Adam?" he asked of her sister-in-law and brother.

"Not yet. Their appointment is in the morning, and they're staying at Uncle Frank's tonight."

"I hope everything is okay."

"That poor girl has been through so much. I just want her to have a nice, easy pregnancy."

"Me, too. Let's turn in early. I'm exhausted."

He'd done three round trips on the ferries that day, which was one more than he usually did lately.

They let the dogs out, shut off lights, locked doors and headed upstairs, peeking in on sleeping little ones before heading into their bedroom.

Joe unbuttoned his shirt and dropped it on the floor.

"Um, hello," Janey said, as she did every night in what had become a little ritual that was one of many that made up her days and nights with him.

Laughing, he bent to pick up the discarded shirt. "Just making sure you're paying attention."

"I'm paying attention, and after growing up with four bovine brothers, I'm not letting you get away with that stuff."

"Yes, dear. You gonna take your bath?"

"I'm too tired."

"Get in bed, and I'll give you a back rub."

"I should be giving you one. You worked twelve hours today."

"So did you. Taking care of kids is no easy job."

"Neither is driving the ferries."

Joe laughed. "It's easy compared to chasing our two wild ones."

"They do give me a run for my money on my days off from the vet clinic, but I wouldn't have it any other way." That had her sobbing again at the thought of spending so much time away from her babies while in school. "I'll never get to see them."

"Aw, hon." Joe wrapped his arms around her. "Yes, you will. It's going to be fine. I'll take very good care of them while you're in school, and we'll have family time every weekend. It's all good."

"They're going to forget about me."

Joe laughed and nudged her ahead of him into bed. Once there, he made her comfortable in his arms, her favorite place to be. "Think about your very first memories. What do you remember?"

"Evan and Adam chasing me around the yard like hooligans."

"How old were you?"

"I don't know. Maybe five?"

"PJ and Viv won't remember living in Ohio. They'll grow up with their mom, a very successful veterinarian, who'll be the most important person in their lives."

"Tied for first with you."

"No, sweetheart. You'll always be first with them, and that's fine with me. You're first with me, too. We'll have a busy couple of years while you finish school, and then we'll come home and settle back into life here, and they'll pick right up where they left off with their grandparents, aunts, uncles and cousins."

"You're sure about that?"

"One hundred percent positive. And they'll be so, so proud of you for finishing school and making your biggest dream come true."

"Being a vet isn't my biggest dream. That one already came true because of you and them."

"And they'll know that, Janey. They already know how much you love them, and they'll always know that. Ohio will be just a brief blip in their lives before we come home to stay."

She took a deep breath and let it out slowly, trying to calm her wild emotions. "I'm sorry to be so over the top about this."

"You're not. I get it, babe. You're going to be really, really busy, and it'll cut into your time with the kids, but we'll make the best of the time we have together, and when you're busy, they'll have me."

She pulled back so she could see his face. "In case I forget to say thank you for this…"

He kissed her. "No thanks needed."

"Yes, Joe, I do need to thank you for everything you've done from the start to make this happen for me. I was thinking downstairs how cool it is that us going to Ohio brought Seamus here, and now he's married to your mom, and they're so happy."

"That's right. That never would've happened without you going to vet school. We have to look at all the positives."

"I'm glad you see him as a positive now."

Joe laughed. "It took a while for me to see him as my mother's partner, but the crazy Irishman has grown on me like nontoxic mold."

Janey lost it laughing. "He's a good guy."

"Yes, he is."

"You told them our plans, right?"

"Earlier today. They were very happy to hear you're going back to finish, even if they'll miss us. They said they'd come visit, too."

"I hope so."

Joe rubbed her back, which helped her relax and decompress. "As long as we have each other, everything will be okay. I promise."

Since that'd been true thus far, Janey decided to take him at his word.

CHAPTER 3

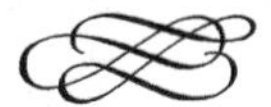

In Providence, Adam McCarthy had been up all night as he tried to think about anything other than the appointment that loomed over them like a dark cloud. Something wasn't right. Abby was almost to the end of her first trimester, but she looked much further along. From the outset of her high-risk pregnancy, David and Victoria at the Gansett Island clinic had advised them to seek out a specialist on the mainland to be doubly sure everything was okay.

They'd made an appointment at Women & Infants Hospital, waited weeks for the date to arrive, and in the next hour or two, they'd know more. Except he wasn't sure he wanted to know.

If something was wrong…

His heart broke at the thought of that. Abby had been through so much before they'd found each other, and even since then, being diagnosed with polycystic ovary syndrome and told she might never conceive. They'd adopted their son, Liam, last winter, but Abby's pregnancy had been a complete shock to both of them.

Their baby was a miracle, and he was determined to do whatever it took to make sure she and the baby were all right. Even if that meant moving to Providence for the duration of her pregnancy. They'd do it if they had to.

They'd hired a young woman named Candice to help run Abby's Attic at the Surf this summer. Candice had been a godsend so far, and if they had to rely on her to finish out the season at the store, so be it. Whatever it took to get Abby and the baby successfully through this pregnancy.

A chirp from the portable crib let Adam know eight-month-old Liam was awake. He went to retrieve him and found that Abby already had him up and was changing his diaper.

"I can do that if you want to sleep for a little while longer," Adam said.

"I didn't sleep at all, so I'm glad to have something to do."

"I didn't sleep either."

They worked together to get Liam washed up, dressed and fed.

"How about some breakfast?" Adam asked.

"I don't think I could eat. Maybe after the appointment. But you go ahead."

"I sort of feel the same way."

They put Liam on the floor in the living room to play with toys while they killed the last hour before it was time to go.

At the hospital, they were taken directly to the ultrasound department for the first of several appointments and tests that would be conducted before they saw the specialist.

Adam held Liam as the ultrasound technician moved the wand over Abby's protruding abdomen. He watched the screen but couldn't make heads or tails out of what he was seeing.

The technician moved the wand around, clicking something on the computer. Each click was like a shot to his nerves. What did it all mean? He took comfort in the very strong sound of the baby's heartbeat. After Mac and Maddie had lost their son Connor in utero, Adam had feared the same silence that had confronted his brother and sister-in-law at a routine ultrasound appointment.

"Excuse me for one minute," the tech said as she left the room.

"What's happening?" Abby asked, her brown eyes gone wide with fright.

"I'm sure it's nothing. You heard the heartbeat. That's what matters." He said what she needed to hear even as he tried to hide his own panic. He'd seen enough movies and videos to know that nothing good ever came of the tech leaving the room.

The tech returned five excruciating minutes later with another woman, who introduced herself as a doctor of radiology.

Adam didn't catch her name and didn't care what it was.

They started the entire process again from the beginning, as Adam and Abby were forced to wait in agonizing silence for someone to tell them what was going on.

Finally, the doctor looked up at them with an odd expression on her face. "Did you undergo fertility treatment?"

"No," Abby said. "Why?"

"Has anyone mentioned the possibility of multiples to you?"

"M-multiples?" Abby asked, gazing frantically at the doctor and then at Adam.

The doctor pointed to the screen. "We're detecting four heartbeats."

Adam's knees wanted to buckle under him. *"Four?"*

Still gesturing toward the screen, the doctor counted. "One, two, three, four."

Now that she pointed to each of them, he could see them. Four. Four babies. *Quadruplets.*

"I have PCOS. They..." Abby choked on a sob. "They said I couldn't have babies, and we... This wasn't supposed to happen."

"Well," the doctor said with a cheerful smile, "there's no question you're carrying four babies, which is why you're showing so early. Sometimes people with PCOS will suddenly drop a bunch of mature eggs. So it can happen. We'll get the ultrasound to your OB so you can figure out a plan going forward. Congratulations, Mom and Dad—times four."

The doctor and tech stepped out of the room, leaving the stunned parents alone.

"Adam," Abby said, gasping. "What did she just say?"

Adam was still trying to process the news himself but forced himself to rally for her sake. "It seems we're expecting quadruplets."

"H-how is that possible? They said we couldn't."

"I know, sweetheart." Still holding Liam, he leaned in to kiss the tears off her face. "It's a miracle."

"No, Adam, it's not a miracle! *Four babies!* What will we do? How will we—"

He kissed her until she stopped talking. "We'll figure it out the same way we have everything else. Now let's get you up and dressed and off to the next appointment so we can ask all our questions."

"I can't remember my own name right now. How am I supposed to ask questions?"

"Your name is Abigail Callahan McCarthy, and you're the strongest person I know. Whatever they tell us, we'll handle it. I don't want you to worry about anything." He helped her sit up and steadied her when she seemed like she might topple right off the exam table.

"I can't be pregnant with four babies. That doesn't just happen."

He smiled at the adorably confused expression on her face. "Apparently, it does."

"You're not allowed to find this in any way amusing, do you hear me?"

"I hear you, but I just want you to remember there're a lot of really awful things we could've heard today. This doesn't really count as awful."

"Spoken by the one who doesn't have to turn into a *beached whale* while having *four* babies!"

He couldn't help it. He laughed.

She punched him in the gut, making him gasp from the surprisingly hard hit.

"Ow."

"Do not laugh, Adam McCarthy, or I swear to God I might actually stab you for doing this to me."

"How is this my fault? I thought I was your hero for getting you pregnant in the first place when they told us that couldn't happen."

"You *were* my hero until I found out you're firing some sort of super sperm."

Adam's smile turned smug. "My boys are rather super."

"Still not funny."

"It's a little funny. Come on, you have to admit it."

"I have to do no such thing, and if you're wise, you'll keep your laughter to yourself. I don't think it's funny at all." She broke down again, her entire body shaking with the force of her emotions. "What is *wrong* with me? All I wanted was to be pregnant, and now I'm freaking out because it's not happening the way I thought it would."

Adam had to bite his lip not to laugh again. He sat next to her on the exam table and put his arm around her. "You're freaking out because we just got the most unexpected news we could've gotten. But we have to be thankful it was an overabundance of good news and not tragic news."

She nodded and wiped her face. "I know. It's just going to take me a minute to wrap my head around it."

"Me, too, sweetheart."

"We're going to have *five* babies, Adam."

"Yes, I heard about that."

"Five babies *under the age of two,* Adam."

"I got that memo."

She elbowed him in the ribs. "You still think this is funny."

"I figure it's better to laugh than cry."

"How are we going to do this?" she asked in a frantic tone.

He took her hand and held on tightly. "We're going to meet with the OB and find out what we need to do to keep you and the football team healthy. Then we'll figure out a birth plan that has you right here when you have them, and we'll recruit grandparents, aunts, uncles and friends to help us survive the first couple of months, and we'll make it work. Somehow."

"You're so rational. How can you be rational at a time like this?"

"One of us has to be."

She elbowed him again. "I can hear you laughing."

"I'm not laughing. Not much, anyway." He brought her closer to him and nuzzled her hair. "It's really your fault, you know."

"I can't wait to hear how it's *my* fault."

"You prayed so hard for a baby that you got four of them."

"I see what you're trying to do, and it's not going to work. It's one hundred percent your fault. Clearly, something is going on with you McCarthy boys knocking up your wives with multiples."

Adam puffed out his chest and received another elbow to the gut that promptly deflated him.

"Let's get moving to the OB appointment so they can tell me how in the hell I'm supposed to carry *four* babies."

Adam got up and used his free hand to help her down from the table. When she wobbled, he put his arm around her until she was steady. "Just hold on to me, sweet girl. I've got you."

"It's a very good thing I love you so much."

"It's a very good thing indeed."

CHAPTER 4

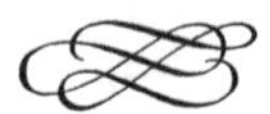

In Los Angeles, Stephanie McCarthy had been up since four in the morning, sitting in front of a huge window that overlooked the Pacific Ocean. Grant's Malibu house, the one thing he'd held on to from his previous life in LA, was one of her favorite places in the world. But even here, she couldn't seem to relax. She couldn't eat or breathe or do anything other than worry about how she would possibly sit through the premiere of the film he'd been working on for the better part of two years.

He'd written her story. Hers and Charlie's, and from all accounts, he'd done a masterful job of bringing their story to life on-screen.

But after having spent fourteen years desperately trying to free her beloved stepfather from prison, she and Charlie were now so far removed from that nightmare that it almost seemed as if it had happened to other people.

Almost…

Some scars couldn't be ignored no matter how well the wound had healed.

She rested a hand over the small bump of her abdomen where her baby was growing bigger by the day, even if she wasn't showing much yet. Victoria Stevens, the nurse practitioner-midwife on Gansett, had told her that was perfectly normal for someone of her slender build. She was right where she should be, or so Vic said, with her baby due in late December.

In truth, she never had shaken the feeling that she had no business having a child after being raised by a woman who thought nothing of beating the hell out of her own daughter. Her mother had been both wonderful and monstrous, and Stephanie had grown up navigating her mother's ever-changing moods.

Charlie's arrival on the scene when she was eleven had been the best thing to ever happen to her, until he'd been accused three years later of the abuse her mother had inflicted.

Stephanie shook off those memories, unwilling to fall into that rabbit hole when her life today bore no resemblance whatsoever to what it had been then. From the minute she'd fallen for Grant McCarthy—which had happened almost the second she met him, if she was being honest—everything had changed for the better. It was only thanks to him and his lawyer friend Dan Torrington that Charlie had been freed and exonerated, and that was the story that would be told in the film *Indefatigable*, set to debut that night.

Tears burned her weary eyes. Her beloved husband had worked tirelessly to write and coproduce the film that would share their story with the world. He'd gone all out to do justice to the epic war she'd waged to free Charlie.

And she couldn't bear to watch it.

"Hey." Grant's voice startled her from the disturbing thoughts. "You're up early."

"Couldn't sleep."

He sat next to her and turned so he could see her face. "Did you sleep at all?"

"Not much." With her head resting against the back of the sofa, she turned to look at him. "Are you excited for tonight?"

"I guess."

"You don't know for sure?"

"I'd be more excited if I didn't sense you melting down about it."

"I'm not."

He gave her a quelling look that made her feel silly for trying to downplay it. He always saw through to the heart of her. "Talk to me, Steph. Tell me what you're thinking, and let's figure it out."

Her eyes flooded with tears that infuriated her. She didn't want to be an emotional disaster area, but past agony resurrected by the film coupled with pregnancy hormones made it impossible for her to combat the overload.

He gathered her into his warm embrace. "Aw, baby, come on. Don't cry. You know it kills me when you cry."

She rested her head against his bare chest, loving the soft fuzz of chest hair under her cheek and the steady beat of his heart against her ear. "Sorry."

"Don't be sorry. I actually expected this to happen."

"Expected what?"

"That when push came to shove, you wouldn't want to see the finished product, and that's totally fine. I understand."

"I wish I did. You've worked so hard for so long. This is the biggest night of your life, and I need to be there."

"This isn't the biggest night of my life."

"Right. You won an Oscar. What am I thinking?"

His low rumble of laughter had her raising her head to see what was so funny.

He tipped her chin up, compelling her to look at him. "The biggest night of my life was the night you finally married me and made me the happiest and luckiest guy in the entire world. Nothing I ever do or have ever done would or could top that."

She sighed. "You still have a way with words."

"I hope so. They're my bread and butter."

"I want you to know how proud I am of you and how hard you've worked to tell our story in a way that's respectful of what we went through."

"It was a labor of love so big, it's the one thing I can't seem to describe in words." He caressed her face. "I want you to stay home tonight."

"I need to be there for you."

"You are. You're there for me every single day. You're the reason I had this incredible story to tell, a story that's resurrected my career, which was flagging badly before you came along with your guts and your grit and your determination. You inspired me, and you're the star of this entire thing, Steph. And while I can't wait for the rest of the world to know what an amazing woman my wife is, I've known that for a long time now. I get that it's too painful for you to relive the past, even for me, and I'd never put you through something that would hurt you."

"That's the thing. I don't know if it would hurt me, and I'm too scared to find out."

"You're not scared. You're protecting yourself from old wounds, and I completely understand that."

"Thanks to you and Dan and so many other people, I've traveled a million miles from the mess I was when we first met and—"

Grant kissed her. "You were *not* a mess. Please don't say that. You're the reason this film is called *Indefatigable*. You refused to give up, no matter how big the mountain was that stood before you. That's what people will see when they watch this film. They'll see the same brave, strong, resolute woman I saw when we first met."

"That's not what you saw," she said with a small smile, desperate for a bit of levity.

He grinned. "Well, after I got past your sexy body and saucy mouth and how you put me in my place like no one else ever has, I saw the rest of you, and I was in awe. I still am."

Deeply moved by his sweet words, she said, "I want to be there for you tonight."

"Let's do this… I'll go to the premiere by myself and send a car to pick you up for the after-party. That way, you can achieve your most pressing goal, which is meeting Flynn Godfrey and Hayden Roth."

Stephanie smiled. "Do you think we'll ever hear the end of Dan talking about Flynn playing him?"

Laughing, Grant said, "Never. I'll be hearing about that for the rest of my life."

They'd cast unknown actors to play Charlie, Stephanie and Grant, but they expected the star power of Flynn Godfrey, Quantum Studios and Hayden Roth's direction to make the film a massive hit. It was already generating Oscar buzz, and it hadn't even been released yet.

"What do you think? Sit out the screening and come to the party?"

"That sounds good. Thanks for understanding. I love you so much, and I'm so, so proud of you."

"I love you more, and I'm prouder of you than you'll ever be of me."

"Wanna bet?"

"Uh-huh." He kissed her lips and then her neck. "Come back to bed for a while."

"To sleep?"

"Sure. Unless something else comes up."

Stephanie laughed at the suggestive way he said that. "When we're in bed together, something else always comes up."

He helped her up and led the way to the bedroom. "I can't help it that you're so sexy, you make me want you all the time."

"So it's my fault, is it?"

"Absolutely." He eased her onto the bed and came down on top of her, careful not to put too much weight on the baby bump. "You make me crazy with wanting you, Mrs. McCarthy."

As she looped her arms around his neck, she drank in the sight of his handsome face, messy hair and scruffy jaw. She loved him like this, the way only she got to see him—completely relaxed, a little messy, incredibly sexy. "You make me just as crazy, and you know it."

"Mmm," he said, kissing her. "That makes us very lucky."

She reached around him to turn her Pooh bear to face away from what was apparently about to happen, making Grant laugh the way he always did when she shielded Pooh from what went on in their bed. "Now, what were you saying?"

He pressed his hard cock against the V of her legs. "It went something like this."

"Tell me more."

"Once upon a time," he said as he kissed her neck, "there was a strong, brave girl who spent years trying to right a terrible wrong." He removed her T-shirt and cupped her breasts, running his thumbs over the tight points of her nipples, which were extra sensitive thanks to pregnancy.

"She was faithful, loyal and true to the one person in her life who'd always been there for her." Drawing one nipple and then the other into the heat of his mouth, he sucked gently on them and nearly made her come from that alone. "Despite every one of the formidable obstacles she encountered, she never gave up on her goal. She sacrificed everything in her pursuit of justice."

Stephanie's heart filled to overflowing as his words moved her every bit as much as his tender touch did. Sometimes she still couldn't believe that this incredible man loved her the way he did.

He removed her panties and settled between her legs where he set out to drive her wild with his tongue and fingers. "And then somehow this strong, brave, warrior woman fell in love with me and changed my life in every possible way."

She came with a cry that echoed through the large room, and then moaned when he entered her in one deep thrust that filled her completely.

Nothing was better than this, than him and them and what they were together. "Grant," she said as she arched into him.

"What, honey?"

"Love you so much."

"Love you more."

She shook her head. "No way."

"Way." He kissed her and kept up the pace until they reached the finish line in a moment of sheer bliss that left her floating in the aftermath.

"Mmm," he said, "now that's how you start a day off right."

THAT NIGHT, Grant sat in the darkened theater with tears in his eyes as he watched Stephanie's story play out on the screen, seeing the finished film for only the third time. The actress had done such a wonderful job of capturing the desperation and frustration Steph had lived through for so many years as she fought an epic battle to free Charlie.

It had been vitally important to him that he and Dan not come off as the heroes of her story. Yes, he'd called his friend Dan, a celebrity lawyer known for his work to free unjustly incarcerated people, and Dan's name had gotten them a new hearing that had resulted in Charlie being set free.

But none of that would've happened without Stephanie and the effort she expended for so many years to save the one person who'd tried to save her and paid for that with fourteen years of his life spent behind bars. Charlie was played to gruff perfection by a newcomer who captured all his rough edges as well as his massive soft spot for the stepdaughter who waged war to save him.

By the time the closing credits rolled and the people in the theater went wild with applause and whistles, Grant was wiping actual tears off his face.

"Holy shit." Dan brushed at the dampness on his own face. "That was fucking *unbelievable,* Grant. Congratulations."

"Hayden gets the credit. He's the one who made it come alive."

"Your words were the magic, my friend. It's going to be a massive hit, and you'd better get your monkey suit ready for award season."

"I thought I knew Stephanie's story," Dan's wife, Kara, said, "but I only knew a fraction of it. That was truly remarkable. Congratulations, Grant."

"Thank you both for being here."

The four of them had flown together to LA for the premiere and were heading home to Gansett tomorrow. No one wanted to miss any more of summer on Gansett than they had to.

"Is Stephanie okay?" Kara asked gently.

"She's great, but she wasn't up for reliving it. Once was enough for her."

"I can totally understand that."

"She's meeting us at the after-party."

"Oh good," Kara said. "She can help us deal with him." She used her thumb to point at Dan. "Flynn Godfrey will be filing for a restraining order by the time Dan is through with him."

"Oh please," Dan said, scoffing. "Who else could've played me so convincingly but him?"

"I heard they tried to get SpongeBob, but he was booked solid," Grant said.

Kara howled with laughter and gave Grant a fist bump. "Good one."

"Flynn's the only actor in Hollywood good-looking enough to pull off Dan Torrington," Dan said.

"Do you see what I've been dealing with?" Kara asked Grant. "He speaks of himself in the third person now, too. I can't deal with him."

"I feel your pain," Grant said, laughing as he stood. "Let's get to the party so I can see my best girl."

"Before we go," Kara said, "I need to hug you and say thank you for doing such an absolutely beautiful job of telling Stephanie's story. We're so proud of you."

Grant returned her hug. "Thank you. That means a lot to me."

"All kidding aside, bro," Dan said. "It's a masterpiece."

"Thanks," Grant said, touched by their praise. "We'll never forget what you did for her."

"One of the most satisfying cases I've ever been involved in. Let's go party."

"He just wants more pictures with Flynn," Kara said, rolling her eyes.

"He's my new bestie," Dan said.

"Well, that's a relief," Grant replied. "I'm finally rid of you."

"You wish."

They greeted hundreds of people in the theater before heading across the street to the hotel ballroom where the after-party was being held.

Grant looked around the vast room before he saw her, sitting alone on a barstool, her back to the crowd that was flooding into the room. He'd know the copper color of her hair and those petite shoulders anywhere, and as he made his way to her, he noted that the color of her dress perfectly matched her hair.

Seeming to sense his approach, she turned, and a smile lit up her face when she saw him coming.

His heart gave a crazy lurch at the sight of her. It had been that way between them from almost the very beginning.

He bent to kiss her and slid his arms around her, relieved to be back with her after a few hours apart. It wasn't lost on him how ridiculous it was that being separated from her for even a few hours had become painful at some point in their time together. "Missed you," he whispered.

"Missed you, too. How was it?"

"Everything I hoped it would be and then some. I hope you're ready to be a star, babe."

"I'm not the star. You are. You wrote it."

"Stephanie, love... You're the star of this show in every possible way. I hope you're prepared for how interested people will be in the woman behind the story."

"Gulp."

Grant laughed. "The Quantum marketing team has a whole bunch of people interested in interviews, and rumor has it that *People* magazine wants to do a cover with us."

"Come on."

"No joke."

"Wow. I just never imagined... Wow."

"And don't look now, but here comes Flynn Godfrey and Hayden Roth, wanting to meet the woman of the moment."

"Don't let me faint."

"Wouldn't dream of it." Grant released her to shake hands with two of Hollywood's most successful men. If there'd been a dream team to work with on Steph's story, the Quantum team was it. "Flynn, Hayden, meet my wife, Stephanie Logan McCarthy."

"Is it okay if I hug you?" Hayden asked. "I feel like I've known you much longer than one minute."

"Of course," Steph said, hugging the handsome Oscar-winning director.

"Your story moved and amazed us all," Hayden said. "It was an honor to bring it to life on-screen. Thank you for trusting us with it."

"Grant said you're the best, and from what I hear, he was right."

"We are the best," Flynn said with a grin, "but your story blew us away from the first time we read the script."

"That was all him," Stephanie said, gesturing to her husband.

"No, babe," Grant said, "it was all you. There's no denying who's the heart and soul of this story."

"I couldn't agree more," Hayden said. "I'm sorry we weren't able to convince Charlie to come. I'd love to meet him, too."

"He's very happy at home on Gansett Island with his new wife," Stephanie said. "They're having a housewarming party Saturday night at their new home. The last thing he wants to do is revisit that time in his life, even though he was supportive of Grant writing the script."

"We're so happy he's found a satisfying new life," Flynn said.

"No one deserves it more," Stephanie said. "What he did for me, what he gave up…" She shook her head. "Grant and Dan don't want to hear that they're the heroes of the story, but without them, we'd never have gotten him out of prison."

"I think I speak for Grant when I say that helping to get justice for you and Charlie was one of the most satisfying things we ever did," Dan said when he joined them.

"I completely agree," Grant said. "Setting you two free and then telling the world what you did is a distant second to getting you to fall in love with me on my list of life achievements."

"That was the easiest thing I ever did," Stephanie said.

CHAPTER 5

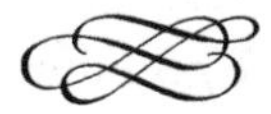

"What a night," Kara said to Dan as he drove them home hours later. "It's so nice to see Stephanie getting such praise for how she refused to give up on Charlie. And Grant for writing such a beautiful script."

"I know. I hope he's ready to add another Oscar to his shelf."

"That'd be so deserved." Kara yawned for the hundredth time since they'd left the party thirty minutes ago. "I'm going to sleep for a week when we get back to Gansett."

"You can't sleep for a week in August."

"Ugh, don't remind me." She had about four weeks remaining until her summer season running the launch service in North Harbor came to an end and she could relax until the spring.

"What's up with you being so crazy tired all the time?"

"That's what happens when I try to keep up with you."

"Seriously, Kara. You're freaking me out with all the sleeping. That's not like you."

"I don't know."

"Is it possible, you know, that you might be... well, pregnant?"

Kara laughed at that. "As you well know, it's more than possible."

"Do you think you are?"

"Could be. It would explain a few things."

"What other things besides being tired?"

"My boobs hurt, my pants feel snug, and I'm hungry all the time."

"Kara! When were you going to tell me you're pregnant?"

"As soon as I confirmed it."

Dan glanced in the rearview mirror before sliding across three lanes on the 5 and taking the next exit.

"What're you doing?"

"Finding a pharmacy to get a test."

"We can figure it out when we get home to Gansett."

"We're figuring it out right now." He drove faster than he should have through a commercial area and took a hard right turn into a pharmacy parking lot. "Lock the doors when I get out."

"Yes, dear." Kara watched him go, sinfully sexy in the tuxedo he'd worn to the premiere, eating up the sidewalk with his always-impatient stride, which was even more so now that he was on a mission to find out if she was pregnant. She giggled to herself, imagining her famous husband buying a pregnancy test. It'd probably be all over the news that she was pregnant before they knew themselves.

He returned ten minutes later carrying a big bag that he passed to her when he got in the car.

Kara looked inside and burst out laughing when she saw he'd bought no fewer than twenty tests. "We only need one."

"I want to be sure."

"I don't have enough pee for twenty tests."

"What do you need pee for?"

Kara lost it laughing again. "You have to pee on the stick to take the test."

"Jesus."

"How can you be thirty-eight and not know how a pregnancy test works?"

"Because I've never come close to being a father, until now."

"Don't get your hopes up. I might just be anemic or something."

"My hopes are up," he said as he drove toward the beach where he owned a house a half mile from Grant's.

"You're driving too fast."

"I'm in a hurry."

"Slow down, or I'll withhold my pee."

"That's gross, Kara."

"*Slow down,* Dan."

He downshifted the two-seater BMW he kept at the house in LA but didn't slow down all that much.

"I was thinking that we should name our first child Dylan," Kara said, "whether we have a boy or a girl. What do you think?"

He glanced over at her. "That'd be perfect," he said gruffly. "Thank you for honoring my brother that way."

"I wish I'd known him."

"I do, too. He would've loved you, but not as much as I do. It's still amazing to me…"

"What is?"

"How everything is so much better since you found me and saved me from myself."

Kara laughed at how he described their meeting. "Is that what I did?"

"You have no idea."

"You did the same for me. After my sister stole my boyfriend and then married him, I thought I'd never want to take another chance, and then there you were in your pink Oxford shirt and your ridiculous loafers, making a complete ass of yourself on a daily basis trying to get my attention."

"Um, hello, I was being totally serious, and you just insulted me."

"Did you or did you not make a complete ass of yourself trying to get my attention?"

"I brought you Diet Mountain Dew. Do you *know* how hard that is to find on Gansett Island?"

"Answer the question, Counselor. Did you or did you not make a complete ass of yourself?"

"I refuse to answer the question on the grounds of self-incrimination."

"Save your legal mumbo jumbo for someone who doesn't know all your BS."

"My 'legal mumbo jumbo' is in hot demand. In case you missed it, Oscar-winner Flynn Godfrey just played me in a movie. And if I may add, he did a good job, but he couldn't quite capture the sexy devil Dan Torrington really is."

"For fuck's sake," Kara muttered. "Do you ever get tired of listening to yourself talk?"

"Nope, not really, and neither do you."

"Yes, I do. I'm officially tired of hearing you talk about what a sexy devil you are and how Flynn Godfrey played you in the movie."

"I can't help that they had to get the handsomest guy in Hollywood to play me in order to do me justice."

"Shut up, Dan."

"Make me, Kara."

Thankfully, they arrived at the house, and she was saved from having to take drastic measures to shut him up while he was driving. He came around to give her a hand out of the low-slung car and steadied her when she wobbled on the ridiculous heels she'd bought for the premiere.

"In case I forgot to tell you earlier, you were a total smoke show tonight, babe. That dress is fire."

"This old thing?" Kara said, glancing back at him as he followed her up the stairs to the door. Their friend Tiffany Taylor had helped her find the perfect dress for the premiere, and Kara had never felt sexier than she did in the clingy black dress that was far more daring than she normally would've chosen for herself. Tiffany had that effect on her—and many others.

"That old thing has had me sporting wood all night."

"Honestly, Dan."

"Honestly, Kara." He put his arm around her from behind and pressed his hard cock to her back to make his point. "Been dealing with that since the first second I saw you in that dress."

"That long?"

"That long, so hurry up and go pee on a stick so we can do something about my stick."

She didn't want to laugh at that, because God forbid she should encourage his juvenile humor, but she couldn't contain the laughter.

He thrust the bag of pregnancy tests at her. "Do at least three of them. I want to be sure."

She took the bag from him, rolled her eyes and headed for the master bedroom, kicking off her heels as she went. Her feet were happy to be rid of them. Sky-high heels were so not her thing, but Tiffany had convinced her she couldn't wear *that* dress without *those* shoes along with the thong she also couldn't wait to be rid of. On second thought, she'd leave that on until Dan saw what she'd worn under the dress he liked so much. Another thing Tiffany excelled at was getting her to buy racy underwear that her husband went wild over.

He was too funny and too sweet and too everything. Despite his over-the-top ego and ridiculous new habit of speaking of himself in the third person, she loved him more than life itself and couldn't wait to give him a baby they'd name Dylan, after the adored brother he'd lost in Afghanistan.

In the bathroom, she shut and locked the door, because she wouldn't put it past him to come in there to watch her pee on the sticks. Her heart gave a little lurch when she realized what she was about to do. She'd suspected she might be pregnant when she missed her last period, but with the trip to LA and the premiere coming up, she'd planned to see Vic when she got back to the island to confirm it. Leave it to her hotshot lawyer husband to beat her to the punch. She shouldn't be surprised. He didn't miss much when it came to her, which was one of the things she loved best about him. He paid attention to her, and he had from the start, noting things like the soda she preferred before she'd given him so much as the time of day.

Her hands shook a little with excitement and nervousness as she opened three of the boxes, got the sticks and read the directions to make sure she did it right. She'd never taken a pregnancy test before, had never had so much as a scare, so this was all new to her, too. But at least she knew you had to pee on the sticks and still couldn't believe *he* hadn't known that!

When she was finished, she set the sticks on the counter and got busy taking off her makeup and brushing her hair.

A soft knock on the door sounded through the room.

Smiling, she went to open it to him. He'd removed his suit coat and bow tie, released the top buttons of his dress shirt and had his arms propped over his head on the doorframe. He was devastatingly beautiful, and even though he knew it, she loved him anyway.

"I can't believe you locked me out."

"Really? You can't?"

His playful scowl only made him cuter than he already was. "What's the verdict?"

"I haven't looked yet." She took his hand. "How about we look together?"

He gave her hand a squeeze. "Let's do it."

"We already did it. That's how we ended up in this boat."

"No one I'd rather be in any boat with, as I proved to you very early on by paying for many a ride on your boat before you were even nice to me."

They approached the vanity with trepidation, as if it might contain explosives that would detonate if they moved too quickly.

Kara looked down at the tests and saw three big plus signs.

"What's that mean?"

"Plus means positive."

"You're pregnant."

"So it would seem."

Dan let out an earsplitting whoop, picked her right up and swung her around, hugging her so tightly, she gasped. "Oh shit, what am I doing? You're pregnant, and I'm acting like Tarzan."

"If you start beating your chest, I might leave you."

He set her down gently, framed her face and gazed down at her. "You can't ever leave me, because you'd wreck me and because you're my whole world. You and our baby..."

She was stunned when she saw tears fill his eyes.

"You've made me so happy, Kara. You and baby Dylan."

Kara curled her arms around his neck and went up on tiptoes to kiss him. "You've made me just as happy."

"Let's go to bed and celebrate."

"Lead the way, my love."

He surprised her once again when he lifted her into his arms and carried her to bed, setting her gently on the mattress and then propping himself on his arms to gaze down at her.

"What?"

"Just looking at my beautiful baby mama."

"I can't believe we're going to have a baby."

"Are you excited?"

She nodded. "And scared."

"Why?"

"The whole pushing-a-pumpkin-out-of-my-body thing is a tad bit terrifying."

"Ugh, do you gotta put it that way?"

"How else should I say it?"

He lowered himself to kiss her, brushing the hair back from her face. "Don't be scared. We'll get you the best drugs money can buy."

"I won't say no to that."

"I'll be right there with you. I have no doubt you'll do great, and you'll make the prettiest baby ever. He or she will be so lucky to have you as their mom."

"And you as their dad."

"This is the best day of my whole life, and not because Flynn Godfrey played me in a movie."

Kara laughed and brought him all the way down on top of her.

"I don't want to squish the baby."

"The baby is fine." She curled her legs around his hips and pressed against his hard cock. "But your wife could use some attention."

"My wife has my undivided attention."

Once upon a time, Kara had thought she would marry a man named Matt, before she found out he'd been secretly dating her sister at the same time he was leading her to believe they were headed toward marriage. Now Kelly was married to him, and Kara was thankful every day that they'd betrayed her, because they'd led her, indirectly, to this perfectly imperfect man.

"What're you thinking?" he asked, studying her in the intent way he had of making her feel seen and adored.

"About the long and winding road that brought us together and how thankful I am for the people who stabbed me in the back and led me to you."

"I'm thankful to them, too, even if I still want to stab them for hurting you the way they did."

"No more stabbing. We've had enough of that." She took hold of the hand that had been sliced open at their engagement party by a knife-wielding Jim Sturgil and kissed the pale white scar that ran the length of his palm.

"Are we really having a baby?" he asked, his expression still awestricken.

"It appears that way."

"When can I tell people?"

"Not for a while. We want to make sure it's going to take."

He'd been rocking against her suggestively until she said that. "What's that mean?"

"A lot of pregnancies end in miscarriage. Surely you must know that much."

"Don't even say that word. Nothing is going to happen to our baby."

"Still... Let's keep it between us for now."

"Ugh, if I have to."

"You do know it takes, like, forty weeks to have a baby, right?"

"That's a long-ass time."

"Yes, it is, and you can't be *extra* the entire time."

He pushed against her suggestively again. "I'm always extra, baby. That's one of the things you love best about me."

She rolled her eyes and gave his hair a gentle tug. "How about less talk and more action?"

"Action is my middle name." He slid a hand under her skirt, encountered the thong and froze. "Well, what have we here?"

"You'll have to take a look and see."

"Don't mind if I do." He pushed himself up so he could help her out of the dress and then sat back on his heels to admire the skin-tone bra and thong Tiffany had chosen for her. "Could I please have a picture of how you look right now? I swear no one else will ever see it but me."

Kara laughed to cover her nervousness. "Sure."

Dan bounded off the bed to get his phone. "Don't move." When he returned to the room, he stopped short at the sight of her... hair loose around her shoulders, propped on her elbows, legs slightly apart.

Before him, she wouldn't have had the courage to put herself on display that way. But he loved her so much and made her feel so desired that it was easy to do things with him that wouldn't have happened with anyone else.

He took a couple of quick photos, tossed the camera aside and hastily undressed before rejoining her on the bed and kissing her with the kind of wild desire that had become part of her everyday life. "Want you so bad, sweet Kara, love of my life, mother of my baby."

"I want you, too. Always."

He was in such a rush, he didn't bother to remove the thong, but rather moved it out of his way and took what they both needed. "*Yes*. God, I was dying for you all night."

No one had ever said things like that to her before he did. He made love to her with urgency and reverence. "Look at me, sweetheart."

She looked up at him.

"Tell me the truth."

"About what?"

"You're not picturing Flynn Godfrey right now, are you?"

Sputtering with laughter, Kara spanked his ass. "Shut up and finish what you started, will you?"

"Gladly."

CHAPTER 6

On Saturday morning, Dara Watkins stood on the ferry's bow and watched the island come into sight as the sea spray brought back memories still so painful, she almost couldn't bear them. Lewis had loved the ocean and their annual trips to North Carolina's Outer Banks, where he'd chased the seagulls, dug holes in the sand and splashed in the surf.

The beach had been one of their happiest places, although everywhere had been happy with him.

Now…

Now she just didn't care.

Oliver had applied for the lighthouse job without consulting with her first, figuring it was a long shot. And when the Gansett Island Town Council had chosen them from all the applicants, he'd been excited about something for the first time in a year of dark despair. So she'd gone along with his plan because it was something to do other than obsess about what used to be. But she simply didn't care. She didn't care about anything or anyone, even Oliver.

She didn't know if he knew that and didn't care if he did.

If it was possible to be completely dead inside while continuing to live, she was the epitome of the walking dead. Her child was gone. Her life had lost all meaning, and a year in a lighthouse on Gansett Island wasn't going to fix what was so irreparably broken in her.

It certainly wouldn't bring Lewis back, which was the only thing she really wanted, to go back to that fateful Sunday, to the peaceful hours before their lives had been shattered. Since that couldn't happen, what else mattered?

Nothing. Not even the husband she'd once adored. Everything inside her was dead, even her love for him, and she didn't care.

With their dog Maisy's leash looped around his wrist, Oliver approached her, holding two coffees, and handed one to her.

She took it from him. "Thanks."

"Does it look familiar?" he asked of the island view.

"Not really. I was twelve the one time I came with my friend's family. I don't remember much about it, except there was ice cream." Even the words *ice cream* were painful now. Lewis had loved ice cream.

Dara fixed her gaze on the rugged coastline of the island and sipped from the coffee cup. For a time after they'd lost Lewis, she'd wanted to end her own life. She'd gone so far as to think about how best to achieve that goal. But then her parents had come to visit, and her mother had tuned in to Dara's deepening despair.

"Please don't put me through what you're going through," her mother had said tearfully. "No matter how bad it gets, please don't do that to me."

Dara had had nothing to say in response to that, but her mother's pleas had ended those thoughts. Since then, she'd been forced to figure out how to stay alive while wishing she were dead so she could be with her baby again.

Before disaster struck, she'd been a prosecutor. Now, she was a shell of that person, someone who'd once had a life in addition to being Lewis's mom. Maybe if she hadn't been so ambitious, she wouldn't have been sealed off in her office when her toddler let himself out of the house that fateful afternoon.

"Looks like a pretty place," Oliver said.

"Yes."

That counted as conversation for them these days. It was all she was capable of—one-word answers and a nod to let him know she'd heard whatever he'd said.

She didn't care what he said.

He'd suffered as much as she had, if not more. She'd been working when Lewis left the house. Oliver had been asleep on the sofa. He blamed himself. Dara blamed him. She hated him for taking a nap, and yes, she knew that was unfair. She didn't care about fairness or anything else.

Her son was dead. What else mattered? Nothing mattered. That's why she didn't care about going to Gansett Island to live in a lighthouse. A change in geography wasn't going to fix what was wrong with her, what was wrong with them.

Maisy nudged at her leg.

Dara scratched the Lab's blond head absently. Sometimes she felt like Maisy was the only one who truly understood how she felt. Maisy had seen it happen and had never been the same. Her heartbreak was every bit as significant as Dara's, and that made Maisy the one "person" Dara still truly cared about.

"Dara."

She realized Oliver had been trying to get her attention.

"They're calling us to the car."

"Oh. Okay."

As she followed him through the large cabin to the stairs, a woman chasing a toddler grabbed him right before he would've crashed into Dara.

"I'm so sorry," the boy's mother said, grimacing. "He's a holy terror today."

Dara had to stop herself from telling her to enjoy every second with her holy terror because you never knew when they might be ripped from your life. She'd been as guilty as the next busy mother of not fully appreciating what she'd had until he was gone. And now she'd give anything for one more chance to chase Lewis, to grab him and hug him and chastise him for trying to get away.

They'd always been so careful with him, she thought as she went down the stairs to the deck where they'd left their car. They'd never let him out of their sight, hadn't taken any chances with his safety and had put him in swim lessons as soon as possible because several of their friends had pools. Their child wasn't going to drown on her watch.

That was the thing she couldn't get past. They'd done everything right, and tragedy had found them anyway. She was bitter about that part of their story. She'd seen friends' kids run wild, unsupervised, and had never let Lewis do things that might get him hurt, or worse. And the bad thing had happened anyway.

As they waited in Oliver's SUV for the cars in front of them to drive off the ferry, Dara wondered what the hell she was doing on this island in the middle of nowhere. "How do we know how to find the lighthouse?" Dara asked.

"Mr. McCarthy, the president of the Gansett Town Council, is meeting us at the ferry office."

In her past life, Dara would've had more questions. Like, how would they recognize Mr. McCarthy, and what would it be like to live in a lighthouse, and what was there to do on Gansett Island? Now? She didn't care. Today was just another day to get through on her way to being reunited with her precious son. That was what she cared about—being with Lewis again and ridding herself of the terrible, desperate ache she lived with every minute of every day. Until that day, she put one foot in front of the other and functioned at the most basic level possible.

They drove off the ferry into an area where people, cars, cargo and bikes converged into a much busier scene than she would've expected for a small island in the middle of nowhere.

Oliver put down the window and asked one of the uniformed employees where the ferry office was.

He pointed at a small shingled building on the far side of the parking lot.

"Thanks." Oliver drove to the building, where a tall man with gray hair waited with a petite blonde woman. "That's him." Oliver pulled into one of the few available parking spaces and got out of the car to shake hands with both of them.

Because the window was up and the AC on, Dara couldn't hear them getting acquainted and made no move to get out to join them. A tap on the window had her putting it down.

"Hi, Dara, I'm Linda McCarthy. I wanted to welcome you to Gansett."

"Thank you. It's nice to meet you." She went through the motions, shook the woman's outstretched hand, did what was expected. That was the easy stuff.

"We're going to show you the way to the lighthouse."

"Sounds good. Thank you."

Oliver got back in the car, and they followed Mr. McCarthy's pickup truck out of the busy downtown area to a far more rural road that wound around the island.

"It sure is pretty," Oliver said.

She hadn't noticed. "Uh-huh."

A short time later, they drove through an open gate and down a long drive that led to the lighthouse at the edge of the coastline. The property was apparently open to the public, which no one had bothered to mention as far as she knew, and the lighthouse itself was a lot smaller than she'd expected it to be. Although, what did she have to compare it to?

Dara got out of the car, took a look around, hoping she might feel a spark of anything, but like always, there was just more nothing.

Linda handed her a set of keys. "The big one is for the gate, which is one of the few official duties the lighthouse keepers have. You're also asked to report the weather conditions to the Coast Guard twice a day and interact with the visitors as you see fit."

"That last part isn't required, is it?"

"Of course not. You can do whatever you wish. No one will be checking. Well, except for the Coast Guard for the weather."

"That's fine," Dara said.

"Come in and let me show you around. It's the cutest place."

Dara followed Linda into the circular building.

"This is a mudroom of sorts. You're welcome to use the beach chairs and anything else that's been left by the previous occupants. Some of our good friends have had this job in the past, and they absolutely loved it."

Linda went up a spiral staircase to the first floor, which housed a galley kitchen and a living room. "The bedroom and bathroom are up there," she said, pointing to the stairs that led to a second floor.

Trying to be polite, Dara went up the stairs to check out the accommodations and noted the king-sized bed and bathroom with a standup shower. It wasn't fancy, but it would do. As she headed for the stairs, her eyes were drawn to the panoramic view of the island and the ocean. She went for a closer look and found herself interested in something for the first time in longer than she could recall.

The view was stunning. From this vantage point, she could see there was a beach at the bottom of the cliff and wondered if it was accessible.

"It's something, isn't it?" Linda asked.

"Sure is," Dara said. "The beach down there... Can we get to that?"

"There's a set of stairs that take you right to it."

Dara nodded and turned to face Linda.

"If there's anything at all that you need, you only have to give us a call." Linda handed over a slip of paper with several numbers on it. "We want you to feel at home here."

"I'm not sure it's possible to feel at home anywhere anymore."

"It is," Linda said. "It's going to take some time, but you'll get there."

Dara looked directly at Linda. In her eyes, she saw compassion and understanding. Oliver had told her about the letter he'd written to apply for the job. "Have you been where I am?"

"Not quite, but I did lose an unborn baby who I've mourned for more than thirty-five years. It's not the same as what happened to you, not even close, but..."

"Grief is grief."

"Yes, I suppose so. I just want you to know... There's an amazing community that lives year-round on the island, and if you'd like, I'd be happy to introduce you to our family and friends. A few of the former lighthouse keepers have interesting stories you might relate to."

In her past life, Dara might've been interested in meeting new people and hearing the stories of the people who'd lived before them in the lighthouse. Now? Not so much. "We'll see what happens."

"Of course. The offer stands. Gansett Island is a great place to live. I hope you'll find some peace here."

"That'd be nice." And with that, she'd said more to this perfect stranger than she'd said to anyone close to her in more than a year. What was there to say?

They went downstairs to where Oliver was having an animated conversation with Mr. McCarthy. That he could smile like that and make conversation with strangers made her want to punch him. What was *wrong* with him?

"We'll leave you to get settled," Mr. McCarthy said. "Did Linda give you our numbers?"

"She did," Dara said. "Thank you."

"Please call if there's anything at all we can do to make you feel more comfortable," he said.

He seemed like a nice man, someone she might've been interested in getting to know if things had been different.

"Thank you for meeting us," Oliver said, shaking hands with them both before he walked them down to see them out.

He returned a few minutes later carrying suitcases that he took up to the second floor. "Wow, the view from up there is amazing," he said as he came back down with more pep in his step than he'd had in months.

Oliver took two more trips to the car, unloading the small amount of personal items they'd packed—bed linens, towels, extra blankets, Maisy's things and some kitchen essentials. Everything else they owned was in storage, waiting for them to figure out what would happen after this year on Gansett.

They'd sold the house where disaster had struck and could live comfortably off the proceeds for a while, but sooner or later, they'd have to go back to real work. She couldn't for the life of her imagine working at the level she had before—or at any level, for that matter.

"Let's make the bed," Oliver said.

She followed him upstairs and went through the motions of putting sheets and a quilt on the bed. They'd been told there was no air conditioning in the lighthouse, but that they wouldn't need it most of the time.

When they were finished, Oliver sat on the edge of the bed.

Since she didn't know what else to do with herself, Dara sat next to him.

"I'm hoping we can find our way out of the nightmare here," he said softly.

"I don't know if that's possible."

It was the most they'd said to each other about their new reality in months of uncomfortable silence on the subject of Lewis and the hell they'd been living in since his death.

"We have to try, Dar. What choice do we have?"

They had no choice, but she didn't want to try. That would take more energy than she could muster.

"Do you want to check out the beach?"

She didn't, but she'd do it so he wouldn't give her that soulfully imploring look that she was so tired of seeing from him. "Sure."

CHAPTER 7

"There it is," Slim Jackson said as Gansett Island came into view, and he experienced the usual feeling of homecoming after being away from his favorite place. They'd spent a rare summer week off-island in Bryn Mawr to celebrate Erin's parents on their anniversary, but it was good to be home. "You got this, babe?"

"Uh, I think so."

"You're ready. All those touch-and-go landings you did in Florida last winter were getting you ready for this." She'd piloted this entire flight, from takeoff in Philadelphia straight through to the approach to Gansett. He was sitting in the right-side seat, acting as her copilot, not that she needed one. His love was a natural with all the sensibilities of a seasoned pilot, and he'd never been prouder of any student than he was of her.

After losing her twin brother in the 9/11 attacks on New York City, Erin hadn't stepped foot on a plane for more than a decade, until Slim had flown her home to Pennsylvania after her father took ill.

"Talk me through it, will you?"

"Nope."

She took her eyes off the "road" long enough to glance at him in surprise. "Nope?"

"You don't need my help. You know what you're doing."

"Don't be silly. Of course, I need your help."

"No, you don't." He crossed his arms to make his point. "Bring us home, sweetheart."

"If it looks like we're going to crash, do something, will you?"

Slim laughed at her sarcastic tone. He loved her sarcasm, her humor, her sweet face and every other thing about her. She was it for him, and he'd never been happier than since she'd come into his life. Teaching her to fly had been one of the greatest thrills he'd ever experienced, and knowing what she'd overcome to get to this point made the victory that much sweeter.

Out of the corner of his eye, he watched her go through the steps he'd helped her to memorize. She paid attention to detail, which was one of many things that made her an excellent pilot. He was about to remind her to call in to the tower when she activated the radio and took care of that.

Slim smiled, his chest bursting with pride as she lined up the final approach and brought them in for a smooth, perfect landing. "Hot damn! Look at you go!"

Her delighted laughter filled him with unreasonable joy. "I did it!"

"You did it. You're ready to solo."

"Hell, no, I am not." She taxied them expertly to the spot on the tarmac where he always parked the plane and cut the engines. "That's not happening."

"Erin, honey, look at me."

She turned to him, albeit reluctantly.

Slim took her chin and looked her in the eyes. "You are *ready*."

"I don't want to solo. I don't want to be licensed. What I've already done is more than enough for me. It's way more than I ever thought I'd ever do. Remember when I didn't think I'd ever get on a plane again?"

"I remember," he said, caressing her cheek. "And I'm so, so proud of how far you've come since then. I don't think I've ever been prouder of anyone in my entire life. You just flew us from Philly to Gansett, Erin. I never touched the controls."

"I know, Slim," she said smugly. "I did do that."

"So why not finish it up? Do the solo, get your license. Imagine how you'll feel when you're holding that piece of paper."

"I don't need that. This—what I just did, what I've been doing for months—it's enough for me. I'll never have the need to fly anyone anywhere like you do, and I don't want to solo."

"Because you're afraid to?"

"Well, yeah, a little bit. Mostly, it's because it wouldn't be any fun if you weren't along for the ride. We both know I could do it if I had to, and that's more than I ever expected to achieve when we started the lessons. You not only taught me how to fly, you took the fear out of it for me. That's so, so huge, and I'll always love you for that."

Slim leaned over to kiss her. He could never resist her, especially when she was telling him she loved him.

She placed her hand on his face. "You're the only passenger I'll ever have, so what's the point of a license?"

"I think it would mean something to you to have it, even if you never use it."

"It wouldn't. I'm delighted to have come this far, to know I could do it if I wanted to, which I don't. You understand that, don't you?"

"I'm trying to. It's something I want for you, but only if you do, too."

"I've given this a lot of thought, and my conclusion is that this, what I just did, is enough. Can you live with that?"

"Of course I can. All I wanted was for you to overcome your fear of flying. That you're also an outstanding pilot makes it that much better."

"I had an outstanding instructor." She kissed him again. "And now we need to get going because we have a party to get to."

"Before we do that, hear me when I tell you that was a beautiful flight, I'm super proud of you, and I love you more than anything."

Smiling, she said, "That's better than any license could ever be, and besides, I already have the best license ever—the marriage license."

"That's true. Best license for sure." He shifted his hand to her rounded abdomen. "How's the Peanut?"

"Doing well, but sitting on Mommy's bladder."

"Let's get going so you can stretch."

They got out of the plane and worked together to tie it down before retrieving their bags from the back. Slim took hold of her hand as they walked to the parking lot, stopping only so Erin could use the restroom. "Best thing I ever did was pick you up on the side of the road that night," he said as he often did.

"Stop saying it like I was a hooker or something!"

"Why stop now? It's tradition. And holy shit, it's hot on Gansett."

"I was just going to say the same thing. The last time it was this hot, Jenny almost roasted to death in the lighthouse."

"I hope the AC is working at Sarah and Charlie's," Slim said. "Or it's gonna be a hot one."

~

"How can it not be working?" Sarah asked Charlie. "It's brand-new."

"I'm working on it, sweetheart. Go do something else and try not to worry."

"Right. Don't worry about the AC not working on the hottest day of the year when we've got a hundred people coming."

"What's not working?" Sarah's son John asked when he came into the kitchen wearing only a pair of shorts in deference to the heat. His blond hair was a mess, and his jaw was covered in scruff. The older he got, the more he resembled his eldest brother, Owen.

"The AC."

"Oh damn. You need help, Charlie?"

"Only if you know how to fix an AC compressor."

"I wish I did." A second later, John called from the kitchen, "Uh, Mom? I don't think it's just the AC. The coffeemaker isn't working either."

"*What?*" Sarah left the utility room where Charlie was working on the AC and went into the kitchen. She stopped short when she noticed the power was off to all the appliances. "Charlie! We've lost power. That's why the AC isn't working. Did we trip a circuit breaker?"

"I'm checking them," Charlie said.

Sarah's cell phone rang, and she took a call from Owen. "Hi, honey. You won't believe what's going on over here."

"Do you guys have power?"

"No, we just noticed it's out. Why?"

"We're out, too. We're hearing the whole island is."

The news hit Sarah like a punch to the gut. "Oh my God. I have a fridge full of food, no way to cook it and it's hot as hell. This is a five-alarm housewarming disaster."

Her youngest son, Jeff, walked into the kitchen, brown hair standing on end, face covered in stubble and, like his older brother, wearing only a pair of athletic shorts. She loved seeing her boys a little disheveled, free to be themselves now that they were out from under the ruthless reign of their military officer father, who'd demanded their children always be "squared away." Whatever that meant.

"What's going on?" Jeff asked.

"The power's out, and Mom's melting down," John said.

"Literally," Sarah said, wiping sweat from her brow. "What're we going to do?"

"Send the boys over to the Surf with Charlie's truck," Owen said. "We've got a couple of grills we can move to your house."

"We need extra coolers and ice, too."

"I'll give you what I can spare."

"Thank you, O. That's great." Sarah's mind whirled with contingency plans. Hopefully, the power wouldn't be out for long and their party wouldn't be a complete disaster. "The boys will be there soon."

"I'll be over to help out in a bit."

"Don't worry about us if Laura needs you at the hotel."

"We're covered for the day so we could be free to enjoy the party. No worries."

"Then I gratefully accept your help."

"See you soon."

Sarah went to plug her phone back into the charger before realizing there was no point. "Boys, your brother wants you to bring Charlie's truck to the Surf to pick up a couple of extra grills, some coolers and ice. Can you do that for me?"

"Sure," John said. "Can we use your grill to make coffee?"

"Do you know how to do that?" Sarah asked.

"Do it all the time when I'm camping."

"Make it a double, bro," Jeff said.

"Coming right up."

While John went out to the deck to fire up the grill she and Charlie had bought for their new house on a trip to the mainland a week ago, Sarah turned to her youngest. "It's a nice surprise to see you here."

"Well, I was invited to the party," he said with a grin that reminded her of Owen. Though Jeff had his father's darker hair and eyes and Owen favored her, there was a hint of his eldest brother in him just the same.

"Of course you were, but I didn't expect you or John to actually come."

"We wanted to be here for you, to help you celebrate this awesome new house."

"It is kind of awesome, isn't it?" Sarah asked as she looked around at the open-concept contemporary with the sweeping ocean views. "We've been here two weeks, and I still can't believe I actually live here."

"You deserve this, Mom. You deserve it all. Enjoy every second of it."

Sarah hugged him. "Thanks, sweetie. Tell me about you. What's going on?"

"Nothing much, which is why it was a good time to come up for a visit."

"Work is good?" Sarah asked as she made a mental list of what she needed to do before the party at two—and wondered how she'd do half of it without power.

"It's a job. I didn't suffer through college to wait tables, but there's nothing happening with the job search. I'm about to give up on Florida and move up here."

"Really? That'd be wonderful!"

"What would be wonderful?" Sarah's mother, Adele, asked as she came in through the kitchen door. Having her parents living in the guest cottage on their property was the best part of the whole situation. They'd been thrilled to accept her and Charlie's offer of a new home on Gansett Island.

"Jeff is thinking about moving up here," Sarah said.

"That would be wonderful indeed," Adele said, kissing her youngest grandchild on the cheek.

Jeff put his arm around his grandmother and gave her a squeeze. "It's no fun in Florida since you guys moved home."

When Sarah had still been trapped in a violent, abusive marriage, her parents had saved Jeff's life by intervening when he became addicted to drugs. He continued to have a tight bond with his grandparents, and Sarah would be forever grateful to them for stepping up for her son when she'd been locked in a hellish marriage. Back then, her parents and children had kept things from her that would've made her nightmare even worse than it already was.

"We do bring the fun wherever we go," Adele said. "I came over to see if you guys have power."

"Nope," Jeff said, "and Mom is freaking out."

She playfully bopped Jeff on the head. "You would be, too, if you had a hundred friends and family coming in a few short hours."

"We'll make it happen, Mom," John said when he came in from the deck with two mugs of coffee. He handed one of them to Jeff. "Don't worry."

"What?" Sarah said. "Me worry?"

"This happened once during the height of the season." Adele and her husband, Russ, had owned and operated the Sand & Surf Hotel for more than fifty years. "I think it was 1973 or 74. We were without power for *days*, but we made do. Somehow."

"Let's hope that doesn't happen this time," Sarah said.

"Did they ever figure out what happened?" John asked his grandmother.

"It was hot like it is now, and the demand for AC overwhelmed the system."

"It must've been upgraded since then," Jeff said. "Right?"

"I can't recall hearing that it was upgraded," Adele said.

"That's not good news," Sarah said, her spirits plummeting. They'd so looked forward to this day and to celebrating with their friends and family. She and Charlie had quietly gotten married over Memorial Day Weekend, so this day was also a celebration of their marriage.

A few minutes later, her daughter Julia came in with her boyfriend, Deacon Taylor, bringing coolers of ice from the Wayfarer. "They closed down for the day due to the power outage," Julia said, "so Nikki sent the ice over. Where do you want it?"

Shane and Katie were right behind them, rolling their grill through the kitchen to the back deck. "Heard you needed grills," Katie said, kissing her mom.

While Katie was blonde, her fraternal twin, Julia, had dark hair. They had fallen for handsome, wonderful men who were nothing like the father they'd grown up with. Sarah gave thanks every day for Charlie, Laura, Shane and Deacon, and hoped her younger four children would eventually find their perfect mates, too.

Charlie appeared next to Sarah, who stood at the massive island in the middle of her kitchen and watched with amazement as her kids stepped up for her. But even their help couldn't quite stem the full-on panic she felt brewing at the thought of entertaining a hundred people with no power. "Whatever you're thinking, knock it off. We've got this. Don't worry about a thing."

"How do you always know what to say to me?"

"I can tell by the way your lips are all tight that you're unhappy. I don't like when you're unhappy."

And that, right there, was the primary difference between her blissful second marriage and the nightmare first one. Charlie loved her and wanted only the best for her and the ones she loved.

He massaged her shoulders with strong hands that touched her only with love and gentleness. "Relax, babe. It's all gonna be fine. Look at them." He tilted his chin to include her kids, their partners, her mother. "Steph and the rest of them will be here in a bit. What else matters?"

"Nothing," Sarah said, relaxing into his loving embrace. "Well, except food poisoning. That matters."

Charlie's bark of laughter made her smile. "We won't let that happen."

CHAPTER 8

Gansett Island Chief of Police Blaine Taylor had looked forward to a rare summer day off with his wife and daughters and a good time with their friends and family at Charlie and Sarah's party. With the power out across the island, he'd been called back to work, which put him in a foul mood.

Jack Downing, the state police officer who was permanently assigned to Gansett, had joined him at the public safety building along with Linc Mercier, the Coast Guard commander who ran the Gansett Island station. They were waiting for Fire Chief Mason Johns to arrive when Big Mac McCarthy came in. As president of the town council, he had a role to play in the conversation, too.

"Well, gentlemen, this is a fine mess," Big Mac said, his trademark humor unaffected by the lack of power during a sweltering heat wave. "I've been making noise about the power grid for years now. No one wants to spend the money to upgrade."

"And no one wants to talk about wind or solar power either," Blaine said. Both had been rejected out of fear of the necessary equipment sullying the landscape and views. "If this goes on for a day or two, people might change their tunes."

"We can only hope," Linc said.

"I've been in touch with the mainland, and they're aware that we're out," Jack said. "I'm waiting for a call back from the power company." Jack was tall, with reddish-brown hair and brown eyes, and according to Blaine's wife, Tiffany, he was a "hot ginger," whatever the hell that meant.

Mason came in a few minutes later, dressed in uniform. "I came as soon as I got your message, Jack. What're we hearing?"

"Not much of anything yet," Blaine said. "We're waiting to hear from the power company and the governor's office."

"Is anyone looking at this as some sort of deliberate act?" Mason asked.

Blaine glanced at Jack, who shook his head. "I don't think so. You'd have to know what you were doing to knock out power to the entire island, and if you didn't know what you were doing, you'd be a fool to mess with the substations. I think it's what Mr. McCarthy said—an old system that should've been updated years ago buckling under increased demand due to the heat wave."

"What's the chance of getting it back before the end of the day?" Blaine asked.

"If past history is any indication," Big Mac replied, "not good. The last time it happened, six years ago, we were out for five days."

The entire group groaned.

"I couldn't believe it didn't happen a couple of years ago with the heat wave that came through," Big Mac said. "Held my breath the whole time it was hot like that."

"What does this mean for emergency preparedness?" Linc asked.

"We've got generators for this building and at the clinic," Blaine said.

"We've got some at the marina," Big Mac said, "but most of them are accounted for."

"Do we need to stop the incoming ferries?" Mason asked.

"I don't think we can do that to the business people who rely on summer weekends for their livelihoods," Big Mac said. "Everyone will have to punt."

Blaine conferred with the others on what they needed to be ready for if the outage lasted a day or two. He didn't want to think about it going beyond that.

"The last time this happened," Big Mac said, "people got nutty after the first day. The bars will do big business."

"Great," Blaine said. Like he didn't have enough trouble with drunks this time of year. "Let's do a test of the 911 and other emergency systems to make sure everything is working on remote power."

An hour later, confident that his subordinates had things under control and with orders to call him if needed, Blaine left the public safety building to resume his precious weekend day off already in progress. He was on the way home when Tiffany called. She'd gone in to her Naughty & Nice shop to check on things before taking the rest of the day off with him. "What's up, babe?"

"Just a little power failure to cut short a day at the shop."

"Did you shut down?" he asked, knowing how important summer weekends were to her business.

"We did. It's just too hot without AC, and it was dead anyway. This heat is sucking the life out of everyone. How are things at home?"

"I had to get my mom to come stay with the girls because I got called into the station when the power went out. I'm on the way home now."

"What're you hearing about the power?"

"That it's not good. The last time this happened, it was out for days."

"I remember that. We'd just moved back to the island. Ashleigh was a baby. It was so hot."

"It's probably going to be like that again. We've got the generator to run the fridge at least."

"You were right, dear."

Blaine laughed. "The words every man loves to hear." He'd insisted they grab one the previous fall in case they lost power during winter snowstorms. He hadn't expected they might need it in the summer, too. "From what I hear, the power grid is old and should've been replaced decades ago."

"Fantastic. So we're in for a siege, then."

"Possibly, but look at the upside."

"There's an upside?"

"Uh-huh. Very sweaty sex."

"How is that an upside?"

"Baby, I can't wait to show you later."

"I'll look forward to that."

"Is the party still on at Sarah and Charlie's?" he asked.

"As far as I know."

He'd no sooner pulled into the driveway than she appeared next to him in her red VW Bug, flashing him the irrepressible grin that was all Tiffany. And damn if his heart didn't still give a happy lurch at the sight of his love, even after all this time together.

He waited for her to get out of the car and held out his hand to her. "Why do I feel like I haven't seen you in weeks when it's only been a few hours?"

"Because you're silly that way?"

"If being obsessed with my sexy wife makes me silly, I can handle that." With his arm around her, they walked inside, where they found a note from his mom.

Took the girls for a walk to the park. Back in an hour or so.

She'd included the time, indicating they'd left ten minutes ago. He'd never loved his mother more than he did just then. Between work and kids and life, the summer was their busiest season, and by August, Blaine was more than ready for it to be over so he could have more time at home with his girls.

He surrounded Tiffany from behind, molding his body to hers.

"Too hot for that, cowboy," she said as she poured a glass of the decaffeinated iced tea she drank when pregnant.

"We have fifty kid-free, work-free minutes *during the day* in *August,* Tiffany."

She fanned her face. "It's hot, Blaine."

"And about to get hotter." He turned her to face him, caressing her cheek and stealing a quick kiss from strawberry-flavored lips. "Hi."

"Howdy."

"Can I convince you to get sweaty with me?"

"Probably. I'm rather easy where you're concerned."

"And I love you that way." Bending his knees, he worked his hands under the skirt of the frilly, feminine dress she'd worn to work and slid them up the backs of silky, soft, toned legs to cup bare ass cheeks. He let out a growl that came from the deepest part of him. She wore the sexiest underwear all the time, including barely there thongs that drove him wild.

"Let's go upstairs," she said with a nervous giggle. "Your mom is apt to bring them back any time."

"She said an hour ten minutes ago."

"Addie might have a meltdown."

"I'm willing to risk it." He was already pushing her dress up and lifting her to sit on the kitchen counter.

"Blaine…"

"Shhh, let me have my sweaty fun." The house was already unbearably warm after only an hour without AC. He ought to stop and open some windows, but that would take time he didn't want to waste when there were much better things they could be doing. Such as pushing her skirt up over her hips and tugging the thong from between her sweet cheeks. Christ have mercy, she was the sexiest thing he'd ever seen, and he had to be the luckiest bastard on earth to be married to her, to be loved by her.

Hooking her right leg over his shoulder, he dove into the sweet, spicy, strawberry-scented haven between her legs.

She let out a sharp cry of pleasure and dropped back onto her elbows, her hips coming off the counter to get closer to his tongue. "We shouldn't be doing this here," she said, gasping when he drove two fingers deep inside her.

"I know. Isn't it hotter that way?"

"Your mom won't think so if she catches us—"

He pushed his fingers into her again, and she gasped before she came hard, her tight channel gripping his fingers. His cock wanted in on this right now. With his other hand, he quickly freed himself and slid into paradise, triggering a second orgasm from her that nearly finished him off.

Not so fast.

He gripped her ass cheeks and gazed down at her sweet face, glistening with moisture. "Isn't sweaty sex fun?"

"Not when I'm waiting for my mother-in-law to walk in any second."

"Stop talking about my mother, or you'll kill a perfectly good boner."

"Nothing can kill your boner."

"Not when I've got you hot, sweaty and naked in my arms in the place where it all began between us."

"If this counter could talk."

He pushed deep into her and loved the way she arched into him and how her legs curled around his hips. "It'd tell quite a story."

"The best story."

"Mmm," he said, losing himself in her the way he always did. "Tell me if it hurts." He worried obsessively about her all the time, but more so when she was pregnant.

"Nothing hurts."

He fumbled with the buttons on her dress, eager to free the spectacular breasts that had become more so since she'd carried Addie.

She helped him with the buttons and released the front clasp on a sinfully sexy bra.

There was something to be said for being married to the island's lingerie queen.

"So fucking hot," he whispered.

"There's no AC."

"That's not why it's hot. You're why. My sexy, gorgeous girl. I love you so much." He buried his face in the curve of her neck where her skin tasted sweet and salty from perspiration. Their bodies glided together in the purest form of pleasure he'd ever found with anyone. Grasping her ass with both hands, he drove them higher and then higher still until they broke with shouts of pleasure that made him glad they were home alone.

He collapsed onto her, being careful not to put too much weight on her abdomen, and sighed when her arms curled around him and her fingers combed through his hair. "Love you more than you'll ever know, Tiff."

"I love you, too. I still can't believe this is my life now, that you're my life."

"Believe it." He flexed his hips to remind her of their connection, which went far deeper than their always-incendiary physical bond. Theirs was a soul-deep communion, and it had been from almost the first time he'd ever laid eyes on her, sitting by her sister's bed in the island clinic, looking so beautiful and so lost.

They'd traveled a million miles together since then, and it would never be enough.

Her heel dug into his ass. "We need to take this party out of public view before your mother and Ash see something that can't be unseen."

"Fine," he said, withdrawing reluctantly from her.

"How can you still be hard after that?"

"How can you still be so sexy and beautiful that you keep me hard all the time?"

She sat up, ran her fingers through her hair and gasped when he picked her right up off the counter, slid her down on his still-hard cock, kicked off his shorts and headed for the stairs. "You're a crazy man."

"Crazy for you, especially when we have almost an hour to ourselves *during the day* in *August*." As he took them up the stairs, he went for maximum bounce, loving the sounds that came from her. In their room, he brought her down on the bed without losing their connection.

With her dark hair fanned out on the bed, her cheeks flushed from heat and pleasure, her nipples tight and her lips red with lipstick, she looked like something out of a fantasy—his own personal fantasy.

She pulled the T-shirt over his head and ran her hands down his sweaty back to grip his ass as he pumped into her, losing himself all over again, as if the first time had never happened. "Tiffany... *God...*"

"Harder."

Just when he thought she couldn't get any hotter, that one word sent him into overdrive, and as he hammered into her, he lost all sense of place and time and anything that wasn't her and them and the magic they created together. It was hot as hell, and with the windows closed to keep in the AC that was now off, it was absolutely stifling, but he didn't stop even as sweat ran down his face and back and stung his eyes. His lips found hers in a greedy, deep kiss that made him feel even more powerfully connected to her.

Afterward, he felt like he could sleep for a week. Even though he was hotter than he could ever recall being, every part of him was relaxed in a way that didn't often happen this time of year when work was nuts for both of them. He, who used to hate winter, now lived for the long, cold days when he could hunker down with his girls for days on end.

Soon, he thought, the season would be over, and there'd be more moments like this one. By August, he was ready. More so this year, for whatever reason. Maybe he was getting older and crankier, and the crap that used to roll off his shoulders seemed to get to him more than it used to. Or maybe he was just so besotted with his wife and daughters that any time away from them—especially time dealing with drunks and other fools—made him bitter.

"What're you thinking?" she asked after a long period of contented silence.

"That I can't wait for this season to be over so we can do more of this and less of everything else we have to do this time of year."

"We're almost there."

"I'm counting the days until Labor Day."

CHAPTER 9

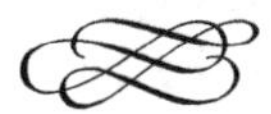

Tiffany's sister, Maddie McCarthy, was counting days, too. On Labor Day, which was only three short weeks from now, she and Mac would move to the mainland with Hailey and baby Mac until their twin girls arrived in mid-September. As she watched Thomas play on the floor with Hailey and their indispensable au pair, Kelsey, who had been a godsend to them since she arrived on the island earlier in the summer, Maddie couldn't bear to think about being separated from Thomas for as long as a month if it came to that.

"She's wonderful with them," Maddie's mom, Francine, said of Kelsey.

"I know. I'm jealous of my own nanny." Not only was she terrific with the kids, she took care of everything around the house and had become a friend to Maddie, who was confined to bed or the sofa until the twins were born.

At twenty-two, Kelsey was a recent college grad, majoring in early childhood development. She had curly reddish-brown hair that she mostly wore up in a bun and hazel eyes that lit up with delight any time the kids did something cute, which was pretty much all the time. Maddie referred to her as their "Disney princess" because she was so sweet that Maddie almost wondered if she was for real until she'd understood that Kelsey was as real as it got. Her heart was pure gold, and she'd made such a difference for them as Maddie's bed rest had fallen during Mac's busiest season. They were both more relaxed since the angel named Kelsey had come into their lives.

"Why are you jealous?" Francine asked.

"The kids like her better than me."

"They like her better than everyone," Francine said, laughing. "She's got the magic touch."

"I should be taking care of my own kids."

"You are." Francine laid a hand over the massive baby bump that seemed to grow exponentially by the day. "You're taking care of these two while you have the very qualified Kelsey taking care of the other three."

"How will I stand to be away from Thomas for a whole month?" Tears sprang to Maddie's eyes at the thought of it. They'd been inseparable since his birth, when she'd been a single mother struggling to get by.

"He'll be just fine with Blaine and Tiffany, and you know we'll help and so will Linda and Mac. He'll be very well loved, and you can FaceTime with him every day."

"I know." Maddie swiped at a tear that made her feel silly for being so emotional. "I love living on this island. You know I do, but sometimes…"

"Trust me, honey. We all feel that way sometimes, when we want something we can't get right now the way people who live on the mainland can."

"Or when we have to move to the mainland for a month to get ready to give birth while leaving one of our babies behind." Earlier in the summer, their lawyer friend Dan Torrington had drafted a document giving Tiffany and Blaine full authority to act as Thomas's parents in an emergency. That they needed such a document had given Maddie nightmares as she counted down to D-Day, as she referred to their departure. "Mac and I debated this a thousand different ways, and we were going to bring him with us until we told him he'd miss the first month of school. He was despondent. More so than he was about not seeing us for a month."

Francine huffed out a laugh. "Welcome to the years when other people start to become more important to your kids than you are. It's hard to take at first."

"Sure is. I remember the first time we were out to dinner, and an adult said hello to him, and I was like, *Who* is *that?* It was the PE teacher at school, who I'd never met."

"They don't stay little for long," Francine said, "and they start to get lives of their own separate from us."

"I'm so not ready for that." Maddie dabbed at her eyes as more tears leaked from the corners. She was on emotional overload all the time lately. "You don't have to babysit me if you have other stuff to do."

"Ned's going to pop by to pick me up shortly. I wanted to see you and the kids."

"Thank you for bringing dinner. I'm getting so spoiled with everyone bringing food. I'm never going to be able to go back to normal after this."

"Everyone is happy to help out. Being on bed rest is a drag, especially in this heat. Why isn't your AC on anyway?"

"The power is out. Has been for an hour now."

"Oh Lord, I hope it's not like the last time when it was out for days. We'll roast to death if that happens."

"I can't imagine being any hotter than I already am. These girls are roasting me from the inside."

"Dad to the rescue," Mac said as he came through the slider that Kelsey had opened to let in some air. "I come bearing a generator."

"For the fridge, right?" Maddie asked, happy to see him as usual. Everything was better when he was around, and it had been that way from the day they met.

"I'm going to rig it up so we get some AC down here, too."

"God bless you. My hero."

Mac came over to the sofa and bent to kiss her. "I can't have my baby mama roasting to death."

"Any word from Adam?"

Mac shook his head. "Not yet."

"Are you worried?"

"A little."

After what they'd gone through losing their son Connor in utero, the thought of that pain befalling his beloved brother and sister-in-law was unbearable, especially since Abby's pregnancy was such a miracle to begin with.

"Are they still due back for the party?" Maddie asked.

"I haven't heard otherwise."

She took a deep breath and released it, saying a silent prayer for her sweet sister-in-law, who'd already been through enough. If anyone deserved a smooth, easy pregnancy, it was Abby.

For her part, Maddie couldn't wait to never be pregnant again. Mac was getting a vasectomy as soon as possible. She was never having sex with him again unless he got that taken care of. "Is the party still on?"

"As far as I know. I helped Laura with their generator earlier, and she said Owen was bringing coolers of ice from the Surf to his mom's."

"Poor Sarah. Of all the things to happen on her big day."

"It'll be fine. Islanders are hardy folks." In a matter of minutes, he had the generator running from the deck, the fridge back on and the low hum of AC filling the room with cool air once again.

"You're the absolute best, Mac."

"I know, right?" he said with the irrepressible grin she loved so much. "How're you feeling?"

"Huge."

"You're glowing."

"I'm sure I'm quite a sight."

"Best sight I've ever seen in my entire life."

"If this is the best sight you've ever seen, your eyes need—"

He kissed the insult right off her lips. "Enough. You're beautiful, and that's all there is to it."

"And that's my cue to get out of here," Francine said when she heard the *toot-toot* of Ned's horn from the driveway. "He must be busy if he's not coming in to see the kids." She bent to accept hugs and kisses from Thomas and Hailey. "Thanks for all you're doing, Kelsey. You're the best."

"Thank you, Mrs. Saunders. This is the most fun job I've ever had."

"We're hoping she still says that when there're five of them," Mac said.

"I will be!" Kelsey said with her usual too-good-to-be-true enthusiasm. "I think I hear Mac waking up from his nap. Who wants to help me get him up?"

"Me!" Thomas and Hailey said as one.

"When I ask them that, they don't even answer," Maddie said when the three of them had gone upstairs to get baby Mac. She looked up at her mom. "Thanks again for the visit and the dinner."

Francine kissed her daughter's forehead. "Hang in there, honey. This too shall pass."

"I've got to go, too," Mac said. "I'm meeting my dad in fifteen minutes. You need anything before I go?"

"No, I'm good," Maddie said with a sigh. She was bored out of her mind but would never tell him that when he was so busy running two businesses.

"I'll be back in plenty of time to help you get ready for the party, and we'll have some good fun with everyone."

"That'll be nice."

He kissed her and tucked her hair behind her ear. "We're in the home stretch, sweetheart. Almost to the finish line."

"Keep reminding me."

"Any time you need to hear it." He kissed her again, got up and went upstairs to give the kids some love before he left, promising to be back in a couple of hours.

Maddie watched him go, envious of his ability to move around freely while she was forced to do nothing at home. She laid her hand over her belly, which was alive with activity at all times from two babies who never seemed to rest. "You girls are going to be holy terrors, aren't you?"

Putting her head back on a pillow, she once again counted her many blessings, which included the twin girls who would soon take over their lives.

As Mac drove away from the house, he was worried about Maddie and how low she seemed as life swirled around her while she couldn't do anything other than use the bathroom and take a quick shower every day. The poor girl was stretched to the limit of her patience with sitting still, even if she understood it was necessary to protect herself and the babies. Bed rest sucked. No way around it, especially with three other kiddos underfoot.

Thank God for Kelsey, who'd been a lifesaver this summer. Hiring her had been the best thing they'd ever done, and he was hoping they could convince her to stay for the winter to help out after the twins arrived. He worked like a madman so his family could have what they needed. Right now, they needed Kelsey.

Not to mention, Thomas, Hailey and Mac adored her, which was a bonus.

Mac drove to the island's northwest corner and pulled into a dirt driveway that took him on a winding path to what had once been an alpaca farm. The place was in shambles, with the roof crumbling, rusted farm equipment scattered about the property and a general aura of neglect clinging to the buildings.

But the potential... That was all he could see after stumbling onto the property the previous winter while out plowing snow. He couldn't get the idea out of his mind, and he'd learned to run with things that interested him as much as this place did.

Big Mac arrived a few minutes later, parking his pickup next to Mac's and greeting his son with the usual big smile, as if they hadn't seen each other in days rather than hours.

"Haven't been out here in years," Big Mac said. "Remember coming for the petting zoo the Conways used to do around Halloween every year?"

"I remember."

With his hands on his hips, Big Mac took a look around. "It's fallen on hard times since they died."

"That it has."

"What're we doing here, son?"

"I'm having a thought..."

Big Mac propped aviator sunglasses on top of his wiry gray hair. "What thought is that?"

"Take a walk with me." Mac led his father through the split-rail fence that was mostly rotted and covered in a thick layer of moss. The grass hadn't been mowed in years and had become a meadow of wildflowers and weeds that led straight down to the water's edge. A gigantic barn made of stone and wood was covered with colorful ivy, and the pervasive stink of alpaca urine filled the air.

"It sure is fragrant," Big Mac said, pulling a face.

Mac laughed. "Indeed. So, you know how we have high-end wedding elegance at the Chesterfield and beach weddings at the Wayfarer?"

"Uh-huh."

"What if we were to renovate this place to offer shabby chic, rustic farm weddings with a million-dollar view of the ocean?"

"What the hell is shabby chic?"

"Rusty farm implements in the wedding pictures, repurposed wood and hay bales." He led his father through a broken door into the vast barn. "Look at this place."

Big Mac pulled a bandanna from his back pocket and put it over his nose and mouth. "It fucking reeks."

Mac laughed at the blunt assessment of the foul odor. "We could do something about that. Imagine the potential. We could turn the far side of the barn into an industrial-quality kitchen and the loft into a wedding-night suite for the happy couples. There could be a stage for bands, and the outbuildings could be used for wedding-party prep. We could put a bar over there and string lights in the trees and set up long, wooden, family-style tables for outdoor dining. I think it could be really cool."

"You've given this a lot of thought, son."

"I was out here to plow last winter and have been thinking about it ever since. We were too busy with the Wayfarer to take on anything new initially, but with that up and running and producing outstanding results, I thought maybe the family might want to take on another challenge." They walked outside and down to where the land met the coast. "Imagine the wedding photos that could be taken here." He gestured to a rusty tractor that had been nearly consumed by weeds.

"Just what every bride wants is a rusty tractor in her wedding photos."

"That's the thing. People who like the laid-back, relaxed vibe of this place would love to have the rusty tractor in their photos. It's a whole other demographic than we see at the Wayfarer or what Lizzie gets for the Chesterfield. I think there's a market for this kind of venue. I got with Nikki about some numbers the other day, and she told me that for every bride she books at the Wayfarer, she turns away ten others because we're at capacity. Lizzie reports similar stats at the Chesterfield. People want to get married here, but there're limits to what's available."

"It's an interesting idea, I'll give you that, and the view is phenomenal. That'd be a big selling point."

"The rusty tractor would be, too," Mac said, grinning at his dad.

"I'd have to take your word on that one."

"Do you think the others would be interested in another project?"

"Based on the results at the Wayfarer this summer, I imagine they'd be intrigued. What's it listing for?"

"One point eight million, but I think we could talk them down. The main building would need to be almost completely rebuilt, and some of the other buildings are in pretty rough shape, too."

"And you'd want to take on the renovations, I presume."

"Correct."

"You guys are booked solid with the reno at the hotel this winter."

"I was thinking we could tackle this after the hotel with a goal of opening the summer after next. I'm super excited about the possibilities here. Maybe in the fall, we do a harvest fair or something with pumpkins and apples, pony rides, hayrides and face painting. Just thinking out loud, but I think we could make it something fun and profitable."

They walked back toward their vehicles, and Big Mac leaned against his. "I love the idea, and more than anything, I love that you love it. However... And don't take this the wrong way, son, but you're about to welcome twins who'll make you a father of five. You've already got a lot on your plate, and this would add a whole other wrinkle."

"I've thought of all that, and of course you're right that a twin bomb is about to go off in our lives, but I can rely heavily on Luke, Shane, Riley and Finn. Any one of them can step in for me as needed. And not for nothing, I do need to keep them all employed year-round, and this would take care of that for another couple of years."

"True."

"If we don't snatch this place up, someone else will, and they'll build yet another fancy big house on the coast. We need something like this. Not only is it tied to the island's history, it brings something we don't have now."

Big Mac scratched at the fine layer of stubble on his jaw. "I really like the idea a lot."

"Yeah?"

"Hell yeah. How about we run it by the family and see what they think?"

"Sounds good to me."

"I love your vision for what's possible and how much thought you put into it. Reminds me of myself when I first saw the marina. I didn't see the sagging roof or the broken windows. I just saw potential."

"I hear I'm a chip off the old block," Mac said.

"That you are, my friend. I couldn't be prouder of the man, father, son and businessman you are."

"Learned everything I know about all those things from you, Pop."

"You learned good, son."

"So tell me the truth about having five kids..."

Big Mac let out a big laugh. "That one you're gonna have to learn for yourself."

CHAPTER 10

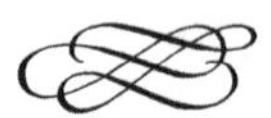

"Give me another big push," Victoria Stevens said to Jessie, the young woman laboring to bring her baby into the world.

Though the clinic's generator had kicked on to provide low-level lighting and monitors, the AC wasn't much to speak of, and it was hot as hell in there.

"I can't," Jessie said, sobbing as tears spilled down her cheeks. "I'm so tired."

Vic bathed Jessie's face with a cool cloth. "You've got this, Jessie. A few more pushes, and you'll be a mom."

She shook her head. "I can't."

"Are you sure there's no one I can call to come be with you?"

"There's no one."

Victoria rarely had a mom deliver alone, but it had happened before. Who, she wondered, would support the young mom and baby when they went home from the clinic?

Jessie began to moan as another contraction started to peak.

"Come on, Jessie. Let's get this baby out. On my count, give me the biggest push yet, and don't let up."

The young woman summoned the last of her strength and determination to give birth to a baby girl, who came out red-faced and squalling.

"You've got yourself a daughter," Victoria said as she wrapped the baby in a blanket and handed her over to her mother. "Congratulations."

"Is she… Is she healthy?"

"I counted ten fingers and ten toes, and she has a healthy set of lungs." Victoria delivered the placenta, placed a couple of stitches and got Jessie cleaned up. "What's her name?"

"I don't know yet."

"I'll give you a minute to get acquainted while I get Dr. David to come in and check her out." Victoria left the birthing room and went to find David, who was in his office, wolfing down a sandwich as he worked on charts and other paperwork that never ended. "Jessie Morgan had a baby girl."

"Everything went well?"

"Textbook, except for the fact that she seems to be completely alone. I asked if she had anyone she wanted to call, and she said there isn't anyone."

"Huh. What do we know about her?"

"Not much. She arrived on the island about a month ago and came to me once for a prenatal check. I don't think she'd had any care before then. I'm a little concerned about sending her home with a newborn and no support."

"Let's go take a look at the baby and see what we can find out."

Victoria followed David back to the exam room. Before she went in, she caught a glimpse of her partner, Shannon O'Grady, coming in the clinic's main doors. "I need a few minutes."

"I'll wait for you out front."

"Thanks." Shannon was so good about rolling with her crazy schedule and the way babies arrived at the most inconvenient of times, such as when she had a lunch date with her love.

Victoria joined David in the delivery room, where he was talking to Jessie about the baby. "We're just going to take a quick look to make sure she's nice and healthy. Is that all right?"

"Sure." She handed the baby over to him, and he took her to a nearby table with a warming light and the items he needed to fully assess her. "She's okay, right?"

"She seems perfect," David said. "We're just making sure. So how long have you lived on Gansett?"

"Just about a month or so. I came to work at the Beachcomber this summer."

"Are you planning to stay for the off-season?" Victoria asked, making an effort to keep the questions casual and friendly.

"I… I'm not sure yet."

"Is the baby's father here with you?"

Jessie shook her head and looked away, sending the message that the subject was off-limits.

"I have to be honest that I'm concerned about you going home with a newborn if you don't have any support," Vic said. "Especially with the power out for who knows how long."

"We'll be okay. I… I'll figure it out. Somehow."

"Do you have a car seat?"

"I don't have a car, so I don't need a seat."

"What about a crib?"

"I was going to use a dresser drawer to start with. My mom did that with us."

"Is your mom around? Could she come and help?"

"She died six years ago."

"I'm sorry."

"Me, too. She was my best friend."

"Do you have a friend here on the island who might be able to help out for a while?"

"Not really. I haven't been here that long."

"Are you staying in the Beachcomber's employee housing?"

"Yeah."

Victoria didn't think that was the right environment for a baby, as the seasonal employee housing tended to be party hot spots. "This community is pretty awesome, and if I put out the word that we have a new mom in need of some help and support, people would be happy to help."

"I'm not looking for charity."

"I'm not offering charity. I'm talking about the kind of help that every new mom needs."

"I… I just don't know."

Victoria squeezed her arm. "Think about it. No need to decide anything right this minute."

David brought the baby back to Jessie. "She's robustly healthy and scored high on all her tests."

"Oh good," Jessie said as she took the baby from him. "That's good news."

The awkward way in which she handled the baby indicated to Victoria that she hadn't had much experience with newborns.

"Make sure to support her head." Victoria adjusted the baby so her head was better positioned. "Her neck isn't strong yet."

"How do people know this stuff before they have a baby?"

"Well, there're books and websites and stuff. I have a couple of books I could lend you, if you'd like."

"That would be great. I don't know much about babies."

"And that's why I'd like to get you some help, Jessie. I know of an awesome group of women who'll take you under their wings and show you the ropes. All you have to do is let them."

Jessie rolled her bottom lip between her teeth. "Are you sure it's not charity?"

"I'm very sure. It's people helping people."

"I guess that would be okay, then."

"Great, while you girls get some rest, I'll make a few calls."

"Thank you."

"It's no problem at all."

David followed Victoria from the room. "What's your plan?"

"My first call will be to Lizzie James."

He snorted out a laugh. "Calling in the big guns."

"Go big or go home. Will you keep an eye on them while I grab a quick lunch with Shannon?"

"Yep."

"You want anything?"

"I'm good. Daisy made me a lunch."

"You're so spoiled."

"I know! I tell her she doesn't have to, but she wants to. She loves her new kitchen so much that she'll take any chance she gets to be in there." He patted his belly, which was as flat as ever. "She's trying to fatten me up before the wedding."

"She's only got a few weeks to go. I hope she's cooking round the clock."

"Every chance she gets."

"You hearing anything about the power?"

"Only that it's out to the entire island."

"Fantastic. It's gonna be a hot night in the old town tonight."

"Sure is. Go have lunch. I'll be here for a while longer."

"Thanks." They were both due to attend Charlie and Sarah's party later, but they'd come in that morning to see patients who worked during the week and couldn't get to the clinic. Jessie had shown up earlier in full labor.

Victoria grabbed her purse from her office and ran out to join Shannon, who was between runs on the ferry. Since he had to leave again at one thirty, they had an hour. "Sorry, sorry," she said when she found him sitting on one of the benches outside the clinic, his face tipped into the sun. "Babies don't care about lunch plans."

"They don't care about anything but themselves," he said in the lovely Irish accent that had become the soundtrack to her life with him. "Selfish buggers." He slung an arm around her shoulders. "How about outside at the Wayfarer today? I heard they're cooking burgers on the grill, but that's about it with the power out."

"A burger sounds good." Since it was only a few minutes away, they walked down the hill into town.

"So what'd she have? A boy or girl?"

"A girl, and the poor thing had to give birth with crappy AC in this hideous heat. What're you hearing about the power failure?"

"That it's island wide and could be out for days."

She groaned. "God, that would suck. It's *so* hot." As they walked, Victoria sent a text to Lizzie James, wife of billionaire investor Jared James, who'd once told her to reach out if she heard of anyone in need. *Give me a call when you have a minute.* Her phone rang ten seconds after she sent the text. To Shannon, Vic said, "Sorry, got to take this."

"Do your thing, love. No worries."

He was the best at rolling with the never-ending demands of being the island's only nurse practitioner-midwife and someone almost always needing her for something.

"Hey, Lizzie. Thanks for calling."

"No problem. How're you holding up over there without power?"

"Not great. The generator is running, but the AC is tepid at best."

"Ugh, hope it won't be out for long. What's up?"

"You mentioned once that I should call you if I encountered someone who could use some help. I have a young single mom at the clinic. She came out to work for the Beachcomber this summer and just had a baby. I don't think she has anyone or anything—"

"Say no more. I'm on it."

"You're the best. She's a bit overwhelmed, to say the least."

"I can only imagine. We'll take care of her."

"Thank you so much, Lizzie."

"Thanks for calling me. I'll come by the clinic this afternoon to see her."

"I'll see you then." Victoria ended the call and put the phone in her pocket, determined to give Shannon her full attention for the rare moment they'd stolen in the midst of a workday. Ever since they'd committed to spending their lives together, he'd been making a huge effort to ensure she was happy—and doing a fantastic job of it by inviting her to lunch between runs, among many other things that had made her feel loved and settled in their relationship.

He was like a different man since he'd unburdened himself to her by sharing the devastating details of his love Fiona's murder and the years of horrific grief that'd followed. More important, though, he'd given himself permission to be happy again, which had been key to their ability to move forward together.

"So my aunt, my mam and my da are talking about coming for a visit in the fall," he said.

"Your aunt who's Seamus's mom?"

"That's the one. My mam and da want to meet the young lady who has me tied to a tiny island in the US."

"You're not exactly *tied*."

"Aren't I, though? Roped and shackled." He made a dramatic display of dragging a pretend ball and chain attached to his leg.

"Be careful, O'Grady. Or your ball and chain won't be friendly at bedtime."

His laughter delighted her. "You know I'm happily chained to the smart, sexy, beautiful Nurse Stevens who saved me from myself by forcing me to fall in love with her."

"I did some of my best work with you."

"That you did, love. So I was thinking, as long as my family is going to be here, maybe we could, you know, make our arrangement a little more... you know, *official*."

Confused and charmed by his stumbling words when he was usually the king of elocution, Victoria looked up at him just as he stopped walking and dropped to his knee right there on the sidewalk in downtown Gansett. "What're you doing?"

He took her hand and brought it to his lips. "I had this whole thing planned for tonight, but I can't wait another minute to ask you..." He looked up at her with gorgeous green eyes filled with love and the hint of sadness that would forever be part of who he was now.

"Ask me what?" she asked, breathless. She needed to hear him say the words.

"Will you marry me, Vic? Will you—"

"Yes!"

Smiling up at her, he said, "I wasn't finished, but 'yes' is a good word."

She reached for him, tugging him up and throwing herself into his arms.

"If you'd let me finish, you would've heard about how much I love you and how completely you saved my life by loving me back."

"I love you just as much, and I can't wait to marry you. Thank you for asking me."

He gazed down at her, smiling as big as he ever did. "Thanks for saying yes. When we get home, I'll give you the ring I got you."

CHAPTER 11

Lizzie gathered her things into the bag she'd brought out to the pool—sunscreen, e-reader, lip balm, water bottle, towel.

"Where're you going?" Jared asked from the next lounge where he'd been dozing.

They'd been enjoying a rare day off together when she got the call from Victoria. She was between weddings at the Chesterfield, and he'd taken the power failure and the subsequent internet outage as a sign that he should take the rest of the day off from managing his portfolio online. "I'm needed in town."

"You're needed here."

Lizzie stopped by his chair to give him a kiss. "I'm needed more there."

"What's going on?"

"Victoria Stevens called from the clinic to tell me there's a new mom with no support of any kind."

Jared reached up to take her hand. "Are you sure that's something you should be getting involved in?"

"I'm fine. I swear." After bending to leave him with another kiss, she walked inside to get ready.

She loved him for asking whether she ought to be going on this mission, especially right now. Their third round of IVF had recently failed, and they were both still recovering from the disappointment that seemed to get bigger with every subsequent failure. This one had been particularly devastating for her, mostly because she wasn't sure she could go through the process again. It'd been grueling—appointments, procedures, shots, tests—and all for nothing in the end.

Lizzie hadn't said much to Jared yet about how she was feeling, but she'd hit her limit, for now anyway. He'd been wonderful through it all, supportive, loving, encouraging, optimistic. She couldn't have asked for anything more from him, but the toll on their emotions had become almost unbearable.

As she took a quick shower and got dressed, she thought about what they'd been through in the last nine months and how they were no closer to having a baby than they'd been at the start. And what was worse, none of the many specialists they'd consulted could tell them why she was unable to conceive.

If only they knew *why,* at least it would make some sense. As it was, nothing made sense. By all accounts, they were a perfectly healthy young couple who should've been able to conceive without a problem. But that hadn't happened, and now the realization was setting in that it might never happen.

Which was the reason for Jared's concern about her getting involved in a situation that involved a newborn. Hell, she was concerned, too, but she couldn't bear to know of someone in need of help that she could easily provide. That's what she did. She got involved and lent a hand to anyone who needed it. She'd married a fabulously wealthy man, even though she'd had reservations about how she could continue to be true to herself while being married to someone with his resources.

What she'd since learned was that she could do a lot of good with his money—or as he liked to remind her, *their* money—and she'd taken full advantage of his willingness to make her happy by investing in things like the Chesterfield Estate and the senior health care facility they'd founded on the island. The center was now fully occupied with residents who'd be living on the mainland, away from their families, without their facility.

Her life with Jared was wonderful in every possible way, except for their inability to have a baby. She knew she had nothing at all to complain about, but her heart ached, nonetheless.

Her gorgeous husband was waiting for her when she emerged from their master bathroom. He sat on the bed, bare-chested, his jaw scruffy and his blond hair messy and still damp from a recent dip in the pool. To look at him in his relaxed state, you'd never guess that he was a self-made billionaire. But underneath his casual exterior was a sharply intelligent, brilliant, loving man.

"Whatcha looking at?" he asked with a playful grin, even as he gazed at her with concern she recognized from the last few difficult months.

"My sexy husband. That's allowed, right?"

"Hell yes, that's allowed." He held out his hands to her, and she went to him, letting him wrap his arms around her as he pressed his lips to her abdomen. "I need a favor."

"What's that?" she asked as she straightened his messy hair.

He looked up at her, his gaze full of love. "This new mom in town who needs help… Let's give her money and stay out of it otherwise."

His softly spoken plea went straight to her heart, leaving a lump of emotion in her throat.

She certainly understood what he was asking her and why, and she'd had the same thoughts herself.

"I love you so much for so many reasons," he said, "but mostly I love your big heart and how giving you are to people in need. But this… This is too much right now, honey."

"I hear what you're saying, and I love you for being concerned about me, but I'm okay. And I'm not just saying that. Yes, I'm disappointed and heartbroken that the latest round didn't work, but I'm trying to accept that it's just not meant to be for us. At least not now."

"You've been so strong, but the last thing you need is to be involved with a newborn."

"Maybe it's just what I need, to see that life goes on even when I'm disappointed and heartbroken. I promise you, if it's too much for me, I'll make arrangements for her to have what she needs and come home. I promise."

He took a deep breath and let it out slowly. "All right." His phone chimed with the tone he'd set for his brother Cooper, a farting noise that always made them laugh, and now was no exception.

"Leave it to Coop to break the tension," Jared said as he released her to fish the phone out of the pocket of his cargo-style bathing suit.

"What's he up to?"

As Jared read the text, his eyes widened. "He says he's coming out on the three o'clock boat so he can be here for Quinn's wedding. I can tell him this isn't a good time for us."

"No, let him come, Jared. He's always fun to be with, and we could use some comic relief around here."

"Are you sure?"

"Positive. It's fine." She leaned down to kiss him. "I'll be back in a while."

"Take care of my sweet Lizzie and her soft heart, you hear me?"

"I will. I promise."

He gave her another tight hug, let her go and then got up to walk her out to the car. "Drive carefully," he said as he closed the door on her silver Land Rover.

She waved as she backed out and headed for town, hoping she could handle this mission she was embarking on.

CHAPTER 12

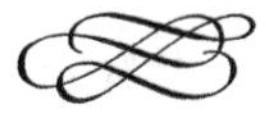

"I'm so hot I feel like I'm going to expire right on the spot," Jenny Martinez said to her husband, Alex, as they worked together at the retail store attached to Martinez Lawn & Garden. While their baby son, George, slept in a portable crib in the back room, they were trying to reconcile the day's receipts by hand since their computer had gone down when they lost power.

"I'm having memories of flying tomatoes," Alex said, grinning as he referred to the day they met.

"I think it's hotter now than it was then, and I wouldn't have thought it possible to be hotter than that."

"We do our best work in the heat." Alex came up behind her to cup her ass and give it a squeeze. "Remember that first week?" He kissed her neck and took a little nibble that sent a zing of sensation through her that converged in a twinge between her legs.

"How could I ever forget?"

"We should do a re-creation out at the lighthouse."

"I heard there are new keepers moving in. We don't need to shock them on their first day."

"Yeah, they might have a problem with us banging one out against the wall of their mudroom."

Jenny laughed at his always-colorful way with words. "Ya think?"

"I'm definitely thinking." He pressed his erection against her back. "I'm thinking of getting sweaty with my baby."

"Do you two ever take a break?" Alex's brother, Paul, asked as he came into the store and caught them in a clinch.

"Not very often," Alex said, tightening his hold on Jenny so she couldn't escape.

"Don't you worry about it breaking off from overuse?" Paul asked his brother.

Alex busted up laughing. "Nope. My motto is use it or lose it." He pushed his erection against her again to make his point.

She'd already received his message—loud and clear.

"In fact, we were thinking about cutting out early today," Alex said. "It's hot as fuck in here, and we've got better things to do than sweat our balls off in this place."

"Point of order," Jenny said. "I don't actually have balls."

"My balls are your balls, which makes them *our* balls."

"Paul, will you please do something about him?"

Paul cracked up. "You knew exactly what you were getting when you shackled yourself to him."

"True," Jenny said with a resigned sigh. "I did."

"Where's my niece?" Alex asked.

"In the car with Hope, where it's cool. We're going to check on Mom and make sure she's okay in the power outage."

"Oh, good call," Alex said. "You want me to go with you?"

"No need. I'll check on her and let you know."

"I'm sure they have a generator at the senior center. Jared and Lizzie thought of everything."

"I hope so."

"I want to see the baby," Jenny said, squirming out of Alex's tight—and sweltering—embrace. She went outside with Paul into the broiling heat to take a peek at baby Scarlett, who was wide awake in a car seat in the back of Hope's car.

Hope put down the window so Jenny could say hi to the baby, and the blast of cold air made Jenny want to climb into the car for relief. "Damn, that AC feels good."

"Doesn't it?" Hope pointed to her dashboard. "Ninety-four degrees."

Jenny reached in to give the baby a finger to squeeze. "How's our little girl doing today?"

"She's been in a great mood since she blew out her diaper and outfit earlier this morning."

Jenny laughed. "That's proof she and George are related. He's famous for that."

"Nothing like a good dump," Alex said from behind her.

"Don't listen to Uncle Alex and his dirty mouth," Jenny said to the baby.

"What'd I say that was dirty?" Alex asked.

Paul went around the car and got in the driver's side. "Get out of my car so we can keep the AC inside," Paul said in a teasing tone.

"Bye-bye, Scarlett," Jenny said. "Enjoy your visit with Grandma."

They waved as Paul drove them toward the main road.

"They've got the right idea," Jenny said. "Take me for a ride, Alex."

He waggled his dark brows. "Happy to, baby. Any time you want."

"Put your horns down, stud. I want a ride *in the car* with *air conditioning*."

"You know how to crush a guy."

"You'll get over it. Go get the car and pick us up."

"Yes, dear." He grabbed another handful of ass and kissed the top of her head before he took off toward their house at the far end of the dirt road.

She watched him go, her heart full to overflowing, the way it'd been since he came into her life during the last heat wave and changed everything a couple of summers ago. Thinking back to that magical week could always make her smile, but she'd been out of sorts since she woke up in the middle of the night after having a disturbing dream that'd cast a pall over her day.

Inside the retail store, she went to the back room to check on George, who was still sound asleep. Her little boy looked just like his dad, with Alex's dark hair and olive-toned skin. He'd brought so much joy to their lives, and they were still hoping to give him a brother or sister. They were doing nothing to prevent that, but it hadn't happened yet, despite one hell of an effort.

That thought made her laugh. Her husband was always in the mood for baby making. She carefully picked up George, who was warm and sweaty, and snuggled him into her arms, hoping he'd stay asleep for a while longer. Like his daddy, he was cranky when he got woken up from a nap. She carried him outside, and when Alex drove up with their SUV, she got the baby buckled into his seat without waking him.

"Nice job, Mom," Alex said.

She got into the front seat, immediately turned up the AC and opened all the vents, basking in the relief of the cool air. "God, that's better than sex."

"I'm highly offended."

"Oh, shut up and let me enjoy this while I can."

"Where are we going on this ride?"

She closed her eyes and let the cool air wash over her overheated body. "Anywhere you want. Just don't turn down the AC."

"Got it. AC is critical—and apparently better than sex."

"For right in this moment. Ask me what's better than sex when it's not a thousand degrees during a power outage."

"I'll definitely get back to you on that."

Alex drove them to the lighthouse, where they frequently returned to walk the property and remember the significance the place had played in bringing them together. He parked in a spot with a view of the vast ocean, which was calm today. "Are you going to tell me what happened during the night?"

Jenny had hoped that maybe she hadn't woken him. Apparently, that wasn't the case.

"You dreamed about Toby, right?"

"H-how do you know that?"

"You said his name. A couple of times."

She dropped her face into her hands. "I'm so sorry, Alex. That shouldn't happen when I'm in bed with you."

He tugged at one of her hands. "Don't do that. Don't apologize to me about something you can't help. I've known from the start that he's part of you." He caressed her cheek and smoothed her hair back from her face. "Was it the same dream? Your last morning together?"

She shook her head. "It was a new one."

"You want to talk about it?"

"Not really, but I know I have to, or it'll ruin me."

"I want to hold you, but we'd have to leave the AC."

"I think I'd give up the AC to be held by you right now."

"I'll meet you outside."

Jenny checked George to make sure he was still asleep before she got out of the running car to meet Alex.

The heat was still intense, but less so with the ocean breeze to temper it a bit.

Alex put his arms around her and encouraged her to lean her head against his chest. "Tell me. Let me help."

It would never come naturally to her to share Toby with him, but he'd made space for her lost love in their lives from the beginning. That made it easier to share her pain with him. "He was in our yard, calling my name. I went outside and couldn't believe he was there." She swiped at the tears that fell despite her urgent desire to keep her emotions under control.

Alex rubbed her back in soothing circles. "What happened then?"

"He said he was sorry he'd had to leave for a time, but he was back now and wanted me to go with him. He said he came right to me as soon as he could." She wiped her face again. "It was so vivid and real. It was like he was really there." Taking a breath, she held it for a second, trying to calm herself. "And then you came walking up to the house, holding George. You asked me who I was talking to. I said, 'It's Toby. He's here.' And I wasn't sure how to introduce him to you. Should I tell him you're my husband? I didn't know, and I felt panicked."

"God, Jenny. I'm so sorry."

"He… He asked who you were, and I had to tell him. I said, 'Alex is my husband, and George is my son.'"

When a sob choked her, Alex tightened his hold on her. "Shhh, honey. It's okay. As painful as it was, it was only a dream."

"It was so, so real."

"I know."

"He asked me to come with him, to leave you and George and go with him. He kept saying he'd come back for me and needed me. I told him you and George need me, too, and I couldn't go with him. I had to tell him no, Alex. Why would I have a dream like that? I hadn't been thinking more about him than I usually do or anything that would cause that."

"I don't know, sweetheart."

"It was so strange to see him there, looking so normal and healthy, as if he'd been away on a long trip or something and had come home to find me married to someone else and couldn't understand how that was possible."

"But you understand how it's possible, because you lived it. You know how it happened."

She nodded. "I do know, but still..."

"It was hard to have to tell him you couldn't go with him."

"It was excruciating. He was so confused."

"Wherever he is, he knows the truth. He knows how much you loved him, how deeply you suffered and grieved his death and how long it took you to move on with me. The Toby in your dream may not have understood, but your Toby... He knows the truth, Jenny."

"Thank you for saying that. It helps."

"I wish there was something else I could say other than I love you, and I'm so proud of how you handled such a devastating loss."

"I didn't handle it well at all."

He placed his hands on her face. "Are you *serious*? You *survived* it, Jenny. That makes you the strongest person I've ever met. Do you know what it's like to be loved by someone who loves the way you do? Who honors both the men you love the way you do? I'm so fucking proud of you, sweetheart. You have no idea how proud I am to be married to someone who loves so fiercely."

"Stop," she said, laughing even as more tears spilled down her cheeks.

"Not until you believe that you're the strongest person any of us has ever known, and we all admire you so damned much. Toby does, too. I know he does. The Toby you loved never would've asked you to choose between him and me. He would've gracefully conceded that things have changed in all the years he was away, and he'd want you to be happy."

"He always said that's all he wanted. To make me happy."

"He knows you're happy with me and George and how much we love and need you. He'd never try to take you away from us."

"Some people might think this entire thing is nuts, that we're actually talking about my fiancé coming back from the dead to take me away from my husband and son."

"Who gives a flying fuck what anyone else thinks? The only thing that matters is that you're okay."

"Thank you for listening and not thinking I'm crazy."

"I'm always happy to listen to you." Alex hugged her tightly. "I love you more than anything." He kissed her lips and then kissed the remaining tears off her cheeks. "You feel better?"

"Yeah, I do."

"Good."

"And by the way, I love you, too."

Alex and Jenny were still standing there when an attractive Black couple came up the stairs from the beach and made their way toward the lighthouse.

"You suppose they're the new keepers?" Alex asked.

"Let's find out." Jenny stepped out of his embrace to walk toward them. "Hi, I'm Jenny Martinez. Are you guys the new lighthouse keepers?"

"We are. I'm Oliver Watkins, and this is my wife, Dara."

Jenny shook hands with both of them. "Great to meet you, and welcome to Gansett. I had this gig for a while before I was married, and it was a lot of fun." She glanced wistfully at the lighthouse that had been so instrumental in changing her life. "That's my husband, Alex. Our son is sleeping in the car, or he'd come over."

Alex gave them a wave.

Was it her imagination, or did the mention of their son make the couple tense? "What brings you to our fair island?"

"A chance for a reset," Oliver said.

Jenny nodded with understanding. "I get that. I was in need of the same thing when I came here. This place was good for me. I hope it will be for you, too."

"Is it always so hot here?" Dara asked.

Jenny laughed. "Not usually, although an earlier heat wave led me to my husband."

"Are you hearing anything about the situation with the power?" Oliver asked.

"Not much except it's apt to be out for a few days if it's anything like past power failures around here."

"That's just great," Dara said with a frown. "If you'll excuse me. It was nice to meet you, Jenny."

"You, too."

After his wife had walked away, Oliver said, "I'm sorry. She… We… It's been a rough year, and…"

Jenny put her hand on his arm. "Please don't apologize to me. I know all about rough years. Hell, I've had rough decades." She pulled her phone from her back pocket. "Give me your number, and I'll text you so you have mine. If I can do anything, anything at all, please get in touch. Wherever you are, I promise you, I've been there."

"That's very kind of you." He gave her his number.

"There," Jenny said. "I sent you a text so you'll have mine. We'd love to have you over for dinner sometime. Shoot me a text when you're settled and ready to meet some people."

"We'll do that. Appreciate it."

"Enjoy your time here. It's a very special place."

"I'm beginning to realize that. Thanks again."

As Jenny returned to where she'd left Alex, his cell phone rang with the tone he'd assigned to Paul. "You mind if I take this?"

"Of course not. Go ahead."

"Hey." Alex took the call while drawing Jenny close to him with his free hand. "What's up?" He listened for a minute. "Yeah, sure. We'll be right there."

"What's going on?" Jenny asked.

"He wants us to come to Mom's right away. He said to hurry."

"He didn't say why?"

"No," Alex said, his jaw tight with tension. "What the hell is wrong now?"

CHAPTER 13

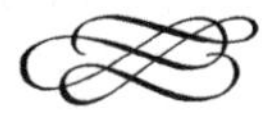

Paul Martinez was afraid to breathe. His mother, the mother who'd raised them with love and discipline and humor, the mother they'd lost to dementia over the last couple of years, was back. She was fully lucid and her old self in almost every possible way. With Scarlett on her lap, Marion absorbed every detail of the granddaughter she'd met many times before now, but this… This was different.

"She's so beautiful," Marion said, her eyes tearful. "Why haven't you brought her to see me before now?"

"I have, Mom."

Marion's brows knitted with confusion. "No, you haven't. And you're married! Why don't I remember the wedding?"

"We eloped, Marion," Hope said, glancing at Paul with amazement.

"And there's a boy. I remember a boy."

"My son, Ethan. You and he are special friends."

"Where is he?"

"He had a sleepover with friends last night, but we'll bring him to see you soon."

"I like him. He's a nice boy, like my Alex and Paul always were."

"Thank you," Hope said. "We're proud of him."

"Is he your son?" Marion asked Paul.

"He's my stepson, but I'm hoping to have the chance to adopt him. I love him very much."

"I can't believe everything that happened while I was away," Marion said. "Where's your brother?"

"He's on his way."

"From Washington?"

"No, Mom. He lives here now. On Gansett."

"What's he doing here? He works at the botanical garden in Washington. He shouldn't be here."

"He's been back for a while now."

"I don't understand. Where am I?" She looked around the room that Jenny and Hope had helped them decorate to look homey and cozy for Marion. "This isn't my home. I need to get home and get back to work."

"You've been unwell, Mom," Paul said gently. "For quite some time now."

She raised the eyebrow that used to convey a wide range of emotions, back before her face became flat and expressionless. Watching her raise that brow hit Paul like a shot to the heart. "Unwell in what way?"

Paul wasn't sure what he should say. Should he tell her the truth, or should he sugarcoat it? He didn't know, so he looked to Hope, who was a nurse and probably knew better.

She leaned in and took hold of Marion's hand. "You have dementia, Marion. It's become increasingly more severe as time has gone on. Alex and Paul did everything they could to take care of you at home. They hired me to be your caregiver, and that's how I met Paul. After a while, it became clear to us that you needed more care than we could provide for you at home."

Hope gestured to the room where Marion lived. "This facility was built by dear friends of Paul and Alex who wanted to help keep you close to them on the island. It's even named for you."

As Marion struggled to process what Hope had told her, Alex and Jenny came rushing into the room, looking terrified. He carried a sleepy-looking George. "What's happening?"

"Alexander," Marion said. "You're holding a *baby*."

Alex looked to Paul as he tried to understand what was going on. "Mom is feeling like her old self."

"*What?*" Alex asked on a long gasp.

"This is Alex's wife, Jenny, and their son, George," Paul said.

"You... You named your son George," Marion said, tearing up over the tribute to her late husband. "And you're married."

Alex sniffed and swiped at the tears that rolled down his face. "This is my wife, Jenny, Mom."

Jenny stepped forward. "It's so, so nice to meet you, Marion."

Alex put George next to Scarlett on her lap.

Both brothers took pictures while they could, both knowing this interlude couldn't possibly last.

Hope stood and leaned in to whisper to Paul. "I'm going to see if Quinn is here," she said of Dr. Quinn James, the center's medical director.

Paul nodded. "Thank you."

After Hope left the room, Paul could only stare at the marvel of his mother appearing to be completely herself after living in a fog of confusion and disorientation for years.

"What is this?" Alex asked him softly while Marion was occupied with the babies and Jenny.

"I don't know," Paul said. "I couldn't believe it when I walked into the room, and she said, 'Hey, Paul, whose baby is that?' I said, 'She's my daughter, Scarlett, Mom, and this is my wife, Hope.' She asked when I got married, and I realized she was lucid. It's been almost an hour."

Hope returned with both Quinn and his fiancée, Mallory Vaughn, who was director of the nursing staff. "I updated them," Hope said to Alex and Paul, who stepped aside to allow Quinn and Mallory into the increasingly crowded room.

"How're you doing, Marion? I'm Dr. Quinn James, and I've been overseeing your care for a while now."

"They... they say I have dementia."

"Yes, you do."

She seemed to be processing that information. "And that means I have trouble remembering things, right?"

"That's right."

"But I can remember my boys and my husband. We live on Gansett Island, and we run our business..."

"You remember right now," Quinn explained in a gentle tone, "but it may not last."

The babies began to get fussy, but Marion waved off their mothers.

"Let me hold them, please." She spoke softly to the little ones, consoling them until they settled and became interested in each other, as they usually were. She looked up at Quinn. "How long do you think it will last?"

"I don't know. I wish I did."

Marion looked to her sons. "Has this happened before?"

Alex nodded. "A couple of times, but never this long. This is… It's such a gift, Mom. We've missed you so much."

Marion broke down into tears as she hugged her grandchildren close while she could.

"I'm going to call Daisy," Hope said to Paul.

"Oh God, yes. I should've thought to do that."

Hope squeezed his arm and left the room to call the young woman who'd been such a dear friend to Marion. Daisy had been faithfully devoted to Marion since the day the older woman showed up on her porch after having walked barefoot into town.

Paul was uncomfortable from the sweat running down his back and face. The AC was on, but not at full speed, and it was warm in the close confines of Marion's room.

"Do you think maybe I could go home for a while?" Marion asked her sons.

They looked to Quinn and Mallory for guidance.

"I suppose that would be all right for a short time," Quinn said.

Paul took his reply to mean the doctor didn't expect the period of lucidity to last much longer. He had his reservations about taking Marion home. Would they have trouble getting her to return to the care center when the time came? And the house was different now. For one thing, he and Hope slept in the room that had once belonged to his parents.

"I'd really like to do that, if you boys wouldn't mind," Marion said.

"Of course, Mom," Alex said, glancing at Paul. "Whatever you want."

DAISY BABSON HAD BEEN SHOCKED to receive the call from Hope Martinez. She grabbed her purse, phone and car keys and was on her way out the door when she nearly collided with David, who was coming in from a morning at the clinic.

"Whoa, what's your rush?" he asked when he kept her from falling by grasping her arms.

"It's the most unbelievable thing! Marion is completely alert. Hope called to tell me. They're all there, and they wanted me to come see her."

"Wow, that's amazing. Do you mind if I go with you?"

"No, I'd love that." Her phone chimed with a text from Hope. "Marion has asked to go home for a little while, so they asked me to meet them there." She returned Hope's text to let her know she'd see them at their home. "Isn't this so incredible?"

"It is, for sure, but it probably won't last. I don't want you to get your hopes up."

"I know," Daisy said with a sigh. "But it's a miracle while it lasts."

"That it is."

David drove them around the island toward the Martinez compound, where the family lived and worked. "What're you doing one month from today?"

"I can't recall. Give me some hints."

He poked her leg, making her laugh.

"Oh! Do you mean marrying the love of my life?"

"That's what I mean. I can't believe it's finally almost here—again."

"Don't jinx us." They'd postponed their wedding, which had been scheduled for last September, after his father had had a massive heart attack.

"Nothing's going to stop us this year, baby. And besides, it's just a party. We're already married in all the most important ways."

"That's very true. If we never had a wedding, it wouldn't change anything."

"Maybe so, but I'm ready to stand up in front of everyone we love and tell them what you mean to me."

"Who would've thought that getting beat up by my ex would lead me to my own sweet, sexy doctor?" Daisy asked with a sigh.

"It's hard to believe everything that's happened since that night. Weird how something so awful can lead to something so great."

"I won't ever profess to being thankful to what's his name, but I am thankful every day that you came into my life and we found each other. You have no idea what a mess I was before I had you to put me back together."

"Likewise, my love. We're very lucky."

She placed her hands over her abdomen. "And about to be so much more so."

"How will we ever stand to wait *nine months*? Ugh."

"It'll go by fast. I'm just glad that I won't be showing yet for the wedding."

"But we'll know there's a special package on board for our big day."

"Yes, we will."

"When can we tell people?"

"After three months. You know how often things go wrong in the first trimester."

"Nothing's going to go wrong."

"And you know that for sure?"

"I do. I feel it in my bones. We're going to have a beautiful baby who looks just like his or her gorgeous mommy."

"Or handsome daddy."

"Let's hope they favor you."

"Stop it. I want handsome sons who look just like you."

David took the left turn into the gates at Martinez Lawn & Garden, drove past the greenhouses and retail store and then took a right toward the house where Paul and Hope now lived.

"Hey, Daisy…"

"Yes?"

"Don't be upset if she doesn't remember you. She met you when she was deep in the throes of dementia."

"I know. I'm prepared to explain to her that we've become friends over the years."

"Dementia is such a cruel disease. The guys are going to get this time with her only to have to lose her all over again."

"I hate that so much for them, but I'm thankful they're getting this interlude with her, even if it's temporary."

They sat there for a few minutes before the family arrived in two cars. Marion was riding in the front seat of Paul and Hope's SUV. Daisy took one look at the older woman who'd become her friend under the strangest of circumstances and could see that she seemed much more alert than usual.

"And already my heart is breaking," Daisy said softly to David as they got out of the car to greet their friends.

Paul helped Marion out of the car, and for a long moment, she stood in front of the house she'd called home for her entire adult life.

"You painted it," she said.

"We did," Paul replied. He stood close to his mother, who wasn't as agile as she'd been before her illness worsened.

"It looks wonderful. I love the flower boxes."

"Those are all Hope's doing. She has your green thumb."

Marion glanced at her daughter-in-law. "They're lovely."

"Thank you, Marion. I hope you know… Paul and I, we've made the house our own, but it's still your house, so I want you to make yourself entirely at home here."

"Thank you, honey. I'm glad that you've made a home for yourselves here. My George and I were always so happy in this house." She looked to Alex. "Where do you live?"

"Jenny and I built a house out by the south fields. We'll take you to see it while you're here."

"I'd like that."

"Mom, this is—"

"Daisy," Marion said, reaching for her. "My friend Daisy."

Relieved that Marion remembered her, Daisy hugged her. "It's so nice to see you, Marion."

Marion pulled back from Daisy and studied her closely. "Are you expecting, honey? Your cheeks are fuller."

Daisy gasped and then laughed. "You found me out."

"I knew it!"

"Congratulations, you guys," Alex said. "That's great news."

"So much for not telling anyone yet," David said, his smile lighting up his lovely brown eyes.

Daisy loved when he smiled like that. It'd taken a while, after they found each other, for him to smile freely, to believe that what they had would last. He'd taken responsibility for the unfortunate way his relationship with Janey McCarthy had ended, but in the end, he'd needed to forgive himself for the mistakes he'd made before he could be truly happy with her or anyone else.

"I'm going to need to feed Scarlett," Hope said. "Should we go in?"

"I'd like to sit on the porch for a while, if that's all right," Marion said.

"Of course, Mom," Paul replied.

The porch had always been Marion's favorite place to pass the time.

They helped her up the stairs and settled her in one of the rockers.

Daisy hung back, wanting to give Marion's sons the opportunity to spend as much time as they could with their mother while she was in this alert state.

But Marion had her own mind and, as usual, wasn't afraid to speak it. "Daisy, come sit by me."

The brothers parted to let her through, and when she sat in the chair next to Marion's, the other woman reached for her hand and held on tight.

"They say I'm not well," Marion said. "That I have dementia."

"Yes," Daisy said.

"How is it that I remember you? That I remember sitting here with you before?"

Daisy looked to David for help in answering the question.

"Marion, I'm David Lawrence, and I was your doctor."

"I don't remember you," she said, giving voice to the baffling mystery of her illness. She'd known David far longer than she'd known Daisy, as he'd grown up with her sons.

"David took very good care of you for a long time, Mom," Alex said. "He was a big part of the reason we were able to keep you at home for as long as we did."

"I'm sorry I don't remember that."

"Don't be sorry, Marion," David said.

"I don't understand what's happening. Why can I remember Daisy, but I don't remember my sons getting married or having children?"

"Dementia is a very complex disease," David said, "and it rarely follows any sort of predictable patterns."

"They said the lucidity won't last… Is that true?"

"I'm sorry to say that it is."

"Will it happen again? Will I remember things again in the future?"

"I don't know that. I'm sorry."

"But it's not likely, is it?"

"No, it's not."

Marion set her jaw and gave a short nod. "Thank you for being honest with me."

"Of course."

Daisy could see that it pained David to have to be honest with Marion, but she gave him credit for his kindness.

"Could I hold baby George?" Marion asked.

"He would love that." Jenny settled the baby on his grandmother's lap. "Would you mind if I took some pictures of him with you?"

"My hair is a mess," Marion said, raising a hand to straighten it.

"No, it's lovely, Marion," Daisy said. "Chloe comes to do it for you every Friday morning."

"Chloe… Does she have pink hair?"

"Sometimes," Daisy said. "You never know what color it will be."

"She's a nice girl."

"She is, and she has a nice boyfriend named Finn McCarthy."

"Little Finn McCarthy? Big Mac's nephew? He's just a teenager."

"Not anymore, Mom," Paul said. "I think he's twenty-seven now."

"Twenty-seven! My heavens. How did that happen?"

They talked for an hour about other island residents, who had married whom, who had children, people her sons had grown up with and other news. At one point, Alex walked to the other side of the porch where he stood looking out over their property, his shoulders hunched.

Jenny went to him, wrapped her arms around him and offered what comfort she could. How cruel it had to be for Alex and Paul to have their mother back while knowing she couldn't stay.

As the afternoon passed, Marion's faithful friends from church came by to see her. Ethan came home with his friends Kyle and Jackson in tow. Ethan delighted Marion, as usual, but she rarely let go of Daisy's hand.

Daisy was honored to be someone who provided comfort to Marion and stayed by her friend's side even as she roasted in the unrelenting heat.

Baby George had sat with his grandmother for more than an hour before he got fussy for his mommy. Despite the heat, the family stayed close to Marion all afternoon.

David put his arm around Daisy and whispered to her, "We're supposed to stop by Charlie and Sarah's."

"We'll do that later. I can't leave Marion. You can go if you want, and I'll catch up."

"I'll wait for you."

~

CHARLIE GRANDCHAMP WORKED the grill in the scorching heat as sweat rolled down his face and soaked his T-shirt. There'd been a time in his life when the heat and sweat would've annoyed him, but it took an awful lot to rile him these days.

He was free, in love with the most amazing woman, and they were surrounded by family and friends in their gorgeous new home. Nothing could get him down today, not even the power failure that had them cooking everything they'd bought for the party and feeding people as they arrived, rather than all at once later as they'd planned.

The only thing he needed to make this day perfect was to see his daughter, Stephanie. He hadn't seen her in a week, since she and Grant left for LA to attend the premiere events for the film that was telling their story to the world. He wanted to know if she'd decided to see it or not. She'd been leaning toward not when she left, and he could surely understand that. He wasn't sure he wanted to see it either, although he was curious about how his son-in-law and the Quantum team had told their story in the film. So he might see it for that reason alone.

Sarah's daughter Cindy joined him at the grill, bringing a large platter. She had light brown hair and brown eyes and a warm smile that made Charlie feel welcome in her life. "Mom said to bring this to you."

"Thank you. Thought you were working today."

"I worked this morning." She cut hair at the Curl Up and Dye salon in town. "I didn't take any appointments this afternoon because I wanted to be here."

"How's Chloe doing?"

"Not so great from what I hear."

Chloe Dennis, who owned the salon, had been dealing with a significant flare-up of her rheumatoid arthritis.

"I'm sure the heat isn't helping," Charlie said as he transferred steak and chicken from the grill to the platter.

"It's not. She's miserable, but Finn is with her and taking good care of her."

"The poor girl. That's an awful thing for someone so young to have to deal with."

"It sure is. She'd been doing really well, so the setback has been devastating."

"I hate to hear that. I'm sure she appreciates you covering for her at the salon."

"I'm happy to do it. She's been so good to me."

"It seems that life on Gansett is agreeing with you."

"It is. I love it here. Having my grandparents, my mom, Katie, Julia and Owen close by is the best. It's been years since we all lived near each other, and now John and Jeff are here, too. It's awesome."

"I'm so glad to hear that, honey. Your mom is thrilled to have you all here."

"It's so nice to see her happy, Charlie. None of us have ever seen that before, and it means so much. You have no idea."

He reached out to squeeze her shoulder. "I have some idea. One of the best parts of marrying your mom is getting seven more kids to love."

"And we get a real father for the first time in our lives. Win-win."

"Hey, what's going on? Are you cheating on me, Charlie?"

He and Cindy laughed as he turned to find his daughter, Stephanie, coming toward him on the huge deck. "Don't be jealous. There's plenty of your old man to go around."

Stephanie walked into his outstretched arms and hugged him tightly.

"Ack, I'm a sweaty mess," he said.

"Don't care."

"Good to see you, kid." She'd been gone only a week, but it'd felt like much longer. Now that they could see each other every day, any day without her felt wrong.

"You, too, Pops."

He pulled back to take a closer look at her. "How're you doing?"

"I'm fine."

"Are you really?"

"Yep. I decided not to see the film."

"That's what I figured you'd do."

"I read about it online this morning," Cindy said. "People are saying it's amazing."

"That's what I've heard, too," Steph said.

"Everyone is going to want a piece of the dynamic duo behind the real-life story," Cindy said.

Charlie had been afraid of that, but he'd kept his concerns to himself so as not to rain on Grant's well-deserved parade. "Where's your Hollywood husband?"

"Inside talking to Sarah and Adele."

"He must be flying high."

"He is. The premiere went really well, the early reviews are awesome, and there's Oscar buzz for everyone involved."

"Good for him. He worked his ass off for a long time." When Charlie had first met Grant, he'd thought the guy might be too fancy and refined for his girl, but over time, he'd seen how devoted Grant was to her, and that was all Charlie needed to know. She deserved someone who'd have her back no matter what. "How'd he feel about you sitting out the premiere?"

"He was totally fine with it. He gets it. He always has."

"That's so sweet," Cindy said with a wistful sigh. "I hope I meet my Grant one of these days."

"Oh, you will," Stephanie said. "And if it happens like it did for us, it'll be when you least expect it."

"Any time now," Cindy said, grinning. "I'm surrounded by happy couples everywhere I go while I wait for Gansett to work its magic on me."

"You'll get your turn," Stephanie said. "I just know it."

CHAPTER 14

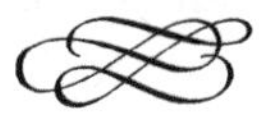

Finn McCarthy stood watch over the kettle, giving thanks for the gas stove that still worked even when the power was out. Their small house had gotten oppressively warm very quickly after the power failed and took the AC with it, which was the last freaking thing they needed when Chloe was already so miserable.

This latest flare-up was a bad one, the worst she'd had since they'd gotten together in May. Other than to go to work, he hadn't left her side in days and wouldn't until she was feeling better. They'd been in touch with her rheumatologist on the mainland, and David Lawrence had been a godsend, too. The doctors had started her on new meds yesterday, and they were praying they'd kick in sooner rather than later.

In the meantime, she hurt, so he hurt.

He took a call from his brother, Riley. "Hey, what's up?"

"How's she doing?"

"Same as yesterday. Just hoping for some relief from the new meds."

"What can I do for you guys?"

"Get the power to come back on? She's even more miserable without the AC."

"I may be able to do something about that. I'll get back to you."

Before Finn could reply, Riley was gone. "Well, all righty, then," he said, amused by his brother as usual.

When the tea was ready, he put it in a spill-proof cup that would keep it warm and took it in to Chloe. She was lying on her side in their bed, her face sweaty, pale and pinched with pain.

"Made you some of that tea you like," he said softly. "Want me to help you sit up a bit?"

"Sure, thanks."

He put the tea on the bedside table and moved carefully to help her. He'd learned how to touch her without hurting her too badly, but right now, everything hurt. When she winced, it broke his heart.

It took a minute to get her settled against the pillows, and by then, her face was even paler than it had been before. His poor baby.

While she sipped the tea, he went into the bathroom, wet a washcloth with cold water and brought it back to bathe her face and neck.

"Feels good," she said. "Thank you."

"You don't have to thank me. I love taking care of you."

She gave him a skeptical look. "I tried to tell you not to cast your lot with me."

"And how'd that go for you?"

"Your own pigheadedness got you into this mess."

"If you're referring to yourself as a mess, that's gonna make me mad."

"What other word would you use to describe my current status?"

"Courageous, defiant, temporarily down but not out."

The right corner of her mouth lifted into a small smile that he took as a major victory. He hadn't seen any hint of a smile in days.

"You didn't sign on for this."

"Yes, I did."

"When?"

"When I said I'd love you forever no matter what. Did you think I was just saying that to get you into bed?"

"If I recall correctly, by the time you told me you'd love me forever, I was already in your bed."

"Exactly." He leaned in to kiss her cheek and the tiny stud in her nose. He loved that little sparkling thing. "I love you all the time, even when you're not feeling well."

"It's not fair to you," she said, blinking back tears.

"We've already had that fight. I won. Let's not have it again, huh?" He kissed her lips. "I'd rather be with you, even when you're not feeling great, than with anyone else in this entire world. So, when you try to get rid of me, it actually hurts my feelings."

She rolled her eyes. "Nice try."

"I mean it. Don't try to get rid of me. I'm not going."

"Suit yourself."

"Thank you, I will." Moving carefully so he wouldn't jostle her, he stretched out next to her on the bed. "It's hotter than a motherfucker."

"How do you know how hot a motherfucker is?"

"It's got to be this hot."

"This has to be what hell feels like."

"I feel so bad. Like it wasn't bad enough before the AC quit."

"I'm okay. Try not to worry. The new meds will work soon."

Finn wanted to ask what happened if they didn't work, but he couldn't bear to ask that. They had to work. That was the only possible outcome. They were still lying in her bed when he heard Riley call from the door. "Is it safe to come into the love shack?"

Chloe grunted out a laugh. "Very safe."

"Come in, Ri." Finn got up, again moving slowly so he wouldn't jostle her, and went to see what his brother was up to.

"I got you a generator," Riley said.

"Seriously? The hottest commodity on this island?"

"Yep."

"Where'd you get it?"

"Doesn't matter. The only thing that matters is keeping Chloe comfortable. Help me get it set up."

They put it on the deck and ran the extension cords that Riley had brought from the deck to the bedroom.

"Hey, Chlo," Riley said softly. "How you doing?"

"Hanging in there. What've you got there?"

"Relief." Riley plugged the window air conditioner cord into the extension cord and turned it on as Finn closed the window he'd opened after the power died.

"You're the best, Ri," Chloe said.

"Couldn't have you suffering any more than you already are, sweetheart."

"Thank you so much."

"Wish there was more we could do," Riley said.

"This is huge," Finn said. "Thanks, bro."

"Let's hook up your fridge, too," Riley said.

Finn followed him to the kitchen, pulled the refrigerator out far enough to get at the plug and waited for Riley to return with another extension cord. "Where'd you really get the generator, Ri?"

"Doesn't matter."

"Is it yours from Eastward Look?"

"Nah, I found it on the side of the road. No one was using it, so I grabbed it for you."

"You're such a liar."

"She needs it more than we do. That's all that matters."

"This will never be forgotten. Thank you so much."

"I can't bear to think of her suffering like this. It's killing me, so I can't imagine what it's doing to you."

"It's been pretty rough, but she's a trouper."

"She sure is. Nik sent some food over to stick in your fridge. Hope that's okay."

"Ah, yeah, Ri. That's more than okay. Thank you again."

Riley gave him a one-armed, half-Nelson sort of hug and kissed the top of Finn's head. "Anything for you and Chlo."

After Riley left, Finn went into the bedroom to check on Chloe and noticed it was already noticeably cooler. Their dog, Ranger, was stretched out on the floor at the foot of the bed, enjoying the AC. Finn sat in the chair he'd dragged in from the kitchen and put next to the bed so he could keep her company. He'd had a pit in his stomach all week knowing the pain had to be awful to put his fierce warrior in bed for days.

"Riley brought us their generator and two tanks of gas."

"That's so sweet of them. I've never had a family of my own before... It's a bit overwhelming the way your family has stepped up for me this week." They'd had a steady stream of visitors, bringing food, books, magazines and treats they thought she might enjoy.

"They love you, almost as much as I do."

"That makes me feel so lucky."

He held out his hand, and she put hers on top of his, which was how they held hands when she was in pain. "You know," he said, "this family could be officially yours any time you say the one word I need to hear."

"And what's that?" she asked with a faint smile.

"Yes. Say yes to forever with me. Marry me, Chloe, and you'll never be alone or lonely again."

"I can't believe you're proposing to me when I'm sick in bed with a condition that's going to plague me for the rest of my life."

"Believe it. I'm asking. Will you marry me?"

She blinked as tears flooded her eyes. "I told you I'd never get married."

"That was before you met me and fell madly in love and realized you couldn't live without me."

That made her laugh, which he'd hoped it would. "You're too charming for your own good—and mine."

"Nah, I'm just right for you, and you know it."

"This last week... This is what's ahead for me, Finn. This is what my life is going to look like. Really good months followed by a flare-up that takes me down for days or weeks or God knows how long. There'll be times I can't work at all. I may not be able to have children—"

Finn stood, leaned over and kissed her, stopping her from completing the list of all the reasons why she was a bad bet. In his estimation, she was the best bet he'd ever made. "I know all that, and it doesn't matter to me. What if it was me who had RA or something else that would take me down for a time? What would you do?"

"I'd take care of you."

"Would you not love me anymore because I had physical limitations? I mean, it's always possible I could get hurt on the job and be more of a burden to you than you could ever be to me."

"Don't even say that."

"It hurts me when you think your condition makes me love you less. If anything, it makes me love you *more* because I get to see how brave you are every single day, how hard you work even when you're in pain. In my mind, I'm awfully lucky to get to live with and love a woman who's as courageous as you are."

"I don't want to hold you back."

"You could never hold me back. Being loved by you makes me feel like there's nothing I can't do or achieve. If you were to leave me, sweet Chloe, you'd ruin my life because I'd have to live with knowing you were out there somewhere without me, maybe in pain, and I wouldn't be able to be the one to sit by your bed and hold your hand and tell you this too shall pass. Who would do that if I wasn't here?"

Her chin wobbled, and her eyes were bright with unshed tears.

Raising her hand to his lips, he gently kissed her swollen, red knuckles. "I know you're preconditioned to believe you have to do this alone, but you don't. If I didn't want to be right here, I wouldn't be. It's really that simple, sweetheart."

"Yes," she said softly.

"Yes, what?"

"Yes, Finn, I'll marry you."

He let out a shout that woke Ranger from a sound sleep to growl at him.

Chloe's smile lit up her face and made him so glad he'd asked her now, when she was feeling poorly and worried that she was a burden. In hindsight, it was the perfect time to ask her.

"Stay right there." He kissed her hand and placed it gently on the bed. "I'll be right back."

He went out to his truck to retrieve the necklace he'd bought for her weeks ago in anticipation of the right moment to ask the question that'd been on his mind for months. Back in the bedroom, he got down on his knees next to the bed and opened the black velvet box so she could see what was inside.

Chloe gasped and covered her mouth. "That's beautiful."

"I bought this a while ago, hoping I'd find the right time to ask you to spend forever with me."

"And you thought this was the right time?" she asked, raising a brow with amusement. "When I can barely move?"

"I thought this was the perfect time, because more than anything, I want you to believe me when I tell you I'm here for the good times *and* the tough times." He took the necklace from the box, put it on her and then sat back to admire how it looked on her. The two-carat diamond was surrounded by amethyst, representing her favorite color of purple. "That no matter how tough it gets, I'm not going anywhere."

"It means a lot to me that you put so much thought into this, knowing it wouldn't be possible for me to wear a ring."

"I wanted something that would tell the world how much you mean to me."

She patted the other side of the bed. "Come here."

Finn went around the bed, stepping over Ranger, who'd gone back to sleep, and stretched out next to her, turning onto his side so he could see her. "You beckoned?"

"Thank you for the beautiful necklace and for everything you said. You have no idea how much it means to me to know I'm not alone anymore, that I have you and your amazing family taking this journey with me. What your brother did with the generator... No one has ever done things like that for me before, and it's all because you love me."

"It's because you're easy to love. Riley loves you, too, and can't bear that you're suffering like this."

"I've never had a brother."

"Now you do."

"When I told you I'd never get married, I meant it."

"I know you did."

"You've shown me something different, something I've never seen before, and not just what's happened between us, but your aunt and uncle, your cousins, your dad and Chelsea, your brother and Nikki. I haven't been around a lot of happy couples in my life, and to see what's possible... The McCarthys made me a believer, but more than anyone else, *you* made me a believer."

"Thank you for taking a chance on me. I promise you'll never be sorry."

"I already know that."

Finn pulled his phone from his back pocket. "Let's take a picture and tell everyone we're engaged." He sat up next to her while she held up her new necklace, the two of them smiling like crazy loons. When he showed the pictures to her, she agreed that any of them would be perfect to share the news with their loved ones.

He cued up a text to the McCarthy family group chat. *Sharing the huge news that the amazing, beautiful Ms. Chloe Dennis has agreed to marry Finn McCarthy!*

Congratulations came flooding in, lighting up his phone with texts that he shared with Chloe.

"Well," she said, "there's no getting out of it now."

"Thank God for that."

CHAPTER 15

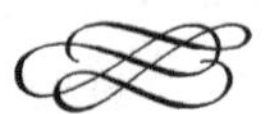

Riley arrived back at Eastward Look and was thrilled to find Nikki home from a morning shift at the Wayfarer. They'd both been working so much this summer that they sometimes went a full day without seeing each other. Those days absolutely sucked. They'd agreed to take this afternoon off so they could go to Charlie and Sarah's party, but those agreements were always contingent upon no crises arising at the Wayfarer that required the general manager's attention.

And there'd been a lot of crises in the first summer since the iconic island hot spot reopened. She'd dealt with everything from alcohol poisoning to drug overdoses to people trashing hotel rooms, day-trippers passing out in the bathrooms and one full-on fistfight between a man and a woman in which the woman had punched the guy unconscious and gotten them both arrested.

Good times.

For the most part, the first season for the new Wayfarer had been a roaring success, but it hadn't been without its challenges. Nikki fully embraced every one of them, acting on behalf of the family she'd marry into in November.

Riley walked into the house to find her in the kitchen they'd renovated together, smiling as she looked at her phone.

"Did you get Finn's text?"

"Haven't checked my phone in a while."

"He and Chloe got engaged."

"*What?* When? I was just there!"

"I guess after you left. You took the generator?"

"I did, and thanks again for agreeing they needed it more than we do."

"That was a no-brainer. I can't imagine what she's dealing with. She doesn't need to be sweltering on top of it."

They'd thrown open the windows at Eastward Look, and while there was a nice breeze, it was thick with heat and humidity that had her hair going curly. He was about to tell her he loved her curls when her phone rang. She grimaced, probably expecting a work issue. But her expression shifted to surprise when she saw the caller ID.

"Who is it?"

"My half sister."

To his knowledge, she hadn't had any contact with her father or any member of his family in the time they'd been together. "Are you going to take it?"

"I guess…" She pressed the green button. "Hi, Kendall. What's up?" Her brows furrowed and her shoulders hunched ever so slightly as she listened to what her sister was telling her. "When?" After another pause, she added, "I'm sorry for your loss." More listening. "No, it's not my loss, too, Kendall. I don't think so. Yes, I'll tell Jordan. Thank you for calling."

Nikki ended the call, put down the phone and glanced at him. "So I guess my father died yesterday."

"*What?* Oh my God. Nik…" When he would've hugged her, she held up her hand to stop him.

"You don't have to comfort me, Riley. He's nothing to me but a bad memory of a childhood spent in chaos."

"He was your father, Nik. It's okay if you feel something after hearing he's died."

"I feel nothing for him."

"What happened?"

"He had a heart attack while driving and crashed on the freeway."

"Oh my God. Was anyone else hurt?"

"I don't think so. Kendall didn't say." She glanced at her watch. "We should get going so I can see Jordan before the party."

"You still want to go to the party?"

"I know it's really hard for you to believe, growing up with someone like Kevin McCarthy as your father, but my father wasn't like yours. He cared more about winning, about defeating my mother, who had mental health and addiction challenges, than he did about us. We were pawns in his chess match and were forced to live with his new family and to see firsthand how he treated the children he actually loved. So, yes, I still want to go to the party."

"Okay."

"I don't want you to think I'm heartless."

"I could never think that about you."

"I feel for his other kids and his wife. They must be shocked and devastated." She kissed his cheek. "I'll be ready to go in a minute. We'll swing by Jordan and Mason's on the way."

While she went upstairs, Riley tried to wrap his mind around what she'd told him. Of course he understood where she was coming from, because he'd heard about her difficult childhood and how she and Jordan had been stuck between warring parents. He knew they blamed their father for most of the drama and had hated living with him and his new family during the school year. But to feel nothing at all when learning of his passing... That was hard for Riley to understand, because for him, losing his father would be one of the most devastating things that could ever happen.

He pulled his phone from his pocket, saw Finn's text and responded. *Huge congrats. So happy for you guys. Welcome to the family, Chloe!* Then he started a second text to only his dad, so as not to send bad news to Finn when he was celebrating his engagement. *Nikki's father died yesterday. She just heard. They were estranged, but she's totally calm about it. Hard for me to understand, because if it was you...*

He sent the text.

Kevin responded a minute later. *Aw, so sorry. That's too bad. Don't worry, your old man isn't going anywhere.*

Please don't. Not done with you yet.

LOL, no worries. Summer needs me.

We do, too. I'm not sure what to make of her non-reaction.

Let her do this her way, son. Her relationship with him was very different from ours. You can't compare the two. She blames him for what happened to her and Jordan as kids. He put them through hell. She's not going to grieve for him the way you would for me. Follow her lead on this and don't expect her to feel things she simply doesn't.

Good advice as always, Doc. Thanks.

Free of charge, too!

HAHA

There'd been a time, not that long ago, when Riley would've resisted his father's advice with every fiber of his being. He and Finn had always known that people paid for Kevin's advice, but he and his brother hadn't been interested in it for themselves. However, the older they got, the more they came to realize that Kevin's advice was usually spot-on, and they were lucky to have him, in more ways than one.

You going to Charlie and Sarah's? Kevin asked.

Heading there now, but stopping to see Jordan first.

See you there.

Nikki came down the stairs looking fresh and pretty in a dress that fell to midthigh, leaving her sexy legs on full display. She'd refreshed her makeup and brushed her long dark hair.

"You look beautiful, as always."

"Thanks. You ready to go?"

"I'm with you, babe."

They went out to his truck, and as they headed for Mason and Jordan's house, Riley wondered if Jordan would be as blasé about their father's death as Nikki was.

Nik adjusted the AC vents to cool herself. "I don't want you to think I'm a jerk, Ri."

"What? I don't. Not at all."

"I certainly didn't want him to die, but when I tell you he's nothing to us… I know that's hard for you to understand. We haven't had any contact with him in years."

"I know, and I get that your upbringing was very different from mine."

"It was a nightmare, mostly orchestrated by him because he used my mother's illnesses against her, and we were the pawns in all that. He hired private investigators to track her doctor's appointments and then used that info in court against her."

"Damn."

"He was relentless in the way he dragged her through the mud, when she was working so hard to get better so she could be there for us. Every time she seemed to be making progress, he'd do something else to undermine her. It went on for years that way, and it was never about us or what was best for us. It was about sticking it to her, because she stopped loving him or some other such bullshit. He doesn't even know what happened to me in college with Griffin, because the minute we were legal adults, we walked away from his madness and never looked back." She paused before she added, "The worst part about hearing he's dead is having it drag up all this old shit I haven't thought about in years."

"I'm sorry, babe. I know those were tough times for you and Jordan."

"It was the worst. Coming here every summer with my mother and grandmother was the only thing that saved us. It's why I love it here so much."

"I'm glad you get to live now in the place that meant so much to you then."

"Me, too, but the only reason I'm still here is because of you."

"You might've stayed. You love it here."

"Nah, I wouldn't have. I think about that a lot. When I came back last winter, it would've gotten very lonely very quickly if you hadn't come over the minute you heard I was back."

"I really did come the minute I heard. I was at the bar with my dad and Finn and some other friends, and something came on the TV about Jordan. Seamus O'Grady said he'd brought Jordan's twin sister over earlier that day."

"He was so nice to me. Everyone was getting sick on the ferry because the seas were so rough, and I wanted to be outside, but he said it wasn't safe. He took me up to the wheelhouse so I could get some air and not be stuck inside with the smell of puke."

"That sounds like him. As soon as he mentioned Jordan's twin being back on the island, I slapped a twenty on the bar, asked my dad to borrow his car for the first time in years and drove so fast to your house that I fishtailed coming in the driveway."

Nikki laughed. "I haven't heard all that before."

"I told you that."

"No, you didn't. I didn't realize you came here one minute after you heard I was back."

"I don't even think it took a full minute. I ran out of there so fast that Finn came after me, asking me what my plan was."

"Did you have a plan?"

"Hell no. I only knew that you were back, and I had to see you."

"You *had* to see me?"

He put his hand on her leg. "It was a need unlike anything I've ever felt. I'd been a mess since you left without saying goodbye."

"I felt so bad about that."

"I know, and look at everything that's happened since I came to find you that night. Wouldn't change a thing."

She placed her hand on top of his. "Me either."

They were getting married at the Chesterfield on Thanksgiving weekend and then going to Italy for two weeks. He couldn't wait to be married to her and for the trip they'd planned with exacting detail.

When they arrived at Mason and Jordan's, they saw Mason's SUV parked in the driveway along with Jordan's BMW and their friend Gigi's white Mercedes coupe. Both women had their cars shipped to the island when they realized they were going to be there a while to film the new season of their show.

"The gang's all here," Riley said.

"So it seems."

Nikki got out of the car, and Riley followed her inside, hoping Jordan took this news as calmly as Nikki had. It was all so strange to him, being unaffected by a close family member's death when something like that would rock his world. The more time he spent with Nikki and Jordan and the more he learned about their upbringing, the more thankful he was for his parents, aunts, uncles and cousins, who'd given him and Finn a dream childhood.

"Nikki," Gigi said, "get in here and settle a fight."

"You'd better side with me," Jordan said, smiling at her sister.

"What's the fight?"

"Who's hotter—Justin Timberlake or Ryan Gosling?" Gigi asked.

Nikki glanced at Riley, who rolled his eyes. "Um, well, I suppose if I had to choose… I'd say JT for the win."

"Oh my God," Gigi said. "You just did that twin ESP shit again, didn't you?"

Jordan high-fived her sister. "Thank you very much."

"I hate you two," Gigi said. "I have no idea why I even hang out with you."

"You love us," Jordan said, giving Gigi a playful shove that had her toppling over on the sofa. That sent them into hysterics.

This was why their TV show was so popular. The two of them were hilarious together.

Mason came into the living room, his hair wet and a towel around his neck. He was wearing only a pair of shorts, with his muscular chest and abdomen on full display, making Riley feel like he needed to get back to the gym—immediately. "Did you ladies decide who's hotter?"

"I won because I said you're the hottest of them all, baby," Jordan said to Mason.

His smile lit up his face. "That's my girl."

"Dear God," Gigi said, rolling her eyes.

"Don't be a nasty old bitch," Jordan said. "It'll give you wrinkles."

"Um, sorry to interrupt your good time," Nik said hesitantly.

Riley knew that Nikki hated to do anything to upset Jordan, who'd fought so hard for her happily ever after with the fire chief. The two of them were so ridiculously happy together, and he was glad to know Jordan would have Mason there to support her if she didn't take the news well.

"What's up, Nik?" Jordan said. "You're doing that frowny thing you do when something's gone sideways."

Nikki crossed the room to sit on the coffee table so she was in front of Jordan.

Mason glanced at Riley as if to ask, *What's this about?*

"So Kendall called me today."

"Huh? How come?"

"She told me Dad died yesterday."

Jordan's face went flat with shock. "What? What happened?"

"They think he had a heart attack while driving."

Jordan took a deep breath and released it slowly. "I don't even know what to say to this."

"I didn't either."

"I'm so sorry, you guys," Mason said. "What can we do for you?"

"Nothing," Jordan said, her expression still blank.

She'd been so animated only a minute ago that it hurt Riley to see her looking like she had after the hideous breakup with her ex-husband.

"We don't need anything," Jordan said. "We haven't talked to him or any of them in years."

Gigi moved closer to Jordan and took hold of her hand. She'd been their friend growing up and had lived through a lot of the drama, so she'd understand better than anyone how strangely this news would hit them both. "Do you guys want to go there? I can get a plane..."

"No," the sisters said as one.

"Absolutely not," Nik added.

"So, um, you might have to," Gigi said.

"*Why?*" Nik asked, sounding horrified.

"Roll with me here," Gigi said. "The press is apt to catch wind of the fact that your father died, and if you guys don't show up, that'll make it a story."

"I'm not going to his funeral," Nikki said. "I don't care who says what about me. I'm not going. I never had a choice back in the day. Now I do, and that's my choice."

"And I totally appreciate why you feel the way you do," Gigi said. "The thing is, though, unless you want to publicly address the estrangement and deal with the questions about that, you have to go. Or at least Jordan does."

Jordan sat with her arms wrapped around her knees.

"Gigi, could I please sit with Jordan?" Mason asked.

"Sure." She moved to one of the other chairs. "I'm sorry."

"Don't be. She needs all of us right now." Mason took the spot on the sofa next to Jordan and put his arm around her.

Jordan leaned into him.

When they'd first gotten together, Riley had wondered if they would stick, because they seemed so different. But the more time he spent with them, the more he saw the deep bond they'd formed. After what Jordan had endured with her ex, it was nice to see her happy and settled with a good guy like Mason.

"God, it's so fucking hot." Gigi fanned her face with a magazine. "How long does it take to fix the freaking power?"

"The last time?" Mason said. "Four days."

"For fuck's sake. I'll die before then."

"You'll be fine," Nikki said.

"This is why I don't belong on a remote island in the middle of nowhere," Gigi said.

They'd spent the summer shooting episodes of their reality TV show *Jordan and Gigi: Marooned on Gansett Island.* By all accounts, they were funnier than ever when lamenting the limitations of island life. The episodes shot on Gansett were due to air over the winter.

"Do you really think I have to go?" Jordan asked in a small voice.

"Let's see whether the press figures out he's your father and make a plan from there," Gigi said. "Nikki, can you text Kendall and tell her you guys don't want to be listed in the obituary?"

"Ugh," Nikki said. "Do we really have to do that?"

"Only if you want to sit out the funeral without causing an uproar."

Jordan gave Nikki an imploring look, letting her know that she was in full agreement about not wanting to go.

Nikki sent the text to Kendall. "Now let's forget about it and go have some fun at Sarah and Charlie's."

"I'm going home to walk around naked," Gigi said.

Riley grunted out a laugh. He'd gotten used to Gigi, but she always cracked him up with the way she said whatever she was thinking.

"Are you going to the party, Jordan?" Nikki asked.

"Yeah, we'll see you there."

Riley followed Nikki out of the house with a sinking feeling that Nikki and Jordan weren't going to get through this loss completely unscathed.

CHAPTER 16

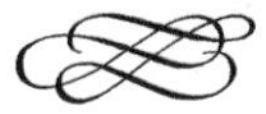

"Talk to me," Mason said when he and Jordan were alone. "Tell me how you really feel."

"Numb. I feel nothing. I know I should, but I don't."

"You're allowed to feel any way you want."

Her phone chimed with a text from Nikki. *Kendall says it's too late. The obituary that includes us has already been submitted to the funeral home and the local papers.*

"Damn it," Jordan said, reading Nik's message to him. "People will think I'm a jerk if I don't go."

"Who cares what people think?"

"I wish I could say I don't, but my career depends upon people liking me and being interested in my life."

"What if you and Nik were to release a statement that says something like, 'Although we were estranged from our father for many years, we send our condolences on his untimely passing to his family and friends.' Something like that."

"That might work. Let me call Gigi."

"Didn't I just leave you, bitch?" Gigi asked when she answered the phone.

"Kendall told Nik it's too late to be left out of the obit, and Mason suggested we release a statement." She passed along Mason's wording. "What do you think? Will that cover us in not attending the funeral?"

"I think it might work. Did you ask Nik?"

"I'll text her. Hang on." She sent a message to Nik outlining the plan and asking if she was okay with it.

Do it, Nik replied.

"Green light from her," Jordan told Gigi.

"I'll write something up and send it over when I get home."

"Thanks, Gigi."

"Anything for you guys. You know that. And even though he was an asshole, I'm sorry you lost your dad."

"Thanks. Love you."

"Love you, too. Always."

Jordan ended the call and turned to Mason. "Thanks for the great idea."

"You would've thought of it eventually. You guys are the experts in managing this stuff."

"I appreciate that you thought of it."

"I'm being selfish. I can't go to LA while the power is out, and there's no way I'd let you go without me."

"I'm not going to LA. Ever since things happened with Zane, I've realized—with a lot of help from my therapist and my grandmother—that I need to protect myself from things that can hurt me. That funeral would hurt me because..." Her voice broke, and she gave herself a minute to gather her composure. "Because in the back of my mind, I always had hope that someday he might see the error of his ways and try to build a bridge with us. And now..."

"Now there's no chance of that."

"Yeah."

He kissed the top of her head and kept his arm around her, even though it was nine hundred degrees in the small house that had become home to her since she'd moved in with him earlier in the summer. She'd never lived in such a small space or been as happy as she'd been there with him.

"I'm very sorry you lost that possibility, sweetheart."

"Me, too."

"If you want to stay home today, we can."

"No, that's okay. You took the afternoon off to go to the party."

"I took the afternoon off to spend it with you. We've both been so busy for weeks that I'm greedy for time with you."

"You spend time with me every day."

"It's never, ever, *ever* enough."

Jordan moved to straddle his lap so she could look him in the eyes when she kissed him. "I never imagined anyone would love me the way you do."

"I love you to infinity and beyond."

"Okay, Buzz Lightyear."

Mason smiled and curled a strand of her long dark hair around his index finger. "Maybe we should stay home and spend this stolen afternoon alone."

"Maybe we could do both—spend some time alone and hit the party later."

"I do like the way you think."

"I do like the way you smell," she said, kissing his neck.

He tightened his hold on her and tipped his head to kiss her.

Jordan had never been kissed the way Mason did it, as if he was dying for her every time he came near her. He made her feel so loved and wanted and accepted just as she was, which had been such an amazing gift.

His big hands cupped her ass and pulled her in tight against his erection. "I want you so bad, all the time, even when it's hotter than the surface of the sun in here."

Jordan laughed and kissed away a bead of sweat that rolled down his face. "Let's go take a sweaty nap."

"Good plan. Can we do it just like this?"

He loved when she was on top of him. "Any way you want it."

"That's a pretty broad statement. You'd better watch out. My imagination is super fertile where you're concerned."

"I'm not afraid of you."

As they moved to the bedroom, he wrapped an arm around her from behind and pushed his hard cock into the cleft of her ass, letting her know what "anything" might entail.

"Okay, I'm scared of that."

Mason laughed. "You never have anything to be afraid of where I'm concerned."

Standing by the bed, he helped her out of her tank top and shorts and then tipped her chin up so he could see her face. "You know that, right?"

"Yes, Mason, I know that."

"Even if we did *that,* I'd make it so good for you. That'd be my only concern. *You* are my only concern."

She reached up to put her arms around his neck, and he helped her by lifting her and curling her legs around his waist. He was so much bigger than her, but he was never intimidating, only ever touching her with love and reverence that made her feel treasured every second they were together—and even when they weren't.

With her wrapped around him, he sat on the bed and kissed her as he cupped her breasts and teased her nipples. In the past, it'd taken a lot for her to become aroused. With Mason, all he had to do was look at her, and she was ready for whatever he wanted. And he always wanted her.

She moved against him, desperate for more as his kisses became more urgent. "Now, Mase. Hurry."

He groaned as he reached between them to get his shorts off while she bit down hard on his earlobe. "Fucking hell, Jordan."

She laughed at the way he said that—one part exasperation, three parts urgent desire.

"Don't laugh at me when it's your fault I'm like this."

"I love you like this."

With his free hand, he squeezed her bare ass. "I love you like this and every other way."

He was so freakishly strong, but he never used his strength against her, not like her ex-husband had. But she wasn't thinking of him or anything other than Mason as he lifted her and brought her down on his cock.

He was big all over, and as always, she had to take him in increments that had her eyes rolling back in her head and her mouth falling open as she tried to breathe through the slight pinch of pain that came before the pleasure.

"Easy, baby. Nice and easy. That's my girl. You're so hot and wet and tight. You make me crazy."

She loved how he talked to her when they were making love. The things he said to her then were raw and real and came straight from his heart. In her wildest dreams, she never could've come up with someone like him or imagined the kind of love he showed her every day. She kept thinking that surely there had to be a downside, but if there was, she hadn't found it yet and was beginning to believe there wasn't one. He was every bit as wonderful as he seemed.

It took a good ten minutes of patience before she was able to take all of him, and as usual, he filled her to capacity.

"If there's anything better than this..."

His gruffly spoken words, whispered against her neck, sent shivers down her spine.

She tilted her hips and began to move, riding wave after wave of desire that seemed to touch every part of her. It was so hot that her sweat melded with his, but neither of them cared about anything other than the heat they created together.

He took her by surprise when he put his arms around her, stood and turned to put her down on the bed, all without breaking their intimate connection.

"Smooth move, Chief."

"I save all my smoothest moves for you, love."

She'd been with him long enough by now to know what was coming, so when he began to power into her, she was more than ready. Her head fell back and her heart nearly stopped from the overwhelming pleasure she found with him every time. Before him, she'd thought it was normal to have okay sex once in a while. Now she got great sex every time, and that was one of many revelations that came from life with Mason.

She'd learned that when she was with the right guy, everything was great.

Jordan wrapped her arms around his neck and kissed him. "Love you so much."

"Love you, too, sweetheart. I still can't believe we get to do this any time we want."

"Apparently, we want all the time."

He laughed as he pushed into her and held still, knowing how that drove her crazy.

Jordan squirmed under him, trying to get him to move, but he remained stubbornly still. "Why do you have to torment me?"

"Because it's fun."

"For who?"

Smiling, he kissed her. "Me, of course."

Jordan laughed. "Mean."

He shook his head. "You love it."

"If you say so."

He reached between them, pressed on her clit and made her explode, taking him with her into breathless pleasure. "I say so."

Gasping and laughing, Jordan gazed up at him, smiling the way she did all the time now. Gone were the days when she'd had to tiptoe around the mercurial moods of an unpredictable, selfish man. She could no longer believe she ever thought *that* was what she wanted. "Thanks."

"Any time, babe."

"Not just for the spectacular orgasm, but for everything. For this sweet, sweet life. I never knew it could be like this until I had you. My whole life was one giant turmoil until you showed me a better way."

"Aw, baby, I should be thanking *you*. You make me feel so lucky every day."

"Even when Gigi and I are forcing you to tell us whether JT is hotter than Ryan Gosling?"

"Even then. You two crack me up." He kissed her again and withdrew from her, but snuggled her in close to him the way he always did after sex.

She loved that almost as much as the sex itself.

"You still want to go to Sarah and Charlie's?"

"Of course I do. You took the afternoon off to go with me."

"We don't have to go if you aren't feeling up to it. Everyone would understand."

"I want to see their new home and celebrate their happily ever after."

"I hope you know that whatever you're feeling about your dad dying, you can tell me. Even if you think it's awful, it's okay to say it."

"I don't know what I feel. I know what I *should* feel, and I just… I just don't. I'm sad that someone's life ended before it should have, but I feel strangely removed from the fact that it's my dad."

Jordan's phone rang in the living room.

"I'll grab it for you."

"Thanks."

He got up and went to retrieve the phone, returning with it held out to her. "Your grandmother."

She took the call from Evelyn Hopper, the woman who'd provided the only stability she and Nik had ever known growing up. She was and would forever be their favorite person. "Hi, Gran."

"Sweetheart, I just heard about your dad, and I'm sorry."

"Thanks."

"Are you guys okay?"

"We're fine. Weird situation, as you know all too well."

"I do," she said with a sigh. "Still... Will you go for the funeral?"

"No. Gigi is preparing a statement for us saying that while we're sorry for his premature passing, we hadn't been in touch with him in years, et cetera. We're hoping it won't become a *thing*."

"I hope not either. Do you want me to come up?"

"You don't have to, Gran. Riley and Mason are taking good care of us. We're okay, but of course we always want to see you."

"I'll be there for Thanksgiving and the wedding."

"Thanks for calling. It's sweet of you to be worried."

"Love you guys. Tell Nik I tried to call her, too."

"She's at a party that I'm heading to as well."

"That'll be good for you, to spend time with friends."

"That's the plan. I'll call you tomorrow."

"Talk to you then."

Jordan ended the call and turned to Mason, who was propped up on his elbow keeping watch over her. "Nice of her to check on us," Jordan said.

"She's a sweetheart."

"She is." Jordan took a deep breath and released it slowly. "I hope it's not going to be a big deal that Nik and I aren't going to the funeral."

"I hope not either."

CHAPTER 17

A little before three, Jared James drove into town, cruising past the clinic to see if Lizzie's SUV was still in the parking lot. It was. He was worried about her getting overly involved in a situation involving a baby after the crushing disappointment they'd recently sustained. They'd been so sure that this time would be different, and when it hadn't been... His heart had broken for her. It was so hard to watch her go through the grueling treatments and end up with nothing to show for them.

He couldn't bear to see her disappointed or hurt or unhappy, and he felt so helpless to fix this for her. Infertility was one thing that all the money in the world couldn't change. He'd confess to having had a limited understanding of the pervasive challenges of infertility until they'd been confronted with it themselves. And now he knew all too well just how many people struggled to conceive and how intense the treatments could be.

They hadn't really talked about their next steps in this journey or whether they were ready to consider alternatives, such as surrogacy or adoption. He was taking his cues from her, and she hadn't seemed ready to talk about it. Not yet anyway, and he wasn't about to ask until she brought it up.

Navigating this situation was like tiptoeing through an emotional minefield, and he was on edge most of the time, hoping he was providing what she needed. Having his irreverent youngest brother underfoot might help to get their minds off their troubles.

He pulled into the parking lot at the ferry landing and walked to the pier to watch the ferry come in. Seamus O'Grady was at the helm, using the aft controls to turn the ferry and back it into port. Jared never got tired of watching the ferries come and go, admiring the skill and precision of the captains who made it look so easy to put the huge vessels exactly where they wanted them.

The cars came off first, followed by a stream of people, bikes and beach chairs.

He kept an eye out for Cooper and waved when he saw him coming, carrying a backpack. Jared wasn't at all surprised to see his good-looking brother surrounded by a group of gorgeous young women, who seemed heartbroken to have to say goodbye to him as they parted company.

The younger man's face lit up with delight when he saw Jared, who'd had a soft spot for the kid from the minute he was born. Of course, Coop knew that and worked it to his advantage. Jared greeted him with a one-armed hug and a noogie.

Business as usual.

His brother's hair was more blond than brown this time of year, his brown eyes were usually sparkling with some sort of mischief, and he'd apparently given up shaving. He attracted women as easily as he breathed—and he had from the time he was about fourteen.

"What's up, old man?"

"Nothing much. Good to see you, punk."

"You, too. Can't believe Q's getting *married*. This I gotta see."

Jared took him by the arm and directed him toward the Porsche. "I know, but he and Mallory are awesome together."

"Yes, they are."

A month ago, Quinn had sent out a text to the family letting them know that he and Mallory were getting married on their shared birthday, which happened to be a Tuesday, with no fanfare, but anyone who wanted to come was welcome. Since then, Mallory's dad, Big Mac McCarthy, had intervened and offered to host a "slightly bigger production" at the Chesterfield. Lizzie had been able to accommodate the request during their sold-out season since the wedding would be on a Tuesday.

His and Quinn's parents were visiting friends in Italy, and their sisters had vacation plans they couldn't get out of on such short notice. So he and Coop would be representing the James family at the wedding. It was almost as if Quinn had wanted it that way, but Jared would never say so to anyone. Quinn tended to keep to himself within their family, especially since he'd lost a leg in combat and hadn't told any of them. He'd been found out when he stepped in a hole on Jared's property, dislodging the prosthetic and reinjuring his leg.

"Can I drive?" Coop asked.

"Hell no."

"Oh, come on. I'll be careful with your baby."

Jared knew he'd regret this, but handed over the keys anyway.

"Whoop!"

"Don't make me sorry."

"Of course I will. That's how I roll."

Jared chuckled at the cheeky reply. He expected nothing less from his baby brother, who wasn't such a baby anymore. "Ain't that the truth?"

Coop started the car and revved the engine. "Fucking A, that's a sweet, *sweet* sound."

"Go easy on my girl. She's old and temperamental."

"Just like you."

"Shut the fuck up."

Cooper laughed, thrilled to get a rise out of Jared. He pulled the car out of the parking space and took off like a shot toward the exit.

"Watch out, will you? There're people everywhere. I don't need to get sued."

"I'm watching. Relax. Your billions are safe."

"Why in the world was I looking forward to seeing you?"

"Aw, you were? You love me. You know it." Coop pulled out of the ferry landing parking lot and took a left, which was the long way home.

Jared wasn't surprised since he didn't let Cooper drive the Porsche very often, so naturally, he'd take the long way. "What've you been doing with yourself since you graduated?"

He'd gotten an MBA from New York University in the spring, and Jared hadn't heard much from him since then, except the occasional text about something to do with the New York penthouse Jared had let him live in while he was in school.

"I've been working on my business plan, which is another reason I wanted to come see you."

"What business plan?"

"The one I developed in school that I've been fleshing out ever since. I think I've really got something cool, and that's where you come in."

"What's it got to do with me?"

"I need investors."

"Jesus, I walked right into that one, didn't I? What happened to the money I already gave you?" He'd set up each of his family members after he struck it rich, and found out how money changed everything, especially relationships with family. Things were better now with everyone than they'd been a few years ago, when he'd felt like all he was to them was a personal ATM. His brothers had never treated him that way, though, and he appreciated that.

"I still have most of it, but my brother the billionaire has taught me to keep the personal and the professional money separate. He's pretty good with money, so I take his advice very seriously. In fact, I've been doing some investing and seeing great results."

Jared was surprised to hear that. "Is that right?"

"Uh-huh." Coop recited a long list of stocks he'd invested in and knew the revenue percentages by heart. "Pretty good, right?"

"Very good. I'm impressed."

"You are? Really?"

"Yes," Jared said, laughing. "I really am. You're doing great. So what's this business idea?"

"After you and Lizzie bought the Chesterfield and turned it into a wedding venue, I got to thinking about how Gansett is a wedding destination, which creates a market for secondary services."

"Like what?"

"Bachelor and bachelorette parties, for one thing."

"What about them?"

Cooper glanced over at him. "I have a formal pitch that I want to practice on you, so can I tell you about it when we're back at the house?"

"Sure," Jared said, realizing his baby brother wasn't a baby anymore. With twelve years between them, Jared remembered every detail of the day his youngest sibling had been born and how adorable he'd been from the beginning. Coop had been a charmer his whole life, and Jared adored him. "Look at you, all grown up and pitching a business to investors."

"I'm twenty-four now," Coop said dryly.

"Twenty-four. How the hell did that happen?"

Cooper laughed and accelerated once they cleared downtown and headed out toward the north end.

"Go easy. You never know what's around the next corner."

"Ain't that the truth."

"In this case, I mean bikes, mopeds, pedestrians."

Cooper downshifted and slowed the car—a little.

"Before we get back to the house, I need to tell you that Lizzie and I have been going through some shit…"

"You're not breaking up, are you?"

"God, no, nothing like that."

"Oh, phew, because you two are like hashtag couple goals for me."

"Is that right?"

"Uh-huh. She's awesome. I want to find someone like her when the time comes."

"That's nice of you to say, and she is awesome."

"So what's the problem?"

"We've been trying to have a baby for more than a year, and it's just not happening. Our third round of IVF just failed."

"Oh damn, man. I'm so sorry to hear that."

"Thanks. It's been rough, especially for her. She's been through hell with the procedures and shots, and all for nothing."

"Yet. It'll happen."

"We're starting to wrap our heads around the possibility that it's not going to happen. We have to find a way to be okay with that."

"Are you, you know, looking at other options?"

"We haven't been, but it might be time for that, too. We're taking it an hour at a time right now. We only found out that the third round failed a few days ago."

"I'm really sorry, Jared. That sucks."

"Sure does. You spend your whole life trying to avoid getting anyone pregnant, and then when you want to…"

"No kidding. I'm sure you guys will figure out a way to be parents.

You've never let anything stand in the way when you set your mind to something."

"Thanks," Jared said, touched to hear himself described that way by his brother. "This has been a tough one. I want her to have everything she wants and needs..." He cleared his throat, fighting back the now-predictable surge of emotion. "I hate that I can't snap my fingers and make this happen for her."

"I hate it for both of you, but you'll figure out a way. I have no doubt."

"Thanks for listening."

"Dude, jeez. It's the least I can do for you with everything you've done for me."

"Do me a favor and don't say anything about this stuff to Lizzie. Let her tell you if she wants to talk about it."

"I won't say a word. Don't worry."

"I just wanted you to know what you're walking into. Lizzie is excited you're coming. She said you're always fun, and we could use that right now."

"I'll do what I can to lighten the mood."

When Cooper drove them into the driveway a few minutes later, Jared was relieved to see Lizzie's car there. She met them at the door with a welcoming hug for Cooper and the usual warm smile for Jared.

"Um, Jared, could I talk to you for just a second?"

"Sure. Coop, give us a second. I'll be right back. Make yourself at home."

"Don't mind if I do," Coop said, grinning as he opened the fridge.

Jared walked outside with Lizzie, who seemed nervous about something. "What's up, babe?"

"So, um, the woman in town who had the baby?"

"What about her?"

"I, ah, hear me out on this... I, um, I brought her and the baby home with me."

"*What?* Lizzie! What the hell?"

"She's living in the Beachcomber employee housing. That's no place for a newborn, Jared. You know what those places are like. It's nonstop parties and STDs and God knows what else."

"How is she even out of the clinic if she only had the baby a couple of hours ago?"

"She insisted on leaving. I think she doesn't have insurance and is afraid of how much it was going to cost."

"I told you to give her money."

"She won't take it."

He ran both hands through his hair, trying not to tear it out of his head in frustration. "I can't believe you brought a baby here in light of everything we're dealing with."

"I'm sorry, Jared. I didn't know what to do. She has nowhere else to go."

"You could've given her money to stay at a freaking hotel, but to bring her here…"

"She needs help. She knows nothing about babies and is in way over her head."

Jared was rarely ever angry with his wife, but this… "I don't think it's a good idea. What happens when you get attached to the baby and she takes off to rejoin her life?"

"I'm not going to get attached."

He gave her a skeptical look. "Please, Lizzie. You always get attached. It's what you do, and it's why I love you so much. Don't tell me you won't get attached and then be heartbroken when they leave, because you will be."

"I'm going to try very hard not to let that happen. You know how impossible it is for me to see people in need and not want to help them."

Jared felt the anger seep out of him only to be replaced by a surge of love for the incredibly compassionate woman he'd been lucky enough to marry. "I do know that, sweetheart, and I love you for it. It's just sometimes I worry about you helping others at your own expense, and I can't bear to see you hurt any more than you're already hurting."

She placed her hands on his chest and looked up at him, using her potent eyes to implore him to see things her way. "I'll be careful. I promise." Tipping her head, she gave him her most adorable smile, the one he was powerless to resist even when he wanted to be annoyed with her. "Do you want to come meet Jessie and the baby?"

He didn't, but he would for her. "Sure." Jared followed her inside to the family room, where Cooper had already found Jessie and was holding her baby.

Coop looked up at Jared. A million questions that Jared couldn't answer were reflected in his brother's gaze.

"Jared, this is Jessie Morgan and her baby girl, who doesn't have a name yet." Jessie had light brown hair and hazel eyes. He figured her to be in her early twenties.

"Nice to meet you both," Jared said.

"Thank you so much for having us. Lizzie… She's just the most amazing person."

"She sure is. I see you met my brother, Cooper."

Jessie's face, which had been so pale he'd been concerned for her, flushed a rosy red at the mention of Cooper.

His brother's superpowers were potent, apparently having an impact even on a woman who'd given birth earlier in the day. Jared didn't want to be curious, but he found himself leaning in for a closer look at the baby. Her eyes were open as she looked around, seeming to take in her surroundings with an aura of serene curiosity. He hadn't had much experience with babies, other than his youngest brother, but even he could see she was an exceptionally beautiful little girl.

"She's gorgeous," Jared said, his voice gruff. "Congratulations."

"Thank you," Jessie said, her chin quivering. "She's so tiny."

"They usually are," Lizzie said.

Jared noticed that she forced a smile for Jessie, but her eyes were bright with unshed tears. Despite her bravado, her heart was breaking all over again, and that was not all right with him.

CHAPTER 18

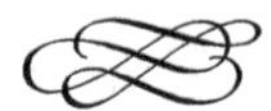

Seamus O'Grady made his way home after completing his last run of the day on the ferries, delivering another rowdy group of tourists seeking summer fun on Gansett Island. Maybe he was getting old and cranky, but the crowds coming these days seemed especially young to him. There'd been a time when drinking and carousing on Gansett would've been his idea of fun. Now he had a whole new definition of fun, and it included watching Kyle and Jackson, the boys he and his wife, Carolina, were raising, play baseball.

Or do anything, for that matter. He was all in on whatever it was they wanted to do. He'd been teaching them how to fish this summer, and they loved it. They loved anything he suggested they do. More than that, though, they loved having his undivided attention, so he gave it to them as often as he could. Easy enough, since he adored every second he got to spend with them.

Quite some time ago, he'd more or less given up on the possibility of becoming a father, and then Kyle and Jackson came into their lives, first as their neighbors. After their mother died tragically young, he and Carolina had stepped up for the boys. The four of them had become a family that also included Carolina's son, Joe, and his family, and Seamus's cousin Shannon and his now-fiancée, Victoria.

He'd been thrilled to get that text from Shannon earlier, after helping his cousin pick out the ring that he'd given Vic.

She LOVED it, Shannon had reported.

That was great news. Seamus adored Vic and how she'd made his cousin smile again, which had once seemed like an impossible task. After Shannon's first love, Fiona, had been murdered back in Ireland, they'd worried that Shannon would never move on with his life—and he hadn't. Not really, anyway, until he came to Gansett to visit Seamus, met Victoria and found a new purpose.

In addition, Seamus loved having his first cousin living nearby and working with him on the ferries. They'd been close at home but became more so after Seamus tragically lost his two brothers when they were younger. Life could really kick you in the teeth, he thought as he let the warm breeze wash over his face, which was why you had to take the joy where you could find it.

His life had been all about the joy since he met Carolina and talked her into taking a chance on a smooth-talking Irishman sixteen years her junior. And since the boys had come into their lives and the grandchildren had arrived, the joy had only multiplied.

He wanted for absolutely nothing, except maybe for more time with the loved ones he'd left back in Ireland. But they made do with FaceTime and Skype and emails and group texts and every other way they could think of to stay in close touch. They made it work, and he was very much looking forward to the visit from Shannon's parents and his own mam. He was still trying to convince his father to come with them.

Seamus pulled into the driveway at home and was surprised to find the yard deserted. Usually, the boys and their crazy dog, Burpy, were running around at this time of day, burning off their overabundance of energy. The stillness had him on edge as he got out of his Gansett Island Ferry Company truck and went inside, carrying three bags of ice that he added to the cooler he'd set up earlier. He'd dropped off six more bags at Charlie and Sarah's on the way home. Their party was in full swing, but he'd wanted to come home to see his own family.

When he walked in, the first thing he noticed was Carolina sitting at the table, looking shell-shocked.

"What's wrong?" he asked, because there was no doubt in his mind that something was very wrong. "And where're the boys?"

"They're playing with Ethan this afternoon. Hope asked if they could come to keep him entertained, because I guess there's something going on with Marion. She was fully lucid earlier."

"Wow."

"Hope said she'd bring them home after dinner."

"Now tell me what's wrong." He couldn't move or breathe or do anything but stand inside the door, waiting for her to drop the boot on him.

"We got a letter," she said, swallowing hard. "From a lawyer in Providence."

"What's a lawyer in Providence want with us?"

"They represent the boys' father, Jace Carson."

Those words sucked all the oxygen out of his body and made his knees buckle. Grasping the countertop, he held on for dear life. "What does he want?"

"To see his sons."

"Just like that? Out of the blue? Where's he been all this time?"

"According to the letter, he didn't know Lisa died. Do you want to read it?"

"No, I don't want to read it." He didn't want to see anything that threatened their standing as the boys' guardians. *He* was their father now, not some sperm donor who'd been nowhere to be found before now.

"Seamus, come here."

"I don't want to do that either." He didn't want to deal with a letter that could endanger their precious family. "If Lisa had wanted him in their lives, she would've asked him to take them after she passed."

"I agree, and we do have options as their legal guardians."

"He can make trouble for us, love. If he so desires… He's their biological father. If he took us to court—" His head was suddenly pounding, probably because he was roasting and on the verge of having a stroke.

"Seamus. Stop. Come here and read the letter."

He did not want to read that letter. If he never read it, he could pretend this wasn't happening.

"Seamus."

Carolina tipped her head and gestured for him to join her at the table, where she'd lit several candles to offset the waning daylight. Since he could deny her nothing, he went, even though he most definitely did not want to.

She handed the letter to him.

He forced himself to read the words, to make sense of the words. The boys' father had only recently learned of Lisa's death as well as the custody arrangement she had made for their minor children. "How is it possible he didn't know? She's been gone for months."

"Which shows how out of touch he is with his children. That's actually a good thing."

"None of this is a good thing. We need to call Dan and get him over here."

"I already did. He's on his way. He and Kara just got back to the island today, so we got lucky."

Seamus was relieved to hear that their highly skilled lawyer friend was coming to help them make sense of this situation. He'd know what to do. He finished skimming the letter, the gist of which was now that he knew that the mother of his children was dead, Jace Carson was interested in knowing more about their living situation.

"She had sole custody," Carolina said. "She chose the people she wanted to finish raising them. We have to believe she knew what she was doing, and this won't change anything."

"It'll change everything."

"How so?"

"They'll know they have another father, for one thing."

"Maybe not. Nothing says we have to let him see them."

"What if we have no choice in the matter?"

"We have a choice. We're their legal guardians."

"He's their biological father."

"Let's not spin in circles before we hear what Dan thinks."

Under normal circumstances, Seamus was never more comfortable than he was with Carolina. These were not normal circumstances, and he was as uncomfortable as he could recall being in a very long time. In fact, he hadn't felt this unsettled since he'd been quite certain that Carolina was going to break his heart. This felt almost as bad as that had.

Then her hand was on top of his, infusing him with her warmth when he needed it most. "I know you're thinking the worst, but try not to go there. There're a lot of miles between this letter and the worst-case scenario."

She was right. He knew it and even agreed with her. But the possibility of that worst-case scenario playing out was a nightmare to him. Losing the boys he and Carolina had poured their hearts and souls into would break him. Losing them would break her, too, even if she was trying to be brave for both of them. It didn't help anything that the house was hotter than the surface of the sun, which only added to the sick feeling churning in his gut.

A sharp knock on the door preceded Dan Torrington's entrance. "I got here as fast as I could after I got your call, Carolina. Had to drop Kara at Sarah and Charlie's." He stopped short when he saw them sitting at the table, probably looking like two disaster survivors. "What's going on?"

Carolina held out the letter to him, and he sat at the table to read it.

Watching his posture become more rigid as he read did nothing to help Seamus's shattered nerves. "Well, that's an interesting development."

"Unsettling is a better word for it," Seamus said.

"I don't think you have anything to worry about. Before Lisa died, she made you guys the boys' legal guardians. She had sole custody, which made it completely her decision."

"He's their biological father."

"Maybe so, but at some point, he either surrendered his rights or lost custody, which removed him from the equation when she was dying."

"So he can't come in now and upend the custody arrangement?" Seamus asked the only question that mattered.

"I can't see how. Lisa was very clear and very specific. The custody agreement is airtight. I made sure of that."

For the first time since he came home to this news, Seamus took a deep breath and no longer felt like he might be having a stroke. "You're *sure?*"

"I wrote it," Dan said with the big, cocky grin that was his trademark. "I'm very sure."

Seamus dropped his head into his hands. "Jesus, Mary and Joseph, I'm getting too old for this shit."

Carolina laughed. "How do you think I feel?"

Seamus reached for her hand. "You're aging in reverse, my love."

"Ha! I wish. Dan, what should we do about the letter?"

"I'll give the lawyer a call on Monday and figure out what they're after. It may be something as simple as assurances that the boys are well and safe."

"What would land on the complicated end of the spectrum?" Seamus asked.

"Let's not speculate about that until we know more. There's no point worrying about something that may not happen."

"If I know my husband, he'll fill the void with horrifying what-ifs and won't get a minute's peace unless you give him the various scenarios, Dan. Trust me, it's better for all of us that way."

"My Caro knows me too well."

"And I have to live with him until you tell us more, so if you can put us both out of our misery..."

Dan laughed. "Got it. Well, he could ask for visitation, and you'd have the right to say no to that as their legal guardians. If he doesn't like that answer, he could file for custody, but that's a remote possibility. Keep in mind, he hasn't been around at all. Lisa never even mentioned him all the times we met about custody and guardianship until I asked about him. She said he wasn't a factor. There was no request for me to notify him of her death or anything else having to do with the kids. To me, that says everything we need to know about who and what he's been to them. I honestly don't think you have anything to worry about. Lisa was very thorough. Maybe she knew it might be necessary at some point."

"That does make me feel better," Seamus said, "but tell me this. What kind of standing would he have in court if he were to pursue custody?"

"Much less than you'd have as the legal guardian chosen by their custodial parent."

Seamus took a breath and released it slowly. "Okay, so..."

"So you need to try to relax and have faith that Lisa took care of things before she died, and her sons are where she wants them to be. That would matter to the court, too, if it came to that."

"Let's hope and pray it doesn't come to that," Seamus said.

"I'll do whatever I can to make sure it doesn't."

"Thank you so much for interrupting your day for us, Dan," Carolina said.

"Not a problem. Do you mind if I take this with me?" he asked of the letter.

"No, please do," Carolina said. "You'll let us know when you have more info?"

"The minute I hear anything, you will, too."

Seamus stood to shake his hand and show him out. "I don't have to tell you what those boys have come to mean to us," he said when he walked Dan to his car.

"No, you don't. We can all see how well they're doing, and that's thanks to you and Carolina stepping up for them the way you did."

"We love them."

"And they love you, too. It's going to be fine."

"From your lips to God's ears."

Seamus waved as Dan drove away, and was still outside, breathing the heavy humid air, when Hope's car pulled into the driveway, bringing his boys home. His heart did a happy jig at the sight of the boys in the backseat with Hope's son, Ethan, who was their best friend. The doors flew open, and boys exploded out of the car like they'd been shot from a cannon. Right behind his boys was their dog, Burpy, who went just about everywhere they did.

They were all talking at once, but he picked up bits and pieces about pizza, swimming, the dog finding something dead in the field at Ethan's house and a treehouse that Ethan's stepfather, Paul, was building for him, and could he build them one at their house, and how many more days of vacation did they have before school started.

That covered the first two minutes they were home.

"*Whoa,*" Seamus said. "Everyone slow down. One question at a time."

"How many more days of summer vacation?" Kyle asked, his missing front teeth giving him an adorable lisp. He had a scab on the end of his nose from when he'd face-planted last week while playing football in the yard.

"About twenty or so," Seamus said.

Kyle groaned. "That's too soon. Why can't every day be summer vacation?"

Jackson and Ethan pumped their fists in support of Kyle's idea, the three of them running off with the dog in hot pursuit.

"Holy moly," Seamus said to Hope, who returned his smile. "To have that much energy."

"I know! If only we could bottle it."

"Thank you for having them."

"Always a pleasure. Ethan adores them."

"Likewise. Our place next time, aye?"

"Aye," she said with a grin. "Hot enough for you?"

"It's unbearable."

"What're you hearing about the power?" she asked.

"Not much, just that it seems to be something in the central line from the mainland."

"That's what Paul's hearing, too." Her husband was a Gansett Island town councilman. "The power company has multiple teams working on it, but they said to expect it to be a couple more days."

"Ugh, great. We brought a ton of ice over on the last boat. Make sure you get some."

"Paul's there now."

Carolina came out to say hello to Hope, who left with Ethan a few minutes later to get home in time for baby Scarlett's next feeding.

He and Carolina supervised the boys playing in the yard for another hour before Carolina told them it was time to come in for baths. As they rounded them up, pissing and moaning the whole time because they hated bath time, Seamus tried to remember what he used to do with himself before these two tiny men took over his life and his heart.

That seemed like another lifetime to him now that the boys and Caro were front and center in his life.

The boys were filthy after a hard day of playing outside in the heat, so Seamus went to supervise the bath, using flashlights and candles to light the room.

"You're like a couple of nasty tea bags," he said, as he did every night, making them laugh. He'd had to demonstrate what a tea bag was and how it made tea before they got his joke, and now they thought it was hilarious. They thought everything he said and did was funny or interesting, which only made him love them that much more than he already did. It was a tremendous responsibility, this job of shaping boys into men, and one he relished with everything he had. Raising them to be decent men was the most important thing he'd ever do, and he intended to give it his all.

"Dirt tea," they said together, echoing a term he used to describe the kind of tea they made.

He helped them wash behind their ears, which was another thing they found endlessly hysterical. *Who got dirty behind their ears?* they asked every night. *Boys who roll around in the dirt all day,* he said.

Tears stung his eyes at the thought of anyone taking them away from him. He'd fight for them until his dying breath, if that's what it came to.

But God, he hoped it didn't come to that.

CHAPTER 19

Abby was stretched out on the bed with the windows open when Adam came to find her, carrying Liam, who was fresh from his afternoon nap. They'd been waiting for him to wake up to leave for the party at Charlie and Sarah's.

"Someone is full of beans," Adam said. "The poor guy was so overheated. I gave him a cool bath to make him feel better."

"Poor baby," Abby said. "Next trip to the mainland, we need a generator."

"I want one of those whole-home generators like my parents got last year. I should've had one put in here at the same time. I wish now that I had."

"Maddie texted to say Mac brought home a generator. They're telling anyone who needs cooler air to come over and bring air mattresses."

"You want to do that?"

"Maybe. Of course we had to lose power when it's hotter than the sun."

"I think that's *why* we lost power. Too much demand for AC taxed the system, which was fragile to begin with."

"It scares me to think we're so vulnerable to something like this. That we can lose power for days on end, and there's nothing anyone can do." Her anxiety had been through the roof since the news they received yesterday about the quadruplets. Coming home to a power outage hadn't helped anything.

"Having the generator will help. I'll get on that right away. Try not to worry."

"Right. What've I got to worry about?"

"Not one thing."

"Are you in denial by any chance?"

"Nope."

"Five kids, Adam. Four infants all at once. Five kids under the age of two."

"Yes, I got that memo."

"And you're totally fine with it?"

"I am, except for the part about you being stressed or uncomfortable, which you probably will be toward the end."

"Do ya think?"

He smiled and moved Liam to his left side so he could reach for her hand. "We've got this, Abs. You and me? There's nothing we can't do if we do it together."

"I feel ridiculous about being so shocked and stressed over this when I prayed for so long to get pregnant."

"Of course you're shocked and stressed after hearing there're four babies in there, Abs. Do you feel like going to Sarah and Charlie's?"

"Yes, I want to go."

"We're ready when you are." Adam helped her up and entertained Liam while she got changed into the lightest-weight dress she owned, not bothering to bring the usual sweater she'd need most evenings on Gansett.

They drove the short distance to Charlie and Sarah's with the air conditioning blasting in Adam's BMW SUV.

"God, that air feels so good. The things we take for granted until we don't have them."

"I know. I'll never take AC or electricity for granted again."

"Yes, you will."

"I suppose you're right."

"I usually am."

Adam laughed as he glanced over at her. "Nice to have you joking again. You had me worried for a while there."

"The shock might be wearing off a bit. Be careful what you wish for, right?"

"For sure," he said, chuckling. "The way I see it is we're incredibly blessed. Not only did we get a miracle that you conceived in the first place, but that miracle is multiplied by four. And we can be one and done with having babies."

"That is *for sure*. Snip, snip, mister."

Adam grimaced. "I'll go with Mac and get the family discount."

"Make that happen ASAP."

"Yes, ma'am."

When they arrived at Sarah and Charlie's, they parked in the street so they could escape if Liam had a meltdown. It was funny to Abby how Adam did that so naturally now. Parenthood changed everything, which caused another thought to occur to her. "How will we take five babies out? We'll need two cars and fifteen people to do it."

"Breathe," he said calmly. "We'll get a bigger car and figure it out. Are you breathing?"

Abby made a dramatic show out of taking a deep breath and blowing it out.

"Do it again. Keep doing it any time you think we can't handle this. We'll have tons of help from grandparents, siblings and friends."

"Several of our friends and many of our family members are having their own babies." Gansett—and the McCarthy family, in particular—was about to experience a baby boom of epic proportions.

"Doesn't matter. They'll all be there for us. You know they will."

"Yes, they will," she said with a sigh. "You're sure we can handle this with two businesses to run, too?"

"I'm positive."

"How am I going to run the Attic with five babies to care for?"

"You hire a manager for a few years, and once we have things under control, you can get back to handling it yourself."

"It'll take us fifteen years to get things under control."

Adam cracked up laughing. "You may be right about that. But let's take it one crisis at a time."

Though she hated to leave the air-conditioned car, she was eager to see Sarah and Charlie's beautiful new home.

Adam retrieved Liam from his car seat, and they walked down the winding driveway that led to the huge contemporary-style house, which wasn't visible from the road. "This place is amazing. I never even knew this was back here."

The house was all windows, gray shingles and cool angles that gave it a cottage-like feel, despite its size. They followed the sound of voices coming from the backyard, which was full of tables, chairs and people.

Victoria Stevens saw them come in and ran over to hug Abby. "Oh. My. *God*! I got the report from the mainland this morning and almost fell off my chair. Abby!"

"I know."

Vic pulled back from her, but kept her hands on Abby's arms. "I'm so, so, so happy for you guys. I was bawling my head off at the clinic. Ask David!"

"Thank you," Abby said, touched by the reaction of the nurse practitioner-midwife who'd been such a source of support to her since the PCOS diagnosis.

"You must be *losing your shit*," Vic said.

"Just a little. Trying to wrap my head around five kids and four newborns. We both are."

"Congrats, Dad. Very well done."

"I did do some good work," Adam said with a smug grin.

"Shut it, Adam," Abby said, even though she loved how excited he was.

"Have you told anyone yet?" Vic asked.

"Nope," Abby said. "We gave ourselves a day to wrap our own heads around it."

"How's that going?" Vic asked, grinning.

"Still not there yet."

"It's going to be fine." Vic put her hand on Abby's arm and gave it a squeeze. "We'll watch you like a hawk and get you out of here well ahead of the delivery. Don't worry about anything."

"Thank you. I'll try not to."

"Come see me Monday, and we'll make a plan."

David Lawrence joined them, shaking hands with Adam. "Congratulations, guys. You had Vic weeping like a baby earlier."

"So we heard," Abby said.

"It's just *so* exciting," Victoria said. "I don't get to monitor quadruplets every day, that's for sure."

Abby glanced at Adam. "I guess we'd better tell our families the big news. We also found out that I'm further along than I thought, which was a surprise. I went from knowing every detail of my cycle and ovulation to not noticing I'd missed a period."

"Once we had Liam," Adam said, "the pressure was off."

"If you knew how many times I've seen that happen," Vic said. "I've never seen it happen with quads, but I do hear of a lot of adoptive parents suddenly finding themselves pregnant after years of trying."

"Glad it's not just us," Abby said. "Well, except for the quads part of the equation."

"We'll watch you very closely, so we can quickly address any concerns."

"What kind of concerns?" Abby asked, immediately on guard against bad news.

"Nope. We're not going there unless or until we need to. For the moment, everything is fine, and it's going to stay that way." Vic looped her arm through Abby's. "Come on, let's get you off your feet, Mom."

Victoria escorted Abby to a circle of chairs where most of Adam's family had gathered, including her sisters-in-law Janey and Stephanie, who were among Abby's closest friends. Also in their group was Adam's cousin Laura, his cousin Shane's wife, Katie, and Maddie, on the lounge chair that went with her everywhere while she was on bed rest.

It occurred to Abby right in that moment that she'd probably be on bed rest before her pregnancy was over, too. Ugh.

"Abby!" Stephanie jumped up—or what passed for jumping in her pregnant state—and hugged her. "We've been so worried! Not a word from you guys after the appointment."

Seeing that they'd arrived, Adam's brothers, parents, cousins and brother-in-law, Joe, came over to see them along with their friend Slim Jackson and his wife, Erin.

"Tell us." Linda McCarthy kissed them and Liam. "Is everything all right?"

"Everything is a little *too* all right," Adam said, smiling at Abby and giving her the floor to share their news with his family.

"One of you had better start talking," Linda said, "before I *expire* from needing to know!"

"You're okay, aren't you, sweetheart?" Big Mac asked.

"I'm okay. In fact, it seems I'm expecting quadruplets."

After a second of complete, shocked silence, the group erupted into laughter and congratulations and more than a few tears as they hugged Abby and Adam.

"Wait!" Maddie said. "I couldn't hear her! What did she say?"

The group parted to allow Adam and Abby to move closer to Maddie. Abby tried not to notice how huge Maddie's belly was with "only" two babies in there. What would she look like with *four*?

"We're having quads," Abby said to Maddie.

"*Oh my God!* Shut up! That's incredible! Congratulations."

"Thank you. We're still in shock, needless to say."

Mac put an arm around Adam. "We McCarthy boys know how to properly knock up our wives, don't we?"

"Shut up, Mac," Maddie said.

"I'd just like to point out that my boys have twice the power of your boys," Adam said.

"Shut up, Adam," Abby said.

Mac and Adam lost it laughing, delighted with themselves and their boys.

"Sorry about them." Linda shoved her sons aside so she could hug Abby. "I'm so, so happy for you, honey. What an amazing outcome after what you've been through."

"Thank you." Abby blinked back tears from the emotional overload of making their news official by telling the family. "I'm going to need all the help I can get."

"Big Mac and I will move in for the first month or two. Whatever you need."

"Could you move in for eighteen or so years?" Abby asked, making everyone else laugh.

"We'll be there for you," Linda said. "Don't worry about a thing."

Linda McCarthy had made her feel like part of their family from the first time Grant brought her home as his new girlfriend, and that had never changed, even during the hard times with Grant and after their breakup. They'd never missed a beat when she and Adam got together, and she considered herself lucky to be a McCarthy, in no small part because of her awesome in-laws. "That means so much to me, Linda. Thank you."

Word about the quadruplets rippled through the gathering, and everyone came over to congratulate them.

"We're so happy for you guys," Erin said when she hugged Abby. "Way to be an overachiever."

"Haha," Abby said. "I never have been before now."

"Yes, you have," Slim said, kissing her forehead. "We can't wait to meet your babies."

"And I can't wait to meet yours," Abby said. "They're going to have to add on to the island school to accommodate all these kids."

"This is amazing news," Laura Lawry, Adam's cousin, said. "Look at you—go big or go home, huh?"

"I'm gonna go big, all right," Abby said. "I'm hoping I won't explode toward the end."

"You won't." Laura was the mother of twins. "You'll just feel like you're going to."

"Awesome."

Charlie and Sarah came over to congratulate them, along with Sarah's sons John and Jeff, who'd come home for the party.

While they were talking to them, Owen Lawry joined them. "What's this I hear? *Four?*"

"That's what they tell us."

"Holy crap." He high-fived Adam. "Well done, my man."

"I'm rather pleased with myself."

"Ugh," Abby said. "Am I going to hear that for the rest of my life?"

"Probably," Owen's wife, Laura, said. "I'm still hearing about his prowess in knocking me up with twins."

"Same." Maddie used her thumb to point to Mac. "It's a good thing they aren't the ones who have to carry and give birth to multiple babies, or they'd be crying like little bitches."

While Mac feigned offense, the others lost it laughing.

"You know she's right, Mac," Adam said. "Our wives are superheroes."

"They are for sure. Have you heard about the no-sex-for-months part of having multiples?" Mac asked his brother.

"Oh yeah," Owen said, "that's the worst."

"Wait, *what?*" Adam said. "No one said anything about that."

"I repeat," Maddie said. "Whiny. *Bitches.*"

"Now you're just being mean to your baby daddy," Mac said, affecting a pout.

Spending the rest of the afternoon with the always-entertaining McCarthys as well as their friends helped to put Abby's fears to rest—for now, anyway.

CHAPTER 20

"I think we have a hit on our hands, sweetheart," Charlie said as he stood with Sarah to survey their guests, who were eating and drinking, talking and laughing, despite the heat and the power failure that had thrown them into chaos earlier. The sun was inching closer to the horizon, promising a spectacular sunset.

"Seems like it," she said. "Thanks to the kids and Seamus for bringing more ice."

"It helps to have well-connected friends."

"For sure."

"Who's that young lady Jeff is talking to?" Sarah asked.

"That's Mac and Maddie's au pair, Kelsey. I hear she's a delightful girl."

"She sure is pretty."

"Indeed." Charlie looked down at her. "Why are you biting that poor lip?"

"I worry about him. Even though he seems to be doing so much better than he was, he's still so young and unsettled."

"He'll find his way, just like the others have. He's doing great, a college grad and lots of opportunities to explore."

"I suppose. Did John say anything to you about an issue at work? I heard him on the phone, but I didn't want to ask."

"He referred to an argument with a superior officer, but I didn't get the details."

"Oh jeez. I hope he's not in trouble."

"I didn't want to pry, so I didn't ask any questions. Just let him know I'm available if he needs to talk. He said he's surprised I'd welcome a police officer into my home after what I went through."

"What did you say?"

"That as Sarah's son, he's always welcome in my home and that I don't blame the police for what happened to me. I blame my ex-wife, who was the one to hurt my daughter and who allowed me to take the blame for what she did."

"Thank you for making him feel welcome."

"Of course he is. He didn't lock me up for someone else's crime. I don't look at him and see all law enforcement. I look at him and see your son. My stepson. A member of our family."

"I love you, Charlie."

"I love you, too, Sarah." He smiled down at her. "Check us out, huh? This amazing house, our beautiful kids, all these incredible friends. How lucky are we?"

"The luckiest people I know."

"Who had the shittiest luck ever until they found each other and everything changed."

She crooked her finger to bring him down for a kiss.

"Um, excuse us, you lovebirds."

She released Charlie and turned to Big Mac and Linda. Sarah's went hot with embarrassment. "Sorry."

"Please don't be," Linda said. "You two are adorable together."

"Not sure how I feel about being called adorable," Charlie said gruffly.

"You should feel pretty good about it," Linda said. "I'm so, so happy for you both. Your house is absolutely gorgeous, and we wish you many, many happy years here."

"Thank you so much, Linda," Sarah said, hugging the other woman.

"Congratulations, guys," Big Mac said. "It's a beaut. One word of advice? Get one of those whole-home generators that're all the rage. We love ours. Damned grateful for it today."

"That's at the top of my list of priorities," Charlie said.

"We're going to check on our new lighthouse keepers," Linda said.

"They just arrived today, and we're worried about them being out there without power."

"It's good of you to check on them," Sarah said.

"Thanks again for having us," Linda said. "It was a wonderful party."

"Thank you for coming and for the gifts that you weren't supposed to bring."

Linda laughed. "Our pleasure. Let's get together again soon. Our place next time."

"We'd love that," Sarah said.

"I'll call you."

After the McCarthys had walked away, Charlie said, "Look at us, making couple friends and everything."

Sarah laughed at the way he said that, with his usual gruff-sounding disdain for everything, which he said was hardwired into his DNA after fourteen years in prison. But he laughed more now, smiled more, joked more and teased her every day. "Look at us, living the dream."

"You said it, sweetheart."

Leaving Charlie and Sarah's, Big Mac directed his truck toward the lighthouse. "Your idea to check on the Watkins was a good one, Lin.."

"They just got here, and it's so hot with no power. It's a heck of a welcome party."

"I hope they accept the invite to stay with us until the power comes back. That was a good idea, too."

"I have all the good ideas," Linda said. "You should know that by now."

"Heh," he said, grunting out a laugh. "I walked right into that one, didn't I?"

"That was a softball."

"How about our Adam and Abby?"

"Quadruplets! It's unbelievable. After what they went through… Life sure can be funny."

"I can't imagine having four infants. That's going to be madness."

"Yep, but we'll all be there to help. We'll get them through it." Linda directed the air-conditioning vent to point directly at her. "It's such a miracle when you think about it. How they told Abby she might never conceive, and now this."

"I was thinking the same thing. I'm so happy for them. They're such great parents to Liam. They'll be fantastic with the squad, too."

"Is that what we're calling them?"

"What else should we call them?"

"Squad works."

A few minutes later, they arrived at the lighthouse property, where the gate was still open. They drove down the long driveway that ended at the lighthouse and parked next to Oliver and Dara's SUV.

As they got out of the truck, Oliver stepped out of the lighthouse and seemed surprised to see them. "Hey, guys. I was just going to walk out and close the gate."

"We wanted to come check on you to see how you're holding up without power."

"We're doing okay. I went into town earlier and got a couple of bags of ice. We're hoping that'll hold us over until it comes back on. Have you heard anything about when that might be?"

Big Mac rubbed the back of his neck as he grimaced. "Could be a couple of days."

"*Days* as in multiple *days*?"

"Afraid so. It was four days the last time this happened."

"Holy crap."

"We feel bad this happened the day you arrived," Linda said.

"It's not your fault," Oliver said. "I suppose we'll survive."

"We were going to ask you," Linda said, glancing at Big Mac, "if you might like to come and stay with us while the power is out. We have a big house with plenty of empty bedrooms and a whole-home generator that's giving us just enough power to run window AC units in the bedrooms on low. It's not ideal, but it's better than nothing. And we'd be happy to have you."

"Oh, well, that's very kind of you to offer. I'm not sure Dara would want to impose that way."

"It's no imposition at all," Big Mac said. "Like Linda said, we're the ultimate empty nesters with bedrooms we're more than happy to share to make you more comfortable than you'd be here with no power."

Oliver seemed to be considering it.

"How about we do this," Big Mac said. "We'll take a walk while you two talk it over. If you decide to stay put, no problem at all. Whatever works for you is fine with us."

"That sounds good. Let me go talk to Dara. I really appreciate the offer. It's just that she's…" He shrugged. "I used to be able to tell you what she'd say about just about anything. But now… I honestly don't know what to expect."

Linda wanted to hug the poor guy. "We understand. It's not at all the same thing, but we lost a child late in pregnancy and had a very hard time afterward. That kind of loss, and certainly what happened to you… It changes a marriage."

"Yes," he said with a sigh. "It sure does. Thank you for understanding. I'll go talk to Dara. We won't keep you too long."

"Take your time," Big Mac said. "We've got nowhere to be." He put his arm around Linda, and they walked away to give Oliver a chance to speak to his wife. "It was good that you told him what happened to us."

"I told Dara earlier. I hope they don't think I was comparing the two. There's no comparison."

"A loss is a loss. Yes, some are worse than others, but I hope it helps them to know we get it a little bit."

"I hope so, too."

OLIVER WENT up the spiral staircase that brought him to the combined kitchen/living room and then went up the second stairway to the bedroom/bathroom. The place was cute, but small. It wouldn't be as easy for him and Dara to avoid each other the way they had at home. Maybe that was a good thing. Who knew? He didn't know anything anymore.

Dara was stretched out on the bed, staring up at the ceiling. Every window was open, but the air was thick with heat and humidity that had sweat rolling down his back. "Who were you talking to out there?"

"Mr. and Mrs. McCarthy came back to check on how we're making out without power."

"That was nice of them."

"They asked if we might want to come stay with them. They have extra bedrooms and a generator that provides some AC."

"Oh."

"I'd understand if you don't feel comfortable staying with people we don't know, but they seem so nice and genuine. Might be nice to have AC in this heat."

"So, you want to go?"

"Only if you do. I want you to be comfortable."

"I'm not comfortable anywhere anymore."

"I know, honey, but it's hot and not looking to break for days. Mr. McCarthy said it might take that long for the power to come back on. By then, we might be dehydrated from sweating." He took her hand and knew a moment of pure happiness when she didn't pull it back. "They told me they lost a baby. Apparently, it messed them up pretty good for a long time."

"She told me that."

"I think they want to help."

"I don't want their help."

"Fine, but I wouldn't mind their AC."

She glanced at him for the first time since he'd come into the room. "You want to go?"

"Yeah, I think I do. They seem like nice people, and it's hot as hell here. Not to mention, they probably have a working fridge and coffeemaker, which we don't have here without power."

"You had me at coffee."

Oliver smiled at the first lighthearted comment he'd heard her make since disaster struck. Her obsessive love of coffee was well documented, and although he was encouraged by her enthusiasm for *something*, it pained him to realize how long it'd been since she'd joked about anything. He gave her hand a gentle tug to help her sit up. "Since we haven't unpacked, it should be easy enough to relocate for a few days."

"And if we're not feeling it, we can come back here?"

"Whatever you want, hon." Oliver meant that. He'd do whatever he could to help her find some peace. The estrangement between the two of them was almost as painful as the loss of their son had been, and he had no idea how to bridge the yawning distance between them so they could find their way back to each other.

He'd hoped that coming to Gansett Island would help to shake things up, but nothing had gone according to plan on their first day.

They gathered their things, bagged up the perishable food items he'd bought at the grocery store earlier and headed down the stairs.

Outside, they found the McCarthys sitting on the tailgate of Big Mac's truck, watching the rather spectacular sunset.

"See what you have to look forward to every day?" Big Mac said, tipping his chin toward the sky.

"It's beautiful," Oliver said. "Dara and I gratefully accept your kind invitation, but we want you to tell us when you've had enough of us."

"Oh stop," Linda said, laughing. "It'll be nice to have the company. You want to follow us so you'll have your car?"

"Sure," Oliver said. "I just need to close the gate on the way out."

"We'll wait for you," Big Mac said.

As they followed the McCarthys to their home, Oliver continued to hope and pray for a breakthrough with Dara, who sat silently next to him, staring out the window, a million miles from him. If the time on Gansett Island didn't work to give them a reset, he didn't know what he'd do next.

CHAPTER 21

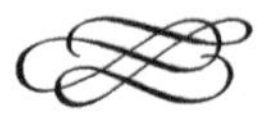

Caught up in a conversation with his father, uncles and cousins about the abandoned alpaca farm Mac wanted to buy as their next family project, Shane McCarthy realized he hadn't seen Katie in quite some time.

Listening to Mac talk about what they could do with the old farm had sparked excitement in Shane, who'd love to renovate another island property that had fallen into disrepair. Mac's enthusiasm was contagious, and they made a plan to get everyone out to look at the place the following week.

Now where had his lovely wife gotten off to? He got up to go find her. "Anyone need anything?"

"Bring more beer when you come back," Riley said.

"Will do."

Shane went inside but didn't see Katie among the women gathered around the massive kitchen island, discussing Sarah's options for backsplash tile.

"Have you seen Katie?" he asked his wife's twin, Julia.

"Not in a while."

"Me either."

"She came in about a half hour ago," Sarah said. "I think she went upstairs."

"I'll find her," Shane said, beginning to worry. It wasn't like her to disappear on him. "You mind if I go up?"

"Make yourself at home, honey," Sarah said with a warm smile.

She was the sweetest mother-in-law any man could hope to have, and he'd loved her long before he married her daughter. They'd spent a winter living close to each other at the Surf, working on the renovations and hanging out with Owen, Laura and baby Holden. That was back when Shane had still been trying to resurface from the nightmare his ex-wife had put him through, and Sarah had been coping with the end of her violent marriage.

Sarah had been a great friend to him then, and after having lost his own mother when he was seven, Shane was thankful to have her in his life to stay.

He went up the stairs and poked his head in a few rooms, but didn't see Katie. Knocking on the one door that was closed, he called for her.

"Don't come in here, Shane," she said, sounding frantic.

Taken aback, he said, "What's the matter?"

"I…"

"Katie, honey… Open the door."

A full minute passed before the lock turned, and the door opened a crack. The first thing he noticed was her red, puffy face and watery eyes. "What's wrong, honey?"

"I… I think I had a miscarriage."

Shane felt like he'd been stabbed in the heart and had to force himself to say something. "Did you… I didn't know…"

"I didn't either," she said as tears rolled down her sweet face.

"Let me in, honey."

"I need to clean the bathroom. There's blood…"

"I'll clean it. Let me help."

The door opened fully, and Shane had to bite back a gasp at how much blood she'd lost. "Katie, sweetheart, let me get Vic."

"No! Just you."

"Do you feel like you could handle a shower to clean up?"

She nodded.

"Okay, let's take it nice and easy." He helped her out of her clothes and into the shower. Alarmed by the amount of blood on the toilet and floor, he said, "Are you sure we shouldn't get you to the clinic?"

"Yes, I'm sure."

Since she was a nurse practitioner and knew better than he did, he yielded to her. For now. If it continued, he'd insist she get treatment.

"I'm so sorry," she said, hiccupping on sobs. "I didn't even know. How did I not know?"

"Shhh, it's okay. You would've figured it out soon." He was trying keep his own heartbreak out of the mix while he tended to her. Under the sink, he found cleaning products and had the bathroom back to rights by the time she shut off the water in the shower.

Shane had a towel ready that he wrapped around her, holding her close to him. "Are you hurting?"

"I was. Now it's more like a dull ache. I thought I was getting my period, but this was way more than that."

"Are you still bleeding?"

"A little."

"How about I go ask Julia if she has anything you can use."

"I can't use tampons. I need a pad. Probably a couple of them."

"I'll ask her to find us some. If she doesn't have some, someone does."

"Don't tell her what happened. Not yet. I need a minute..."

He kissed her forehead. "I'll tell her you're having a bad period."

"Thank you. I'm sorry. I know this is gross."

"Don't be sorry, and it's not gross. I'm just glad you're okay."

"I'm heartbroken." Her chin wobbled as her eyes filled. "We were going to have a baby, Shane."

"We'll have others. The good news is that now we know we can." They'd been trying for a while, so it was a bit of good news mixed in with the sorrow. "This one wasn't meant to be for whatever reason, but we'll have babies, sweet Katie."

He held her while she sobbed, and when she finally calmed, he settled her on the closed lid of the toilet and went to find Julia.

She was outside on the deck, talking to Owen about the set they planned to perform and figuring out how to work around not having power for Julia's keyboard or their microphones.

"Hey, Julia." Shane gestured for her to come to him. "Katie's upstairs and having a bad period. She needs pads. Do you have any?"

"Let me check my bag. Is she okay?"

Shane followed her inside. "I think so. She just feels lousy."

"That stinks." Julia rifled through a massive tote bag and found three individually wrapped pads at the bottom. "Would you rather I delivered them?"

Shane forced himself to smile. "I got it. I'm not easily intimidated by girl things."

"Tell her to let me know if she needs anything."

"I will. Thanks." He went back upstairs, moving quickly to get to her as fast as he could. In the bathroom, he handed her the pads. "Julia to the rescue."

"I can always count on her and that suitcase she carries around."

"Do you need clothes? I can ask your mom for something."

"No, I managed to protect my clothes."

"I'll, ah, just give you a minute."

When she emerged from the bathroom, dressed but still pale and looking shocked, he guided her into one of the guest rooms and encouraged her to lie down for a bit. He shut the door and sent a text to Julia, telling her where they were and asking her to run interference for them. *Katie isn't feeling well, so we're going to chill up here for a bit. Tell your mom?*

Will do.

Shane opened the windows so they wouldn't suffocate from the heat and stretched out next to Katie on the bed. His phone chimed with another text from Julia that included the eye-roll emoji.

Mom was freaking out that maybe Katie had food poisoning. Assured her it's girl trouble. Tell her we said to feel better.

Katie curled up to him, resting her head on his chest.

Shane put his arms around her. "How do you feel?"

She sniffled. "Sad, empty, achy."

"I'm so sorry, sweetheart."

"I've helped so many patients through this very thing, but until it happens to you..." She took a shuddering deep breath and let it out slowly.

"As soon as it's safe to try again, we will."

"Thank you for being so great. You deserve hazardous-duty pay after walking into that nightmare."

Shane chuckled. "It wasn't that bad, and I always want to be wherever you are, especially when you need me."

"I need you all the time, but I might need you even more the next few days."

"I'm right here, sweetheart."

CHAPTER 22

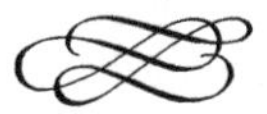

Alex drove home from the senior care center with tears running down his face. Of course it couldn't have lasted. He'd known that but had held out hope, nonetheless. They'd gotten four hours of complete lucidity before Marion had once again retreated into the cruel bitch of dementia, asking where she was, who they were and when her husband, George, would be home.

As quickly as the lucidity had arrived, it'd been snatched away.

He was so thankful for the time they'd gotten, but losing her again had knocked the wind out of them all. He'd offered to drive her "home" to the center, which had been dreadful. She'd been confused and disoriented and screaming for his late father. The very capable staff had encouraged him to leave, assuring him they'd take good care of her.

It fucking sucked.

They'd gotten just enough time with her to see what kind of grandmother she might've been to the kids.

He pounded his hand against the steering wheel until pain shot up his wrist.

The sun had nearly set by the time he pulled into the driveway to Martinez Lawn & Garden, the business his mother and Paul had been running only a few short years ago. He hooked a left behind the retail store, pulling up in front of the house he and Jenny had built.

His mother hadn't gotten to see it. He'd hoped they'd have more time.

Alex sat for a long while, once again pondering the irony of him meeting Jenny and Paul meeting Hope because of their mother's illness. He sure as hell never would've moved home to Gansett or been cutting grass at the lighthouse if his mother hadn't gotten sick. Hope had come to the island to help care for Marion at home.

The cruel sadness of those twists of fate wasn't lost on him, that in her brief moment of lucidity, Marion had finally gotten to meet the daughters-in-law who wouldn't be her daughters-in-law if she hadn't become ill.

He had no idea how long he sat there, lost in thought, before Jenny knocked on the passenger-side window.

Alex unlocked the door and hastily wiped the remaining tears off his face.

Jenny slid into the seat, holding the remote baby monitor. She immediately directed the AC vents toward her sweaty face. "Are you okay?"

"Never better."

"It was bad?"

"Horrible. When I left, she was screaming for my dad."

Jenny winced. "I'm so sorry, Alex. What can I do?"

He reached for her hand. "This helps."

She squeezed his hand. "I wish there was more I could do."

"I was just thinking how there'd be no me and you without her illness, no Paul and Hope. No Ethan, George or Scarlett. How fucked up is it that we have these happy lives because she got sick?"

"She seemed so pleased with the family we've created in her absence."

"She did." He swiped angrily at another tear, wishing they would fucking stop. "It's just so unbearably sad."

"It's sad and unfair."

He nodded, appreciating that she understood. Of course she did.

"Life can be sad and unfair, but it's also sweet and joyful, often all at the same time."

"Today was such a tease," he said on a long sigh.

"I think you should try to see it as a gift. She got to meet me, Hope, the kids. Really meet us, not just exist in the same space with us. We got to talk to her and get to know her better. I'll never forget that time with her or stop being thankful for it."

"I'm thankful for all of that. Please don't get me wrong."

"I know, it's the having-it-yanked-back part that's tough."

"Yeah." He took a deep breath and held it for a second before releasing it. "We can go in."

"It's so much nicer out here in the AC."

"We're getting a generator ASAP."

"You won't hear me arguing."

He looked over at her. "Thanks for being there for me and my mom today. Having you by my side makes everything easier than it would be without you."

"Same."

"It might take me a minute to shake this off."

"Take as many minutes as you need and tell me what I can do to help."

"I love you, Jenny Martinez."

"I love you, too, Alex Martinez, and I'm so very glad we met, but I'll always be sorry your mom had to get sick for us to find each other."

"Me, too. Can we go in?"

"Whatever you want to do."

"You know what I want to do?"

"Gee, let me guess," she said as she followed him from the hot outdoors to the hotter indoors.

"I want a re-creation of our first sweaty week together."

"Is that right?"

"Yep."

Inside the door, he turned to keep her from progressing into the house, backing her up until she was pressed against the wood door he'd hung himself. He took the baby monitor from her and placed it on the table where they kept their keys. "We were talking about the mudroom at the lighthouse earlier," he said as he kissed her neck. "That was where my obsession with the lighthouse keeper began."

"Did it?"

"You know it did. Shortly after she pelted me with tomatoes."

"That was my finest hour. And to think, the boys at school used to say I threw like a girl."

Laughing, he said, "Not that day." He unbuttoned her shorts, pushed them down and shoved a hand into her panties. Back when they were first together, he used to worry about his lack of finesse at times like this, when he wanted her so badly, he burned from it, but she told him she loved him with or without finesse. It was a good thing, because tonight he needed her as much as he wanted her, craving the connection he found only with her. That connection soothed and comforted him on days like this, when the enormity of his mother's illness was too much to bear.

"*Yes*, Alex," she said on a sigh. "Right there."

He knew exactly where to touch her, how to make her scream from the pleasure they found together. Waiting until she was right on the verge of release, he withdrew from her only long enough to free his hard cock from his shorts and plunge into her, which sent her flying.

Somehow he managed to hold on through her release as sweat rolled down his face and burned his eyes. Or maybe those were tears. What did it matter, he wondered, as he pumped into the woman he loved more than anything or anyone. Where would he be by now in this situation without her to keep him sane, to fill his life with joy and love, to light the darkness?

"Jenny…"

She wrapped her arms around his neck and kissed his cheek and then his lips. "I'm here. I'm right here."

"Love you so much."

"Love you more."

He shook his head, his fingers digging into the dense flesh of her ass as he pounded into her. His sweat mixed with hers as they moved together with the practiced ease that came from years together. He'd never had that ease with anyone else. "It's so fucking hot."

"Mmm, sure is."

"I meant the temperature, but this is pretty hot, too."

Jenny smiled. "'Hot' is the word of the day."

Alex slowed his pace, lifting her and letting her slide down the length of him repeatedly until her head fell back, connecting with the door with a loud *thunk*. "Ouch. Are you okay?"

"Very okay. Don't stop."

The need he heard in those few words lit a new fire in him, and when he reached between them to coax her over the finish line, he was right there with her, surging into her as he came with a groan. When he'd recovered enough to be sure his legs would hold their weight, he said, "Hold on to me."

Her head was on his shoulder, her arms looped around his neck. "Holding on."

Alex kept a tight hold on her as he lifted her off the door, stepped out of his shorts and walked them to the sofa, where he came down on top of her while maintaining their connection.

"Fancy," she said, smiling up at him.

"You liked that?"

She pushed the sweaty hair back from his forehead. "I like it all."

"Thanks for being there for me today."

"I'm here for you every day, not just the good ones."

"Thank God for that. I never would've survived this situation with my mother without you here to keep me sane."

"Yes, you would have."

He shook his head. "No way. You're the secret to my success. You and George."

"We love you."

"I love you, too." He kissed her softly, intending it to be a quick one, until her mouth opened to his tongue, and suddenly, round two was underway. That's how it always was between them. They could never seem to get enough of each other. He was thankful every day that he'd gone to the lighthouse to mow the lawn and had been pelted by her tomatoes. She'd been so mad at him for waking her up at the crack of dawn.

"What're you thinking?" she asked, gazing up at him with eyes that looked at him only with love. Well, except for when he irritated her, often on purpose, because that was fun, too. Everything was fun with her.

"I'm thinking about the tomatoes," he said as he moved slowly in her. "You have no idea what you saved me from by throwing tomatoes at me."

"I do know. I was right there with you in the pits of despair."

He put his arms around her and nuzzled her neck. "Everything was better after I found you."

"For me, too."

"Even days like today."

Jenny wrapped her arms around him and held on tight to him as they moved together like dancers in perfect harmony. "Especially days like today."

He held on tighter to her and took them on a sweet, sensual ride that ended in gasps of pleasure that echoed through the room. They were a sweaty mess, but he felt better than he had when he got home. "Thank you for this, for us, for having my back with my mom. All of it."

"Yours is my favorite back in the whole world," she said as she ran her fingers through the sweat that had formed at the base of his spine.

"We're getting a fucking generator."

CHAPTER 23

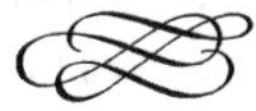

Luke Harris held his sleepy daughter, Lily, while his wife, Sydney, said goodbye to their friends. He wondered if anyone else noticed how fragile Syd seemed lately, since the accident at the marina at the beginning of the summer. She'd inadvertently driven her car over the bulkhead into the water with Lily strapped into her car seat. Mason and Blaine had gotten them out, but not before they'd all been severely traumatized by the rising water inside the car. When he thought about what might've happened if it'd taken Blaine and Mason a few more minutes to get there, or if they hadn't been able to rescue them in time…

He'd had his own nightmares about those scenarios and could only wonder if she had, too. If so, she wasn't talking to him about it. He kept hoping she'd bounce back, but she hadn't. Not really. She'd done a great job of pretending to be fine, but he knew her too well for her to get away with it.

She'd had a nice time at Charlie and Sarah's party, had enjoyed a few glasses of wine with their closest friends and was as relaxed as he'd seen her since the incident.

After they got home and put Lily to bed, he was going to see if he could get her to talk it out with him. He hoped he wasn't making a huge mistake by forcing the issue, but he couldn't bear to see her suffering in silence any longer.

As they drove home, he tried to think of how he might broach the subject with her. He was nervous about it, which was further indication that things were off between them. Talking to her was the easiest thing he'd ever done—and for someone who'd been quiet with other people his whole life that was saying something. He was never nervous or uncertain around her. The fact that he was both those things now meant this conversation was long overdue.

The accident had happened almost three months ago, but nothing had been the same since then. He'd noticed that Syd went out of her way to avoid driving herself and Lily anywhere unless it was absolutely necessary. That couldn't continue. She had a booming business as the island's only interior decorator, and with her biggest job yet—the redecorating of the McCarthys' hotel coming this winter—she couldn't be afraid to drive with their daughter in the car.

When they got home, he let their dog, Buddy, out while she gave Lily a bath.

Then they snuggled in their bed to read her a couple of stories.

At the end of a busy day, Lily was tired and fell asleep during the second story.

"Want me to put her in the crib?" Luke asked.

"Sure."

Luke carefully lifted the sleeping child and carried her into the next room to put her down for the night. Sometimes when he looked at her, he still couldn't believe she was real. He ran his fingers through silky hair that was the same copper color as her mother's and gave thanks, as he had every day since that awful ten minutes at the marina, that Blaine and Mason had gotten to them in time.

They'd immediately installed a new curbstone in the spot where it had occurred, but Luke couldn't bear to look at the area, even after all this time. He woke in a cold sweat at least once a week after having dreamed about the two of them being trapped in a sinking car and him unable to do a goddamned thing to save them.

He forced himself to breathe through the now-predictable wave of nausea that hit him every time he relived those endless moments of watching the car fill with water while his wife and daughter were trapped inside.

Syd blamed herself. She'd been on the phone when her foot slipped off the brake onto the accelerator. No matter how many times she was reminded that it'd been an accident, she couldn't get past the fact that she'd caused it. And that was at the crux of their problem. She had to forgive herself before she could move on.

He returned to their room, where she was sitting up in bed, her ever-present iPad propped on her knees as she took care of some work.

Luke unbuttoned his shirt and stripped down to boxers before using the bathroom and then sliding into bed next to her. "Hey," he said.

She smiled at him. "Hey, yourself."

"Can we talk?"

"Uh-huh." She continued to tap away on the iPad.

"Syd."

She glanced his way.

"I want to talk to you."

She put the iPad on her bedside table. "Is something wrong?"

"Yeah, baby. Something is wrong."

Her expression conveyed confusion and alarm. "What?"

He gave himself a second to choose his words carefully, knowing how important it was to get this right. "I'm worried about you."

"About me? Why?"

"You haven't been yourself this summer."

"What does that mean? Who have I been?"

"Syd. You know what I'm talking about. Since the accident..."

She held up her hand to stop him. "I don't want to talk about that."

"Sweetheart, we need to talk about it."

She covered her ears and put her head down on her knees. "I can't."

Luke sat up, put his arms around her and brought her into his embrace. "We have to. Nothing has been right since that day, and I can tell you're suffering. I can't bear that for you. Or me, or Lily. We need to talk about it and figure out what we have to do to get past it."

"I'll never get past it. Ever."

"You will, but first you have to *deal* with it."

"How do I do that when every time I close my eyes, I see the water rushing in and Lily trapped in her seat and no way out all because I wasn't paying attention to what I was doing while my child was in the car? How do you suppose I deal with that?"

"By talking about it. By confronting what happened and why it happened and forgiving yourself the way everyone else has."

"I'll never forgive myself for nearly killing my child. In a *car*. After what's already happened to me in a car, you'd think I'd know better."

"Sydney, baby, there is no relation to what happened to your family and this accident. Someone got drunk and decided to drive, and that's what killed your family. You made an honest mistake—"

"That nearly *killed* Lily!" She pulled free of him. "I'll never forgive myself for that, Luke. Not *ever*."

"You have to."

"I can't."

"Would you consider seeing Kevin about this?"

She shrugged. "Not sure what good a psychiatrist would do. He can't erase the horrible memories."

"Maybe he could help you figure out a way to live with what happened so you can go forward without being afraid of something like that happening again."

"That's the thing. The next disaster is always right around the corner, waiting to snatch away everything I care about."

"No, honey. No, it isn't. You can't live your life being afraid like that. It'll ruin everything."

"I don't know how to be anything other than afraid. The accident reminded me not to get too comfortable in my happy new life."

"We need to fix that for you so you can find some peace. Maybe we should go see Kevin together."

"Why do you say that?"

"It wasn't easy being outside of that car, helpless to do anything to save my family."

"Oh God, Luke," she said, her voice breaking. "I've made this all about me. I'm so sorry."

"It was an *accident*, Syd. An accident. It wasn't your fault. It just happened. And now we need to find a way to live with it without being tormented this way. Can we please make an appointment with Kevin?"

She thought about that for a long moment before she gave a reluctant nod.

Filled with relief, Luke hugged her and kissed the top of her head. "We're going to get through this, sweetheart. I promise."

"I hope so."

It was only the first step of what would probably be a long journey, but he was thankful she was willing to take it and determined to do whatever it took to help her feel better.

CHAPTER 24

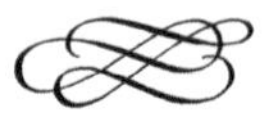

Long after his family was in bed, Paul Martinez sat on the sofa, nursing his second glass of whiskey and thinking about the extraordinary afternoon with his mother. When he and Hope had taken Scarlett for a regular visit, he'd noticed right away that something was different, and when he'd realized she was fully aware, he'd been so stunned he hadn't known what to do at first.

"Call Alex," Hope had said. "Hurry."

It still felt surreal, even hours later, that his mom had been almost completely herself for those few hours. If he hadn't seen it with his own eyes, he wouldn't have believed it was possible. And then, with dementia being such an unrelenting bitch, Marion had left them just as quickly, lost again to the confusion as if someone had flipped a switch.

He wasn't sure if he was thankful for the brief respite or resentful. His emotions were a jumbled mess.

When he heard Scarlett stirring, he went to tend to her so Hope wouldn't be disturbed. He changed her and gave her a bottle of the milk Hope had pumped earlier.

Paul loved being a father to Scarlett and Hope's son, Ethan, and was so grateful his mother had gotten to meet his family, to know he and Alex were happily settled with wives they loved and children they adored. He hoped she'd taken that knowledge with her to wherever it was she went when she was lost to them. He hoped it gave her comfort to know they were doing well and living happy, productive lives.

She'd asked about the landscaping business she and their father had started more than forty years ago and had been relieved to hear that he, Alex and Jenny had kept it growing and thriving in her absence. For a short while, it'd been like old times, talking about the business with her. The two of them had run it together back in the day, before he started to notice her forgetting important things and dropping balls she'd juggled effortlessly only a few months earlier.

That'd been the start of it, and she'd declined so rapidly that he'd been forced to ask Alex to come home to help in what still rated as one of the worst phone calls he'd ever had to make.

Paul had no idea how long he'd been rocking the baby before he realized she was asleep. He stood to put her back in her crib and waited to make sure she was settled before tiptoeing out of the room. He encountered Hope in the hallway.

"I was just coming to check on you guys," she said.

He kissed her forehead. "You're supposed to be sleeping."

"It's too hot to sleep. I heard her wake up, and then you didn't come back to bed."

"I haven't been to bed yet."

"Oh. Are you all right?"

He shrugged. "I guess."

She took his hand and led him to their room, the room that had once belonged to his parents. It had taken him a while after his mom moved to the first care facility she'd been in on the mainland to feel right about using her room.

They'd completely redecorated the room to make it their own, but even after all this time, sometimes it still felt odd to be sleeping in there.

Hope snuggled up to him in bed. "What can I do for you?"

He put his arm around her. "More of this."

"Even if it's too hot to snuggle?"

"It's never too hot to snuggle."

"I wish there was something I could say to make you feel better."

"It's okay, hon. There's nothing anyone can say or do to make this situation better. It is what it is. I'm just glad she got to really meet you and the kids."

"Me, too. I'm also thankful it happened when she was here on the island rather than on the mainland. We might not have been able to get there in time."

"That's a good point."

"Even in the worst of situations, there're often silver linings to be found."

"Thanks for helping me to see them." He caressed her back and ran his fingers through her silky hair. "When we were on the way to see Mom earlier, you told me you wanted to talk to me about something when we got home. We never got a chance to do that."

"It's okay. It'll keep."

Paul ran a hand up and down her arm, marveling at the softness of her skin. "You'd better go ahead and tell me, or I'll be awake all night worrying about whatever it is."

"It's actually good news. I heard back from my divorce attorney about our request for you to adopt Ethan."

Paul nearly stopped breathing. "And?"

"He spoke to my ex-husband's attorney and told him what we wanted. The attorney presented it to him, and he agreed to sign off on it with one condition."

"What's that?"

"He wants an annual update on Ethan with photos."

"How do you feel about that?"

"I'm okay with it if it means there's no chance he could ever again try to get visitation."

Ethan's father had gone to prison after being convicted of the statutory rape of a high school student. He was due to be released at some point in the next year, which had precipitated their adoption request.

"So that's it? I can adopt him?"

"We need to get with Dan and figure out details, but his father won't block it as long as I send him the annual letter and picture."

"This is the best possible news. I'll call Dan in the morning about getting it moving."

"My son is very lucky to have you as his father, Paul."

"I'm the lucky one. He's the best kid ever. I love him so much."

She moved in to kiss him, and he kept her there with an arm around her shoulders.

His other hand slid down over her nightgown to cup her ass.

She smiled against his lips. "It's too hot for this."

"It's never too hot for this."

"I think it might actually be tonight."

"No," he said, kissing her until he'd won her over to his way of thinking.

"How do you do this to me every time?" she asked when he'd removed her nightgown and begun to kiss his way down her body.

"My special powers."

"They're potent."

Paul hadn't expected to laugh tonight, but leave it to her and the news about Ethan's adoption to give him something other than grief to focus on. With her legs hooked over his shoulders, he set out to show her what she meant to him, using his tongue and fingers to bring her to a quick orgasm.

"So potent," she said, gasping in the aftermath.

He kissed his way back up to her breasts, tasting both nipples before pushing his cock into her. "Ah, God, that's the best feeling in the whole world."

"Mmm, so good."

"So sweaty."

She huffed out a laugh. "Sweaty but good."

Being overheated had never been more worth it, he thought, as he came down from the incredible high they found together.

"I need a cold shower," she said.

"That can be arranged. In a minute, though. I need more of this first." He held her closer, his heart beating hard from exertion and love. So much love.

She hugged him tightly and ran her fingers through his hair. "I've got plenty of this. Any time you need it."

"All the time."

"That works out well, because I need you just as much."

His heart might be broken once again over his mother's unrelenting illness, but Hope had helped him see how much he had to be thankful for, too.

CHAPTER 25

After waking up Sunday morning in Atlanta with a full week off to spend with his wife, Evan McCarthy was ready to put months of planning into motion, hoping to pull off a surprise his amazing Grace would never forget. And the best part? The song he'd written about her had made it all possible. She'd made everything possible for him, and now he was ready to repay the favor for the many sacrifices she'd made so they could be together while he toured.

He'd been able to reach for the brass ring, all because of her encouragement, her insistence that he chase the dream and her willingness to travel with him. Every night for months, he'd appeared onstage with Buddy Longstreet, Taylor Jones and Kate Harrington, had spent time with them, their families and the musicians that supported them all. To say he was living the dream would be putting it mildly, but the only way this dream could've come true was with Grace by his side.

She'd put her own dreams on hold to support his, turning her pharmacy over to her friend Fiona to manage while she was off-island.

And now, the day he'd been anticipating for so long was upon them, and he couldn't wait another minute to put plans into action. He kissed her awake. "Gracie."

"Mmm, ten more minutes." She was super grumpy in the morning since she'd been pregnant. While she'd been spared the morning sickness that so many of their friends and family members experienced, she was tired all the time.

"I ordered breakfast."

One beautiful brown eye opened. "What'd you get?"

"The French toast you liked the last time we were here."

"You remembered that?"

"I remember everything that makes you smile the way that French toast did."

Her eye closed again, and she snuggled deeper into the covers. "Best husband I ever had."

He pushed a hand under the covers to caress a sensitive breast, making her gasp. "You gotta get up. We have to be somewhere right after breakfast."

"Where do we have to be? I thought we were on vacation."

"We are, and it's a surprise. Now get your sexy ass out of bed and get packed. I'm taking you on an adventure."

"I thought we were staying here for the week."

"We were. Now we're not."

They'd talked about going home for the week, but decided not to since that would require devoting two of their seven days off to travel. Because Grace had been so tired, they'd decided to stay in Atlanta and hang out at the hotel until they had to be in Orlando the following weekend. She'd insisted she'd be fine if he decided he wanted to go somewhere else, which was the reason he knew she wouldn't mind that he'd made surprise plans for them.

His Gracie was nothing if not a good sport. She'd proven that over and over again during the rigorous tour that'd taken them to thirty cities since the beginning of July. He hoped the week at home would be restorative for them both. As an added bonus, he'd be home for the last-minute wedding of his sister Mallory. He'd gotten a text from her two weeks ago, letting him know that she and Quinn were tying the knot on their upcoming mutual birthday.

Mallory had asked him to sing at the wedding, and he was honored she'd asked.

"Is it the kind of adventure that includes sleep?" Grace asked. "Lots and lots of sleep?"

"As much as you want, but first you have to get up."

"All right, all right. I'm getting up."

But she didn't move.

"Grace..."

"Evan..."

"I love you. Get your ass up."

Mumbling and grumbling, she sat up, pushed her dark hair back from her face and forced her eyes to open.

"There she is. My gorgeous wife."

"I feel like I've been drugged or something."

"Vic said it should get better in the next trimester."

"God, I hope so. At least I'm not puking my guts up like Abby has been."

"I got a text from Adam. They had their appointment on the mainland, and you won't believe what they found out." His brother had also mentioned the power failure on the island that was now in its second day while the temperatures stayed at roast level. Hopefully, the power would be back on by the time they got home.

"Nothing bad, right?"

"Nope, nothing bad. In fact, they found out they're expecting *quadruplets*."

"*What?* Seriously? How'd that happen?"

"The old-fashioned way, which makes it a true miracle."

"After everything they went through... That's incredible."

"From what Adam said, they're still in shock. Five kids under the age of two..."

"Holy *crap*. Abby must be freaking out. To go from not being able to conceive to quads..."

"I know."

"Well, I've certainly got no business complaining about being tired from carrying one baby. Imagine how she's going to feel."

"She's going to need a ton of help."

"Fortunately, both families are there and can pitch in."

"Adam said my parents offered to move in with them for the first month or two."

"That's so great. They'll need that kind of help. Five babies..." She shuddered as she got up to head for the shower. "Dear God."

The news from home had only added to Evan's good mood this morning, knowing what his brother and sister-in-law had endured after hearing she might never be able to conceive. And now this… What an amazing development. Evan couldn't wait to see them and the rest of his family later that day when he surprised Grace with the unscheduled trip home, among other things.

They ate breakfast in their suite, checked out of the hotel and took a car service to the airport.

"When are you going to tell me where we're going?"

"When we get there."

"What's with all the mystery?"

"You'll see."

By prearrangement, the car delivered them right onto the tarmac where a small private jet waited to take them home.

"What's all this?" Grace asked.

"Your chariot, my love."

"Since when can we afford to fly private?"

"Since your song went to number one and stayed there for twelve weeks. This is all your fault."

She smiled even as she rolled her eyes. "My fault. Whatever you say."

He placed his fingers on her chin and met her gaze. "There's no 'My Amazing Grace' without my amazing Grace." Kissing her, he added, "You're the secret to all my success, and now I want to spoil you a little bit, so will you please let me?"

"If I must."

"You must." He followed her out of the car, helped the driver with their bags and then walked with her up the stairs to the plane. They were greeted by the pilots and flight attendant and given VIP service on the two-and-a-half-hour flight. When the pilot announced they'd be landing in thirty minutes, Evan opened his backpack and found the item he'd bought on the sly a week ago in anticipation of this moment.

"What's that?"

"The blindfold I need you to wear for a short time."

"What is going on, Evan?"

"Good things." He kissed her as he put the blindfold in place. "Only good things."

"Can I blindfold you later?" she asked.

He went immediately hard at the thought of her taking that kind of initiative. "Any time you want, baby." Grasping her hand, he placed it on his hard cock so she could feel what her innocent question had done to him.

She snorted with laughter. "You're so easy."

"Only with you."

The plane made a smooth landing on the island right on schedule at one o'clock. His dad's best friend, Ned Saunders, was picking them up and under strict orders not to say a word until they'd reached their destination. Grace would know Ned's voice anywhere, and he wanted to at least *try* to keep the fact that they were home a secret until they got to where they were going.

He helped her off the plane and into the broiling heat that had gripped the island for days now and had most likely caused the island-wide power failure. They'd lived through a few power outages growing up here, usually when it was hot like this.

Evan had donned a ball cap that he pulled down over his face, hoping he wouldn't be recognized in the terminal. They got lucky. The place was nearly deserted. As they walked out the main door, Ned's woody station wagon was parked at the curb. He greeted Evan with a big grin and a thumbs-up that their plan was coming to fruition.

"When will I know where we are?" Grace asked as Ned drove them to their destination with the AC on full blast. "It's obviously somewhere hot."

"You'll know in a few minutes." He felt like a little boy on Christmas. In addition to the surprise he'd arranged for Grace, the hit song had also allowed him to buy Ned out of the Island Breeze recording studio that Ned had graciously funded at a time when Evan was convinced his career in music was never going to happen.

Ned hadn't wanted him to return the money, but he'd accepted it when he realized it was important to Evan. He would never forget the lifeline his beloved extra uncle had extended to him at a time when he'd badly needed a purpose. The studio had been a surprise success and was now being run by Evan's good friend Josh.

Everything had changed in the last couple of years, but the best change was the woman who was now at the center of his life. She owned his heart and soul, and he couldn't wait to show her what she meant to him.

One more minute, and they'd be there. They'd be home.

Ned took a left turn onto a dirt road that ended in front of a huge contemporary home that sat on the coast, overlooking Long Island Sound. At night, they'd be able to see the Newport Bridge lit up in the distance. About a year ago, they'd attended an open house at what Grace had deemed her "dream house."

She'd laughed about the sheer impossibility of it as she oohed and aahed over the custom cabinetry, the teak accents, the inground pool and spacious yard. It had five bedrooms and seven bathrooms, a media room, a wine cellar and a dining room big enough to host their entire family. It'd sold shortly after they'd toured it, and when it came back on the market a few months later, Ned had called him to let him know. He'd been instrumental in helping Evan pull this off by acting as his local representative during the purchase.

Evan was elated as he got out of the car, hugged his beloved friend and then went around to help Grace out.

She wobbled a bit before getting her bearings.

He kept his hands on her arms until she was steady. "Are you ready for your surprise, love?"

"Very ready. Is that the ocean I smell?"

"Maybe."

"Can I look now, Evan?"

"You can look."

She removed the mask, blinked a couple of times as her eyes adjusted to the bright sunlight and then gasped. "We're home? On Gansett?"

"We are, and we're home in more ways than one. Remember this house?"

Her eyes widened. "What about it?"

"You loved it so much. We both did."

"Evan... *What've you done?*"

"It's ours."

She screamed and launched herself into his arms. "You're not serious!"

"I'm as serious as a heart attack. It's ours. The baby needs a bedroom." The loft above the pharmacy where they'd been living until now didn't have room for a baby.

"Oh my God! Evan!" She hugged him so hard, she nearly broke his neck.

He'd never had a better hug.

Behind her, he saw Ned grinning like a loon as he looked on. "Ya done good, kid."

"I thought someone bought it," Grace said, releasing Evan so she could include Ned.

"They did, and when it went back on the market, Ned called me to ask if we were still interested. That's when I got the idea to surprise you."

"Best surprise ever!"

"I'm so glad you think so. On the flight, I started getting a little panicky over buying a house without you knowing about it."

"You knew how much I loved it when we toured it that day." She glanced up at him, her dark eyes shining with unshed tears. "Is it really ours, Evan?"

"It's really ours, and it's all because of you. Because you loved me so perfectly that I had to write a song about you, a song that went to number one and stayed there long enough to make all our dreams come true. None of this happens without you, my amazing Grace."

"None of it happens without *us*."

"I'm thankful every single day that my amazing Grace is such a stickler for doing the right thing that she had to come back to Gansett to pay me back for buying her a ferry ticket home."

"I wouldn't have been able to live with myself if I didn't pay you back," she said in the prim, haughty tone he loved so much.

"I wouldn't have been able to live with myself if you hadn't come back." He took her hand to lead her toward the front door. "I was going to come after you."

"What? You were? You never told me that before."

"Yes, I did."

"No, you didn't. I would've remembered that."

Evan used the key Ned had given him to open the front door. After ushering Grace inside, he turned to wave to Ned. Evan would call him when they were ready for a ride to the pharmacy in town, where they'd left Grace's car and his motorcycle. Also thanks to Ned, they had what they needed to spend the rest of the day and the night at their new home —food, beverages and a bed. As always, Ned had been an excellent partner in crime. He hadn't dared clue in any of his family members, as they wouldn't have been able to contain the surprise.

As they went into the foyer that was the size of their apartment over the pharmacy, Grace looked around, taking it all in once again, her eyes big with wonder. "I never dreamed anything like this, Evan. Or anything like you."

He put his arms around her. "Welcome home, love."

CHAPTER 26

Big Mac invited Oliver to attend the morning meeting at the marina, which happened closer to noon on Sundays.

"What takes place at this so-called meeting?" Oliver asked.

"Very important business," Big Mac said gravely.

"Otherwise known as coffee, doughnuts and bullshit," Linda said.

Oliver laughed. "That sounds like my kind of fun. You mind if I go, Dara?"

"Of course not. Have fun."

"We'll be just down the hill," Big Mac said to Oliver, "so you can escape whenever you've had enough of the BS."

"Good to know." Oliver gave Dara a kiss on the cheek. "See you in a while."

After the men left, Dara took her coffee and wandered to the deck to check out the view of New Harbor.

Linda gave her a minute before she followed, bringing her own coffee. "That's our marina," she said, pointing, "and our hotel."

"You've got your own slice of heaven here."

"We do. We're very lucky to live and work in such a beautiful place."

"When Oliver first told me we'd been hired to run a lighthouse on a remote island in Rhode Island, I thought he was crazy. What would we *do* on a remote island? But there's a peacefulness to this place."

"There is for sure. I'm glad you can see that, especially now. It's a little crazy this time of year when the tourists are here, but after Labor Day, it settles down quite a bit. Mac and I have a wonderful family and a big circle of friends who'll welcome you with open arms, if that's what you want."

"I don't know what I want. Every day feels like a new endurance test. Just get through it. That's the goal."

"That's a tough way to live."

"Believe me, I know."

Linda didn't want to push Dara to talk more than she wished to, so she sipped her coffee and watched Big Mac's truck arrive at the marina and park in the same spot he used every day. They were nothing if not beholden to a routine, especially in the summer when the marina and hotel required their constant attention.

Later this afternoon, Linda was going to Mac and Maddie's to help out with the kids so Mac could spend some time at the office with his assistant. Julia Lawry had done a beautiful job organizing the construction and marina businesses since Mac hired her in May. She'd been a godsend to him, and for that, everyone was thankful. Mac's stress level had been a big concern since the incident in the spring.

"How did you… Get back to normal, or what counted as normal, after you lost your baby?"

"We didn't. We had to invent a new normal. Nothing was the same. The loss of a nearly full-term baby was so shocking, and it took us a long time to get past it. We went on to have five children, but we still think about the one we lost, even after all these years."

"I'm sorry that happened to you."

"Thank you. Our son Mac and his wife, Maddie, went through the same thing. They went in for a routine ultrasound with their third child, and there was no heartbeat. That was a very difficult time for them, but thankfully, they were able to move forward. They've since had a third child and are expecting twins in September. But they still mourn the child they lost, and they always will."

"People tell us we should have another baby, as if that would fix everything."

"It wouldn't, but I can tell you for sure that a baby would bring new joy to your life. The baby certainly wouldn't replace your Lewis, but you might find a new sense of purpose. It did for us, and Mac and Maddie found comfort in the two children they already had when they suffered their terrible loss."

"A baby would give me something new to worry about."

"That's certainly true. My kids are all in their thirties, and I worry as much about them now as I always have. That never ends."

"Perhaps Oliver and I just weren't meant to be parents. I've had to accept that possibility since... Well, it might just be better for us to remain childless."

"Why do you say you weren't meant to be parents?"

"Look at what happened to Lewis on our watch."

"Dara, honey, we've only just met, but I already know for sure that you were a loving, devoted mother, and Oliver was a loving, devoted father. What happened to Lewis was an *accident*."

"He let himself out of the house while we were both there."

"It was an accident. You both thought you'd done everything possible to keep him safe. It never occurred to you that he'd do what he did. Why would it?"

"He was always getting into stuff, but when he napped, he barely moved for at least two hours. That was the only break we got. Otherwise, we were chasing him."

"Sounds like my oldest, Mac. He was a terror as a toddler. We told him all the time he was lucky he got siblings."

Dara laughed. "That about sums up my Lewis. We'd been talking about trying for a second, but he was running us ragged."

"You said he was a good napper."

"The best. He never fought it because he'd basically worn himself out by naptime."

"Had he ever before done anything like he did that day?"

"No."

"So why would either of you think you ought to be paying special attention during that time?"

Dara shrugged. "We knew he was obsessed with the new kid who'd moved in across the street."

"But would it have occurred to you that he'd try to go over there by himself?"

"No. But it's hard not to blame myself—or Oliver. We were both home when it happened."

"You know it's not your fault, right? The two of you would've done anything in your power to keep him safe. Sometimes things just happen, and there's no good reason or explanation for it. What happened to Lewis was a tragic accident."

"I feel so responsible. I was prepping for a big trial. My mind was completely consumed with work. Maybe if I hadn't been so wrapped up in my job..." She shrugged. "I think about that a lot."

"It wasn't your fault, Dara. Parents must work in order to provide food and lodging and clothing for their children. I have no doubt that Lewis felt very loved by both his parents."

"We loved him so much," she said, wiping away tears.

Linda put an arm around the younger woman, hoping the comfort would be welcome.

Dara leaned into her. "Thank you for listening. It helps to talk to someone who gets it. So many people have wanted to help us, but they don't understand. It hasn't happened to them."

"Lewis was a lucky little boy to have you and Oliver for his parents. You should try to take the time here as a reset. Make some new friends who didn't know you as his parents. You may find that helps."

"It's already helping."

"I'm so glad you came to our island and that we had a power failure."

Dara laughed even as she dealt with more tears. "Me, too." She looked over at Linda. "Thank you for listening and talking about this. So many of the people in my life can't handle their own grief over losing Lewis. They have no space available for mine."

"I have all the space you need for as long as you need it."

"That means so much to me. I didn't expect to come here and make new friends."

"When you're ready, I have a lot of good friends and family who'll be happy to meet you, to welcome you and Oliver into their circle, and to make you feel at home here."

"I wouldn't have thought I'd want to be welcomed into anyone's circle, but after meeting you and your husband, that actually sounds rather lovely."

"We'll make that happen. You just say the word."

"Thank you, Linda."

CHAPTER 27

"Everyone, this is Oliver Watkins. He and his wife, Dara, are our new lighthouse keepers. Oliver, this is my buddy Ned, my brothers Frankie and Kev, my oldest son, Mac, and our business partner, Luke Harris."

The guys greeted Oliver with handshakes and welcoming smiles.

"Let's get the man a coffee and some of Linda's famous doughnuts." Big Mac was determined to show the younger man a good time and make him part of their morning gathering—if he wished to be, that was. "Cream and sugar?" he asked Oliver.

"Just cream is great. Thanks, Mac."

"I'll get them, Dad," Mac said.

"Thanks, son."

"You hafta call him Big Mac," Ned said, "or it gets mighty confusin' round here with this one." He used his thumb to point at the younger Mac, who was now inside. "And *he's* got a son named Mac, too. It's a mess."

Oliver laughed. "Gotcha."

"The world needs *more* Mac McCarthys, not fewer," Big Mac said.

"You keep tellin' yerself that," Ned said.

Mac returned with a tray containing coffees for himself and Oliver and a plate of doughnuts for the table. "Thank goodness for generators."

The men dove into the doughnuts like wild seagulls.

"Get in there, Oliver," Kevin said. "You can't be shy in this group."

"Don't mind if I do." He helped himself to one of the sugary confections, took a bite and moaned. "Holy hell, that's good."

"Right?" Big Mac said. "Linda gets all the credit for the doughnuts that are such a big part of this place. She started making them right after we were married, and before we knew it, people were coming back year after year for more of them. I swear they did more to make this place a hit than anything else."

"Ya did yer share, too," Ned said between bites.

"This place was a falling-down wreck when my little brother found it, had a big idea and made it a reality through sheer grit," Frank said.

Oliver took in the bustling marina, full of boats and people and activity on the docks. "Quite an operation you've got here."

"It's a special place," Kevin said. "This marina and this island. From the first time I ever visited my big brother here, I was eager to come back. The last time I came, I decided to stick around, and here we are."

"The McCarthy brothers back together again," Frank said, raising his coffee cup to Big Mac and Kevin. "Along with our adopted fourth," he said of Ned.

"Do yourself a favor, Oliver," Mac said, "and don't listen to too much of what goes on with the four of them. You may find yourself in need of bail money if you do."

"He's fulla crap," Ned said. "Stick with us. We'll show ya a good time."

"Are we still fishing this afternoon?" Frank asked.

"That's the plan," Big Mac said. "You're welcome to come along, Oliver."

"That's very nice of you. Let me see what Dara wants to do today before I commit to anything."

"Spoken like a wise man," Kevin said.

"What brings you to our fair island?" Frank asked as he helped himself to a second doughnut.

"My wife and I were in need of a reset after we lost our three-year-old son."

"Oh God," Kevin said. "I'm so sorry.

The other men chimed in with their condolences.

"Thank you. It happened more than a year ago, but we're still reeling.

When I saw the ad for the lighthouse keeper's job, something about it spoke to me. I'm hoping we can start over here and figure out a way forward."

"You've come to the right place," Mac said. "We have so many friends and family members who've come here at difficult times in their lives and found peace in this place."

"That's good to hear," Oliver said. "We're in bad need of some peace."

"If there's anything we can do…" Kevin said.

"Kev's a therapist," Big Mac said. "A damned good one, too, from what I hear."

"Wow, you guys have it all here, huh?"

"We have everything you need," Big Mac said.

"Except fer power," Ned said, making everyone laugh.

As Big Mac watched Oliver join in the laughter, he had a feeling his island was going to be good for his new young friend.

CHAPTER 28

Seamus was up long before the boys and Caro and had already drunk two cups of coffee he'd brewed on the gas grill by the time she joined him on the deck.

"Another scorcher," she said, grimacing at the heat.

"Looks that way."

"Still no power?"

"Nope."

"We need a generator for the next time this happens."

"I already made some calls about getting one installed this fall."

"Did you sleep?"

"Nope."

"Seamus…" She sighed as she lowered herself into the chair next to his. "You can't make yourself sick over this."

"Too late." He got up, poured her a cup of coffee and handed it to her. "I wouldn't trust the cream at this point."

She made a face at the thought of drinking it black.

"I've been thinking…" Seamus returned to his seat, shifting so he could look directly at her. "What if we allowed the boys' father to see them, but we introduce him as a friend of ours, not as their father. We could offer him that in exchange for him leaving us be. Then later, when they're older and more settled, we could tell them who he really is, and it'd be up to them whether or not they wish to continue seeing him."

"What if he wants more than that?"

"He can't have more than that. We're their legal guardians."

"He could challenge us in court."

"I don't think he will. There's a reason Lisa kept him out of their lives and didn't even consider contacting him when she knew she was dying. He knows what that reason is, and it probably wouldn't take much digging on our part to discover what it is. What do you think of my idea?"

"I worry the boys will resent us someday for not telling them who he is from the beginning."

"I think we could say—truthfully—that we wanted the chance to get to know him and make sure he'd be a good influence in their lives before we told them the truth. There's also a chance he might want to see them once, and we'll never hear from him again. If we tell them who he is, and he disappears after seeing them, then they have someone else to mourn."

"That's true." She reached for his hand and linked their fingers. "You seem calmer than you were yesterday."

"On the outside, maybe. Inside, I'm still a mess of fear and anxiety."

"You're hiding it better today."

"I keep reminding myself of what Dan said, how the law is on our side because Lisa made us their legal guardians. I'm trying to have faith in that."

"You're a wonderful father, Seamus. Those boys are so lucky to have you."

"You really think so? Half the time I feel like I'm making a regular mess of it."

"I really think so, and you're not making a mess of it. They adore you. They follow you around like two little puppies, hanging on your every word and watching everything you do."

"I love them so much."

"And they know it. I think you should pitch your plan to Dan so he has that information if he needs it when he talks to the other attorney."

"You'd be willing to let him see them under the conditions I mentioned?"

"If it meant keeping everything the way it is now, I'd be willing."

"And we agree that not telling them who he is, not now, anyway, is the right thing to do?"

"I think so. If he continues to come around, we'll owe them the truth at some point. But not yet. It's too soon after they lost their mother."

"I'm glad we're in agreement."

"Do you feel better?"

"Much. It helps to have a plan." He withdrew the cell phone he'd charged overnight using a portable charger and texted Dan.

Call me when you have a minute to talk strategy.

Dan called a few minutes later, and Seamus pitched the idea to him. "What do you think?"

"That could work. Let me contact the attorney first thing tomorrow morning and see what he wants. I won't offer anything until we know what he's after. I'd also want to know why Lisa cut him out of their lives before we open the door to possible visitation."

"That's a good point." And one he should've thought of.

"I'll call you the second I'm off the phone with him."

"Thanks, Dan. Appreciate the help with this."

"No problem at all, my friend. Keep breathing. It's going to be okay."

"Thanks for the reminder. Talk to you tomorrow."

"He likes the idea," Seamus told Carolina. "He'll keep it in mind if need be."

"That's good. Now let's try to relax and enjoy your day off."

Seamus felt better after formulating a plan with Carolina and discussing it with Dan. However, he wouldn't rest—or relax—until he knew for sure the potential threat to his family had been neutralized.

CHAPTER 29

Awaking to sunlight streaming in through the blinds he'd left open, Cooper James stretched and jumped out of bed, pulling on a pair of shorts before using the bathroom that adjoined his room. His brother's island house was sweet and much homier than the ultrahip contemporary penthouse Jared had made available to Coop while he was at NYU.

He'd had some rad parties at that place, not that Jared knew anything about that. Like he'd care. Ever since he'd married Lizzie, his brother had spent almost no time in the city, preferring this cozy house on the island he'd retreated to when he decided to leave the Wall Street rat race.

Jared was happy here. Anyone could see that. That was due in large part to his adorable wife, who was one of the nicest, most genuine people Coop had ever met. Take what she did yesterday, bringing a young mother and her newborn home with her while she herself was mourning yet another failed round of IVF.

That took a special kind of person, capable of putting aside her own pain to step up for someone else. And Lizzie was a very special person.

Coop wandered into the kitchen and was surprised to realize he was the first one up. That never happened when he was around his family. Thanks to a whole-home generator, Coop was able to make some coffee that he took outside to the pool deck. He stopped short at the sight of a goddess swimming in Jared's pool.

Who in the hell was *that*?

She wore a white bikini and cut through the water with a smooth, efficient crawl stroke and flip turns that indicated swim-team training.

He was mesmerized watching her as he sipped from his coffee mug. The girl could've been an Olympian with the way she ate up the water.

By the time she finally came to a stop at the end of the pool where he was standing, he was seriously intrigued. When she removed her goggles and looked up at him, his heart nearly stopped. What in the ever-loving fuck was Gigi Gibson doing in his brother's pool?

"Hey, cutie," she said. "What's your name?"

"Uh, Cooper?"

"You're not sure?" She pulled herself up and out of the pool with practiced grace.

He tried and failed not to gawk at her smoking-hot body, finally diverting his gaze so he wouldn't embarrass himself. His very own wet dream was standing before him—and dripping wet. Stuff like this didn't happen to mere mortals like him.

"Hello? Earth to Cooper, if that's your name."

"It is. Cooper James. I'm Jared's brother."

"Now that you mention it, I see the resemblance."

"Wh-what're you doing here?" He never, ever, ever felt nervous around women, but this wasn't just any woman. This was *the* woman, his hall pass, the one he canceled plans for so he could watch her show.

She pointed to the garage apartment. "I live here."

"You live *here*? On *Gansett Island*?"

"For a few more weeks."

"Why?"

"Jordan and I are shooting the new season of our show here. You see, it's like this. My girl came to Gansett after her disastrous marriage ended, fell in love with the tall-as-a-motherfucker fire chief, and next thing I knew, she wanted to film the show here rather than in LA, and so here I am."

How had he not heard about this? Perhaps because he'd been working night and day on his business since he graduated and hadn't paid much attention to anything else. "I can't picture you two anywhere but there."

"No one can, which is what makes it fun to do it here. We wrap in three weeks."

"And then what?"

"I'm heading home."

"Will that be the end of the show?"

"We're not sure yet. I guess that depends on how this season is received."

"I'm sure it'll be great. You two are amazing together."

She raised an eyebrow. "You watch our show?"

"Sweetheart, every red-blooded man in America watches your show. I can't believe I'm standing here talking to Gigi freaking Gibson."

Placing a hand on her hip, she struck a pose. "In the flesh."

"Uh-huh, I see that." Cooper wasn't one to ogle famous women or indulge in one-sided crushes that had no hope of ever coming to fruition. He was more of a realist when it came to women. Gigi Gibson was so far out of his league as to be laughable, but she was, in fact, standing before him in the flesh, which gave him the courage to make his next move. "You want to hang out later?"

"And do what?"

"I'm sure we can find some trouble together."

"I've been here for months and haven't found any trouble yet. If there's a more boring place in this world than this island, I haven't seen it."

"Aw, come on. Gansett's not that bad."

"When you're used to LA, it's bad."

"I suppose that's true. I live in Manhattan."

"So you know what I'm talking about."

"I do, but there's something charming about this place. It's relaxing."

"It is, and it's beautiful. I definitely see why people love it. But it's not my jam long term."

"Fair enough. So are we hanging out later?"

She gave him a thorough looking-over, so thorough he nearly ended up sporting wood from the way she studied him. "I suppose we are."

"I'll pick you up at seven."

Smiling, she said, "You're awfully cute. Are you even legal?"

"I'm twenty-four," he said, offended.

"Such a baby."

"How old are you?"

"Twenty-nine."

"Oh damn. That's kinda old for me. I might need to reconsider this plan to hang out."

"Really?" She seemed genuinely surprised.

"No, not really," he said, laughing. "I'll see you at seven."

"See you then."

As she walked away—really, it was more of a strut than a walk—he stood frozen in place, taking in the beautiful sight of the back of her, laid nearly bare by a thong bikini.

He was definitely sporting wood after that show.

When she reached the stairs to the garage apartment, she looked back, caught him staring and flashed a satisfied grin.

The woman was too sexy for his own good. As soon as he got himself under control, he went inside to find Jared and Lizzie had gotten up while he was living out his own personal wet dream outside. "Jared, I need to borrow the Porsche later."

"That's not happening."

"Let him have it, Jared," his new best friend Lizzie said. "What is it you always say? It's insured."

Jared's scowl took in both of them.

"Where you going, anyway?" Lizzie asked.

"It seems I have a date with Gigi Gibson."

"Oh dear God," Jared said. "She's *way* too much woman for you, little brother."

"She's just the right amount of woman for me," Cooper said with a dirty grin.

Jessie came into the kitchen, carrying the baby and looking as if she hadn't slept at all. "Is there coffee?"

"Coming right up," Lizzie said. "How do you like it?"

"Cream and sugar, please."

"You got it." As Lizzie fixed the mug for her, she glanced at Jessie over her shoulder. "Were you up all night?"

"Pretty much."

"I read that babies often get their days and nights mixed up the first few weeks," Lizzie said, "which is why you have to sleep when she does."

"I need to go to work."

"You can't work the day after you gave birth, Jessie."

"If I don't work, I don't get paid."

"Don't worry about money," Jared said gruffly. "We'll take care of whatever you and the baby need."

Jessie's chin wobbled. "I can't let you do that."

She was such a sweet girl, and Coop found himself wanting to know more about her and how she'd ended up a single mom on Gansett Island.

"It's already done," Jared said. "Don't worry about anything."

"Are you people for real?" Jessie asked as she took the seat Jared pulled out for her. "You just help people you don't even know?"

"She does." Jared used his chin to indicate his wife, smiling as he looked at her. "She helps people all the time."

"Using his money," Lizzie said. "Spending his money to help others is one of my favorite hobbies."

"And she's exceptionally good at spending *our* money to help people," Jared said.

Lizzie beamed at him as she delivered Jessie's coffee to her at the table. "You can stay here as long as you need to."

"I can't do that. You guys don't need a newborn screaming your house down."

Jessie couldn't know how true that was, Cooper thought, amazed by his brother and sister-in-law's ability to extend such generosity to a new mother while dealing with their own private grief.

"Thank you," Jessie said, seeming on the verge of tears.

"Here," Coop said, "let me take her while you have something to eat. Lizzie's eggs are to die for."

"Oh, um, are you sure?"

"I'm sure." Coop took the baby from her and settled her in the crook of his elbow. She was a cute little thing with a bow-shaped mouth and feathery eyebrows that came together in an expression that made her look confounded. "Good morning, my little peanut. What's this I hear about you keeping your mommy up all night?"

While the others ate breakfast, Cooper walked her around the spacious house, keeping up a nonsensical conversation with her. She seemed interested in everything he said. Although he'd been an uncle for years, he hadn't given much thought to having kids of his own. That fell into the "maybe someday" category for way off in the distant future.

"You're good with her," Lizzie said, leaning against the doorframe as she watched him.

"I've been an uncle since I was fourteen," he reminded her. "My older sisters have five kids between them."

"Ah, yes, that's true."

"She's a cutie."

"She sure is," Lizzie said wistfully.

"Why did you bring her home if having a baby here was going to hurt you, Lizzie?" He knew she wouldn't mind that Jared had told him what they were going through.

Lizzie shrugged. "She needed somewhere to go. We have room."

His heart went out to her. "Lizzie…"

"I'm okay. I swear."

She said what he needed to hear, but heartbreak was written all over her face.

"Do you want to hold her?" Coop asked. He had no idea if he should offer that, but then again, he was clueless about how to navigate this situation.

"Um, sure. I'll take a turn. Go have some breakfast."

Cooper transferred the baby to her. "You good?"

"I'm good."

He was hesitant to walk away, but after a minute, he left the room to return to the kitchen.

"Where's the baby?" Jared asked.

"Lizzie has her."

He got up and went after his wife.

"Tell me the truth," Jessie said. "Is it really okay that I'm here?"

"It's okay," Cooper said, hoping he spoke the truth.

CHAPTER 30

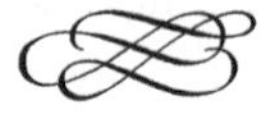

Jared found Lizzie in the living room, sitting on the sofa with the baby on her lap. His heart ached as he wished she could have that experience with their baby rather than with a stranger's child. "Babe."

She looked up at him, her face the picture of devastation that she quickly tried to hide from him. "Hey."

"What're you doing?"

"Holding the baby so Jessie can eat."

"Cooper was doing that."

"I'm all right, Jared."

"No, you're not, so don't even try to tell me that. I know better."

When she didn't argue with him, she confirmed his suspicions. "Let's give the baby back to Jessie and go for a ride."

"Where do you want to go?"

"I'll show you." He carefully retrieved the baby and kissed Lizzie's forehead. "Go get ready."

"Okay."

Jared went to the kitchen and transferred the baby to Jessie, who had finished eating. Then he went to their bedroom to join Lizzie in the shower, certain that some of the water on her face was from tears. He put his arms around her and held on tight, wishing there was some magic wand he could wave to give her what she wanted so badly.

No words were exchanged as they held each other under the stream of hot water.

A short time later, they left the house in his car for a ride around the island. The roads were busy that Sunday morning in August, but soon the island would be quiet again. Jared was ready for that. He, who'd once thrived in the hustle and bustle of New York City, had grown to crave the peaceful quiet of off-season Gansett Island.

They ended up at the Chesterfield, the estate they'd bought and turned into a wedding venue that Lizzie ran. He'd insisted she hire help so she didn't have to sacrifice every weekend all summer to the business.

"What're we doing here?"

"I want to show you something."

"Okay..."

She followed him inside where their dedicated team was preparing for the day's wedding, which was set for two o'clock. Thankfully, they'd installed a generator when they'd done the renovations, or they'd have been forced to cancel.

"Thank God for the generator, huh?" Jared said.

"Seriously. Imagine having to tell a bride and groom that their big day is canceled due to a power failure."

"I'd rather not have to think about that."

He led her up the grand staircase and then up a smaller set of stairs to the third floor. He used a key in the door of the apartment that'd been vacant since his brother Quinn had moved in with Mallory.

"What're we doing here, Jared?"

"Two things. One, I wanted to get you out of the house, and two, I wanted to remind you that this place is available. We can set up Jessie and the baby here with everything they need and let her live rent-free for as long as necessary."

Lizzie took a seat on the navy sofa she'd chosen for the apartment. She'd seen to every detail of the renovation personally, turning the outdated estate into a showplace that had brides and grooms waiting up to eighteen months to get married there.

His wife was a sparkling gem, and her sadness wrecked him.

"I'm sorry I brought them home with me."

He sat next to her. "Please don't be sorry, sweetheart. I know you can't help yourself when you see someone who needs help. I love you so much for that."

Tears spilled down her cheeks. "I thought I could do it, that it wouldn't be any big deal. But you were right."

After putting his arm around her, Jared kissed the top of her head. "I can't bear to see you hurting."

"I know, and you've been so great through all of this. I've been thinking it might be time to think about adoption. I'm not saying I'm giving up on having a baby, just that maybe we should explore other options, too."

"What about surrogacy?"

"I wouldn't rule that out."

Jared breathed a sigh of relief, because this was the first time that she'd entertained the possibility of alternative paths to parenthood. Frankly, he wasn't sure if he could handle watching her go through another failed round of IVF.

"Tomorrow, we'll see what's involved with all of it and get the ball rolling." That was where he excelled—seeing a challenge and finding a way to address it. The act of doing something—*anything*—to bring them closer to their dream of being parents would make them both feel better about their failure to conceive. He honestly believed that.

Brushing her hair aside, he placed a kiss on her neck in the place that always made her melt. This time was no different. "So we'll move Jessie to the apartment?"

"In a day or two, when she's feeling stronger."

"That works for me."

CHAPTER 31

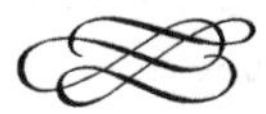

As another busy summer weekend came to a close, Gansett Island Harbor Master Deacon Taylor brought his boat into the public safety dock and tied it up. After shutting down the engines, radio and other equipment, he checked the lines one more time and then bounded up the dock, eager to see Julia after a long day apart.

He ought to go home to wash off the sweat, salt and sunscreen before he went to find her, but he was too excited after missing her all day. It was funny, really, how domesticated he'd become this summer, since he met the love of his life and found the missing piece to the puzzle that'd been his existence before her.

And *existence* was the keyword. Before her, he'd merely existed. With her, he was fully and completely alive in a way he'd never been without her.

Her stepsister, Stephanie, had hired Julia to play the Sunday cocktail hour at Stephanie's Bistro, insisting on paying her to do something Julia would've done for free for the sheer joy she got from playing the piano and singing for an appreciative audience.

And the audience was super appreciative. Stephanie's was *packed* any time Julia was scheduled to play. Many of the customers ended up staying for dinner, which made the arrangement a win-win for both sisters.

Deacon dashed up the stairs to the Sand & Surf Hotel and nearly ran into Owen Lawry, who was coming out the door.

"Hey, man." Owen, who owned the hotel with his wife, Laura, held the door for Deacon. "What's your rush?"

Deacon pointed to Stephanie's Bistro, cocking his head so he could hear the sublime sound of Julia's voice.

"Ah, of course. My beautiful sister."

"It's been a *long* day at the office," Deacon said, grinning.

"Don't let me stand in your way."

"Have a good night," Deacon said to Owen.

"You, too."

Any night with Julia was the best night he'd ever had with anyone. Months after they first got together when he'd "kidnapped" her from her sister Katie's wedding, Deacon was still waiting for the magic to wear off, for the extraordinary to become ordinary, the way it always had in every past relationship. He'd come to believe that wasn't going to happen with her.

He stepped into the crowded Bistro and found his love on the small stage at the front of the room, sitting at the sleek baby grand piano with their dog, Puppy Pupwell, curled up at her feet.

The black Lab puppy they'd saved when they found him swimming in the ocean and then adopted together had gotten big over the summer, topping forty pounds at his last checkup. Julia was sad that she could no longer carry him around like a baby.

Even though every window and door in the place was thrown open to capture the ocean breeze, the heat was intense inside. But no one seemed to care about the heat as they listened to Julia.

Leaning back against the doorjamb, Deacon drank in the sight of his loved ones. Their little family was the greatest joy of his life. Listening to her sing and watching her become more confident in her amazing talent was a close second. She was performing "Fallin'" by Alicia Keys, a song she'd been practicing on the keyboard he'd bought for her to use at home. He'd ordered it online and waited with the kind of anticipation that used to be reserved for Christmas morning until it finally arrived a week later.

He'd had it set up in their small apartment over his sister-in-law's dance studio when Julia came home from work at Mac's office. Deacon would never forget the way her face had lit up at the sight of her very own keyboard, the first one she'd had since her asshole father had gotten rid of the piano she'd loved.

That had been a very good day, one of many very good days he'd had with her since Katie and Shane's wedding. Crashing that wedding and "kidnapping" the maid of honor had been the best thing Deacon had ever done. They were planning to look for a bigger place in the fall, when things calmed down a bit for both of them. He'd told her that wherever they landed, there needed to be room for a baby grand so she could play any time she wanted.

"She's amazing," a guy standing next to Deacon said.

"She sure is."

"Wonder why she's not playing for bigger crowds than this."

"I'll bet she's perfectly satisfied playing here." Julia loved performing at the hotel that had been her summer home growing up. Those summers with their beloved grandparents had been the only respite she and her siblings had gotten from their violent, unpredictable father.

"Do you know her?"

"I do."

"Is she seeing anyone?"

"She is."

"Bummer. He's a lucky guy."

"And he knows it."

The guy gave him a curious look before moving on.

Hands off. She's mine. Deacon kept the thoughts to himself. Watching her blossom over the last few months had been the ultimate satisfaction as she took control of her life and devoted herself to the things she loved, especially him.

Deacon was so damned lucky to be loved by her. Because he was watching her so intently, he was aware of the exact moment she spotted him. Her smile lit up her face and his world. He stayed right there until she finished her set with a slow, sultry version of "Bohemian Rhapsody" that had everyone in the room riveted to her. The audience exploded into applause that made Julia flush with pleasure and embarrassment.

She'd yet to become completely comfortable with the way people reacted to her performances.

Julia blew a kiss to the crowd, collected Pupwell and made her way to

Deacon, stopping here and there to acknowledge the praise of her adoring fans.

And then she was smiling as she went up on tiptoes to kiss him. "Hey, sailor. Buy a girl a drink?"

Deacon put his arms around her and held her close, thrilled to be back with her after hours apart. "Anything you want, sweetheart."

"Oh, *anything*?"

"Anything at all."

"I have everything I need right here with you and Pupwell."

"You want to eat out or go home?"

"Let's go home. I'm tired."

Deacon kept his arm around her as they headed out of the hotel in the sultry heat that felt more like midday even though it was nearly eight o'clock.

"How much longer is this heat wave sticking around?" she asked.

"Another day or two."

"Ugh, I can't stand it. It makes me feel so *wilted*."

"You didn't look wilted on the stage. You were magnificent, as always."

"Aw, thanks. That's nice to hear, but I was sweating the whole time. I probably reek."

"Me, too. I'm a salty, sweaty, crusty mess."

"I see a very cool shower in our future."

"Mmm, yes, please."

They walked through town to Blaine and Tiffany's property, strolling down the long driveway past his brother's house to the garage in the back. Deacon followed Julia up the stairs, his gaze landing on the sweet ass that swayed as she moved. She was so effortlessly sexy. She would say she was too thin, but he thought she was perfect. What mattered to him was that she was healthy, and according to Dr. David, she was doing great after suffering with eating disorders for most of her life.

Deacon was well aware that the lack of chaos in their happy life together was key to her good health, and he intended to do whatever it took to keep it that way.

Inside their apartment, which was hot like an oven that'd been left on all day, she fed Pupwell and then headed for the bathroom to join him in the cool shower.

"God, this feels like heaven," she said when they were standing under the water.

"It sure does," he said, running his hands over her.

Smiling, she said, "I meant the shower."

He kissed her. "I meant you."

Sliding her hands up to curl around his neck, she kissed him back. "I had a feeling you weren't talking about the shower."

"I'm always talking about you." He grasped her ass and lifted her against the cool tile wall. "Since it's too hot to do this any other way…"

"I'm all in."

"I'm about to be all in."

Julia sputtered with laughter. He loved to make her laugh, to make her sigh from pleasure, to make her scream—when the windows weren't open to his brother's backyard, anyway.

He pushed into her and had to hold completely still to keep from coming too soon. It was always that way with her, intense and hot, so incredibly hot, even when they weren't in the middle of a heat-wave induced blackout.

"Are you okay?" she asked when he held still much longer than usual.

"Trying not to lose it too soon."

"It's okay if you do."

"No, it isn't. Not before my baby gets what she needs."

She tightened her hold on him. "I have everything I need and more than I ever dared to dream."

His heart skipped a crazy beat every time she said those words to him, reminding him of how much both their lives had changed since they found each other. He closed his eyes and counted all the lucky stars that had put him on Gansett Island at the same time as her. When he thought about how easily he could've missed ever meeting her… He pushed all the way into her, loving how her mouth fell open and her head tipped back, exposing her gorgeous neck. "I couldn't wait to get to you after work. I practically ran to the Surf from the dock."

"I was so happy to see you, like it'd been a month rather than a few hours."

"So many hours. Too many. We need a vacation after the season so we can do this all day."

"Mmm, let's do that."

"Anywhere you want to go."

"I've never been anywhere, so whatever you want."

What he wanted was to give her the world, to make up for every hurt she'd ever suffered in her life before they found each other, to give her children and a home and a life of comfort and security. In other words, everything she'd never had before.

"I'd be perfectly happy to spend an entire week right here with you and Pupwell." But he would find them somewhere awesome to go so they could see more of the world.

"That sounds like heaven." Her fingernails scraping against his scalp sent a shiver down his spine.

Deacon reached down to where they were joined to help her along, stroking her until she clamped down on his cock and came with a sharp cry of pleasure that demolished his control. They weren't doing anything to prevent conception, and every time they had sex, he hoped that maybe this would be the time he could help make another of her wildest dreams come true.

It hadn't happened yet, but they were having fun trying.

The water had turned icy cold while they were getting busy, but icy cold had never felt so good until he realized Julia was starting to shiver. "Let's get you warmed up, darlin'."

"I never imagined I could be cold today."

He withdrew from her and put her down carefully, making sure she had legs under her before he let go to get out and find towels. "You'll be sweating again in ten minutes."

Deacon wrapped her in a towel and kissed her. "Best shower ever."

"We keep topping ourselves."

"I hope we keep that up for the next fifty or sixty years."

"I'd be down with that."

He kissed her forehead and then her lips again. "I'm down with anything that includes you and me forever. In fact…" He directed her toward the apartment's only bedroom and sat her on the edge of the bed.

"In fact, what?"

"Hold that thought a minute." Still bare-ass naked, he went to his dresser and found the velvet box he'd hidden weeks ago, waiting for the right moment to ask the most important question of his life. If you'd told him six months ago that he'd be dying to shackle himself to one woman for the rest of his life, he would've laughed his ass off. Since meeting Julia, however, he understood why sane men went crazy over the women they loved. Crazy had never felt so good.

His need for her only grew exponentially with every day he spent with her, and he was wise enough to know that keeping her by his side forever was essential to any chance he had to be happy. After giving himself a second to get his shit together, he turned to find her watching him with the curious, wary look that had been permanently etched into her gorgeous face when they first met.

Deacon hadn't seen that in a while and didn't want to be the cause of it now. "Nothing bad, darlin'. Only good things from now on, remember?" He told her that any time she seemed worried or afraid or anxious. "So turn that frown upside down."

She smiled, which made her eyes glitter the way he liked them best. He never wanted her to be worried about anything, even if he knew that was a rather lofty goal.

Kneeling before her, he kept the box hidden in one hand while he used his free hand to bring her down for a kiss. "You know how much I love you, right?"

"I think I do."

"Actually, you probably don't know the full extent of how you occupy every available space inside me."

"Deacon," she whispered, her eyes sparkling with tears.

He often teased her about being a waterworks, but he wouldn't change a thing about her, even how she teared up at corny commercials on TV. She was perfect for him.

"When I'm not with you, I'm counting the minutes until I can see you again. When I'm with you, there's nothing else I want or need. And you know how much it means to me to be your shell, to protect you from anything that can ever hurt you. I was hoping that maybe you might, you know, agree to marry me."

He held up the square-cut diamond ring he'd chosen with Blaine and Tiffany's input and held his breath waiting to hear what she would say.

Tears spilled down her cheeks as she stared at the ring for the longest time before shifting her gaze to his face.

"If you don't like it, we can get—"

She kissed him. "I love it. I love you, and yes to marrying you. One thousand percent yes."

"That's a whole lot of yes," he said, weak with relief.

She smoothed the wet hair back from his forehead. "You weren't really worried about what I'd say, were you?"

"Not that so much as getting the ring right. I was a bit obsessed with that, actually. Tiffany assured me you'd love it."

"She was right. I do. But I loved what you said even more than I love the ring. That's the stuff that really matters to me. You know that."

"I do know, and I promise to always keep you safe, my sweet Julia, and to do my very best to make you happy every day."

"You couldn't offer me anything that would mean more to me than that, but you could put that sparkly ring on my finger any time now." She held up her hand and waggled her fingers.

Smiling, Deacon took it out of the box, slid it on her left hand and then sat back to admire the way it looked on her. "Perfection."

"Just like us."

He hugged her tightly. "Just like us."

CHAPTER 32

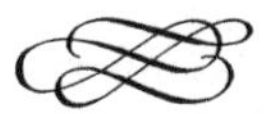

After talking it over with Dara, Oliver decided to accept Big Mac's invitation to join him and the other guys for an afternoon of fishing. He couldn't remember the last time he'd enjoyed anything more than those hours on the water with his new friends. The guys were fun, funny and obviously close to each other.

Big Mac's son Evan texted while they were out to let his dad know that he and his wife, Grace, were back on the island. Watching the older man's joy at hearing his son was back in town tugged at the grief that had become such a big part of who Oliver was after losing his son. It made him ache for things that would never be.

"Aw, shit," Big Mac said. "I'm sorry, Oliver. I shouldn't have gone on about my son that way."

"Oh, please," Oliver said. "Don't do that. You're rightfully excited to see your son."

"Still... I could've been less over the top about it."

"Yer over the top 'bout everythin'," Ned said dryly, breaking the tension by making everyone laugh.

"I don't want you guys to worry about what you say in front of me. I've got to get back to some semblance of normalcy."

"You're not on any timeline," Frank said. "Took me years to take a deep breath after my wife died of cancer, leaving me as a single dad to my kids, who were seven and nine."

"I'm sorry you lost her."

"And I'm sorry you lost your son."

"Thanks. It's been a bitch, to say the least. Since nothing else was helping, my wife and I are here looking for a fresh start."

"You've come to the right place," Kevin said. "Gansett is great for resets."

"He oughta know," Ned said. "Came here fresh off a split with his wife o' thirty years and ended up remarried with a new baby girl."

"True story," Kevin said with a grin. "And I couldn't be happier. That's not to compare my situation to yours. There's no comparing. I just mean that being in this beautiful place with these fools turned out to be just what I needed."

"I can see how that might be the case," Oliver said.

"You're welcome with us any time, every day, whatever you want," Frank said. "If you need a band of brothers, you've got one, my friend."

Moved nearly to tears by the kind words, Oliver could only nod.

"And if you need someone to talk to about it all, Kev's your guy," Big Mac said. "He's an outstanding therapist, and we're lucky to have him practicing right here in our little neck of the woods."

"No pressure," Kevin said. "If you need me, I'm here. Either way, we'll be fishing and coffee buddies."

"That's good to know on both counts," Oliver said. "My wife and I... It's been a struggle to get through the days since we lost Lewis."

"I can't even imagine," Kevin said. "My heart goes out to you both."

"Anyway," Oliver said, "I didn't mean to bring down the mood."

"You didn't," Big Mac said. "Don't worry about us. We're here for you in any way that you need while you're part of our community and even after you've moved on. Unfortunately for you, my friend, once you're stuck with us, you're stuck with us forever."

"I can attest ta that," Ned said. "They stick like glue."

"You like being stuck with us," Big Mac said to his best pal.

"Yer right about that."

"Actually, that's rather comforting," Oliver said. "We've been surrounded by well-intentioned people who want to help but only make things harder for us by adding their grief to ours. It's a relief to make some new friends."

"We'll see if yer still saying that in a few weeks," Ned joked.

Oliver smiled. He'd done a lot of that since he'd joined them for coffee that morning. "I'm sure I will be."

~

LINDA TALKED Dara into coming with her when she went to help out with Mac and Maddie's kids so Mac could get some work done at the office. Everyone had been pitching in to help them since Maddie had been put on bed rest. Kelsey had been such a godsend, but Sundays were her day off. Francine took the morning shift on Sundays, and Linda relieved her after lunch.

"How long have you all been doing this?" Dara asked as they rode the short distance to Mac's house in Linda's yellow VW Bug.

"Since May," Linda said.

"That's quite a commitment."

"With three kids six and under, they need the help."

"Wow, and now she's having twins."

"The last three pregnancies weren't exactly planned. That includes the child they lost. We were so happy to hear she was expecting again after that, and then the twin girls were a huge shock. She's been telling my son for months that he's getting the snip before he comes near her again."

Dara laughed, and the sound of her own laughter took her by surprise. It'd been a very long time since she'd laughed at anything. "That's funny."

"She's dead serious. Five kids is her limit."

"Can't say I blame her. That's a lot."

"It was a lot for us, but ours were spaced out a little more than theirs. It's going to be a wild couple of years for them. We also heard that our son Adam and his wife, Abby, who've had fertility challenges, are expecting quads."

"Whoa. Did they do IVF?"

"That's the interesting part. They didn't. They adopted a little boy last winter, and a few months later, boom, she's pregnant. They just found out about the quads this week."

"What a shock."

"For sure, but they're trying to see it as a miracle."

"No other way to see it. Your family sure is interesting."

"Aw, thanks. We love them. In other news, Mac's daughter is getting married on Tuesday. Mallory and her husband-to-be are both turning forty-one that day and decided to celebrate by getting married."

"That's cool. Mallory is Mac's daughter?"

"Right. He ended a brief relationship shortly before we met and found out almost forty years later that he'd fathered a child with her. Now *that* was a shock."

"Holy cow. What did he say? What did *you* say?"

"My husband has the biggest heart of anyone you've ever met. As soon as he met her, he put his arm around her and made her part of our family. I followed his lead, and not for nothing, Mallory made it easy. She's a delightful, accomplished woman. She fits right in with us, as if she's always been around. We see her as one more person to love."

"That's an amazing story. You have two other sons, right?"

"That's right. Evan is a musician, and he's married to Grace. They've just come back from touring with Buddy Longstreet."

"*Seriously*? *The* Buddy Longstreet?"

"The one and only. Have you heard the song 'My Amazing Grace'?"

"Evan McCarthy. *He's your son?*"

"Sure is. And Grant McCarthy, who wrote the movie *Song of Solomon* is our son as well."

"No way. I loved that movie. It's one of my all-time favorites."

"Mine, too. He and his wife, Stephanie, are expecting a baby, and so are Evan and Grace. Evan surprised Grace with a new home on the island, and we're all going there tomorrow night for a party for Mallory and Quinn, but also so we can see the new place."

"I really love your family."

"We do, too." Linda glanced over at her. "Mac and I started with the ultimate heartache and then went on to have five wonderful children, plus the bonus of Mallory much later. I've always been thankful we were able to push through our grief to discover that we had a lot of living and loving left to do. The children we had after we lost our first helped to soothe our broken hearts."

"It's good to know that can happen. Sometimes I wonder if I'll ever feel happiness or joy again."

"You will."

"Maybe," Dara said. "It's so hard to find joy in anything anymore."

"Perhaps you need to create your own joy."

"I hear what you're saying, and you make very valid points."

"I don't want to overstep."

"Please don't worry about that. You and Mac have been a breath of fresh air for Oliver and me. He texted to tell me how much fun the fishing has been."

"Those guys always have fun. They'll be good for him. And my girls and I will try to be good for you."

"So far, so good."

"That's nice to hear. Come along and meet my lovely daughter-in-law and grandchildren."

Linda led the way up the stairs to the deck and let herself in through the sliding door. A boy and a girl came rushing toward her and wrapped themselves around her legs.

"Thank God you're here," an older woman said.

Dara assumed she was Maddie's mother, Francine. She had red hair and greenish eyes that twinkled as she looked down at the baby she was holding.

"Rough morning at the ranch?" Linda asked.

"Busy morning. And Maddie's not feeling well. She's upstairs in bed."

"Do we need to call Vic?"

"She says not to. She's nauseated."

"Poor thing." Linda bent to kiss the little boy and picked up his sister. "This is my new friend, Dara. Dara, meet my partner in crime, Francine, my grandsons, Thomas and Mac the Third, and this little princess is our Hailey."

"So nice to meet you all," Dara said.

"What's for lunch, Grammy?" Thomas asked as he ran off to play with his trucks without waiting for an answer.

"Francine, you're off duty. Dara and I are on the job."

"Praise the Lord. These little people have run me ragged this morning."

"What're we gonna do when there're two more of them?" Linda asked, kissing Hailey's neck until she giggled.

"We're going to need to hire some additional grandmothers," Francine said in her typical blunt style. She went upstairs to check on Maddie and came back downstairs to report that she was asleep. After kissing her grandchildren, Francine told Linda she'd check in with her tomorrow to see what was needed and then headed out the slider to the deck.

Linda put Hailey down and got busy making lunch for the kids, which she served on paper plates at the kitchen table just as Mac began crying for his bottle.

"I can do it," Dara said after Linda had changed his diaper.

"Are you sure?"

"I'm sure."

Dara took the baby and settled into a chair.

He looked up at her with inquisitive blue eyes. From the photos she'd seen at Linda and Mac's, he looked just like his father.

Linda brought her the bottle. "If it's too much for you, please just say so."

"I'm okay, but thank you."

"No, thank *you*. This granny only has two hands."

"I'm happy to help." A million memories overwhelmed her as she fed the baby. How many times had she done this with her own son? He'd stubbornly refused to breastfeed, having had a mind of his own from the very beginning.

While Linda colored with the other kids at the table, Dara tended to the baby, entertaining him until he began to rub his eyes and whimper, signs she recognized as a baby who needed a nap.

"I'll take him up," Linda said, "and check on Maddie. Will you keep an eye on the monkeys?"

"Sure thing." Dara sat with Thomas and Hailey at the table and got to work on the picture Linda had been working on.

"What's your favorite color?" Thomas asked.

"Orange. How about you?"

"I like orange, too. Hailey likes black. She colors everything black. Who does that?"

Sure enough, Hailey was going to town on a picture of a flower with a black crayon. Her concentration level was admirable.

"Everyone likes different things," Dara told him. His inquisitiveness reminded her of Lewis, whom they had called the question factory. The memory made her smile rather than cry, which was a welcome relief, since she couldn't allow herself to break down in front of these precious children. "Are you excited about your baby sisters?"

"Ugh, no," Thomas said, wrinkling his cute little sunburned nose. "One sister is *more* than enough."

Hailey stuck out her tongue at him.

"See what I mean?"

"I see, but at least you'll have Mac."

"He's just a baby. He can't do nothing."

"That's temporary. You'll be chasing him around in no time."

"But there will still be *three* of them and *two* of us. Mommy says no more babies."

Dara had to force herself not to crack up laughing.

"Daddy says it's my job as the big brother to take care of them all."

"He's right about that."

"Do you have babies?"

Dara held back a gasp at the shot to the heart. "No, I don't." There was no way she could explain Lewis or what'd happened to him to this child, so she didn't try.

"You'd be a nice mommy."

"You think so?"

He smiled and nodded.

"That's nice of you to say."

"When can we watch TV again?" Thomas asked, bored with the coloring.

"As soon as the electricity comes back on."

"It's lame without TV."

"Sure is."

Linda came back downstairs. "Thomas, are you talking Dara's ear off?"

"How can I talk her ear off? Ears don't come off."

"He's in a literal stage," Linda said to Dara. "It's an expression, sweetheart. A figure of speech."

"What does that mean?"

"It means it's something people say, but it can't really happen," Dara said. "When your Grammy asks if you're talking my ears off, she means are you talking a lot."

"He talks a *lot*," Hailey said.

"Be quiet," Thomas said.

"You be quiet."

"None of that," Linda said, "or we'll all have quiet time in our rooms."

Thomas shot Hailey a foul look, full of sibling disgust.

"Business as usual around here," Linda said. "Feel free to take my car if you want to escape. I wouldn't blame you."

"Nah, I'm fine. It's good to have something fun to do. Maybe you guys can come over to play at my lighthouse sometime."

"You have your own lighthouse?" Thomas asked, eyes gone wide.

"For the next year, it seems I do."

"That's awesome. Can we go, Grammy?"

"We'd love to do that," Linda said to Dara.

"Great, it's a plan, then." It was nice to have something to look forward to, Dara thought, thankful to her new friend for taking her in and giving her hope.

So far, Gansett was proving to be good for her shattered soul.

CHAPTER 33

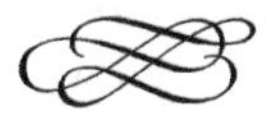

On Monday evening, the entire clan gathered at Evan and Grace's new home for a combined bachelor and bachelorette party for Mallory and Quinn. After another day without power, everyone was starting to get cranky, but they put their best foot forward for the bride and groom.

Mallory appreciated that her family went all out for her, despite the blackout, and she was eager to see Evan and Grace's new home.

"Holy shit," Quinn said when they pulled up to the huge house with the three-car garage, gorgeous landscaping and a to-die-for view of the ocean. "I need to get busy writing and recording music."

Mallory laughed. Things had been so hectic at the senior center as they grappled with the blackout that he hadn't seen his younger brother Cooper, who'd arrived a couple of days ago. "Aren't you busy enough, Dr. James?"

"I'm plenty busy, but I'm doing something wrong if this is the house your brother bought with music money."

"You're doing everything right, and we can buy ourselves a nice house when we're ready."

"We can't afford this."

"We don't need this."

He looked her way. "I do have the money Jared gave me when he first struck it rich. I've never touched it because it felt kinda weird to take money from my little brother, but he wanted to share his largess with us. So we have that if we want something really fabulous."

"I don't need really fabulous. I've been perfectly happy in my sister's little cottage. As long as you're there, I'm set."

"That makes you rather easy to please."

"You know it."

"I do know it, and I appreciate it more than you can imagine."

"Same. I love our stress-free, easy life together. You and me and Brutus make for a perfect little family."

From the backseat, Brutus grunted in agreement.

They'd brought him because it was too hot to leave him home alone. The poor guy had been suffering in the heat.

"Let's go to our party!" Mallory said as she got out of the car and led the way up the elaborate stone walkway to the front door.

Evan and Grace were there to greet them with hugs and kisses and excitement for their wedding.

"To hell with the wedding," Mallory said. "Show us this house!"

"To hell with the wedding, she says the day before," Quinn muttered.

"Oh hush, you know I'm kidding. Sorta."

Grace laughed, hooked her arm through Mallory's and said, "Let me give you the grand tour."

"Can you believe you live here?" Mallory asked.

"It's going to take a year for me to believe I live here."

After the women had walked away, Quinn sized up Evan. "Way to lay down the gauntlet with the best wife surprise in the history of wife surprises."

"I did a rather good job, didn't I?"

"Don't make it worse by being smug."

Evan laughed and gestured for Quinn to lead the way to the deck, where every form of beverage was chilling in coolers.

"Soda, water and seltzer are in that one," Evan said.

"Thanks."

Quinn chose a lemon seltzer and cracked it open. "I've had enough of this freaking heat wave."

"I hear you. It's like someone set the thermometer to roast."

"For *days*."

"How're you guys holding up at the center?" Evan asked.

"Hanging in there, thanks to two generators, but they're just enough for lights, low-level AC and the refrigerators. The residents are grumpy about being without TV and internet service. And I feel for them. It's their lifeline to the world."

"That sucks."

"It really does. Thankfully, our part-time activities director, Jordan Stokes, has been coming up with all sorts of fun things for them to do, but I'm and I'm hearing it could be another couple of days."

"For what?" Grant asked when he joined them on the deck.

"Power," Evan said, filling in his brother.

"No way. We're about to sweat to death in our house. No sign of even the slightest breeze there."

"Stay here," Evan said. "The breeze off the ocean is pretty good, and this place has a generator."

"I may take you up on that," Grant said. "The heat is making Steph sick."

"My house is your house," Evan said.

"This place is crazy, and I'm actually pissed with you."

"About what?"

"I was going to look at this place when we got back to the island."

"Snooze ya lose, brother," Evan said.

"You're being smug again," Quinn said.

"He gets like that," Grant replied as he found a beer and took a long drink. "Damn, that tastes good." He caught himself and glanced at Quinn. "Sorry. Don't mean to drink and gloat."

"No worries, man. I don't even want it anymore." After so many years in recovery, alcohol of any kind held little appeal to him. "Don't ever worry about drinking in front of me or Mallory. It's all good."

"Did you guys hear the news about Adam and Abby?" Grant asked Quinn.

"We did hear. It's amazing."

Adam joined his brothers and future brother-in-law on the deck, holding his son, Liam. "Let's face it. My boys are the most powerful of all the boys."

"Oh my God," Evan groaned. "Is that what we're in for forever?"

"I'm afraid so," Grant said. "He's been insufferable for days."

"He's been insufferable a lot longer than that," Evan said.

Adam made a suggestive motion with his hips and free arm that had his brothers gagging. "I got the *goods*. *Four* babies. Top that, a-holes."

Grant sighed. "I want to have him killed, but I don't want to have to raise his five kids."

"I'd help you hide the body," Evan said.

"Why do they want to kill you now, Adam?" Abby asked when she and the other women came out to the deck.

"He's talking about his boys and his prowess at knocking you up with four babies," Evan said. "Congratulations, by the way. I think."

Abby laughed and tipped her cheek up to receive a kiss from her brother-in-law. "He won't be thinking about his so-called prowess when we have five babies underfoot."

"Did I or did I not do a spectacular job of knocking you up, love?"

"You're starting to sound like Mac," Abby said.

"Who's sounding like me?" Mac asked when he came out carrying Hailey and baby Mac. "All my stuff is trademarked. No one can use it without express written permission."

"Oh shut up, Mac," Evan said. "Do you ever get tired of listening to yourself?"

"No, not really, and hello to you, too, brother. Welcome home."

Evan took baby Mac from his brother and leaned in and kissed Hailey, who let out a happy squeak at the sight of her uncle. So he took her, too. "It's okay to like Uncle Evan better than Daddy. Everyone would understand."

"*Puleeze*," Mac said. "They're on Team Mac forever. And PS, nice house."

"Thanks," Evan said. "We're still trying to believe we actually *live* here."

"It'll feel like home in no time," Grant said. "I wanted to tell you all that we're going to premiere the film here on Friday night. Fingers crossed the power is back by then. Everyone is invited to the theater to see *Indefatigable* with an after-party at the Bistro."

"I can't wait to see it," Evan said. "I read the article and review in the *LA Times*. They loved it."

"The reviews have been awesome so far," Grant said. "We're excited for the release."

"I'm hearing Oscar buzz for my brother," Mac said. "Couldn't be prouder."

"Thanks," Grant said, "but Steph and Charlie are the stars of this story."

"By all accounts, you did a beautiful job bringing their story to life, and you should be very proud of that," Evan said.

"I am," Grant said, "but I'm even prouder of her. When you see the full extent of what she endured... It'll blow your mind."

"Looking forward to it," Mac said.

"This place is awesome," Mallory said when she joined the others on the deck. "Congratulations, Evan. You made your wife very happy."

"She's made me very happy. Without her, there's no number one hit and no cool house. There's no nothing."

Quinn put his arm around Mallory. By this time tomorrow, they'd be married. That was still hard to believe. He'd never pictured himself married to anyone until she came along and changed everything.

She smiled up at him. "What level of nonsense has been happening out here?"

"The usual level."

"My brothers are nothing if not entertaining."

"Speaking of brothers, here come mine."

Jared and Lizzie came onto the deck, followed by Cooper, who had a gnarly wound on the right side of his face.

"What the hell happened to you?" Quinn asked his youngest sibling as they exchanged a side handshake-hug combination.

"Ugh, go easy," Cooper said, wincing when Quinn patted his back.

"He's got two broken ribs," Jared said, "to go along with the mess on his face, and he's not talking about how it happened, but apparently, the fire department was involved."

Quinn told himself he shouldn't laugh, but how could he not?

Jared joined him while Cooper scowled at them both and then grimaced, in obvious pain.

"The best part," Jared said, "is he was on a date with Gigi Gibson at the time."

"Leave him alone, you guys," Lizzie said. "He's injured."

"And probably mortified," Jared said.

"I'm getting a drink," Cooper said. "You guys can eff off."

"I want to know what happened so bad," Jared said after Cooper walked away, "but he's not saying."

"I can find out from Mason," Mallory said, pulling out her phone.

"Or better yet, you can ask him in person." Quinn used his chin to direct her attention toward their friend the fire chief, who'd arrived with his girlfriend, Jordan. She was Gigi's best friend, so there was bound to be more info forthcoming.

Mason and Jordan greeted the others before making their way to Mallory and Quinn. He'd become one of their closest friends and would be serving as one of Quinn's groomsmen tomorrow.

"There's the happy couple," Mason said.

"We want the skinny on Gigi and Cooper, and we want it now," Mallory said.

"Uh, I've been sworn to secrecy by my beloved," Mason said.

"Oh, come on!" Mallory protested. "Someone knows what happened."

"You'll have to hear it from him," Mason said. "I'm not talking, or Jordan will cut me off."

"Honestly... Are you that far gone?"

"Yep. Ready for the big day?" Mason asked, apparently eager to change the subject.

Quinn had no doubt that Mallory would get the details during her next EMT shift.

"So ready," Mallory said, beaming with happiness.

After losing her first husband suddenly years earlier, she'd told him she never expected to get married again until they found each other. So much had happened since Quinn had accepted Jared and Lizzie's offer to be the medical director for their senior care facility. He'd come close to saying no, fearing the confines of island life, not to mention living close to family members for the first time since he joined the army after medical school. He liked doing his own thing and valued his privacy, but living near Jared and Lizzie had been fun. They left him alone. He left them alone. And when they were together, it was always a good time. He'd found a friend in his younger brother and a delightful extra sister in Lizzie.

And then he'd found Mallory, and his entire life changed.

"You're quiet," Mallory said to him between conversations with family and friends.

"Just thinking about everything that's happened since I came out here to work with Jared and Lizzie and how I almost said no to their offer."

"That would've been tragic."

He kissed her temple. "Indeed." Looking down at her, he said, "This time tomorrow..."

"I can't wait."

"Me either."

LAURA LAWRY WAS WORKING the front desk at the Sand & Surf Hotel when one of her guests, Piper Bennett, returned from an outing in town. Laura did a double take when she realized Piper's face was bruised and her lip was bleeding,

Laura rushed around the registration counter to provide assistance. "Oh my God! What happened?"

"I... A guy... He..."

"Shhh, okay. You don't have to talk about it if you don't want to."

With the poor woman trembling violently, Laura helped her into the sitting room off the lobby.

"We need to call the police, Piper."

"No," she said, blinking back tears. "I can't."

"The chief of police is my close friend. He'll know what to do. Please let me call him. Whoever did this to you shouldn't be allowed to get away with it."

Piper folded shaking hands in her lap.

Laura forced herself to stay quiet, to give the other woman a chance to wrap her mind around the fact that she was a victim of a crime. She would've rendered first aid, but after having been through this before with Owen's mom the night she arrived on the island, Laura knew it was important to let the police see the woman's injuries.

"If you're sure that's what I should do..."

When she'd checked in the day before, Piper had struck Laura as a sharp, intelligent woman. She suspected shock was dulling her senses at the moment, making her uncertain.

"It's the right thing."

Piper nodded and tightened her folded hands.

"I'll be right back."

Laura went to her office off the lobby and put through the call to Blaine's cell phone.

"Hey, Laura. What's up?"

"I have a guest staying at the Surf who's been attacked. I'm not sure what happened, but she's bruised, her lip is bleeding and she's obviously in shock."

"I'm on my way."

"She's hesitant about police involvement."

"I understand. We'll take good care of her. Be there in a few."

"Thanks, Blaine."

As Laura stepped out of her office, her husband, Owen, came down the stairs with their three children in his arms. How he managed to carry them all was a constant source of amazement to her.

"Ready to go to the party?" he asked.

"I don't think I can go."

"What's up?"

Laura quickly filled Owen in on what'd happened. "She told me yesterday she was in need of a getaway after her fiancé canceled their wedding and dumped her. And now this... Blaine is on his way."

"That's awful."

"I need to stay with her."

"Of course. I'll take these guys over to Evan's for a little bit. They can blow off some steam with their cousins."

"I'll meet you there if I can."

He kissed her. "Keep me posted."

"I will." After kissing him and her kids and seeing them off, she rejoined Piper in the sitting room. "Can I get you a drink of water or anything?"

She shook her head. "No, thank you."

Laura sat with her while they waited for Blaine. Fortunately, he didn't make them wait long. When she heard voices in the lobby, Laura went to greet him and Jack Downing from the state police.

"We were together," Blaine said.

"I don't want to overwhelm her. She's pretty shook up."

"I'll wait out here," Jack said.

Laura gestured for Blaine to follow her into the sitting room. "Piper, this is Blaine Taylor, chief of the Gansett Island Police Department. Blaine, this is Piper Bennett, a guest here."

"Hi, Piper," Blaine said, taking a seat across from her.

"Th-thank you for coming."

"Of course. Can you tell me what happened?"

Piper glanced at Laura.

"I can leave you two to talk."

"No! Please don't go."

Laura sat next to Piper. "I'm right here, and I'll be right here for as long as you need me."

Piper broke down into gulping sobs.

They waited until she'd collected herself by taking a series of deep breaths. "Just when you think things can't get any worse."

"I'm so sorry this happened on our island," Blaine said.

"It was my fault. I was acting out by partying with strangers. I went to his room, knowing I shouldn't be doing that, and when he attacked me..."

"This was not your fault, Piper," Blaine said. "Going to a man's room isn't an invitation to be attacked, but I do have some good news for you."

"What's that?"

"If you can tell me where you were when this happened and what room it was, we'll be able to find him and arrest him for assaulting you."

"It... It was the Harborside. Room thirty-two."

"And his name?"

"Chris."

"Hang on for one second." Blaine got up and left the room, returning a minute later. "The state police will pick him up."

Piper dropped her head into her hands, her shoulders shaking with sobs. "I never should've gone with him, but he seemed so nice and sweet. I just needed to feel better."

"Did he rape you, Piper?" Blaine asked gently.

She shook her head. "I managed to fight him off and get out of there before he could."

"Do you require medical attention?"

"I... I don't think so."

"I'd like to take some photos of your injuries for the record," Blaine said. "It will help us to make a case against him."

"Okay," Piper said hesitantly. She grimaced as Blaine took several photos.

"I'll get our first aid kit." Laura retrieved the kit from her office and brought it to the sitting room. She gently tended to Piper's cut lip and applied ointment. She offered an ice pack for the bruise blooming on Piper's face. The incident brought back memories of the night Sarah had arrived in even worse condition after being beaten by her now ex-husband.

"Thank you," Piper said, pressing the ice pack to the bruise.

"I'm going to need you to take me through it, from the minute you met him until you escaped his room," Blaine said, pulling a notebook and pen from his pocket.

Laura sat with Piper while she told the story of what'd happened.

Blaine asked a lot of questions, and Piper answered every one of them, her resolve seeming to strengthen with every passing minute.

By the time they emerged from the sitting room an hour later, Jack had returned.

"He's on ice at the station," Jack said. "Asking for a lawyer."

Piper wrapped her arms around herself. "What will happen now?"

"We'll charge him with assault and attempted sexual assault," Blaine said. "At some point, if it goes to trial, we'll need you to testify. But that won't be for a while."

"Thank you for coming and for acting so quickly," she said, her gaze shifting to take in Jack, too.

"I'll be in touch," Blaine said.

"If there's anything we can do," Jack said, handing Piper his card, "please feel free to call."

"Thank you both."

"Yes, thank you." After Laura saw them out, she turned to Piper. "Come upstairs to my place. I'll make us some tea."

"I don't want to put you out any more than I already have."

"You're not." Laura put her arm around the other woman, feeling as if they were friends after the last couple of hours. "I want to help if I can."

"You've been so kind. I really appreciate it."

"I'm so sorry this happened," Laura said as they walked up the stairs to her apartment on the third floor.

"It's not your fault."

"Before we go inside, I need to tell you… I have three kids. I have no idea what our place looks like."

"Please, don't worry about it. I have nieces and nephews. I know what it's like with little ones."

"Here goes nothing." Laura used her key in the door and stepped into an immaculate space. "And once again my husband proves why he's the best." Not only had Owen changed all three kids and gotten them ready to go out, but he'd cleaned the apartment, too. It even smelled fresh and lemony.

"I'm impressed," Piper said.

"Have a seat. Make yourself comfortable. And I don't even have to warn you to watch out for hidden peanut butter sandwiches."

Piper smiled as she sat on the sofa.

Laura made tea for both of them, giving thanks once again for the gas stove that had served them well during the power outage, and carried the mugs to sit with the other woman.

"Thank you." Piper took a tentative sip, wincing when her sore lip connected with the edge of the mug. "You've gone above and beyond."

"It's no problem at all. We're always on duty and happy to do whatever we can for our guests."

"My grandparents used to stay here. There was a couple named Adele and Russ who they were friendly with. Do you know them?"

"They're my husband's grandparents. They live here on the island."

"It's wonderful that they've kept the business in the family."

"The hotel was their wedding gift to us."

"Wow."

"Anyway, enough about me. What can I do for you? Is there someone I can call?"

"No, I don't want to call anyone. They're already worried enough about me."

"I was thinking about you after you checked in yesterday. I was once exactly where you are… Only I was actually married when I found out my new husband was still hooking up with women on a dating app."

Piper's eyes widened with shock. "How did you find out?"

"One of my bridesmaids saw him and made a date with him under another name, thinking it had to be a joke. But it wasn't. I found out shortly after that I was pregnant."

"Okay, you win."

Laura laughed. "It's not a competition. I only tell you this to let you know that despite how it might seem at the moment, you will get through this. I promise you will."

"That's good to know. What happened today was so not me. I don't do random hookups. Not that there's anything wrong with that. It's just never been my thing."

"You didn't do anything wrong. You must've had some fun with him before you agreed to go to his room."

"We had so much fun. He made me laugh, which I wouldn't have thought possible. It felt good to laugh, to feel desired again. It was stupid. I know better than to take those kinds of chances."

"I'm going to continue to tell you that it wasn't your fault until you believe me."

"That might take a while," Piper said, wiping away a tear.

"You're welcome to stay here as long as you need to. Take whatever time you need to heal and figure out your next step. We're happy to have you."

"That's very kind of you." She placed her teacup on the table. "Thank you again for the support, the friendship, the tea. I appreciate it more than you know."

Laura hugged her. "I'll check on you in the morning. In the meantime, call extension thirty from any of the house phones if you need me during the night. Please don't hesitate to call."

"I won't. Before I go, one quick question."

"Sure."

"What's the story with Jack the hot cop?"

Laura laughed. "Is he a hot cop? I hadn't noticed."

"Liar. No one is *that* married."

"Haha, very true. I may have noticed once or twice that Jack is a very hot cop, but don't tell my husband I said that."

"Your secrets are safe with me."

"He did give you his card if you need anything..."

"I don't think I'm in the right headspace to need anything from him. But it's nice to know that guys like him and Blaine and your Owen are out there."

"I don't think his offer came with an expiration date," Laura said with a cheeky grin. "If you don't have anywhere to be, you ought to stick around for a while. You never know what's going to happen on Gansett Island."

"Since I quit my job to move to where my supposed-to-be husband lives, I don't have anywhere to be at the moment."

"We can keep you busy here, if you're interested in hanging out for a while. This is the point in the season where my college helpers start to leave me shorthanded, so if you think you might be interested, let me know."

"I'll think about that. Thanks again, Laura. I'll see you in the morning."

"See you then."

Laura walked her to the door and watched her go, shoulders hunched. She imagined she'd looked a lot like that when she came to Gansett for her cousin Janey's wedding. That was the week she met Owen, and everything changed. She hoped that Piper would find someone who loved her the way she deserved to be loved—maybe even Jack, the hot cop. How funny would that be? One thing was for certain—her ex-fiancé was obviously a fool.

She sent a text to Owen to let him know she was free and to ask if she should meet him at Evan's.

Jon is melting down. We're heading home soon. I can handle them at home if you want to come for a bit.

I'll see everyone tomorrow at the wedding. Text me when you get here, and I'll come down to help herd babies.

Will do.

Being alone in the apartment was such a rare thing that Laura took advantage of the opportunity to put her feet up on the table and read a magazine for the thirty minutes she had before Owen texted to tell her they were home.

She went downstairs, said hello to Tara, the college student who was minding the front desk, and went outside to walk around the hotel to the parking lot in the back where Owen had parked the navy blue SUV they'd bought earlier in the summer. Toting three little kids around required a big vehicle.

Her little Jonathan's face was red and his eyes wet. "What's the matter with my sweet boy?" she asked as she freed him from his seat.

"He was out of sorts the whole time," Owen said.

Laura kissed his forehead. "Probably the heat getting to him."

"I hope that's all it is," Owen said.

Poor Owen seemed stressed.

He carried Joanna and Holden while Laura followed him up the stairs with Jon and the diaper bag over her shoulder. After seeing three little ones through baths and bedtime, their exhausted parents crawled into bed.

"What happened with the guest?" Owen asked.

"She reported the attack to Blaine and Jack, and they arrested the guy."

"I'm glad they got him. I hate that things like that can happen here."

"Blaine would tell you our little island isn't immune from assholes."

"That's for sure."

"How was the party?"

"It was great. Wait until you see Evan's new house. It's unbelievable."

"I can't wait to see it. Are Mallory and Quinn excited?"

"You know them. They're kind of low-key, but they were smiling all night."

"I sent her a text to apologize for missing the party."

"I told her you had a situation with one of the guests, or you would've been there."

"I feel so sorry for Piper. The poor girl is going through an awful breakup, and then this had to happen. I invited her to stay for as long she'd like and even offered her a job if she wants to work."

"That's nice of you, hon."

"I've certainly been where she is. I was thinking earlier about the day after Janey's wedding. Remember?"

Owen turned on his side and smiled as he smoothed the hair back from her face. "How could I ever forget the day I found you outside this hotel, standing in the pouring rain, looking like a little girl lost?"

"I was *so* lost then."

"So was I, and I didn't even know it until you found me."

"It's amazing how one of the worst days of my life turned into one of the best. I'll never forget those early days we spent here together when I was so sick and pregnant with another man's child, and you were right there for me the whole time. And when you decided to stay with me for the winter…" Laura fanned her face. "Most romantic thing ever."

Smiling, he said, "I wasn't even trying to be romantic. I just knew I couldn't leave you."

"Maybe Piper will find her Owen on Gansett Island."

"Wouldn't that be something?"

Laura thought of what Piper had said about Jack, but kept it to herself for now. "Sure would."

CHAPTER 34

For most of Monday, Dan Torrington had played phone tag with the attorney representing Kyle and Jackson's father.

"You have to understand," the attorney said when they finally connected while he was at Mallory and Quinn's party. "My client only recently learned that their mother had died. He wants to be sure his sons are being well cared for."

Dan had walked away from the others to take the call, fearing that Seamus would actually have a stroke if they didn't get this worked out soon. "From all accounts, he was nowhere to be found when she was alive. The boys don't even know him. I assume that was by design on her part. And not for nothing, a court saw fit to give her full custody. I also assume there were good reasons for that."

"He had some difficulties and made mistakes he regrets."

"If I run his record, what am I going to find?" Dan asked, already knowing the details but wondering whether the lawyer would be honest with him.

"You'll find he had some trouble earlier in his life, but he's moved on from that."

"What kind of trouble are we talking?" Dan asked.

"He battled drug addiction for years and did some time for possession. He's off probation now with a good job and a home that he owns. He was still battling addiction and on probation during the years he was with Lisa, but he hasn't been in any trouble since he got out of jail."

"I appreciate you being honest with me, but you have to understand that my clients have provided a good home for the boys and have helped them through the difficult loss of their mother. Disrupting them at this point wouldn't be in their best interest."

"He wants to see his sons."

Dan had held off on presenting Seamus's plan until it became clear that they were at a stalemate. "I have an offer for you, and I want to be clear—this is the only offer we're going to make. My clients have full custody of the boys as well as the resources to fight for them if it comes to that. The boys' mother, who had full custody, chose my clients—not yours—to raise them after she died. You and I both know that any judge would respect the provisions their late mother made for them."

"Okay, what's your offer?"

"The O'Gradys are willing to allow him to visit them, but not as their father. They would be told he's a friend of theirs who wanted to meet them. They'd allow him to visit twice a year, and when the boys are older, they'd be told who he really is and be offered the opportunity to have whatever relationship with him they chose to have."

"That's an awfully big ask."

"It's a big ask for him to show up at this point making demands when those kids don't even know him. Where's he been for the last seven years?"

"I'll present the offer to him and get back to you."

"We'll look forward to hearing from you."

Dan had no sooner ended the call when Seamus pounced. "What'd he say?"

"He's going to take your plan to his client. The father had some drug issues and did time for possession. He was still using and was on probation when he and Lisa were together."

"Ah," Seamus said. "That explains a lot. What did the attorney say when you told him our plan?"

"That it was a big ask, but I pointed out that him showing up after all these years making demands is a big ask, too."

"Sure as fuck is."

"In his defense, he didn't know until recently that Lisa died."

"He has no defense. Where's he been all this time?"

"I said the same thing. I also made it clear that you have both the resources and the wherewithal to fight him."

"Damn straight. Most of the time, I try to pretend that my lovely wife isn't loaded, but I wouldn't hesitate to ask her to pay for something as important as this."

Carolina curled her hands around Seamus's arm when she joined them. "I would gladly pay for anything that would keep those boys with us."

"Ah, love," Seamus said. "You shouldn't sneak up on me that way."

"Why not when you do it to me all the time!"

"She does have a point."

Dan laughed and gave Seamus's shoulder a squeeze. "I know it's futile to tell you not to worry, but I really think it's going to be okay. He doesn't have a leg to stand on, and he knows it. The attorney knows it, too, which is why he agreed to take the plan to his client. I'll let you know the second I hear anything from him."

"I'm sure it makes a hell of a difference to have you representing us," Seamus said. "The other guy must've been, like, *seriously*? *The* Dan Torrington? That right there tells them we're not fucking around."

"Oh, he knows we're not fucking around. I've got you covered. I'll be in touch tomorrow. And now I'm going to go find *my* lovely wife. You guys try to have a nice evening and get some sleep. I feel very confident that everything will be fine."

"Thanks, Dan," Carolina said. "We really appreciate you."

"Happy to help. This is totally my thing, making sure the law works the way it's supposed to. Have a good night."

"You, too," Seamus said.

Dan left them and went to sneak up on Kara, who was talking to Linda McCarthy, Tiffany Taylor, Janey Cantrell, Grace McCarthy, Sydney Harris, Abby McCarthy and Maddie McCarthy, who was stretched out on a lounge.

Kara startled and then relaxed when she realized it was him. "I've told you to quit doing that," she said with amusement in her voice. "He loves to scare the crap out of me."

"Evan does that, too," Grace said. "What's up with that?"

"We like how you swoon with fear and then fall into our arms," Dan said, earning an elbow to the gut from his beloved.

Dan gasped and then laughed. His wife didn't suffer fools, especially him.

"Was that the attorney you've been waiting to talk to?" Kara asked him.

"It was. All good for now. More to come tomorrow." With his lips close to her ear, he said, "Want to call it an early night? I'm exhausted."

She looked back at him with a cute little smile that he loved so much. "Are you exhausted or horny?"

"Am I allowed to be both?"

"I suppose so. Let's say our goodbyes."

That he got to leave every party for the rest of his life with the beautiful Kara Torrington was the best thing to ever happen to him. *She* was the best thing to ever happen to him. As he watched her laugh and talk with their friends as she said good night, he felt like one lucky son of a bitch to be going home with her—and to be expecting a baby with her.

Life was good and only getting better with every day he spent with Kara.

CHAPTER 35

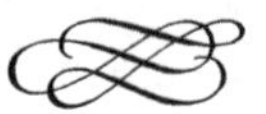

"I'm worried about how tense you are," Carolina said as they watched the boys run on the lawn with Thomas, his cousin Ashleigh, and Ethan. Burpy was in hot pursuit as usual.

"I'm better now that Dan talked to the lawyer. It's good that they know we're willing to do whatever it takes to keep them with us."

"Like you said, getting a call from Dan Torrington sends a certain message."

"Sure as hell does. We're fortunate to have him on our side."

"Which is why it's probably safe to get some sleep tonight."

"I'll do my best. This whole thing has made me realize just how much those two little scamps have come to mean to me."

"You already knew how much they meant to you. And they know it, too. They see the way you rush home from work to take them fishing or on some other kind of adventure. They see it in the way they have your full attention all the time and how you include them in everything you're doing. They hang on your every word and watch you intently. You've become the most important person in their lives."

"You're right up there with me, love."

"They love me. I know that. But they *worship* you, and it's the most wonderful thing I've ever seen. They couldn't have a better father, and they'll never ever choose anyone else over you, no matter what happens with this guy. They'll remember who was there for them when they needed him most."

"Ah, love, you're going to make me weepy."

"Then I'd better get you out of here before you embarrass yourself."

"Probably not a bad idea." Seamus whistled for the boys, and they came running, as they did whenever he called for them. When he'd married Carolina, who was sixteen years his senior and the mother of a grown son, he'd known he was sacrificing fatherhood to be with his true love, and that'd been fine with him if he got to be with her.

Never in his wildest dreams did he imagine the family they had now, with Kyle and Jackson as well as Carolina's son, Joe, his wife, Janey, and their kids, PJ and Vivienne. Joe had told them a few days ago that they were planning to go back to Ohio so Janey could continue vet school. They would miss them something awful, but they'd be back for Christmas break and home next summer.

With two little monkeys clinging to him, Seamus followed Carolina as they said good night to the others and promised to see them tomorrow at the wedding.

Later on, after he'd supervised two dirty boys through baths and bedtime and let the dog out one last time, Seamus settled into bed next to Carolina and stared up at the ceiling. After losing his younger brothers—one to cancer and the other to an overdose—many years ago, Seamus had all but given up on praying, but he dusted off his faith and said a silent prayer to the Almighty, asking for His help in keeping those boys with him and Caro, where they belonged.

Only then did he close his eyes and try to get some rest.

CHAPTER 36

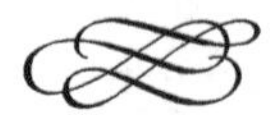

According to her father, Mallory Vaughn was "as Irish as Paddy's pig." At least on the McCarthy side of the family. Her late mother had been English and Dutch, and since finding her father two summers ago, Mallory had filled in the blanks on his side of the family. Despite her Irish heritage, however, Mallory wasn't superstitious, which was why she spent the night before her wedding with her fiancé.

Looking over at Quinn as he slept with one arm tossed over his head, she gave thanks for the twisted strokes of fate that'd brought him into her life.

After her first husband had dropped dead at age twenty-seven, Mallory hadn't expected to marry again. But meeting Big Mac McCarthy had changed her life in every possible way and had led her to Dr. Quinn James, who'd be her husband by the end of this day, which was also their forty-first birthday.

When they'd hatched the plan to get married on their joint birthday, Mallory and Quinn had intended to host a casual cookout in her brother Mac's backyard. But when Big Mac had heard that plan, he'd asked permission to host her wedding at the beautiful Chesterfield Estate.

"I missed every single thing with you," he'd said. "Please let me do this for you."

He had been so sweet and so sincere that Mallory had tearfully agreed to let her father give her a wedding. Because their birthday fell on a Tuesday this year, they had no trouble booking the sold-out Chesterfield a month ago. Since then, Lizzie James and her team had pulled off a miracle. Mallory couldn't wait to see the final result of weeks of meetings and phone calls and emails. With Lizzie in charge, she had no doubt it would be beautiful.

She kissed Quinn's shoulder and then his lips, rousing him out of a sound sleep.

His golden-brown eyes popped open, and a smile lit up his handsome face. "Morning, beautiful. Happy birthday. Happy wedding day."

"Happy everything," Mallory said, sighing when he wrapped his arms around her. In all the years since she'd lost Ryan, she'd never felt as at home anywhere than she did with Quinn. "We need to get moving if we're going to catch a meeting before the festivities start." They made a point of beginning every day with an AA meeting in town and rarely missed a day.

"How about we take a run and end up there?"

"Sounds good to me."

They got up, got dressed in running clothes and headed off, taking the long way into town and arriving at the nondenominational church where the meeting was held each morning. Their regular group, which included their good friend Mason Johns, was already seated in the circle when they came in, wiping off sweat. The heat wave continued unabated, but the basement where they held the meeting was cooler than most places.

Their friends offered a round of applause for the bride and groom that embarrassed Mallory and Quinn. They grabbed bottles of water off the refreshment table and sat away from the others, since they were sweaty from running.

Nina, the woman who facilitated the group, gestured to them. "This is what dedication looks like, my friends. On a day when Mallory and Quinn certainly have better things to do, they're taking the time to come here first. Let that be an example to all of us on days when we feel like we have better things to do than come to a meeting."

After the meeting, they jogged home at a slower pace to shower and have breakfast, which consisted of cold cereal with milk from the cooler they'd kept iced for days.

"I'm seriously over this power failure," Quinn said. "It'll be nice to get off this island for a few days and rejoin the twenty-first century already in progress."

"Indeed," Mallory said. "I'm starting to miss hot water, even if cold showers are the only thing keeping us from melting. Thank goodness they have a generator at the Chesterfield so I won't look like a sweaty mess in the wedding pictures."

"You couldn't be a sweaty mess if you tried."

"No need to pour on the charm, Dr. James. In case you hadn't heard, I'm somewhat of a sure thing where you're concerned."

"That doesn't mean I'm going to lower my game." Quinn came over to where she was standing at the kitchen sink. "I'm going to get out of your hair now so you and your girls can do your thing. But I just wanted to tell you, before things get crazy, that I love you and that loving you has been the highlight of my life so far."

"Let me turn around so I can see your handsome face."

He stepped back so she could turn and link her arms around his neck.

"That might be the nicest thing you've ever said to me, and you've said a lot of nice things to me."

"I mean it. You're the best thing to ever happen to me, and I can't wait to be married to you."

"Same to you. I was thinking this morning about how when Ryan died, I thought that was it for me when it came to love and marriage. Until there you were, giving me a second chance to have it all."

He kissed her and hugged her tightly for a long time. "Don't be late."

"Wouldn't dream of it."

Quinn was going to Jared's house to hang out with his brothers until it was time to go to the Chesterfield. Mallory was getting ready at home, with her sister, Janey, serving as her maid of honor and her cousin Laura and longtime best friend, Trish, rounding out the wedding party. Trish, an accomplished photographer, would also be taking the photos. She was due to arrive on the ten-thirty boat, after shooting a wedding the night before in Boston.

Mallory hadn't seen her since before she first came to Gansett and couldn't wait to introduce her friend to Quinn, Big Mac, Linda and the rest of her new family. For many years, Mallory's family had consisted of her mother and Trish. Now she had more relatives than she could count and loved being part of the big McCarthy family.

Janey and Laura arrived together, along with Cindy Lawry to do Mallory's hair. She'd intended to wear it down, until the heat wave struck, and she and Cindy had changed their plan, deciding to go with an updo in deference to the heat.

A few hours of primping later, Mallory stood before the full-length mirror in the Chesterfield's bridal room and gave herself a critical once-over. "Not bad for a forty-one-year-old broad," she said, laughing at her own choice of words.

"Not bad at all," Big Mac said from behind her.

Mallory caught his eye in the mirror and smiled the way she did every time she saw him. All her life she'd wondered what her missing father might be like, but nothing could've prepared her for the reality of him. He was one of the most wonderful people she'd ever known, and she loved him dearly.

"You look beautiful, honey," Linda said when she came in behind her husband. "That dress is perfect on you."

"Thanks to Tiffany," Mallory said of the dress that was sexy but classy, too, with spaghetti straps holding up a slinky bodice. It had minimal adornments and a two-foot train, but the showstopper was the back, which was completely bare. Tiffany had convinced her the dress would be sensational, and she was right. Mallory loved it and was fairly certain Quinn would, too. "Only she could help me order the perfect dress online and have it fit like a dream."

"She sure is good at what she does," Linda said. "The two of you got it just right."

"I'm glad you like it." Mallory held up the skirt as she walked the short distance to a table where Lizzie had left two boxes of flowers. She removed a wrist corsage from one of the boxes and gestured for Linda to come to her. "Since my own mom can't be here today, I was hoping you might be willing to stand in for her." Mallory slid the corsage onto Linda's wrist.

"I'd be honored," Linda said, visibly moved.

"I'll never have the words to properly thank you for the way you've welcomed me into your family. You never so much as hesitated to make me feel a part of things when you certainly didn't have to, and I'll *always* be thankful to you for that."

Linda hugged her carefully. "We had no idea that we were waiting for you to make our family complete. You made it easy to welcome you, and we love you very much."

"You're going to make me cry," Mallory said, smiling.

Linda laughed as she dabbed at tears. "You started it."

The two women shared a laugh as they made good use of the tissues Big Mac handed them.

"I'll see you downstairs," Linda said, leaving the room after kissing them both.

"That was very nice of you to include her that way." Big Mac looked as handsome and polished as she'd ever seen him, in a dark navy suit, a white dress shirt and light blue tie that complemented his blue eyes.

Mallory pinned a white rose boutonniere on his lapel and then looked up at him. "I love her as much as I love you. Thank you for this beautiful day."

"We love you, too, and it's our pleasure to give you this day. Thank you for letting me be your dad today and always. Linda was right, you know. We were waiting for you to make us complete." He kissed her cheek. "Happy birthday, my sweet girl, and all the best of everything to you and your new husband."

Mallory dabbed at new tears, hoping she hadn't completely ruined her makeup. "Thanks, Dad." Calling him that would never get old.

Lizzie came to the door, looking beautiful in a red dress with her blonde hair in a bun. "We're ready when you are, sis."

Mallory was delighted to be getting her as a sister-in-law and Jared and Cooper as brothers-in-law. She didn't know the rest of the James family as well as she knew them, but looked forward to spending time with the rest of them.

Big Mac extended his arm to Mallory. "You don't need anyone to give you away, but I'm so glad you asked me to."

She tucked her hand into the crook of his elbow. "I waited a long time to have a dad. I'm not missing anything else with you."

QUINN HAD THOUGHT he was prepared for this day, to see Mallory as a bride on the arm of her beloved father. But as he stood on the lawn of the Chesterfield with the ocean behind him, he realized nothing could've prepared him for how beautiful and happy she looked as she and Big Mac appeared on the back porch.

Janey, Laura and Trish had preceded them down the aisle, with one of Trish's colleagues handling the photos for this part of the day. Quinn had met Mallory's longtime friend via FaceTime chats, but hadn't met her in person until today.

Mallory's dress was a knockout, but he hadn't expected anything less from his gorgeous bride. She wore her dark hair up and never looked away from him as she came toward him on the arm of her dad.

With Jared, Cooper and Mason standing by his side and their bow tie-clad dog, Brutus, sitting at his feet, Quinn fought his emotions as he reflected on the journey that had brought him to this day. He'd fought a difficult struggle to regain mobility and to overcome the deep depression and alcoholism he'd descended into after losing a leg in combat.

When Jared and Lizzie had invited him to Gansett Island and offered him the job as medical director at the senior facility, he'd expected to give the place a year, maybe two, before moving on to something else. That was before he met Mallory and found a whole new life for himself. Now he couldn't imagine anything better than every day with her at home and at work.

In the front row, Mason's girlfriend, Jordan, was providing FaceTime coverage of the wedding for his parents and sisters, who'd been unable to change their plans in time to make it to the island. Quinn was thankful to Jordan for thinking of the idea and making it possible for the rest of his loved ones to be there in spirit.

Big Mac walked Mallory to the end of the aisle formed between two rows of seats. He kissed his daughter's cheek and shook Quinn's hand. "Be happy, you two."

"That's the plan," Quinn said as he took hold of Mallory's hand.

After Big Mac had gone to sit with his wife in the front row, Quinn took a good long look at his beautiful bride. "Holy smokes," he said. "Stunning."

She surprised the shit out of him by turning to show him the entirely bare back of her dress, shooting him a smile over her shoulder.

Quinn fanned his face dramatically as everyone else laughed.

Mallory's uncle Frank, a retired Superior Court judge, presided over the service. "Friends and family, near and far," Frank said, with a gesture toward Jordan and the FaceTime call with Quinn's family, "we're gathered today for the marriage of my beautiful niece Mallory Vaughn and Dr. Quinn James. Today is also our bride and groom's birthday. They were born on the same exact day, which makes this an occasion forty-one years in the making."

Quinn glanced at Mallory in the same second she looked at him, both of them smiling at the many twists of fate that had delivered them to this moment.

"Mallory and Quinn have written their own vows, and I'm just here to make it legal," Frank said. "Mallory, when you're ready."

She handed her colorful bouquet to Janey and then turned to face him, taking hold of both his hands and looking up at him with the love and affection that had become essential to him. "I remember the day we met so vividly," she said. "It was a summer day a lot like this one, only not quite as hot. We were out running when we encountered a motorcycle accident and discovered we both had medical training. I recall being so impressed by your cool competence during a crisis, but I also happened to notice that you were rather hot."

Quinn laughed even as he felt his face flush with embarrassment.

"Neither one of us could've known what that first meeting would lead to or how intertwined our lives would become over the next few months. I was in a bad place that day, having just been laid off from a job that I'd loved for fifteen years. I was grappling with a lot of emotion over the secrets my late mother had kept from me while getting to know my father and my new family. By all accounts, that was probably the worst possible time for me to meet the man of my dreams. But there you were, and I'm so thankful our paths crossed that day and that we've gotten to spend almost every day since then together. Everything about us feels so right to me, so easy, so perfect. I love you more than anything, and I look forward to forever with you."

Quinn used his sleeve to blot the tears she'd caused with her heartfelt words. "I remember that day, too. I remember every detail, especially how lucky our patient was to have a trauma surgeon and emergency room nurse first on the scene after he crashed his motorcycle. It's hard to imagine anyone getting luckier than that, and yet I was the one who truly got lucky that day. You say you were in a bad place when we met. So was I. I'd sunk into a deep, dark place after losing my leg, and it was only after

I met you that I was able to share that pain with someone and truly begin to recover. You not only helped to save that motorcyclist's life that day, but you saved mine, too, in so many ways, mostly by giving me a reason to smile, to hope, to make plans, to fall in love and have this amazing new life that I never expected to have." Quinn leaned his forehead against Mallory's. "You make it so damn easy to love you, and I can't wait for everything with you."

They were both a weepy mess, but he couldn't have cared less about that as they laughed through their tears and exchanged rings before Frank made it official.

"By the power vested in me by the State of Rhode Island, it's my great pleasure to introduce for the first time as husband and wife, Dr. Quinn James and Mrs. Mallory Vaughn James. Dr. James, you may kiss your bride."

"Don't mind if I do," Quinn said.

CHAPTER 37

Sitting on the stupid lounge chair that allowed her to be part of everything while on bed rest, Maddie McCarthy watched her sister-in-law Mallory marry Quinn James as she timed pains that could no longer be called anything other than contractions. This couldn't be happening, she thought, not in the middle of Mallory's wedding, not when the twins weren't due for another month.

Thankfully, Mac was occupied with watching his sister get married while keeping their kids from distracting from the proceedings, so he'd yet to notice his wife grimacing in pain every eight minutes. He was going to lose his mind when he realized she was in labor.

Maddie withdrew her cell phone from her purse and sent a text to her sister, Tiffany. *As soon as the ceremony is over, please come here. I need you.*

After Quinn kissed Mallory for what seemed like five full minutes, they turned to face their guests, smiles stretching across their faces as they made their way down the aisle to rousing applause for the newlyweds.

Carrying her daughter Addie, Tiffany stood and rushed over to Maddie. "What's wrong?"

Maddie took a second to see where Mac was and saw him holding Hailey and baby Mac while he said something to Thomas.

"Maddie?"

She looked up at her sister. "I'm in labor."

"No, you're not."

"Yes, I really am." As if to make her point, a contraction picked that moment to take her breath away. She breathed through it as she broke into a cold sweat.

"Since when?"

"About an hour, since right after we arrived. Is Victoria here?"

"She is. Do you want me to get her?"

"Yeah, and hurry up about it." The last thing Maddie wanted to do was anything to disrupt Mallory's day, but her baby girls apparently had other plans. She was terrified about them arriving early. They were supposed to be in Providence long before the due date, not once again on a remote island, and once again without electricity. She forced herself to remain calm, to not give in to the hysteria bubbling just below the surface.

Tiffany returned with Victoria and without Addie.

"Did your water break?" Vic asked.

"Not yet, but for the last hour, I've been having contractions that I thought were Braxton Hicks, but they're eight minutes apart."

"I need to get you inside and examine you. Do you think you could walk?"

"I can do it."

Victoria and Tiffany helped her up.

"Be careful, Tiff," Maddie said to her sister, who was also pregnant.

"I'm fine," Tiffany said. "Don't worry about me."

Maddie whimpered when another contraction made it so she couldn't move.

"That was only six minutes after the last one," Tiffany said.

Time seemed to slow down at that point as others on the lawn began to notice something was going on. Maddie happened to look up and catch the exact moment when her husband realized something was wrong. The stricken look on his face told the story for both of them. This couldn't be happening again.

Victoria and Tiffany got Maddie up the stairs and into a main floor sitting room.

"I don't have gloves," Victoria said.

"It's fine," Maddie said.

"Let me go wash my hands before I touch you."

When she returned, Victoria performed a quick exam and discovered Maddie was fully effaced and six centimeters dilated. "Holy crap. You don't mess around."

"What's happening?" Mac asked when he came into the room, his face ashen from shock and dismay.

"I think we're going to have some babies today," Victoria said.

"No," Mac said, shaking his head. "It's too soon."

"The babies seem to have other ideas, and it's not at all unusual for twins to arrive early," Vic said. "Tiffany, go get your husband. Tell him to hurry."

While Maddie contended with another contraction, Mac rushed to her side, dropping to his knees beside the sofa where she was stretched out. "I'm so sorry," she said as tears rolled down her face. "This came out of nowhere. I was fine earlier." But when she thought about it, her belly had felt tight for days, her back had been aching worse than usual and she'd been nauseated. Perhaps she'd been in labor without realizing it.

"Stop," he said. "Don't be sorry. You and I don't know any other way to have babies except the crazy way." He kissed her and brushed away her tears. "Everything will be fine. I promise."

She appreciated him making an effort to stay calm for her when he was probably losing his shit on the inside.

Blaine came into the room, consulted with Victoria and made the decision to call for the life flight helicopter to get Maddie to Providence, in case neonatal intensive care was required for the babies. With the power out on the island, they didn't want to take any chances.

Just hearing those words, *neonatal intensive care*, was enough to spike the expectant parents' combined anxiety.

The next few minutes were a blur of activity and people and contractions and tears and then finally the roar of the helicopter as it landed on the lawn adjacent to where the wedding had just been held.

As soon as she and Mac were loaded on the chopper, the overwhelming need to push became impossible to stop. The first of their twin girls was born as the chopper lifted off from Gansett Island. Her sister followed twelve minutes later as they approached the landing pad at Women & Infants Hospital in Providence.

The medics on the chopper told them the girls were small but breathing on their own, which was a huge relief, even if there were still other concerns.

Maddie was exhausted after giving birth to the twins and couldn't seem to stop crying from the powerful wallop of emotion and the whiplash from how it'd happened. So much for the calm, rational, well-orchestrated delivery they'd planned. If there was any silver lining to the babies coming early, perhaps it was that they wouldn't have to be separated from Thomas.

"Are you all right?" Maddie asked Mac.

"I can't believe you're asking *me* that. You're the one who just gave birth to twins on a helicopter."

"I know how these crazy births freak you out."

"The only thing I care about is that you and the girls are okay. And the good news is, this is the last crazy birth we'll ever have."

"Snip, snip," Maddie said, referring to the vasectomy he was scheduled to have in September.

"After this, I'm actually looking forward to the snip," Mac said.

"Go with the girls," Maddie said when they landed. "Stay with them until you know how they are and then come find me."

He bent to kiss her. "You're amazing every day, but today in particular. I love you so much. Thank you for all our children." And then he was gone in a rush of action that had the babies being whisked off the chopper in a flurry of movement and people and urgency that had her anxiety flaring again.

As Maddie was taken off the helicopter, she prayed their babies would be okay.

MAC WAS in a state of disbelief. One minute he'd been telling his son that he had to be quiet for a few more minutes, and the next he noticed something happening with Maddie. The realization had left him briefly frozen in shock before he shook it off, passed his kids to his parents and ran for his wife.

The episode reminded him too much of the night Hailey was born in the middle of a tropical storm, on an island, in a power failure, with the only doctor off-island—or so they'd thought until Janey remembered her ex-fiancé, Dr. David Lawrence, was in town. That time, David had come to the rescue. Today, the helicopter had saved them.

If you'd told him that morning he'd be at Women & Infants, separated from Maddie and waiting to hear that his daughters were okay, he wouldn't have believed it. But nothing in his life with Maddie had ever been predictable, so why should this be?

He paced in the hallway outside the NICU, his phone chiming with texts from worried friends and family on the island, and waited impatiently for news about the babies. He took only one call, from his father.

"Hey."

"How are you holding up, son?"

"I'll be better when we know how the babies are."

"They were already born?"

"On the helicopter."

"Holy shit. Is Maddie okay?"

"She seems fine. She was incredible, as always. We're just waiting to hear how the babies are. They're a month early..."

"I know, but we have to have faith that they're going to be all right."

"Hope so."

"Let me know the minute you hear anything, and I'll keep everyone else in the loop."

"Will do. Tell Mallory and Quinn we're sorry for disrupting their day."

"Don't give it another thought. She already said they're thrilled to share their birthday and their wedding day with the twins. Everyone just wants to hear that the girls and Maddie are fine."

"I'll be in touch as soon as I know anything more."

"We'll be waiting to hear, and don't worry about the kids. Mom, Francine and Tiffany have them covered. Ned and I are helping, too."

"As long as you and Ned are on the job, they're in good hands."

"That's what I say, too!"

Leave it to his dad to make him laugh, even when he was stressed. "Love you, Pop."

"Love you, too, son. Tell Maddie we're thinking of her and the girls and that we already love them."

"Will do."

Mac waited another hour, pacing from one end of the small room to the other a thousand times before a nurse came to find him.

"Mr. McCarthy?"

"Yes."

"Would you like to see your daughters?"

"Yes, please, and if possible, I'd like to know how my wife is doing."

"I'll see what I can find out."

Mac followed her into a room where he was provided a gown, mask, gloves and even booties to put over his shoes. When he was ready, she led him into a large room full of incubators and beeping machines. The girls were in side-by-side incubators, hooked to numerous machines and monitors, a sight that completely overwhelmed him.

"Are they…"

"They're doing remarkably well," the nurse told him. "Baby number one is just over five pounds, and her Apgar scores are good. Baby number two is four pounds, six ounces. Her scores aren't quite as good, but it's nothing to worry about. We want to keep them here for observation for at least forty-eight hours to monitor their oxygenation and other vitals."

"So, they're going to be all right?"

"They're going to be just fine. Do they have names?"

Filled with relief, Mac nodded. "The older of the two is Emma Linda, and her sister is Evelyn Francine."

"Those are beautiful names. I'll make a note on the charts."

Mac stared down at two perfect little faces. "They're named for their grandmothers and great-grandmothers."

"They appear to be identical."

He wiped away tears that were equal parts relief, joy and love. For the fifth and sixth time, counting the son they'd lost, he was amazed by how his heart expanded to make room for more people to love. Identical twins. He and Maddie had read about how identical twins were truly a miracle, whereas fraternal twins tended to run in families.

For the longest time, he stared down at their two miracles until the nurse returned with news about Maddie.

"I spoke to the charge nurse on her floor, and she's doing well but receiving a transfusion, as she lost quite a bit of blood after the birth. She's in room four twelve if you want to go check on her."

"Thank you so much. Would it be okay if I took some photos of the babies for their mother and the rest of our family?"

"Of course."

Mac focused the camera on his phone on their cute little faces and got two good photos that didn't include any of the wires or monitors. "I'll be back in a little while."

"We'll be here."

Outside the NICU, he removed the protective gear and stuffed it into a garbage can before making his way to the elevator and the fourth floor, anxious to get to Maddie and see for himself that she was really okay. He came off the elevator and went straight to the nurses' station. "I'm looking for room four twelve. Madeline McCarthy?"

"Third door on the left."

"Thank you." He went into the room, which she had to herself, at least for now. Maddie was asleep, but all he could see was how pale she was. A bag of blood hung from the IV pole, along with other bags of medication. Mac sat next to her bed and covered her cold hand with his. He watched her sleep for a long time before she finally stirred, opening her eyes and turning to him.

"How are they?"

"They're beautiful." He found the photos he'd taken and showed them to her.

Maddie stared at the little faces, going back and forth between the two pictures.

"The nurse said they're doing great. Emma is just over five pounds, and Evelyn is four pounds, six ounces. They're breathing independently, and their scores were mostly good. She said they also appear to be identical."

"Which means they'll be working against us as soon as they realize their power."

"Damn, I hadn't thought of that."

"I had a lot of time on bed rest to think about what it'll be like to have three teenage girls at the same time. I may require medication to get through that."

"We'll get you whatever you need."

"I'm so relieved to hear they're doing well. I was so scared because they were early. Now that I know they're okay, I can start to celebrate never being pregnant again. I've had enough of bed rest, lounge chairs, sore boobs and watching other people take care of my kids. This is a big moment for me, the end of an era."

"The team and I couldn't be prouder of our amazing captain. She's done some great work these last few years." He leaned over the bed rail to kiss her. "But honestly, Madeline, on a freaking *helicopter*?"

She laughed. "I had to top Janey having Viv on the ferry."

"Well played, my love. You know that topping Janey is a blood sport in the McCarthy family."

"I do know that, and I took one for the team by having the babies on the chopper. You have to admit, it makes for a good story."

"I'll only admit that I'm glad it's over and the three of you are okay. That's all that matters. Can I send a picture of the girls and their names to the family?"

"Please do. They must be going crazy with worry."

"I talked to my dad a while ago and told him the babies had been born and that all is well."

"I hope you asked him to apologize to Mallory and Quinn for us, too."

"He said no apology necessary. She already said how cool it is that she and Quinn will be sharing their big birthday and anniversary with their nieces."

"That is cool."

"He also said that the kids are fine with them and your parents and Tiffany."

"That's good. I hope they weren't too traumatized by the whole thing."

"I'm sure they're fine with everyone telling them not to worry." He kissed the back of her hand, being careful to avoid the IV needle. "You know what else is kind of cool about having the babies early?"

"Gee, I can only imagine..."

Waggling his brows and smiling, he said, "We're six weeks closer to *you know what.*"

"'You know what' isn't happening until that thing gets snipped, so while we're here, maybe you ought to move up your appointment if you're hoping to get back in the saddle any time soon."

"He really hates it when you call him a *thing*," Mac said, affecting a pout.

"Tell him to stop being a baby and get himself snipped. No snippy, no nookie."

"All right, all right, I hear you. You don't need to enjoy this so much."

"Are you *kidding*? I've been pregnant for most of the time we've been married. You're damn right I'm going to enjoy this, and I fully expect you'll milk it for all it's worth and be a great big baby over it."

"They're gonna take a *knife* to my junk. How do you expect me to feel?"

"I just pushed two pumpkins through my hoo-ha. I win. Today and every day. So, if you're looking for sympathy for what will be a tiny little scab on your pee-pee," she said, using Thomas's word for penis, "you're gonna have to look elsewhere."

"I had no idea I was married to such a mean and nasty woman."

Maddie lost it laughing and then winced from the pain. "You know exactly who you're married to."

"Yes, I do, and I wouldn't trade her for anything, even when she's being mean to my pee-pee."

"Tell him I'll make it up to him, after the snip."

"Ohhh, he just stood up to cheer that news. He can't wait. He's missed you."

Maddie rolled her eyes. "It doesn't take much to make him stand up and cheer."

"Not when you're around, and especially when he's had to be on his best behavior for *months*."

"Oh, the *sacrifices* he's made."

"Glad you recognize them."

"I do recognize them. Thanks for all you did to get me through this pregnancy. I know it wasn't easy on any of us."

"Please don't thank me. You're the wonder woman of this story. Thank *you* for my two perfect little girls."

"Let me see the pictures again."

They spent the rest of the day talking to Thomas and Hailey on the phone, napping, looking at pictures, checking on the babies, exchanging texts with family and friends and giving thanks for their perfect, *complete* family.

CHAPTER 38

After they got the good news from Mac in Providence, Ned went looking for Francine and found her in one of the stylish little rooms on the Chesterfield's first floor. She was sitting with baby Mac, who'd been frightened by the helicopter and had been inconsolable after his parents left. The baby was asleep in his grandmother's arms, and Francine was singing softly to the little guy while he slept.

Ned leaned against the doorframe and watched her with the baby. She was such a wonderful grandmother, and it gave him pleasure to see her with the kids. She'd told him how much she'd missed with her daughters because she'd had to work so much to support them after her jackass husband left. It also gave him pleasure to know that because of his years of house flipping, she'd never have to work another day in her life. She could devote herself to her daughters and their *seven* grandchildren, with an eighth one on the way.

He pushed off the doorway and went to join her on the sofa, taking pains not to jostle the baby. For a guy who'd never had kids of his own, Ned had become rather adept around babies and little ones.

"Have you heard anything?" Francine asked, her brows furrowed with worry.

"Big Mac talked ta Mac." Ned kept his voice down so he wouldn't disturb little Mac. "Emma Linda and Evelyn Francine were born on the chopper."

"Oh my Lord! Are they all right?"

"The babies are small but healthy, and they're keeping 'em in the NICU fer at least forty-eight hours to keep an eye on 'em."

"And Maddie?"

"Mac said she lost some blood durin' the delivery, so they're givin' her a transfusion. But otherwise, she's fine."

"Thank goodness," she said, exhaling a deep sigh of relief.

Ned pulled out his phone to show her the photos Mac had sent. "This beauty is our Emma, and this little doll is Evelyn, named in part for her Grandma Francine."

"It's so sweet that they did that," Francine said, looking a little misty. "My mother's name was Evelyn."

"I remember that, and Linda's mother was Emma."

"They did good."

"Sure did, and it's such a relief ta have it done and over."

"You said it. Hopefully, we only have to go through this one more time."

"Hope so, 'cause it's awful tough on the grandparents."

"That's for sure. You're the best grandpa ever. The kids are so lucky to have you."

She twisted him up in knots when she said things like that. "I'm the lucky one ta have this amazin' family at my age."

"And the best part is we get all the fun and none of the work."

"That's right," he said, chuckling. "We're still gonna keep tryin' ta have one of our own, though, right?"

She giggled as her face turned bright red, the way it always did when he said things like that. He loved to make his pretty redhead blush. "Stop it."

"Never." He'd waited a lifetime for her and their family, and he planned to enjoy every second with them.

CHAPTER 39

"I've been thinking," Frank said as he twirled his fiancée, Betsy, around on the dance floor.

"About?"

Frank looked down at her, marveling as he did every day about how lucky he was to have found her after so many years alone since he lost his young wife, Joann, to cancer. "About you and me and making some plans."

"What kind of plans?"

"The kind where we get to spend forever together."

"I thought we'd already made those plans."

"I'm talking about making it official and tying the knot. What do you think?" He'd surprised her over breakfast one morning last spring with a ring and a proposal that'd made her cry. Since then, they'd had a busy summer and hadn't given much thought to a wedding.

"I think that's a fine idea. With all the weddings you preside over, it's probably time you got one of your own."

"My brother Mac has offered to get internet ordained so he can preside over our wedding when we're ready."

"Of course he has," she said, laughing. "He'll do a great job."

"I told him he can only marry me and you. I don't need him cutting into my gig."

"No one can replace you, Your Honor. When are you thinking to have this so-called wedding of ours?"

"That depends on what kind of shindig my bride wants."

"Small and simple works for me."

"That'd work for me, too, except there's nothing small or simple about the McCarthy family."

"True. What do you propose?"

"What do you think about late October at the Wayfarer? The season will be over, the tourists will be gone, and we'll have the place to ourselves again."

"You mean *this* October?"

"Yep. I don't want to wait another year to marry you, Betsy Jacobson. It won't take much to pull it off for this October."

"That's like *two months* from now."

"Right, and all you need to do is buy a sexy dress and show up on time. I'll talk to Nikki and figure out the rest."

Before she could respond to that, a collective shout erupted from the other guests.

"What's going on?" Frank asked his son Shane, who was dancing with his wife, Katie, next to them.

"Power's back on."

"Oh, thank goodness," Frank said.

"Thank goodness is right," Katie said. "I can't take another night in this heat without air conditioning."

"She's not kidding," Shane said, smiling at his wife. "She's a bear without her AC."

"Guilty as charged," Katie said. "It's been awful."

The air in the big room already felt cooler as the air conditioning came back on with full force.

"Shane, will you please talk to your father and tell him we can't plan a wedding in two months' time?"

Katie laughed. "Oh, how fun!"

"He's crazy," Betsy said, rolling her eyes.

"He's crazy about you and can't wait to be married to you," Frank said.

"Aww," Katie said. "That's so sweet, and we can pull off a wedding in two months. Of course we can."

"You're all crazy," Betsy said.

"And you already know that," Shane said, smiling. "So, you'd better be sure before you marry into the circus known as the McCarthy family."

"Hey," Frank said. "Don't try to talk her out of it. I'm already batting way above my pay grade with her."

"That's true," Shane said, his expression deadpan.

While Frank sputtered with outrage, the others laughed.

Owen and Laura came over to see what was so funny.

"Dad's trying to talk Betsy into marrying him in two months," Shane told his sister. "She thinks he's crazy, and Dad is worried about me trying to talk her out of it. Oh, and she's way out of his league. Now you're caught up."

"A wedding in two months?" Laura asked. "That's doable. Let's have it at the Surf. I'll take care of everything. Late October is beautiful."

"Every one of you is crazy," Betsy said, her dark eyes glittering with amusement, "but I know when I'm outnumbered. Laura, I'd love to get married at the Surf. Shane, there's nothing you can say to talk me out of marrying your dad. Sorry. And, Frank, stop thinking you're marrying up. I'm the one who's marrying up. Not only do I get you, but I get your beautiful family, too. So yes to late October, yes to everything, including the McCarthy family craziness."

Surrounded by friends and family, Frank put his arms around her and kissed her as if they were alone, while the others whooped and hollered. He couldn't wait to make her his wife.

CHAPTER 40

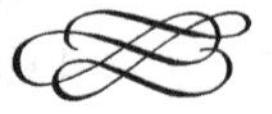

"Best day ever," Quinn said as he danced with Mallory. "I can't believe you're finally my wife. I can't believe I finally *have* a wife."

"Better late than never, I guess."

"I was waiting for you. I'd never met anyone I could imagine being married to until you bowled me over." He punctuated his sweet words with an even sweeter kiss that had their guests cheering for the bride and groom.

"If I can have everyone's attention," Jared said when the song came to an end.

Quinn put his arm around Mallory to escort her back to their seats at the head table. "I'm sorry for whatever's about to happen here."

Mallory laughed. "I can't wait to hear what he has to say."

"Lizzie and I want to thank you all for being here today and extend our thanks to our hosts, Mr. and Mrs. McCarthy, for this beautiful day in honor of my brother Quinn and his lovely bride, Mallory. I've rarely met two people who were more destined for each other, right down to sharing the same exact birthday, not to mention the same profession. From the day he met you, Mallory, Quinn was a different man. He was brighter, lighter, funnier, happier. He smiled more than I've ever seen him smile, and he's never stopped smiling in all the time you two have been together. I've begun to believe he never will."

The sound of a screaming baby had everyone shifting their gazes to the doorway, where a young woman stood with a baby, a frantic look on her face. "I'm… I'm sorry. Lizzie. I need Lizzie."

"Excuse me," Lizzie said as she got up from her seat and rushed over to the other woman.

"Who's that?" Quinn asked Jared.

His brother's jaw clenched with tension. "Someone that Lizzie is helping out." Jared appeared to make an effort to shake off the interruption. "Anyway, where was I? Ah, yes, I was about to say here's to Quinn and Mallory." He raised a glass of champagne in a toast to them.

"May you have many happy years together."

Other guests toasted the bride and groom, while Jared's gaze was fixed on the doorway as tension rolled off him in waves.

Quinn wondered what was really going on.

LIZZIE GUIDED Jessie into one of the salons and closed the door. She noticed right away that Jessie's face was puffy, and her eyes were red from crying. The baby was in equally rough shape, her little body trembling from crying so hard.

"I'm so sorry to interrupt your brother-in-law's wedding," Jessie said, her voice catching on a sob. "But I can't do this. I can't take care of this baby. I have no idea what I'm doing, and nothing I do satisfies her. I need you to take her."

Lizzie couldn't bring herself to move. Here was the line in the sand that she'd promised Jared she wouldn't cross. "I can't take her, Jessie. She's your daughter."

"I don't want her. I know that makes me sound like a monster, but I never wanted her. I made one mistake… *One mistake.*" She broke down again into sobs that shook her petite frame. "Please, Lizzie. You could find a good home for her. I know you could."

"I… I can't do that. I just… I just can't."

"I'm sorry to do this to you. I appreciate everything you've done for me, but I'm afraid I might harm her." She placed the baby on the sofa, kissed her forehead, dropped the diaper bag on the floor and pushed by Lizzie on her way out of the room.

"Wait! Jessie, wait!" In the time it took Lizzie to pick up the baby and follow Jessie, she was already out the door to a cab waiting in the driveway. In a state of complete shock, Lizzie watched the cab leave as she tried to calm the hysterical baby.

It was almost as if the little one understood what was happening.

She was still standing in the doorway to the main entrance ten minutes later when Jared found her.

"What's going on?" he asked from behind her.

"Jessie… She said she can't take care of the baby, that she's afraid she might harm her." Lizzie turned to face him.

His expression conveyed shock when he saw her holding the baby. "No way, Lizzie. There's no way…"

"I know, that's what I told her. But she put the baby down and rushed out of here so quickly that I couldn't stop her from leaving. That was about ten minutes ago."

"We need to go after her."

"We can't leave the wedding." Although it was his brother's wedding, Lizzie had seen to many of the details personally and needed to be there.

Jared thought about it for a minute. "I'll ask Cooper to go." He turned and walked away, striding purposefully back into the ballroom to find his younger brother.

Lizzie snuggled the baby closer, bouncing her carefully, instinct kicking in as her heart raced with implications and dismay. "Don't you worry about anything, sweetheart. We'll make sure you're well taken care of."

Jared returned with Cooper in tow and handed him the keys to the Porsche. "She left in a cab about fifteen minutes ago. Find her. If she's not at our place, check employee housing at the Beachcomber."

"What if she's not at either place?" Cooper asked.

"Check the ferry landing. We can't let her leave the island. God knows how we'll ever find her if she does."

"I'm on it," Cooper said.

"Bring her back to the house if you find her. Text me, and we'll meet you there."

"What if she doesn't want to come?"

"Call me," Jared said. "We'll come to you."

Blaine Taylor joined them in the foyer. "Everything all right?"

"Not really," Jared said, filling the police chief in on what had happened.

"Did you catch the number on the cab?" Blaine asked Lizzie.

"I didn't, but it was yellow."

"Sedan or station wagon?"

"Sedan."

Blaine removed his cell phone from the inside pocket of his sport coat and put through a call. "This is Chief Taylor. I need to know who just made a pickup at the Chesterfield and where they went." He listened for a second, nodded and said, "Thanks. Appreciate the info." To Jared and Lizzie, he said, "They went right to the ferry landing."

Jared checked his watch. "Son of a bitch. She probably made the six o'clock boat. What the hell do we do now?"

"I can call Child Protective Services on the mainland," Blaine said. "But they probably won't get here until tomorrow."

"No," Lizzie said. "Don't call them. She'll end up in the system. I've seen that happen too many times to let it happen to her." She'd ran a homeless shelter in New York City before they were married and was well versed on such things. "Jessie asked me to take care of her, and I'm going to do it. She'll come back when she's had a minute to calm down. She'll come back."

"Lizzie, we're not keeping her."

"I never said anything about keeping her. I said I'm going to take care of her until her mother comes back."

"And what if she never comes back? What then?"

"I don't know, but we can't let her go into the system, Jared."

"Why can't we? That's what the system is for."

"Because we can take care of her."

"She's not our child, Lizzie, and you know as well as I do why this is a very bad idea."

Lizzie couldn't stand to see him so upset, but she also couldn't bear the thought of this poor helpless baby sent to strangers. Not when she had the wherewithal to care for her. "We'll just take care of her until we find out more about Jessie."

"Could you guys give us a second, please?" Jared asked Blaine and Cooper.

"Of course," Blaine said.

The two men walked away, seeming relieved to let Jared and Lizzie have their argument in private.

"We can't do this, Lizzie, and you know why."

"We can help Jessie until she gets herself together."

"We've already helped Jessie, and this is the thanks we get? She dumps her baby with us and expects us to take care of her? I don't agree with this at all. What's going to happen when she comes back and wants her baby, and you've already fallen in love with her? What happens then?"

"I don't know! I just know that she asked me to help her, and I'm going to."

"Regardless of what I want?"

"Of course I care about what you want. You know I do."

"I'm asking you to turn this baby over to Blaine and let him figure out what to do. That's his job."

The baby had fallen asleep in her arms, her little body warm against Lizzie's chest. "I don't want to do that. I want to give Jessie time to realize she made a mistake, without involving the authorities."

"You know I'll support you in anything you want. Always. But this is too much. I'm scared to death you're going to get your heart broken in this situation, and it hurts me to see you hurt."

"I love you so much for that, Jared. I really do. But I can't turn this helpless child over to the authorities and live with myself. I need to do this for the baby and for Jessie."

She understood why he felt the way he did. Of course she understood. It was a huge risk for her to get involved in a situation like this. But she was already involved and would stay that way until she was sure the baby was safe.

He put his arm around her and went through the motions of being supportive, but she could tell by the tension radiating from him that he was deeply conflicted. And with good reason.

CHAPTER 41

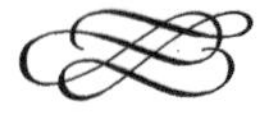

Dara was sitting on the back deck at the McCarthys when Oliver returned from a trip into town.

"Good news," he said. "The power's back on."

"That's great news. Should we go to the lighthouse?"

"I suppose we could."

"I feel bad leaving without saying goodbye to Mac and Linda." They had been at his daughter's wedding all afternoon.

"We could leave them a note and invite them to dinner at the lighthouse to thank them for having us."

"That's a good idea. Let's do it."

She followed him upstairs to pack their things and strip the bed. They put the sheets and towels in the washing machine and started it.

Back downstairs, Oliver found a pad of paper and a pen.

Mac and Linda,

The power came back on, so we decided to get out of your hair. We can't thank you enough for having us and for your friendship since we arrived. If you're available, please come to dinner at the lighthouse tomorrow night, any time after six. If tomorrow's not a good day, just give us a call or text to reschedule. The sheets and towels are in the washer. Thank you again for your hospitality.

"How should I sign it?"

"Sincerely, Oliver and Dara."

He signed the note and left it on the counter by the coffeemaker. Then they ushered Maisy out of the house and drove "home" to the lighthouse. Oliver had been there earlier in the day to open the gate, which remained open as they drove through.

"I may as well lock up," he said, putting the car in Park to get out and lock the gate.

As Dara gazed at the lighthouse, she realized she already felt different about coming there than she had on the day they arrived. The time with Mac and Linda had been priceless, a thought she shared with Oliver when he got back in the car.

"I agree. Being with them was very special."

"Will you keep going to the morning meeting?"

"If you don't mind."

"I don't mind. You seemed to enjoy it."

"I did, and you seem to like spending time with Linda and her grandchildren."

"I wouldn't have thought that was something I'd want to do, but I was enjoying her company so much that when she asked me to go with her, I did. And I really loved it."

"Look at us, making friends and having fun, and that's in just the first couple of days."

"I like it here. I feel less… raw here."

"Me, too. Doesn't hurt that the people are great."

"No, it certainly doesn't."

It was the longest conversation they'd had since Lewis died and almost seemed like the old days, when she'd felt like she could talk to him about anything. Oliver had been her best friend since the day they met, and she'd missed him. Before tragedy struck, she would've thought that nothing could ever come between them. She knew better now.

They got out of the car, and Maisy ran ahead of them toward the door. Even she seemed to have new pep in her step after a few days on Gansett Island.

Dara followed Oliver and Maisy into the lighthouse and up the spiral staircase to the second floor where they unpacked their bags and got settled. "Home" was another thing that had been fraught with peril since they lost Lewis. Dara couldn't bear to be in their home without their little boy. She'd stayed with her parents for months, until their financial reality became such that they had to sell the house anyway.

Before they came to Gansett, they'd been basically living separate lives within the same small space. Here, they had no choice but to sleep together, since there was only one bed. Maybe that would turn out to be a good thing. It couldn't get any worse, that was for sure.

Dara sat on the edge of the bed, not sure what to do with herself now that they were back at the lighthouse. When Maisy nudged her, she scratched between the dog's ears.

"Do you feel like going into town and having dinner?" Oliver asked.

The hope she heard in his voice and saw in his expression moved her to agree. "Sure, that sounds good."

His face lit up with the first genuine smile she'd seen in longer than she could remember.

"Hey, Ol?"

"Yeah?"

"Come here, will you?"

He came to sit next to her on the bed.

"I was just wondering if we could..."

"What, honey?"

"Would you hold me?"

For a second, he seemed so surprised that she wondered if he'd do it. But then he wrapped his arms around her, drawing her in close to him and reminding her that he'd always been her home. She breathed in his familiar scent and rested her head in the curve of the shoulder where she fit so perfectly.

"Feels good," he said.

"Feels like coming home."

"Dara..."

"Don't. Let's just do this and go to dinner and celebrate a good day. Okay?"

"Yeah, that's okay."

CHAPTER 42

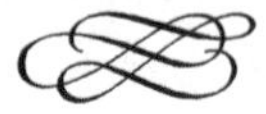

It'd taken nearly a week to schedule an appointment with Kevin McCarthy, but now that the appointed time was upon them, Sydney was unreasonably nervous. Seeing a therapist reminded her too much of the unbearable months that'd followed the deaths of her first husband and their two children.

That it'd nearly happened again was too much for her to handle, and no amount of therapy was going to change that.

"Luke filled me in on why you're here," Kevin said.

His warmth and calming demeanor helped to set the tone, but the agitation inside her was hard to ignore.

"How about we start by you telling me about the accident from your point of view and how you've been feeling about it in the months since."

The last thing in the world Sydney wanted to do was revisit the terrifying minutes in which she'd been convinced that she and Lily were going to die. Only the eager, expectant, hopeful look on Luke's face could get her to bare her soul this way. She ran through the events of that awful day, from leaving home with Lily and stopping to see a client on the way to lunch with Luke at the marina.

"One minute we were sitting in the parking lot, and the next we were in the water. I banged my head on the steering wheel, so it took me a minute to snap out of it to realize we were in big trouble. And then Luke and Big Mac were there. They couldn't get the doors open, and the windows wouldn't work." She paused before forcing herself to continue, to give voice to the unspeakable. "The one thing I remember most vividly, other than the panic and disbelief, was thinking that at least this time I'd get to go with her."

Luke gasped.

"I'm so sorry." Syd took his hand as she looked at him. "I hate that I thought that and not about what it would do to you to lose us, but it was such a relief to know I wouldn't have to live through the nightmare again."

"That's a very heavy thing to have to carry around with you, Syd," Kevin said.

"All of it is. That it even happened in the first place…" She shook her head. "That's the part I just can't get past. My daughter almost *died* because of me."

"I've tried and tried to help her see that it wasn't her fault," Luke said.

"What if we put a different spin on it?" Kevin asked. "What if we allowed Syd to take the full blame for what happened—"

Luke's eyes flashed with anger. "Wait a minute."

"Hear me out." Kevin held up a hand to stop his friend. "Syd, you're already blaming yourself. You believe it was completely your fault, so what if we all agree that, yes, it was? You left the car in Drive, your foot slipped off the brake and hit the gas, and you're the one who put that car in the water. Does it make you feel any better to have other people agree with what you already believe?"

"It does," Syd said, surprised to realize that was true. "I feel like I need to be held responsible."

"Okay, then we'll hold you responsible, but only if you agree to consider the possibility that you made an honest mistake. Anyone who's ever driven a car understands the potential for costly mistakes. A foot slips off a brake, and a car accidentally rolls through an intersection. Those are honest mistakes, as opposed to a driver who thinks they can easily make it through a caution light before it turns red, or that it's no big deal to exceed the speed limit. Do you see the difference?"

"I do, and logically, I know I'd never do anything that might put Lily in harm."

"Isn't that the most important thing?" Kevin asked. "That you'd never do anything that might harm her? If you're able to take responsibility for causing the accident, then you have to also accept that it wasn't intentional."

"Wow, he's good," Syd said to Luke.

He grunted out a laugh. "He sure is."

Kevin smiled as he leaned forward. "You can do both things at the same time—blame yourself for the accident while acknowledging that you'd never do anything to harm your precious daughter. You're a wonderful mother, Sydney. Anyone who knows you can see that."

"She's everything to me," Syd said softly. "My beautiful second chance."

Luke gave her hand a squeeze.

"You know better than anyone how things can happen, things we never see coming," Kevin said.

"I hate those things."

Kevin chuckled. "If you hate the bad things, then you have to also hate the good things. We've all lived long enough by now to know this life gives us plenty of each, and there's often much more good than bad."

Sydney thought about that for a minute. "I suppose you're right."

"I propose we continue to meet and talk it out until you start to feel better about what happened," Kevin said. "However long it takes, I'm here."

"Thank you, Kevin. I'll admit that I was reluctant to come, but I can see how it might help to air it out."

"Then that's what we'll do."

KEVIN SAW them out half an hour later, pleased by the progress they'd made in their first meeting. He'd sent them home with instructions to continue talking about what happened that day, how it had affected them both and how they felt about it. In his years of practice, he'd found that giving voice to those feelings could help people to deal with them.

After he recorded his notes on their session and a few things he wanted to cover with them in the next one, he left the office to head home to his girls, eager to see them after an afternoon at the office.

When he got home, Chelsea was sitting on the sofa, breastfeeding baby Summer. Chelsea lit up when he came in, giving him a feeling he'd never felt before he'd had her. He kissed her and then Summer, whose eyes popped open and then danced with pleasure at the sight of her daddy.

"What's going on around here?"

"The usual after a good nap for both of us." Chelsea had talked about wanting to go back to work at the Beachcomber, but he'd encouraged her to take more time with the baby. She was so used to having to take care of herself that it had been an adjustment for her to let him take care of her.

They'd decided she'd go back a couple of nights a week next summer.

In the meantime, they were enjoying every minute with the baby girl who brought them such joy.

"How was work?"

"Good," he said, "but nothing is better than this."

Summer had wrapped her little hand around his finger, squeezing tightly, the way she always did.

"How would you feel about one more?"

Kevin stared at her. "Ah..."

Chelsea laughed right in his face. She did that a lot. "Not right this minute, but maybe in a year or so."

"I'm getting old."

"You are not. Age is just a number."

"I'm going to be fifty-four, Chels."

"I know that, but when I see Riley and Finn together, I want Summer to have that, too. A sibling close in age that she can grow up with and be best friends with the way they are."

"You do know how to keep me on my toes, Mrs. McCarthy."

"I can't let you get too comfortable," she said, smiling.

"Before we had Summer, I secretly thought I was insane for starting over with another family when my boys are almost thirty."

"It wasn't so secret. We all knew you were in a panic over it."

Smiling, he said, "Since she arrived, it's like none of that even matters. She's so perfect and so beautiful, and I'm completely in love with her. So, if you wanted to have another one, I'm fine with that. As long as we do it soon."

"We'll do it soon."

"I'm available to provide stud services on a moment's notice."

She lost it laughing. "Duly noted, stud."

"It's a good thing I love you so much," he said, kissing her.

"It's a very good thing."

CHAPTER 43

With the power back on, the scheduled island premiere of *Indefatigable* would go on as planned Friday night, which left Stephanie with the same dilemma she'd confronted in LA. On Thursday afternoon, she stopped by Charlie's house, hoping to get a minute alone with him.

She found him in the garage, setting up tools on the pegboard over the new workbench she and Grant had bought him for his birthday. He kept his silver hair in a buzz cut and was wearing a Gansett Island tank-style shirt that put his arm muscles and tattoos on full display.

"Hey," she said. "Hope I'm not disturbing you."

When he turned to her, his face lit up with a big smile that made his blue eyes sparkle. He smiled a lot these days and had mostly shed the hard edges he'd brought home with him from prison. "Hey, kid. Come in. And PS, it's not possible for you to disturb me."

From the time he first started dating her mom when Stephanie was eleven, she'd thought that everyone should be so lucky as to have a Charlie in their lives. He held out his arms to her, and she walked into his embrace. Being able to hug him any time she wanted never got old.

"It's looking good," she said of the workbench and arrangement of tools.

"Getting there."

"Where's Sarah?"

"Over at the hotel helping Laura with something." He tipped his head and gave her a probing look. He'd always been able to see right through her. "What's on your mind, Stephie Lou?"

She *loved* when he called her that. "The premiere."

"Ah, I wondered if that was it. I heard from three different reporters this morning before breakfast. I'll be glad when the hubbub dies down."

"Did you tell Grant that you've been getting those calls? He can ask the studio publicity people to deal with that."

"They're the ones that gave them my number."

"Oh crap. You want me to tell them to stop calling you?"

"Nah, it's fine. I give them a quote, and they go away."

"I wonder why they don't call me."

"Probably 'cause your husband told them to leave you alone. He's seen how tender you are about this. We all have."

"I'm not *tender*," she said disdainfully. "I'm just..."

"Pregnant? Hormonal? Emotional? Tender? All of the above?"

"Very funny, Charlie Bear."

"So all of the above, then, huh? Plus, a trip down Unpleasant Memory Lane on top of all that other stuff, and you've got yourself a predicament."

"Something like that. I want to be supportive of Grant and Dan and you and everyone involved in the telling of our story, but I just don't know if I can bear to relive it. I feel like we've traveled a million miles since then."

"We have. For sure. Sometimes I even forget about it, you know? Like it's noon before I remember I used to be locked up."

"That's good. I don't want you thinking about that."

"I'll probably always think of it. It's part of my story, just like you and your mom are part of my story. But I don't think about the bad stuff so much anymore."

"I don't either. There's so much better stuff to think about now, for both of us. That's why I've been kind of reluctant to reopen that door."

"Which is totally understandable. When I think about it now, I'm not sure which one of us had it worse—me on the inside or you on the outside fighting our battles by yourself."

"You had it much worse. At least I was free."

"Were you, though?"

Leave it to him to cut through the bullshit. Stephanie looked up at him. "Are you going to the premiere?"

"Don't know yet. Figured I'd decide the day of." He took her by the chin and gently compelled her to look at him. "Maybe we ought to go together and get it over with, hmm?"

"Don't do that for me."

"Who else would I do it for? I think you actually want to see this project that Grant has poured his heart and soul into over the last two years."

"I do. He's worked so hard. If it was about anything else…"

"I know that, and so does he. How about we make a date of it, you and me? I'll pick you up and even buy your popcorn."

Stephanie could always count on her Charlie Bear to make her laugh and to give her exactly what she needed. "Remember our very first 'date'?"

He thought about that for a second. "I'm not sure which one was first."

"You took me to see *The Little Mermaid*, and you said I could have any snack I wanted."

Nodding as he smiled, he said, "And you stood at the counter for so long trying to pick something that we almost missed the start of the movie."

"That was the first time anyone had ever told me I could have anything I wanted. I picked Milk Duds, and every time I've had them since then, I've thought of that, the first time my dad took me out, just me and him, and how special you made it for me. How special you made everything for me." She forced herself to look at him. "If you wonder why I spent fourteen years obsessed with getting you out of jail, it was because of the Milk Duds, because of *The Little Mermaid* and the dance classes you paid for and took me to and the things you taught me about bugs and nature and animals. It was all of it. You were *everything* to me, and you still are."

He took a few steps to close the distance between them, put his arms around her and gave her one of the Charlie Bear hugs she'd missed so much during the years they'd been apart. "You're everything to me, too, kid," he said gruffly. "Always have been, always will be."

"How about you pick me up at the Bistro around six thirty tomorrow?"

"It's a date."

CHAPTER 44

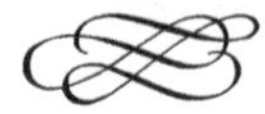

Seamus and Carolina had spent two agonizing days waiting to hear if the boys' father would accept their offer. Dan had called them Thursday night to say they had a deal, that Jace Carson had agreed to the plan that would allow him to see the boys twice a year. When they were both of age—or sooner if all parties agreed—they'd be told Jace was their biological father.

If he stuck around that long, that was.

In exchange for access to the boys, Dan had required Jace to sign a release that stated he wouldn't challenge the custody arrangements Lisa made before her death. It had been a great relief to Seamus and Carolina to hear that Jace had signed that document.

Jace had wasted no time in requesting his first visit, and he was due to arrive within the next few minutes. Seamus had arranged for Joe to take his afternoon runs on the ferry so Seamus could be home with his family. He'd spent a few hours online, getting to know the man who'd fathered the boys and had learned of a long struggle with drugs that'd briefly landed him in jail.

By all accounts, Jace had been clean and sober for some time and had become an advocate for others struggling with addiction. From photos posted to social media, Seamus learned that Jace had blond hair like his sons. In fact, Kyle looked just like him, which led Seamus to wonder if

Kyle would notice the resemblance. The boys were smart and bright, and not much got by them.

"If they figure it out," Carolina said when he shared his concern with her, "then we'll tell them the truth sooner rather than later. The only thing that'll matter to them is that they're safe and secure in their home with us."

From where they sat at the kitchen table, they could hear the boys running around outside with Burpy barking as he tried to keep up with them. They often joked that they never had to wonder where the boys were because they could always hear them and the dog.

"You don't think we're doing the wrong thing by not telling them the truth from the beginning, do you?" he asked.

"No, I think it's the right thing to wait. They've been through so much and have settled into their new life with us. Now isn't the time to do anything that would disrupt that."

"Helps to have the advice of a professional mother to rely upon."

"I don't know if I'd call myself a professional mother, but I do recall what it was like to move here with Joe after we lost his dad and how important it was to keep things on an even keel for him."

The sound of a car arriving outside had them moving quickly to go out to greet their visitor. Jace emerged from the back of Ned Saunders's cab, and the first thing Seamus noticed were forearms covered in ink. The boys were fascinated by tattoos and would certainly want an up-close look at Jace's.

Seamus could hear the boys and the dog playing on one of the paths that led into the woods that were their playground. They'd been given strict guidelines about how far from the house they were allowed to go and were good about doing what they were told.

Jace paid Ned for the ride and thanked him.

Ned gave a little toot and a wave before backing out of the driveway.

As Jace walked toward them, Seamus noticed that he moved like Jackson did, his stride almost impatient. He shook hands with Seamus and Carolina. "Thank you for having me."

Seamus appreciated the man's manners, even if he was predisposed to dislike him on sight. "I'd say it was no problem, but..."

"Oh, you're Irish."

"Aye, that's right."

The two men sized each other up, almost like prizefighters about to face off.

"The boys…" Jace said. "They're doing well?"

"They're doing wonderfully," Carolina said, "after a rough couple of months following their mother's death."

"I… I didn't know she was sick. I felt awful when I heard about what'd happened."

"It was a very difficult time," Carolina said. "But the Gansett Island community stepped up for her and the boys, and we got them through it."

"I'm sorry I wasn't here to help. I've had some… problems, but I'm better now. I understand it was a lot to ask to see them, but I only learned that Lisa had died when I tried to reach out to her about seeing the kids. I wanted to wait until I'd gotten my life together before I got in touch with her, and then I found out it was too late."

Jace seemed genuinely sad about Lisa's death. "This is a nice place you've got here," he said.

"We added on after we took in the boys," Carolina said, gesturing to the new part of the house. "We wanted them to have room to spread out."

"Are they here?"

"If you listen carefully," Seamus said, "you can hear them off playing in the trees. They love to be outside."

"I remember that from when they were little. Always wanted to be outside."

Seamus put his fingers in his mouth and whistled for the boys, who came running, as they always did when he called for them. He wondered how old they'd be when that stopped.

They burst through the brush, two towheads with sunburned noses and missing front teeth. Burpy was hot on their trail, barking as usual. Seamus often thought it was a good thing they didn't have close neighbors with all the racket the kids and dog made. The house where Lisa and the boys had lived was the closest one to them, and it was several hundred yards up the road. A new couple lived there now.

"Kyle, Jackson and Burpy, I want you to meet a friend of mine. This is Mr. Jace. Can you say hello?"

He held his breath, waiting to see if either of them would recognize the man, but they didn't seem to.

Both boys said hi and shook Jace's hand the way Seamus had taught them. They were working on making eye contact when they were introduced to new people. So far, the handshaking was going better than the eye contact.

Seamus could see that Jace was impressed by the handshakes and perhaps a bit emotional about seeing his sons for the first time in years.

"Can we please have a snack?" Kyle asked Carolina.

She'd been working on their please-and-thank-you game. "Sure," she said. "Let's go inside and wash our hands."

"Come on in," Seamus said to Jace. "Can I get you something to drink?"

"Just some water would be great. Thank you."

While Carolina supervised the boys washing up in the bathroom, Seamus poured three glasses of ice water, got out juice for the boys and cut cheese to serve with crackers and grapes.

The boys came out of the bathroom and dove into the snack like two savages who hadn't seen food in a year. "Easy, mates," he said. "We have a guest, and the polite thing is to let the guest go first."

"Sorry," Kyle said around a mouthful of cheese and cracker.

"No worries," Jace said, seeming amused by the boys.

Carolina joined them at the table, and over the next hour, Jace asked the boys about their life on Gansett Island, about their school, their friends, the TV shows they liked and their favorite food.

Seamus had to give Jace credit. He made a genuine effort to get to know the boys and truly listened to everything they had to say. And when he asked if they would show him their favorite toys, the boys were happy to lead the way to their new playroom that Seamus had told them to clean up earlier in anticipation of their guest's arrival.

"He seems like a nice guy," Carolina said when she and Seamus were alone in the kitchen.

"Aye, he is. I like how he gave them his full attention." Still wary, however, he went to check on them in the playroom and found Jace sitting on the floor while the boys showed him all their toys.

Though he was glad the visit was going so well, Seamus still felt out of sorts over the situation. Carolina had wisely said that allowing Jace into their lives meant giving the boys one more person to love them. He was no threat, or so Seamus told himself.

An hour later, Seamus drove Jace back to town to catch the last ferry off the island. They were both quiet on the short ride.

"Thank you so much for this," Jace said when they arrived at the ferry landing. "You'll never know what it means to me to be able to see them."

"I'm glad we could figure something out."

"It's obvious that they're very happy with you and your wife, and I'm not looking to upset them any more than they've already been. I'd like to give you my number just so you have it, and if you're inclined to send some pictures once in a while, I'll always be happy to get them."

"I can do that."

They exchanged contact info and then shook hands.

"You know," Seamus said, "I was prepared to hate you simply because you're their real father. But after having met you, I don't hate you."

Jace gave a gruff laugh. "Well, thanks for that. And by the way, it's very clear who they consider their real father, and from what I can see, they're lucky to have you."

"That's nice of you to say."

"I've made a lot of mistakes in my life, big mistakes that hurt a lot of people. I'll always be most sorry for the mistakes that hurt Lisa and my boys. I've learned in recovery that we can't undo the past. We can only try to do better in the future. That's my only goal."

"I can see that."

"And I can see my sons are happily settled with two people who love them very much."

"We do love them. They've changed our lives entirely."

"Thank you for stepping up for them and for Lisa when she needed you."

"Stepping up for them was the second-best thing I've ever done, after marrying my Carolina."

"Thanks again for having me."

"I'll be in touch."

Jace shook his hand and got out of the truck.

Seamus watched him join the line to get on the ferry, waiting until Jace presented his ticket and got on the boat before he pulled out of the parking lot and drove home, filled with a powerful sense of relief. After having met Jace and learned he was a decent sort of bloke, Seamus felt better about welcoming the man into their lives.

When he got home, Carolina was supervising the boys as they ate spaghetti and meatballs, their adorable little faces covered in sauce, as usual.

Carolina gave him a welcoming smile, and Seamus felt himself finally relax for the first time since they got the letter from Jace's attorney.

He took a seat at the table, and Carolina brought plates for both of them.

"Thanks, love." To the boys, he said, "Thank you for being so nice to my friend. He really liked you guys."

"He was nice," Jackson said around a mouthful of meatball. "Can he come back to play again sometime?"

"Aye," Seamus said. "He'll be back."

CHAPTER 45

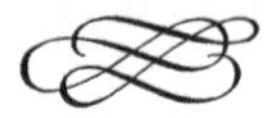

Late on Friday afternoon, Grant McCarthy was home alone when he received a delivery of flowers. "Thank you," he said to the young man who'd brought them from the island florist.

"Have a nice day."

"You, too." Grant took the vase of multicolored roses into the kitchen, placed them on the counter and then found the card.

Since we didn't know what to send a fancy award-winning screenwriter on his big night with the hometown crowd, we hope roses will do. We're so proud of you, Stephanie and Charlie and so sorry to miss the premiere. We can't wait to see the movie! Love you, Mac & Maddie + 5

Touched by the gesture and the sweet words, Grant put through a call to his older brother.

"Hey, bud," Mac said. "How's it going?"

"I should be asking you that. Thanks for the flowers. You guys didn't have to do that."

"Yes, we did. We feel bad about missing it."

"You've got the best possible excuse. I'll make sure you get your own private screening when you get back."

"We'll look forward to that."

"How are Maddie and the babies today?"

"Everyone's doing well. The girls are still in the NICU for the time being, but we're told that's a good thing because they can keep a really close eye on them there. They want to keep them another week or so, and then we'll move to Frank's house for another week so we can be close to the hospital if need be. That's the plan at the moment, anyway. Of course, we're dying to get back to the other kids, too."

"They miss you, but they're doing okay."

"Thank God for Mom, Francine, Tiffany, Kelsey and everyone else who has helped. It takes a village to have twins on the mainland when you have three little ones on an island."

"I can only imagine."

"Are you ready for tonight?"

"As ready as I'll ever be."

"How about Steph?"

"I don't know, she hasn't said much about it. I'm trying to play it cool with her. I don't want her to feel pressured to see it if it'll hurt her."

"Sounds like the best way to play it."

"I have to be honest. I've been kind of caught up in the details and so excited about the way it came together that I hadn't given enough thought to how it would affect her to see her story played out this way."

"She was foremost in your mind the whole way through, Grant. I have no doubt about that. It's an amazing story, and she and Charlie deserve all the praise and publicity they're getting—and so do you. I'm hearing there's lots of Oscar talk attached to this film."

"Ack, don't even say it. You'll jinx us."

Mac laughed. "I won't say it. I'll just wish you all the best."

"Thanks again for the flowers."

"Break a leg, bro."

"Give Maddie and the babies a kiss from us."

"Will do. Talk soon."

Grant took a shower, shaved and got changed into a dress shirt and khakis, which were much more in keeping with the Gansett Island vibe than the tuxedo he'd worn to the Hollywood premiere. He thought about stopping at the Bistro on his way to the theater, but decided not to because he honestly didn't want Stephanie to feel pressured.

Friday nights in August were busy at the restaurant, so she might not make it, and he was fine with that. After spending the better part of the last two years fully immersed in her story and Charlie's, Grant understood better than just about anyone how painful it might be for them to see the film.

He loved them both too much to ask more of them than they'd already given to make this project possible. Besides, Stephanie had offered to host the after-party at the Bistro, so she was probably overseeing last-minute details.

When he arrived at the theater, he was greeted by a crowd of family members and friends that included his parents, siblings, uncles, cousins, Dan and Kara Torrington, and just about everyone else he knew on the island. He couldn't think of anyone who wasn't there.

They applauded when he walked in, embarrassing him with their effusiveness.

Grant spent a few minutes greeting his guests before making his way to the stage in the front of the room. He'd thought a lot about what he wanted to say to this hometown group about Stephanie and Charlie and the film. When he had their attention, he stepped up to the microphone his brother Adam had helped him set up earlier.

The theater was rather basic, and as such, he'd enlisted Adam to make sure everything was good to go. He couldn't help but wonder what his friends in Hollywood would think of the Gansett Island theater. They would look down their noses at it, but it was right here in this musty room with the folding chairs and the headlights shining through the windows that he'd fallen in love with movies and visual storytelling.

"Good evening, everyone, and thank you so much for being here for the Gansett Island premiere of *Indefatigable*. As most of you know, *Indefatigable* tells the story of my wife Stephanie's fourteen-year effort to free her stepfather, Charlie Grandchamp, from unjust incarceration. After meeting Stephanie, hearing her story and falling in love with her, I thought I understood what she'd been through. But it was only when I delved into the writing of the screenplay that I found out I only knew a fraction of it. The more I learned about Stephanie and Charlie, the more I loved and respected them both for not only surviving an ordeal that would've ruined lesser people, but for who they are now in the aftermath of this story. We named the film *Indefatigable* in honor of Stephanie's unyielding determination to right a terrible wrong, against the greatest of odds. Ladies and gentlemen, this is *Indefatigable*."

While the audience applauded, Grant left the stage and went to sit in the front row next to his parents. His dad patted him on the back and beamed a proud smile as the opening credits played.

Two hours and twenty-one minutes later, the closing credits began scrolling as the audience burst into wild applause.

Grant noticed both his parents mopping up tears.

"It was magnificent," Linda said. "Even after all this time that we've known Stephanie… I still had no idea."

"Congratulations, son," Big Mac said. "It's a triumph for everyone involved."

"Thanks, guys. So glad you enjoyed it." Grant returned to the stage to accept a standing ovation. "Thank you so much, everyone. I have so many people to thank. First and foremost, to my parents, Mac and Linda, who told me I could be anything I wanted, even a screenwriter. The team at Quantum Productions, especially Hayden Roth, Kristian Bowen, Jasper Autry and the incomparable Flynn Godfrey, who brought this story to life, along with the incredible cast and crew and all the many people involved. I want to send a special shout-out to my friend and attorney extraordinaire Dan Torrington, without whom this story might've ended very differently."

Grant paused to lead another rousing round of applause for Dan, who stood and took a bow.

Then Grant saw them, Steph and Charlie… in the back, standing against the wall, side by side as they'd been from the beginning of their incredible story.

His heart skipped a beat when he saw Stephanie wiping tears from her face as she smiled and clapped for Dan, who'd saved them both by intervening in Charlie's case.

"Finally," Grant said, contending with a huge wave of emotion that he battled through, "I'd like to acknowledge my beautiful, courageous wife, Stephanie Logan McCarthy, and her beloved stepfather, Charlie Grandchamp." He held out his arm to indicate their location in the back, and everyone turned to face them as they applauded.

Grant came down off the stage and headed down the center aisle.

Stephanie met him halfway, nearly leaping into his outstretched arms.

She held on tight to him as she whispered in his ear, "It was incredible. Absolutely *incredible*."

It was the best review he'd ever gotten—and the only one that mattered.

~

THE AFTER-PARTY at the Bistro was packed with friends and family, celebrating Stephanie and Charlie, both of whom seemed to be enjoying the limelight.

Julia Lawry was doing a set onstage with her brother Owen and Evan. The three of them were magic together.

"What a night," Big Mac said to Linda as he sat with her, Adam, Abby, Grant, Stephanie, Grace, Joe and Janey.

Charlie and Sarah were holding court at another table, with her parents, Russ and Adele, along with Jeff, John, Cindy, Katie, Shane, Laura, Frank and Betsy.

"What a *week*," Linda said. "Did you ever hear any more about what caused the power failure?"

"Apparently, it was due to lightning striking a substation on the mainland. Took them a few days to figure out where the problem was and then another couple of days to get it fixed."

"Everyone who doesn't have a generator is talking about getting one."

"I'm so glad we got ours after the last big blizzard."

Oliver and Dara were sitting with Ned, Francine, Kevin, Chelsea, Riley, Nikki, Finn, Chloe, Mason and Jordan. Over dinner at the lighthouse the other night, they'd convinced their new friends to come to the premiere and the after-party so they could introduce them to more island residents. So far, they'd met the Martinez brothers and their wives as well as Slim and Erin and many of their other island friends.

"They seem to be having a nice time," Big Mac said, using his chin to direct her attention to the Watkins. He'd asked his brothers and Ned to help make them feel welcome.

"They do. I'm glad they agreed to come."

"Me, too. They seem to really like it here so far."

"What's not to like?" Linda asked, grinning.

"There's nothing not to like about Gansett Island. It's good to see Chloe out and about, too. Kev said the new meds are giving her relief."

"I'm so glad to hear that. I hate to see her suffering. We had a meeting yesterday about the new spa at the hotel. She has so many great ideas. It's going to be awesome when it opens in the spring, and she's going to be a wonderful manager."

"Mac's getting ready to start the renovation—and as soon as they finish that, they'll get to work on turning the alpaca farm into another venue. That place was too great to pass up."

"I love the idea of making that a wedding venue."

"Me too. Did you ever hear what happened to Cooper James's face?"

"From what I'm told, he's not talking, and neither is Gigi, but apparently, they've been inseparable the last few days."

"Very interesting. Who's that gal talking to Jack Downing?"

"Her name is Piper Bennett. Laura hired her to work at the Surf in the off-season."

"Ah, I see." If he didn't have the skinny on the latest Gansett Island news, his wife usually did. "And what's the latest with Jared and Lizzie and the baby?"

"I heard he hired an investigator to try to find the baby's mother, but so far, no luck."

"That's a sticky situation."

"Sure is, especially since they've been struggling to have one of their own, but keep that between us."

"Oh God. What a mess."

"I know," Linda said, sighing. "I hope they aren't going to get their hearts broken."

"I hope not either."

"So Adam told me a secret earlier," Big Mac said. "You wanna hear it?"

"Duh. Yes!"

Smiling, he leaned in closer to her so only she could hear him. "They had another ultrasound, and it seems the babies are two sets of twins."

"No way. Did they say if they're boys or girls?"

"They think four boys."

"Oh my Lord! They're going to have five sons!"

"I know, right? Is the world ready for five more McCarthy boys?"

"No, it most definitely isn't, but I still can't wait to meet them."

"Me, too." Big Mac said. "Never a dull moment around here."

"And that's why we love it so much."

~

A Gansett Island Short Story

Dr. David Lawrence and Daisy Babson
Request the honor of your presence on September 8
at five o'clock in the evening at the Wayfarer on Gansett Island

Reception to immediately follow

ON THIS DAY one year ago, the skies had been dark and stormy, matching David Lawrence's mood as he'd paced the hallways in the ICU at Rhode Island Hospital, waiting to hear if his father would survive a massive heart attack. His dad had been airlifted off the island three days prior—three days before David and Daisy's wedding day.

They'd had to postpone the wedding, deciding to hold off and do it on the same date this year. Today had dawned crystal clear with cloudless blue skies and bright sunshine. Nothing stood in the way of him marrying Daisy later today. As the saying went, the third time was the charm. His wedding to Janey McCarthy had been canceled years ago, and it had taken him a long time to move forward with his life after that self-inflicted wound.

In the end, though, it had turned out for the best. Janey was happily married to Joe Cantrell, and by the end of the day today, David would be married to his true love.

For there was no doubt whatsoever that Daisy was the one he was meant to love forever.

His phone chimed with a text from Janey. *Happy wedding day to you and Daisy. Joe and I are sorry we can't be there to help you celebrate. We're so happy for you both. xoxo*

There'd been a time when Joe and Janey would've been the last people to wish him well. But after he'd saved the lives of Janey and their infant son PJ, he'd been forgiven for cheating on her and ruining everything between them. That was in the past now, and things had worked out the way they were meant to for both of them. He truly believed that.

Thanks so much, he texted to Janey. *We'll miss you guys. Hope all is well in Columbus.*

The studying is killing me, but I hear it'll be worth it someday. She added a grimacing emoji.

You got this, Dr. Cantrell.

Thank you! Have the best day ever! Send pics!

Will do. Thanks for reaching out.

It felt good and right to hear from Janey that day. She'd been his best friend for thirteen years, and losing her friendship had been the most devastating part of their breakup. He was thankful to have earned it back.

At four o'clock, David donned his tuxedo and headed for the Wayfarer to meet his groomsmen, Alex and Paul Martinez and Shannon O'Grady.

He hadn't seen Daisy since the previous evening, when they'd held their rehearsal dinner at Dominic's restaurant, and he couldn't wait to see her. The day without her had been long and boring, much like his life had been before she came along to make everything better.

When he got to the Wayfarer, Alex and Paul were already there, dressed in tuxedos.

"You two clean up well," he said to the brothers.

"I sent him back to get the dirt out from under his nails," Paul said, earning a shove from his brother.

"That's bullshit," Alex said. "Jenny had already given me a manicure." He blew on his nails and shined them up on his tuxedo jacket.

"Thanks for doing this, you guys."

"We were honored to be asked," Paul said. "Now you've got to tell us which one is the best man so the winner can gloat."

"No way," David said. "I'm not choosing. You're both my best men."

"Damn," Alex said. "I was so sure you liked me better."

"No one likes you better than me," Paul said.

Alex waggled his brows. "Jenny does."

"She can have you."

"She has me *a lot.*"

"Ew, shut up."

Amused by the brothers who'd been his friends since middle school, David said, "How's your mom today?"

"She was having a tough day earlier," Paul said, "but was doing better by this afternoon. I heard Daisy was in to see her, and that always cheers her up."

It didn't surprise David to hear Daisy had made time for Marion, even on her wedding day.

"Oh crap," Alex said. "Speaking of Daisy, I almost forgot that she asked me to give you this." He withdrew an envelope from his inside pocket and handed it to David.

"Thanks. I'm gonna just go…" He gestured to the far doors that led to a patio on the beach.

"We'll be here."

David went outside and found a seat away from the activity that went into preparing for a wedding. Nikki Stokes was in the middle of the action, supervising her staff.

He opened the envelope and pulled out a page covered in Daisy's distinctive handwriting.

My darling David,

By the time you're reading this, we'll be very close to the moment we've looked forward to for so long now. I can't wait to be your wife, to have forever with you, to have babies with you, to have everything with you. From the time we first met when I was at my lowest, you've always made me feel so safe and so loved. You were the first person in my whole life to ever make me feel the way I do when I'm with you. It would be impossible for me to describe that feeling in words. All I can say is it's the best feeling I've ever had.

I love you so much. More than you'll ever know. Can't wait to see you and say, "I do."

Daisy (soon-to-be) Lawrence

David wiped away the tears that'd filled his eyes as he read her sweet words. He was the lucky one, and he knew it. Making her happy every day for the rest of their lives was the least he could do after all she'd given him.

An hour later, he stood on the patio with Alex, Paul and Shannon as the sun headed toward the horizon. In the front row were his parents and sisters, who'd stood by him during his battle with lymphoma and the terrible darkness that'd followed his breakup with Janey. His father was doing great and had lost thirty pounds since his near-fatal heart attack.

His close friend and colleague, Victoria Stevens, was the first one down the aisle, wearing a gorgeous pale orange silk gown and grinning like a lunatic at David as she came toward him. She gave her fiancé, Shannon, a sultry look that had Shannon clearing his throat.

Vic was a nut, but David loved her. She'd been the first to encourage him to pursue a relationship with Daisy, and he was so glad he'd let her push him toward his true love.

Jenny and Hope Martinez were next, followed by Maddie McCarthy, who was Daisy's matron of honor. A month after delivering premature twins, Maddie was doing great. The babies were home, and Mac and Maddie were settling into life as the parents of five small children.

David had written a referral earlier that week for Mac's vasectomy on the mainland and had been entertained by Mac's many thoughts on the matter. The procedure was scheduled for the following week.

The ladies looked beautiful in the orange gowns that Daisy had agonized over until he'd told her she should have the color she liked best and not worry about what anyone else thought.

Daisy came into view, on the arm of Mac McCarthy, whom she'd asked to walk her down the aisle because she was afraid that she'd trip from being so nervous.

She'd never been more beautiful, and David had to remind himself to breathe as she came toward him wearing a sexy yet classy dress that was absolutely perfect on her. There were beads and pearls and other adornments, but he saw only her—her brilliant smile, the tears in her eyes and the glow of happiness that surrounded her.

She was an angel come to life, and she was all his.

As she took his hand and looked up at him with eyes full of love, David decided she'd been well worth the wait. The third time was indeed the charm.

~

THANK you so much for reading what I'm calling the "Frankenbook," because it included more than forty points of view and forty-five chapters. Phew! My early readers tell me it worked wonderfully, so I hope everyone who reads this one agrees. It was SUPER FUN to write this full-cast story that gave me a chance to catch up with all the characters and couples we've come to love over the first twenty-two books, and to introduce some new characters who'll be populating the next few books.

A very special thanks to my beta readers, Anne Woodall and Tracey Suppo, as well as Sarah Hewitt, family nurse practitioner, who checks the medical info for me. My longtime editors, Linda Ingmanson and Joyce Lamb, are always so great about making time for me when I need them, and I so appreciate their dedication. Thanks to my Gansett Island beta team: Betas: Betty, Lyn, Katy, Gwen, Michelle, Kelly, Andi, Jaime, Juliane, Doreen, Mona, Jen, Tammy and Laurie. You guys are awesome!

Thank you my team—Julie Cupp, Lisa Cafferty, Tia Kelly, Jean Mello, Nikki Haley, Melissa Saneholtz, Janet Margot and Ashley Lopez for all you do to keep things running smoothly behind the scenes.

Finally, a special thanks to my amazing READERS, who've propelled Gansett Island to book TWENTY-FOUR with NO END IN SIGHT! Coming up next is Cooper and Gigi's story, Temptation After Dark. Turn the page to see the cover and click on the link to preorder to read it later this year. Thanks again for your support of Gansett Island!

xoxo

Marie

ALSO BY MARIE FORCE

Contemporary Romances Available from Marie Force

The Gansett Island Series

Book 1: Maid for Love *(Mac & Maddie)*

Book 2: Fool for Love *(Joe & Janey)*

Book 3: Ready for Love *(Luke & Sydney)*

Book 4: Falling for Love *(Grant & Stephanie)*

Book 5: Hoping for Love *(Evan & Grace)*

Book 6: Season for Love *(Owen & Laura)*

Book 7: Longing for Love *(Blaine & Tiffany)*

Book 8: Waiting for Love *(Adam & Abby)*

Book 9: Time for Love *(David & Daisy)*

Book 10: Meant for Love *(Jenny & Alex)*

Book 10.5: Chance for Love, *A Gansett Island Novella (Jared & Lizzie)*

Book 11: Gansett After Dark *(Owen & Laura)*

Book 12: Kisses After Dark *(Shane & Katie)*

Book 13: Love After Dark *(Paul & Hope)*

Book 14: Celebration After Dark *(Big Mac & Linda)*

Book 15: Desire After Dark *(Slim & Erin)*

Book 16: Light After Dark *(Mallory & Quinn)*

Book 17: Victoria & Shannon (Episode 1)

Book 18: Kevin & Chelsea (Episode 2)

A Gansett Island Christmas Novella

Book 19: Mine After Dark *(Riley & Nikki)*

Book 20: Yours After Dark *(Finn & Chloe)*

Book 21: Trouble After Dark *(Deacon & Julia)*

Book 22: Rescue After Dark *(Mason & Jordan)*

Book 23: Blackout After Dark *(Full Cast)*

Book 24: Temptation After Dark *(Gigi & Cooper)*

The Green Mountain Series

Book 1: All You Need Is Love *(Will & Cameron)*

Book 2: I Want to Hold Your Hand *(Nolan & Hannah)*

Book 3: I Saw Her Standing There *(Colton & Lucy)*

Book 4: And I Love Her *(Hunter & Megan)*

Novella: You'll Be Mine *(Will & Cam's Wedding)*

Book 5: It's Only Love *(Gavin & Ella)*

Book 6: Ain't She Sweet *(Tyler & Charlotte)*

The Butler, Vermont Series

(Continuation of Green Mountain)

Book 1: Every Little Thing *(Grayson & Emma)*

Book 2: Can't Buy Me Love *(Mary & Patrick)*

Book 3: Here Comes the Sun *(Wade & Mia)*

Book 4: Till There Was You *(Lucas & Dani)*

Book 5: All My Loving *(Landon & Amanda)*

Book 6: Let It Be *(Lincoln & Molly)*

Book 7: Come Together *(Noah & Brianna)*

The Treading Water Series

Book 1: Treading Water

Book 2: Marking Time

Book 3: Starting Over

Book 4: Coming Home

Book 5: Finding Forever

The Miami Nights Series

Book 1: How Much I Feel *(Carmen & Jason)*

Book 2: How Much I Care *(Maria & Austin)*

Book 3: How Much I Love *(Dee's story)*

Single Titles

Five Years Gone

One Year Home

Sex Machine

Sex God

Georgia on My Mind

True North

The Fall

The Wreck

Love at First Flight

Everyone Loves a Hero

Line of Scrimmage

The Quantum Series

Book 1: Virtuous *(Flynn & Natalie)*

Book 2: Valorous *(Flynn & Natalie)*

Book 3: Victorious *(Flynn & Natalie)*

Book 4: Rapturous *(Addie & Hayden)*

Book 5: Ravenous *(Jasper & Ellie)*

Book 6: Delirious *(Kristian & Aileen)*

Book 7: Outrageous *(Emmett & Leah)*

Book 8: Famous *(Marlowe & Sebastian)*

Romantic Suspense Novels Available from Marie Force

The Fatal Series

One Night With You, *A Fatal Series Prequel Novella*

Book 1: Fatal Affair

Book 2: Fatal Justice

Book 3: Fatal Consequences

Book 3.5: Fatal Destiny, *the Wedding Novella*

Book 4: Fatal Flaw

Book 5: Fatal Deception

Book 6: Fatal Mistake

Book 7: Fatal Jeopardy

Book 8: Fatal Scandal

Book 9: Fatal Frenzy

Book 10: Fatal Identity

Book 11: Fatal Threat

Book 12: Fatal Chaos

Book 13: Fatal Invasion

Book 14: Fatal Reckoning

Book 15: Fatal Accusation

Book 16: Fatal Fraud

First Family Series

Book 1: State of Affairs

Historical Romance Available from Marie Force

The Gilded Series

Book 1: Duchess by Deception

Book 2: Deceived by Desire

ABOUT THE AUTHOR

Marie Force is the *New York Times* bestselling author of contemporary romance, romantic suspense and erotic romance. Her series include Gansett Island, Fatal, Treading Water, Butler Vermont and Quantum.

Her books have sold more than 10 million copies worldwide, have been translated into more than a dozen languages and have appeared on the *New York Times* bestseller more than 30 times. She is also a *USA Today* and *Wall Street Journal* bestseller, as well as a Speigel bestseller in Germany.

Her goals in life are simple—to finish raising two happy, healthy, productive young adults, to keep writing books for as long as she possibly can and to never be on a flight that makes the news.

Join Marie's mailing list on her website at marieforce.com for news about new books and upcoming appearances in your area. Follow her on Facebook at www.Facebook.com/MarieForceAuthor and on Instagram at *www.instagram.com/marieforceauthor/*. Contact Marie at *marie@marieforce.com*.

CPSIA information can be obtained
at www.ICGtesting.com
Printed in the USA
LVHW052018290121
677862LV00011B/1244